The

John Needham

Copyright © John Needham 2016
All Rights Reserved

Some places and locations referred to in this work of fiction do
exist, but all characters are entirely fictitious and any resemblance
to real people, living or dead, is purely coincidental.

John Needham was born in Rutland in 1943 and brought up in Stamford, Lincolnshire. After study at Leicester College of Art he spent the first twenty-five years of his working life in graphic design and copywriting. Later he pursued his lifelong passion of renovating old houses, to end his career in landscape gardening.

Since retiring he has written three non-fiction books: two on house renovating and an autobiography, *Wishing for the Better, part one of which is published.*

In fiction he has written *Convergence, Forebears, The One of Us* and *Secret Shame,* in addition to *Awakening,* a short anthology of short stories. *The Flautist* is his fifth novel.

He lives in west Wales with his spaniel, Sali.

For Jenny, as always.

Finale

The piano concerto ends its final, jaunty rondo movement with its familiar E-flat major coda. *Yes,* I think, letting out a long, deep sigh of satiation, *Beethoven certainly knew how to do an effective finish.* There's a brief moment of almost uncertain silence, as if we in the audience are not quite sure it *has* finished. But we are, of course. I (and, it's a fair bet, everyone else here at the Barbican too) know Ludwig's *Emperor* like the back of my hand. Beside me, my companion sighs happily. Well, it can't be entirely happily, so soon after recent events, I imagine. The pleasure we've just shared must have been rather bittersweet. I glance at her, catching her eye, which has suddenly moistened. She returns my look, offering a little smile. Reaches for and briefly squeezes my hand.

But then the spell is broken and the audience explodes into rapturous applause. I can see her sitting there in her new black (and surprisingly expensive, I found) Christmas-present evening dress with its demurely cut v-top and thin straps over her white shoulders. Stupidly, I find myself pausing in my clapping to raise a hand in a wave. I know that she knows where we are sitting, because she'd scanned the audience when she came onto the stage at the beginning and spotted us and grinned. I gave her a little wave of encouragement then too. But the house lights are still turned low, so I don't know whether she'll be able to see us at the moment.

No matter, though. She looks radiant; cheeks flushed with pleasure, eyes bright, glancing sideways to the other musicians, sharing some sort of special musicians' rapport, I suppose. This is her fourth concert now but, she tells me, she still reaches quite a high. Artistes often feel that at the end of a performance, apparently, and I can certainly believe it in her case.

I feel my throat tighten. I'm so proud, so pleased for her. She certainly deserves this exhilaration . . .

First Movement

Allegro – moderato

Chapter 1: 2011

The theatre of Juilliard Music School was heaving with people. Leah struggled through the horde of excited students, each one clutching a diploma to their chest, reverentially, as if they'd found the Holy Grail (which they probably had, in a way) to her parents and Shay. The grin on her face would have put the Cheshire Cat to shame. The expressions on her mother's and Shay's faces matched her own, although her father's was polite but less enthusiastic. But she knew why that was; he was a bit disgruntled that she'd only gained a C in piano and a B in flute. He'd expected no less than an A with Distinction, after spending so many dollars on her education as she hadn't qualified for a free scholarship. He'd hoped for a better return on his investment. Not that, in his eyes, being a musician was a particularly relevant qualification for inheriting the Solomon Weisman chain store empire one day, so she couldn't see why not fully making the grade was such a big deal for him.

Oh well; he'd just have to lump it. She'd tried her best, although Shay being in her life had been rather a distraction lately. Especially after his proposal. She could hardly believe her luck. Such a hunk of a guy and with such great prospects, to boot, wanting to marry plain-Jane Leah!

'Well done, honey!' Carmel enthused as she reached them, taking her to her thin-as-a-rake, expensively-attired body, into an embrace that was more theatrical than sincere (they were not a very tactile family) and air-kissing her left cheek, careful to neither spoil her lipstick nor red-stamp Leah's flushed skin.

'Yes, well done,' Solly and Shay chorused.

Her mother released her grip (well, she mustn't overdo things). Leah looked at Shay, trying to gauge his expression. He certainly looked pleased, although he did seem rather more buoyed up of late about his job offer with a significant salary rise and generous bonuses and fringe benefits than her graduation. Or about the wedding in the offing, for that matter. Well, that was to be expected, she supposed. He was quite a go-getter, much to her Dad's approval. She wasn't sure how demonstrative to be with her fiancé; felt a little inhibited in her parents' presence. Although why the hell she should be, she had no idea. But perhaps it was their suffocating over-protectiveness; watching her like a hawk (especially Dad) throughout her teenage years, carefully monitoring her boyfriends, all two of them, making sure they were Of The Faith and morally impeccable. Marrying out would have been completely out of the question.

'Aren't I the clever girl then?' she chirruped rhetorically, moving towards him.

He grinned. 'Yeah. You certainly are.'

He held out his arms but there was no embrace. He simply placed his hands on her slender biceps, closed the distance and also targeted her cheek for a kiss, slightly irritatingly, but at least his lips made contact, briefly, which was something anyway. He moved away and she took his hand with her free one, glancing at her father. There would be no point in expecting any sort of embrace from *him,* even on this special occasion. But he was still smiling, in a slightly rictus sort of way. He looked fidgety though, as if wishing he were someplace else. Classical music was not really his thing though, as he frequently reminded her. Old fogey that he was, Sinatra was more his bag.

'Okay then,' he said, raising the bushy eyebrows above the piggy eyes in his jowly face, 'is that it then? Can we go now?'

'Well, yes, I think so,' Leah replied dubiously, disappointed. 'I think the rest of it is just mingling, socializing. But I think there's to be a Class of 2011 group photo; that sort of thing.'

He grunted; looked disgruntled. 'Oh. Okay. Yeah, I suppose you have to have that.'

'And there's the individual photos too.' Leah tried to press her advantage home. 'You know: "clever offspring, just graduated, posing with diploma" sort of thing.

Solly Weisman looked impatient. 'Ah, come on. We don't have to mess around with that now, do we? I'll arrange a proper studio shoot for that. Get our PR people to organize it. I've got a table booked for us at Da Silvano to celebrate, right now.' He paused; conceded, 'Well, we'll wait for the group shot then, as long as they aren't too long about it, then get outta here. I'm famished.'

Leah sighed; contemplated her corpulent, controlling father. *Yeah, it's always about you, isn't it! What you want. But this is my day, for God's sake. My special day. Can we do what I want, just for once?* But aloud she said, 'Yes, okay then Dad, it's a deal.'

Henrico the trusty chauffeur was waiting with the Mercedes in the parking lot and the glide across town to the restaurant didn't take long. Solly phoned ahead to let William, the manager, know they were on their way, so he'd be there ready, fawning, to suitably welcome them. Not that there'd been any problem about losing the booked table; it was paid for and theirs for the entire evening, whether they actually made use of it or not, and with Solly's prestige and spending power they would have been welcome whatever time they showed up. Even if it were five minutes before the staff's end of shift. Da Silvano catered to a very select clientele indeed, with prices to match.

Sure enough, he was there at the door, smiling his obsequious smile, wringing his hands, smarming. Leah detested his servility.

'Good evening. Mr Weisman,' he oozed, 'Mrs Weisman. Miss Leah. Mr Goldstein. How are we this fine evening?'

'Just fine, William, just fine.' With the prospect of food and a bottle or two of good champagne, plus a few whisky chasers in prospect, Solly's good humour had returned. 'I'm ready to eat a horse. Well, a cow, anyway!'

Solly chuckled at his own *bon mot* and William dutifully laughed too, although he'd already heard it *ad nauseum*. He led them to their table in the centre of the dining room, so chosen the better to be noticed by the other notables in that evening, including a sprinkling of B-list starlets and their sometimes middle-aged beaus. Leah would have preferred a position less conspicuous. William took their orders personally (well, only the very best service for the famous retail entrepreneur!). Solly, predictably, ordered a humongous T-bone steak, very rare, with fries. Shay, not to be outdone, did the same. Carmel opted for a smaller one, properly cooked. Leah, defying her father's contemptuous stare, ordered a mushroom goulash.

The wine waiter arrived, although the wine order was also a foregone conclusion: 1998 Clos d'Ambonnay, one bottle to be going on with, and a bottle of good malt. The waiter scurried away and quickly returned with the whisky. The champagne would follow, he said, after it had had a few minutes on ice. Solly wanted to begin serious drinking now though and he and Shay were poured generous measures. The womenfolk, neither of whom liked whisky, would have to twiddle their thumbs and wait.

But then the champagne arrived too, sweating, nested in its ice-filled bucket, and the waiter popped the cork, frothily filled their flutes and retired. Solly raised his, leading the toast. 'To you, Leah. Congratulations!'

Carmel and Shay murmured agreement. They drank. It was, Leah had to admit, a very fine champagne. Although to be truthful, she'd never tasted a really cheap one (well why would she have?) so she had no point of reference really.

As if suddenly remembering the point of the occasion, Carmel said, 'Well, that's your education all finished now then, honey.'

'Yeah, I suppose so,' Leah agreed, not quite knowing how to respond. It was a pretty self-evident statement, really. Not that her schooling had been all that remarkable. For all her parents' wealth, and it was considerable, money couldn't ensure academic brilliance. She'd been to a top private school where she'd not exactly excelled in any subjects. None of the academic ones, at least. And she'd hated sport. But music had been another matter. She'd taken to it with a passion. She'd been learning piano obsessively since the age of eight (she'd been given a baby grand for Christmas when she was ten) with a dedication that was astonishing and had quickly become technically proficient. Then at fourteen had fallen in love with the flute and had soon mastered it too (so her Christmas present that year had been a high-end Muramatsu, because one of Dad's friends had advised him that it was a good brand); only the best was good enough.

But both her piano and flute teachers had advised, delicately, that whilst she was good technically, she lacked sensitivity and some feel for interpretation. Dad hadn't been too bothered about that, as he regarded Leah's passion for music as a schoolgirl thing, much like wanting a pony, which she'd probably grow out of. And anyway, as their only child now, since tragically losing her brother, little Isaac, to meningitis at a few months old (Mom had absolutely refused to try for another child after that), she was in line to take over the reins of the Solomon Weisman dynasty. As Dad saw it, she didn't want to have her head turned too much by thoughts of a musical career. Her future, after all, lay in retail.

She'd pestered Mom though to go to Juilliard, which would involve them paying her not inconsiderable fees as she wouldn't get in on merit. But then free scholarships were reserved for the talented high-potential children of the poor, and it had to be admitted that she was in neither category. But her (and Mom's) secret hope had been that Juilliard would teach, would somehow inculcate the emotional dimension her music-making lacked. And it had worked to some extent, although it was one of the school's tutors' frequently rehearsed maxims that you couldn't teach genius. You either had it innately or you didn't. And if you were no Mozart, the next best thing was loads of hard work. There was no reason why she shouldn't become a reasonably accomplished and employable orchestra player.

But a soloist?

Well, no. Forget it.

Mom had worked on Dad, and finally he'd relented and she'd gone to music school. And she'd really tried, even neglecting piano to some extent to try and focus all her energy on the flute, and had managed a B, which was still pretty respectable, and today was her big day. *She* felt she'd achieved something anyway, even if her too-demanding father didn't.

She was brought out of her reverie by her parents talking in unison although not saying the same thing. Mom was saying, 'And your next big thing now is the wedding. I can't wait for that.'

Whereas Dad, the ritual of the congratulatory toast over, had already changed the subject – subject as in 'Leah' – completely and had turned his attention to Shay. 'So, when do you start the new job, did you say?'

Shay preened. 'In three weeks. I'll have to fly over there well before then of course to sort things out, especially accommodation-wise.'

'Yeah, of course you will' Solly agreed, already reaching for a refill from the whisky bottle. 'Will you be looking to live in the city itself, or somewhere out in the sticks? Surrey's very nice, as I recall. Stayed in a very nice hotel there once. Very olde-worlde, but genuine. Been a manor house once, we were told. Although it had all the essentials, all the mod cons. Jacuzzi. Hot tub. And great landscaped grounds with a nine-hole golf course. Even a swimming pool, which is something you don't always see in Britain. They don't have the weather for it.' Solly never used five words when sixty-five would do.

'Well I think we should go for something in town, so as to be close to the job, although Lee fancies country life, I know.' Shay glanced at Leah with something approximating to an apology.

'I think you're right,' Solly opined. 'I imagine you'll be working pretty long hours. You bankers do. You don't want the little lady to be waiting up until midnight for you to come home, do you?' It didn't occur to him to include his daughter in the conversation.

Leah fought down irritation. They were discussing her and Shay's future, the pair of them, as if she wasn't present. And of no account. And hogging the conversation, as usual. What about her own plans, dreams for her career? She raised her voice, trying to compete with her father's gravelly foghorn. 'Yes, it's quite my year, one way and another, isn't it? I can't believe I'll be Mrs Goldstein in five month's time. And turning twenty-one next month too. It's all happening!'

Carmel said something in reply, but her voice was drowned out by Solly and Shay, who were talking loudly and animatedly on their mutually favourite subjects: business and money, and she didn't catch it.

'Yes,' Shay was enthusing, 'there are some very nice apartments in Canary Wharf, which is only a stone's throw from the bank. It'll be nice to be able to walk to work. Apparently, they've really developed the former docks area – what do they call it now? Docklands, that's it – in recent years. Added a shi – er, shedload of value to the place. A lot of the property gets bought by foreigners as an investment. Well, you can't blame them really; with the London property market so buoyant, it's a no-brainer. I might consider doing that: borrow as interest rates are so low over there, so I could easily afford to service a loan, and put it into property. It really would be a win-win.'

'Yeah, very astute of you, young man.' Solly nodded approvingly. 'I can see you've a very sound business head on your shoulders.' He was growing to like his daughter's fiancé more and more at each meeting. He leaned forward, conspiratorially, and lowered his voice to slightly less than a boom, as if the entire restaurant might be listening in. 'As a matter of fact, I'm seriously thinking of expanding into Europe: the UK and possibly Germany to begin with. There's got to be a market for my high-end stuff over there, I'm sure. Certainly in London, anyway, and probably in Berlin. It has to make sense.'

'I think you're right,' Shay agreed, nodding his handsome, dark, curly-haired head too. 'With a Conservative-dominated coalition government in charge in Britain, the economic environment's highly conducive to quality retail. There might be some necessary corrective austerity measures in place there just now, like there are here, but there's plenty of money swilling around the system at the top.'

'Quite right,' Solly enthusiastically agreed. 'The only reason I haven't considered getting into Europe before is the lack of a good, reliable man to head up the overseas operation. But with you joining the family, and with your background and track record so far, well hell, a few years down the line, who knows?' He grinned, showing the party several gold premolars. 'Take my meaning?'

Shay was taken aback. He hadn't seen this coming. 'Well, yes Sir. I think I do.'

'After all,' Solly continued, now on his second glass of champagne (and three whiskies already downed too), and flushed-faced, the pores on his bulbous nose and his bald pate glistening with sweat, 'left to herself, Leah isn't all that interested in taking over the reins, but I did want to keep everything I've worked for in the family. So here's the way to do it.'

'Er, right. Yes!'

Solly expanded his theme. 'So the way I see it, Yishayah, you can think of yourself as a kinda spearhead, trailblazer, getting to know the market for me, the lay of the land if you will. And maybe arrange some finance on the right terms, so we can really put some serious money into the project. Give it a couple of years at the bank then join me as Director of European Operations. And after that, the sky would be the limit, if you take my drift. Waddya say?'

Shay was having difficulty taking in the full implications. 'O-kay . . . yes, thank you, Mr Weisman. Well that certainly gives me food for thought . . .

'No, "Solly", please.'

Weisman's tone became abruptly maudlin. Alcohol often had that effect on him. 'Yeah, well. As I suppose Leah has told you, I don't have a male heir, sadly – '

Shay interrupted. 'Yes, she did say. I'm sorry.'

Solly looked downcast; shrugged his heavy shoulders. 'Well; God's will, I suppose. It's just the way things have panned out. But maybe you coming into our lives is God's will too. Who knows?'

'Um; yes. Perhaps. It's certainly a golden opportunity you're offering me . . . Solly.' Shay wished he would change the subject. This was embarrassing.

Carmel clearly thought so too. 'Yes, well anyway, honey, that's something for the future. This is Leah's evening, remember?'

Solly smiled. Reached for the whisky bottle again and recharged his and Shay's glasses, as a waiter appeared with their food. 'Yeah, you're right, I guess.'

Carmel continued, quickly, before he changed his mind and resumed his empire-building, seeming herself to forget the point of the celebration too. 'Yes, we've got the wedding to think about before then. There's so much to plan! There's the Rabbi; you and Yishayah will have to speak with him, and the synagogue to book. And Leah's bridal gown. And something for myself. Not too eye-catching of course. We mustn't detract from the bride! And the invitations. How many people should we invite?'

Carmel paused for breath. Leah tried to get a word in to remind her mother about graduating, but she was in full flight now.

'Yes, we'll have to decide on the venue, won't we, as it'll depend on the number of guests. And bridesmaids to organize, and a Matron of Honor. And you two will have to think about where you'd like to go for your honeymoon. Somewhere nice. We'll pay for that, naturally. Oh, there's so much to think about; I'll be a nervous wreck by the time the day arrives!'

'Okay, well calm down, Mom,' Leah said, exasperated. She wanted to be talking about her career prospects this evening, not her nuptials. 'It's not going to be a huge society wedding now, is it? Shay and I aren't exactly celebrities, are we? Not movie stars or anything!'

'Well, no,' Carmel conceded, huffily, 'but your dad and I have a certain social standing all the same and we want to give you a nice kiddushin; one to remember!'

Leah forced a smile. 'Fine, and thanks for that, but today was my graduation, remember? Can we talk about that?'

'Yes of course, honey. But what is there to say? You've done wonderfully well and got your diploma, and that's it, isn't it?'

'Well, no, not really! I'd like to think this is just the beginning, not an end. I've not just left some sort of smart Swiss finishing school you know; I've got my entire career ahead of me!'

'Okay,' Carmel said, placating, 'I know your music means a lot to you, although I would have thought your marriage and move to England was top of the agenda at the moment. That's all very exciting too, isn't it?'

Leah sighed. 'Yes, of course, but the marriage is months away, although the move isn't. I want to be over there as soon as Shay has got us a place fixed up. And see about an orchestra job there. That would be good. I've applied for one or two vacant posts I've seen advertised, but I don't know whether I'll get either of them. One with the London Symphony Orchestra and the other with a much smaller outfit I haven't heard of, but I don't really expect to get either of them. Not with my lack of experience and not being British. But I expect there'll be something, even if it's not an orchestra. Like session work; things like that'

The condescending smile had left Carmel's face. She said coldly, 'Oh, that's your plan, is it, to move over there straight away; not wait until you're married? Live in sin?'

'Well yes, obviously. And it's not "living in sin", as you so quaintly put it. Honestly, Mom, you are so last-century!'

'Yes, well it doesn't seem five minutes since you were my little girl, and now you can't wait to leave your father and me.' A tear sprouted at the corner of Carmel's eye. She carefully wiped it away without smudging her mascara.

'Yeah, and you still are to me, honey,' Solly's less-than-dulcet tones cut in. 'We'll miss you.'

Leah sighed again.

Chapter 2

Leah stood at their hotel bedroom window gazing out at the foaming River (no, *Afon,* give it the Welsh word) Dee burbling busily and surprisingly noisy below. She sighed happily. 'Isn't this just *gorgeous,* honey?'

Shay moved close behind her, pressing groin to bottom (as he often did when they were naked, when it was wonderful); wrapped his arms around her waist. Rested his chin in the nape of her slender neck. 'Yeah, very nice.'

He was getting over his irritation that there was no car parking at the Glyndwr Hotel at this tiny back-of-beyond place, Llangollen, in North Wales, a part of Britain he'd barely heard of. To his amazement, there was only parking for the proprietors and delivery trucks and they'd had to leave the car in a municipal parking lot and tote their suitcases themselves without so much as the offer of a bellboy to carry for them, over a precarious-looking chain suspension bridge to the riverside hotel.

But Leah thought it divine. The perfect place to be in the fall, with the leaves yellow and russet and ochre on the trees, clinging stubbornly on for a few final glorious days before they'd be stripped away by the next strong gust of wind or rain shower. Along the river high hills rose sentinel, receding like huge green open egg boxes into the distance. They'd flown over the previous day, after the wedding, direct to Liverpool airport from JFK. She would have liked a quiet, no-fuss wedding somewhere really romantic in Britain, but had been outvoted. And as Mom and Dad had paid for it all, and they, Shay and Shay's parents had wanted a New York venue, in a proper Synagogue, it was fair enough, she supposed.

They'd overnighted in Liverpool and then in a hired car driven south today, crossing the border into Wales with its cute bi-lingual *Croeso y Gymru* sign soon after Chester, then done a right at Ruabon into wonderful hill country and onto an absurdly narrow single carriageway B road, as the Brits called them, past the soaring stone arches of a high, elegant and dramatic aqueduct over the Dee. It carried a canal (another British quaintness; they must have been a painfully slow means of travel, at the walking pace of the towing horse) over the river to shadow its northern bank westwards to Llangollen. The crossing was called Pontcysyllte, according to her guidebook, a name that looked impossible to pronounce.

And then the arrival here, and Shay's little temper tantrum, barely concealed, because there were no flunkeys waiting to bow attendance. But he seemed to be over it now. She turned to face her new husband and wrapped her arms around him too. 'Okay; I know you would rather we'd just gone to somewhere hot and exotic, but this is different, a new experience, don't you think?'

'Well, yeah, it's that all right, I'll grant you,' Shay conceded. 'I hadn't realized Britain was so . . . varied, I must admit.'

'That's the nice thing about it. I know it hasn't got really spectacular sights like our Grand Canyon and stuff, but for a small island it packs a lot in. So my guidebook says, anyway.'

'I suppose it does, if you like sightseeing. So what are we going to do here then? This is your part of the honeymoon. It's up to you.'

That was certainly true. They'd haggled over where to go. Leah wanted it to be something like this: getting to know her adoptive (if only for a few years) country. She wanted to explore it. Shay on the other hand just wanted a beach somewhere expensive and select and wall to wall sunshine to work on his tan. So they'd compromised. Leah would choose the first five days and Shay the second. Poring over road map and guidebooks, she'd devised a mini-tour of Britain, beginning at Liverpool and going south into Wales (hence Llangollen now, because it looked interesting); then further west into Snowdonia; then back into England and down through Shropshire and Hereford and Worcester to

Stratford upon Avon and sampling a little Shakespearian culture: overnighting there and taking in a performance at the theatre the following day. Then overnighting again before heading for the golden-stoned, chocolate-box Cotswolds region of Gloucestershire.

Then on to the Vale of White Horse in Wiltshire to see the chalky stylized Celtic figure cut in the hillside at Uffington before joining the M4 motorway for the final leg back to London and their penthouse apartment in Canary Wharf. Then a short intermission there before boarding their flight to French Polynesia and Shay's sea and sun. That was the plan. It had something for each of them.

'Okay,' Leah said, 'well I thought we might do a canal boat trip this afternoon; what do you think?'

'Hold on, Lee! It's twelve o'clock now.' Shay looked down at his watch. 'Twelve-fifteen, and we've only just got here; can't we chill for a bit?'

She snorted dismissively. 'It's okay, there's plenty of time. I checked. There's a trip leaves at two o'clock. They do lunches on the boat, so we can eat then. We can have a look round the town while we're waiting.'

'Well, all right then; I suppose so,' Shay said, sounding distinctly doubtful. He'd already grumbled not entirely good-naturedly that she was trying to pack too much into the first days.

'Oh, come on! It'll be fun!' Leah cajoled, her voice high like a little girl's. 'It goes back along the canal, the way we came in, and goes over that high aqueduct we saw: Pont . . . thingy. It's quite an experience going over there, apparently. Then the trippers return by road, in a bus. Or you can get a bus to the far end and the canal boat back. You'll enjoy it!'

Shay smiled, conceding defeat. 'Okay, let's do it. Anything to keep Mrs Goldstein happy!'

They left the hotel and wandered into the little grey stone town. Fall might have arrived but it was still alive with a generous sprinkling of tourists, probably because of the mid-term school break. This would no doubt be the final spasm of commerce before winter exerted its chilly grip and the shops closed for the season though. The village was remarkably spick and span; it was clearly quite a tourist honey pot. Leah could see why. Apart from the scenery and the canal, it boasted another attraction: a conserved steam railway. She would have liked a ride on it too, but the tight itinerary didn't allow it. And there were other delights in other places planned, after all.

With fifteen minutes to spare they found the wharf, from which the feeder canal fed water into the main one. A brightly-painted narrowboat (as the British called them) was tied up at the quay and tourists were already taking their seats aboard, as if fearful that it might leave without them. They found the ticket office for the boat tripping. The smartly-uniformed young woman behind the glass asked for their booking details.

'Oh,' 'We haven't done. We only arrived in Langollen a short while ago,' Leah said, alarmed, mangling the strange name horribly, 'we thought we could just turn up.'

The booking clerk sighed patiently. 'It does say in our brochure and on our website that trips are pre-booked. So is lunch, if you want it.'

She consulted a list. 'And I'm afraid the two o'clock outward trip is fully booked anyway. Sorry.'

'Oh,' Leah repeated. 'Dammit.'

The young woman suppressed a smile and looked apologetic. She was used to this. She scanned her lists again. 'But I could book you for the return trip. It's still got some vacant seats. It means taking our courtesy coach to Froncysyllte, at the far end, which is included in the price. It leaves here at three fifteen. Would you like to do that?'

Shay opened his mouth to speak but Leah beat him to it. 'Yes, that sounds good. We'll do that. Thank you.'

'Good.' The clerk beamed. 'Can I have your names, please? And would you like to order cream tea?'

'Oh, yes please!' They'd only lived in England for four months, pre-nuptually, but Leah knew what that quaint British custom, with its scones with cream and jam and cakes, involved. She gave their names and they left the booking office.

'Great; so now we've missed lunch!' Shay grumbled, looking around hopefully, as if a McDonalds might suddenly appear. He could murder a hamburger.

Leah shushed him with a dig in the ribs. 'Come on now, misery-guts. It's not a big deal. We can go and find a café and get something to eat to keep us going. There's bound to be somewhere still open.'

So they returned to the town and found an eating place, and ate burger buns (with ham for him and cheese for her) and buttered *bara brith,* a Welsh delicacy: dark treacly fuity bread, and drank enormous mugs of strong milky tea, in the British style, although Shay would have preferred something alcoholic. Then after more time-killing wandering around the town, they returned to the wharf, to climb aboard the coach, joining pensioners and (distastefully for Shay) families with noisy excited children, for ferrying to the unpronounceable Froncysyllte.

Finally they were aboard the boat, the same one they'd seen back in Llangollen, according to its nameplate: *Thomas Telford.* It must have arrived before them. Obviously it plied back and forth between Llangollen and . . . the other place but return trips were not on offer. The punters could only sample its stately delights as a one-way trip, starting at either end, with the coach used to complete the return (or deliver travellers to the start).

They ensconced themselves in the saloon, sitting at a table across from a family of three: a middle-aged man with crown-thinning hair as curly and ginger-streaked-with-grey as his (presumed) plumpish, Mediterranean-looking wife's was jet-black and straight. Against the window opposite Leah sat their presumed child, a girl eight years old or so who had clearly inherited her raven hair and almond eyes from her mother. Leah fished out her guidebook again as they waited for the boat to set off. She'd read something about Llangollen being famous for an international music festival. She found the item again. Yes, it happened regularly, apparently. 'Hey, Shay,' she said, 'This sounds interesting. They do a big music gig in Langollen (horribly mispronouncing it again) every year. "The Langollen International Music Eyestedfod" Or however you pronounce it. It's another of those pesky Welsh words.'

The fellow-tourist across the table smiled a friendly smile, the margins of his hazel eyes wrinkling quite fetchingly. He spoke. 'Close. It's Eisteddfod. "Aye-steth-vod." Something like that.' He pronounced the 'th' hard, like in 'the'. 'And it's "Thlan-gothlen." Approximately.'

Leah laughed. (Shay scowled.) 'Ah right: thanks for that! I'm just a stupid American tourist, so what do I know?'

She tried copying the man's pronunciation tips, repeating the words several times. The stranger laughed too, as his (wife?) glowered bad-temperedly. He prompted her again, several times, until she was making a reasonable fist of it. 'That's it!' he said finally, 'you've got it, pretty well!'

Leah was enjoying the lightened mood. 'Thanks again! But you don't sound Welsh, not that I'm any expert in accents. Er . . . are you?'

The stranger chuckled again. 'Good grief no. Otherwise I'd get the pronunciation right. I'm a fellow Celt, but from across the water. Another branch of the family, so to speak.'

'From Ireland,' he added, as if to make it crystal-clear.

'Ah, right. Yes, I can tell now you say so.'

They regarded each other, smiling. It was nice to be chatting to someone personable, after Shay's grumpiness. Leah said, 'And do you know anything about this, er, Eisteddfod thing, then?'

'No, not a lot, except that they have musicians and singers performing from all over the world. It's a big event. Very colourful, because it's traditional folk music.'

'Sounds wonderful!' Leah enthused. 'I'd like to see it sometime.'

Her travelling companion regarded her steadily. 'Are you a musician then, by any chance?'

Leah laughed wryly. 'Well, I try to be. It's getting the work that's the hard part though. I'm a flutist.'

'Oh, really? A budding James Galway, are you? We say "flautist" over here, by the way; we pronounce it properly.'

There was a teasing undertone to the words though, they weren't disparaging. It was just banter. She could tell from his twinkling friendly eyes and grin. What did the Irish call it now? 'Joshing', was it? Something like that. It was fun, anyway. She batted back, grinning, rather surprised at her own boldness, although he seemed to take it in good part, 'Yes, well I can see you're the expert in pronunciation! Okay then, wise guy, "eether, either, neether, neither. Let's call the whole thing off". And no, I'm no budding Galway. For a start I'm not Irish and for seconds I'll never be as successful as him. So I'm told, at least.'

The stranger straightened his face and looked sympathetic. 'Well, there's a world of difference between commercial success and good musicianship and fulfillment, I would have thought, sure. No disrespect to our James, of course, but he had a load of luck as well. It's achieving what you want from life that measures success though, and not necessarily huge wealth, isn't it?'

'Well it's pretty important as far as I'm concerned, my friend.' Shay put in aggressively.

The Irishman shrugged, raised his hands in a peacemaking gesture and said no more.

The engine of the canal boat suddenly burst into throbbing life and they were cast off. The *Thomas Telford* began its leisurely progress, slowly picking up speed. Further conversation forgotten, Lea gazed out of the window, drinking in the lush scenery as it slid slowly past. An automated commentary began, welcoming them to the trip and giving information about canals in general and the Llangollen waterway in particular. And telling (demonstrating the correct pronunciation) about Thomas Telford, the Victorian engineer who had overseen the building over two hundred years ago of the amazing aqueduct they would soon be crossing. The voice rattled off statistics: *third iron viaduct to be built in the world; at one thousand and seven feet long and one hundred and twenty-six feet above the River Dee, the longest and highest in Britain.* And so on. Then came a warning that passengers of a nervous disposition or suffering from vertigo might prefer to sit on the right-hand, towpath side of the boat where there was a railing, because there was nothing at all on the left, no visual or actual barrier, just the low lip of the iron trough that held the water. Although, the narrator assured, it was perfectly safe.

Leah's heart did a minor nosedive. She and the child were by the window. On the left. Oh well; as the commentary said, it was perfectly safe. The boat couldn't possibly fall off and plunge to the river below. Irrational feelings of insecurity were all in the mind. Really, they were. And sure enough, three minutes later an ornate iron railing appeared outside the window, at right angles, beyond which there was no barrier on her side and then the ground was dropping steeply away, down, down into the river valley. Ahead, through the front windows, the canal with its towpath on its right was die-straight into the distance but there was no land on either side. Just a void. It was as if the canal had suddenly leapt into empty space.

Now her chest was jolted by an adrenaline rush. *Ohmygod, it was scary!* And then the child noticed the disappearance of terra firma too. She took a stricken look out of her window, hesitated for a moment, the colour drained from her face and then she screamed. Hers wasn't the only voice as people suddenly found themselves apparently airborne. There were squeals of delight and mock-alarm all around. But hers was pure panic. Her eyes widened in terror and her scream became constant. On the other side of the Irishman, the Mediterranean woman complained impatiently, *'Stai zitto, Bella! Non essere sciocca!'*

The father turned to her. 'Hey, hey, It's all right, love! You're quite safe!'

But the panic had really taken hold. She wouldn't be quieted. She was still staring masochistically into the void, and now the river, far below. Leah impulsively reached out a hand to cover one of hers. 'Yes, come on, honey. It's okay! Just don't look!'

But still the child continued. The Irishman pulled her onto his lap and clasped her face into his chest, so that she couldn't see the terror; stroked her hair. 'Come on now. Calm down. Deep breaths now. Come on.'

Leah said, 'You're all right. Imagine you're not here. You're safe home, with your dad. He'll keep you safe. Think of something really nice.'

She began singing, softly, something her Grandma Ruth had sung to her when she was little and frightened about anything (like her parents fighting): *'Raindrops on roses and whiskers on kittens, bright copper kettles and warm woolen mittens.'*

After a while the little girl's screaming became intermittent; then it stopped. She looked across at Leah, interest in the singing winning over her fear. Leah sang Maria von Trapp's song all the way through to the end, *'. . . and then I don't feel . . . sooo bad.'*

Beside her, Leah sensed Shay heaving a long sigh of relief. He was probably embarrassed by the commotion. The Irishman had been watching her intently, an unknowable expression on his friendly open features. He let go of the child for a moment to theatrically applaud. 'Bravissimo! There, wasn't that nice Bella? Being sung to by the nice lady?'

Bella nodded shyly. Leah held her attention away from the heart-stopping drop outside until they reached the end of the aqueduct (quite honestly, she wasn't very keen on looking to her left either). Courage regained, the child scrambled off her father's knee to resume her seat by the window, glancing at Leah now and then with a tiny timid smile.

The catering staff brought their cream teas: a proper china pot for the tea and scones, both English-style and flat, disc-shaped ones ('Welsh cakes', their Irish companion informed), pots of cream and strawberry jam and a plate of assorted fancy cakes. Embarrassment threatened when Leah thought they'd have to eat watched by their travelling companions, but fortunately they had ordered refreshments too. Bella had regained her composure fully now, and ate her own and half of Leah's share of the cakes.

An hour and a half later they were back at Llangollen (Leah knew how to pronounce it now) Wharf. It was time to part from their shipsin-the-night companions. They hovered uncertainly. The Irishman looked Leah steadily in the eye. He had a disarming way of doing that. 'Well thanks for what you did with Bella. That really was very kind of you.'

Leah smiled. 'Oh, it was nothing, really. My pleasure.'

He smiled again. 'Oh but it was. You should be a music-therapist! I appreciated it. Right then; enjoy the rest of your trip; 'bye.' His wife smiled too. Bella grinned cheekily.

''Bye then,' Leah replied. The trio turned and left them, heading back towards the town.

Shay cheered up at the prospect of an evening meal in the hotel. As they were still in post-wedding celebrating mode, and it was their honeymoon after all, they ordered a bottle of the best champagne the establishment had to offer. It wasn't comparable in quality with what they were used to, but it was fizzy and boozy, that was the main thing.

At ten o'clock, having also polished off a bottle of Chablis (and in Shay's case three whiskies too) in the lounge bar, they stumbled unsteadily to their room. A full moon was hanging in the sky, as if specially ordered, perfectly positioned outside the undrawn drapes to cast its silver beams into the room, and they left them undrawn and fumbled urgently out of their clothes and into each others' arms, and slightly too quickly, Shay trembled and groaned and his embrace became a bear-hug of orgasm, and he gave up his seed.

Later they climbed beneath the duvet and lay entwined, a cat's cradle of overheated limbs. Leah sighed. 'Well that's day one of the rest of our lives over, Mr Goldstein. How was it for you?'

Shay grinned in the moonlight. 'Okay, yeah, pretty good.' He was feeling extremely mellow.

'You weren't too bored, were you?' Leah asked, just a tad anxiously.

He hesitated, but only briefly. 'No; the ride over that aqueduct was quite white-knuckle. Not sure I'd want to be standing on deck on that boat, steering, though. Wouldn't do to lose your footing and fall off the thing on the one side, would it?'

Leah laughed. 'No; me neither. No, it wouldn't!'

'Shame about that kid screaming it's head off though. The parents shouldn't take them if they're going to do that.'

Leah looked at her husband, shocked. 'But she was only little. And she was really scared. I don't blame her, really. Poor little mite.'

'Uh! Well she shouldn't have been on there then, should she?'

Leah felt a faint icy finger of annoyance stabbing her chest. Shay wasn't showing a lot of empathy. 'Ah, come on Shay! I don't suppose her parents anticipated how heart-stopping it was going to be any more than we did. It's one thing reading about it in a tourist brochure but a different thing in real life!'

'Yea, well you certainly fixed her with your singing that God-awful song, didn't you? Perhaps that guy was right; you should use your musical talents doing music therapy for disturbed kids, or something. I hope none of our kids are such wimps.' He grunted. 'Okay, let's get some sleep, shall we? I suppose you've got another action-packed day lined up for us tomorrow.'

He untangled his arms and legs and turned his back. Soon he was snoring, leaving Leah staring up at the moonlit ceiling. Angrily, she got out of bed and drew the drapes across. The romantic mood was over. She returned to bed and tried to settle to sleep too, feeling just a tiny irrational twinge of loneliness.

The next morning they set off driving westwards, to Snowdonia. No, the planned activity wasn't as energetic as Shay had slightly sneeringly suggested. Leah would have liked to walk to the top of Snowdon, Wales' highest mountain, but that would have involved buying a lot of proper gear: walking boots, rucksack, correct clothing and the like. More importantly though, she would have had to persuade Shay. She knew he wouldn't be interested. She didn't want to push her luck. But there was a narrow-gauge railway that ran right to the top of the mountain, according to the tourist literature. He surely wouldn't object to that.

So they took it, but it was slightly disappointing. The mountains of the Llanberis Pass were majestic, the beetling heights impressive and the lovingly restored diminutive steam locomotive of the Snowdon Mountain Railway cute in its busy, puffing way, but halfway up the train found itself in low cloud and the promised spectacular view from the summit remained just that. The tea-and-snack taken at the summit café and the return journey in the company of more children, some of them fractious and disappointed, were largely silent affairs. Shay sulked and cast her frequent glances heavy with mute I-told-you-so accusation.

The hotel stay was fine though (at least Leah thought so) and the weather fine (for which she gave silent Heavenward-directed thanks) for the journey back through the mountainous spine of Wales to the hilly east and over the border into England. And the sun stayed with them through the verdant western counties and on through the pretty, quaint towns of Ludlow and Leominster and Worcester, to the Bard's magnificent half-timbered birthplace: Stratford-upon-Avon.

And the hotel in Stratford was certainly up to scratch, Shay confirmed approvingly. He put on a cheerful face looking around the town the following morning and driving to Warwick eight miles away in the afternoon to see the castle. He indulged Leah in the performance of *Macbeth* back in Stratford in the evening. And the final leg: the picture postcard Cotswolds and the White Horse, were to his satisfaction too.

Back in the apartment at the end of that final day, they collapsed into bed almost too tired to make love. But that was fine. Tomorrow they could relax; return the car to the hire company, do laundry, sort clothes and pack for honeymoon, part the second.

Leah lay in the huge feather-soft bed (it probably was one) waiting for Shay to come out of the shower to join her. She'd done nothing all day except lounge by the pool in her new bikini, basted with sunscreen. They'd opted for the most expensive villa. Well, Dad was paying. She had to confess; the hot weather and the glamour and the exoticism certainly did things for your love-life. Stimulated it big time.

Shay came out of the en-suite, naked, rubbing his hair dry. It was only day two and already he was bronzed like a god and achingly desirable, except of course for a narrow genital triangle beginning only just above his pubic hair. He dropped the towel on the floor, pulled the thin white sheet aside and climbed in beside her, lifting his left arm to invite her to snuggle in. She did. He sighed contentedly. 'It's quite a place, this, you've got to admit, Lee.'

Leah sighed too, although hers was not entirely one of contentment. Yes, the sex was terrific. And the luxury. And it was a relief to see Shay cheerful. But to be honest, she was a little bored. But then this was what marriage was all about, after all, wasn't it? Compromise.

She swept the sheet away and straddled him and his quickly growing tumescence, as his hands reached for her. 'Yes, honey.' She said, suppressing a second sigh, 'it is.'

Chapter 3

Leah could have cheerfully throttled Leo. If the record producer had made them play through the piece once he must have done so twenty times. To say that the man was a perfectionist was to put it very mildly indeed. It was hardly as if it were a major, important work; simply an eighteen-bar instrumental section mid-way through a love song. The band had got all their parts laid down and now Leo Matthews was buggering around being a pain in the butt with the session musicians: Maddy on first violin, Sam on second, Mel on viola, Charlie on cello and herself, the only woodwind player. There was supposed to be another wind player, a saxophonist, apparently, but they hadn't showed, which wasn't pleasing Leo terribly much and probably explained why he was giving them such a hard time. He'd grumbled about unreliable fucking session players and said, well, they'd just have to do it as yet another track when she deigned to show and splice it in.

Leah secretly thought that having both a flute and a saxophone featured was a bit over the top anyway; have one or the other, fine, with the strings as background texture, but not the two of them. She didn't think Leo was much of an arranger really, if he considered that the two worked well together. The strings, she and a piano would have been better, although the keyboard player in the band had an ersatz, electronic one. She meant a proper, acoustic instrument though. But then it wasn't for her to say. She was just the hired help; the lowest of the low, working for a flat (and hardly excessive) fee no matter how well the album did. There'd be no nice fat royalty for her, Maddy, Sam, Mel or Charlie.

Her reverie was interrupted by Leo saying, exasperated, 'Now come on guys; this isn't really all that difficult! You, flautist, what's your name now?'

'Leah,' she said, coldly.

'Okay, Leah. So let's have some feeling in it, can we? Some emotion. I want this to soar. It's a bloody love song, remember?'

Leah could have cheerfully given him the finger, pompous little prat that he was, and stormed out, telling him to stuff his pathetic little ditty where the sun didn't shine, but she bit her lip, nodded and said, 'Okay, right,' and turned back to the beginning of the instrumental part. She couldn't afford the luxury of musical integrity; it was a little bit of work and sustenance for her self-esteem, if nothing else. It was hardly that Shay and she needed her to earn an income as well, with his very generous salary and bonuses and all the rest of it, but she needed to show him that she could contribute; be an earner in her own right.

Leo counted them in and they played the piece through again, with Leah trying to summon every last grain of expressiveness she had. He finally declared himself satisfied. 'Okay, boys and girls, that'll do it. That's better, er, flautist.'

He'd forgotten her name again, already. He looked questioningly through the glass at Gary the sound engineer, who gave him the thumbs up. Leah sighed with relief. It seemed the product of their blood, sweat and tears was safely, finally committed to the digital. Leo was still grumbling though. 'It's a pity the saxophonist couldn't be arsed to put in an appearance, but there we are. We'll just have to do it separately.' He reached into his back trousers pocket for his wallet and took out a thick wad of fifty-pound notes, peeling off and handing two to each of them. Leah felt slightly repelled, as if paying them informally, tax free (unless they were honest and declared it), cash-in-hand were somehow slightly sleazy; put them on a par with nudging and winking tradesmen like self-employed plumbers, or something.

Their usefulness now at an end, without so much as a thank you-and-goodbye, Leo left them to join Gary for the alchemy of the mixing process. They put their instruments in their cases, donned their coats, hats and scarves and made for the door. Out in the street a chilly December wind greeted them, the same one that had been lurking outside on their arrival. The group stood in a woe-sharing huddle for a moment.

'Well God was in a foul mood today,' Charlie complained, resting his cello case on the pavement. 'Miserable git.'

'Yeah,' Sam agreed. 'As if our little contribution's going to make that much difference; all eighteen bars of it.'

'Oh well,' Leah sighed, 'It's something, I suppose. We have to be grateful for the crumbs that fall from the table of rock n' roll, I guess.'

'All the same it beats me, Leah, why you're lowering yourself to do this crap; you being Juilliard-trained, and all that,' Maddy put in. 'I should have thought with impeccable credentials like yours, you'd get work anywhere.'

Leah laughed bitterly. 'Yeah, well maybe I'd stand a better chance back in the States, but there aren't so many orchestras or ensembles over here.'

They were interrupted by the arrival of a flustered vision of loveliness: a female one with a woolly hat, long blonde hair cascading over her green parka, blue anxious Nordic eyes and a glamour model figure. It was clutching a saxophone case. Charlie and Sam took immediate appraising interest. She addressed the group in general in a twangy Southern-States accent, 'High guys! Ya'all are obviously musicians. Is this where the session for Vagabond's latest offering to the world is at?'

Charlie grinned. 'Yes . . . and no! Right place but it's over, finished. You're too late, love.'

The newcomer's face fell. 'Oh, *shit*. It's not, is it? I got here as fast as I could. I'm not used to your London subway though. Can't make any sense of the maps. They're a complete mystery. Found myself on the wrong line twice.'

'Underground,' corrected Sam.

'What? Oh, yeah. Right. "Underground."' The girl sounded peeved at the pedantry. 'Well, whatever, looks like I've messed up, anyway.'

Leah said, 'No, you'll be okay. Leo said he'd do the saxophone part separately.'

'Really? God; that's a relief. I'd better head in then.' Glamour model glanced gratefully at Leah. 'Thanks.'

'You'd better grovel though,' Mel advised, 'he's not in the best mood. He's just been giving the rest of us a hard time.'

'Oh, Jeez!' the American said. 'Right, I will. Best Little Miss Contrite expression on then.' She moved towards the double blue, paint-peeling doors. Abbey Road this was not. 'See you guys around then. Wish me luck!'

'You may need it,' Maddy remarked, a little cattily.

'Well thanks a bunch for that,' the girl muttered, opening a door. 'If I'm not out in five hours, send in a rescue party.'

Leah felt sorry for her compatriot, even though she was a brash Southerner who sounded like a refugee from Nashville. 'I'll come back in with you; I'm not in any great hurry to be anywhere.'

'Really? Right, thanks. Cool. I'd sure appreciate that. Don't really want to face the ogre alone. United we stand, and all that.'

The others were drifting off in various directions, calling See-You-Laters. Leah and her companion entered the studio, where Leo and Gary and the members of the band were still crouched over the recording deck, mixing. Leo looked up, scowling at the interruption, before his expression gave way to one of blatant admiration.

Leah shouted through the open door to the inner sanctum, 'Your saxophonist has arrived; lost her way a bit on the Underground.'

Leo came out into the studio, grinning. 'Hi there! Grace, is it? Well better late than never!' His bad mood had miraculously vanished. The band was taking a sudden interest in the new arrival too.

Grace expelled a sigh of relief. 'Yeah, right. Hi. Sorry I'm late and sorry to mess you around. I had slight travel difficulties. I expect I should have taken a cab really, or something.'

Leo beamed munificently. 'Think nothing of it, dear girl. Happens to the best of us. We'll do your part separately, no problem at all. Give yourself five to collect yourself and we'll make a start.' He looked at Leah. 'And what are you doing back here, er – '

'Leah,' Leah reminded him again. 'Just here to observe, if that's okay?'

'Well yeah, as long as you keep quiet.'

'Like a mouse,' Leah assured, through gritted teeth. She was feeling homicidal tendencies rising again.

Grace put down her instrument case; divested herself of coat, hat, gloves and scarf. Her petite shapely figure wrapped in a knitted woolen top and tight jeans was to die for, Leah thought ruefully, unlike her own skinny gangling frame. Leo handed her the score. Grace looked it over. By the time the saxophone part was separated out, there wasn't a great deal of it: just six bars. Hardly worth her coming, really. She fitted her mouthpiece and played a few scales, warming up, loosening her fingers, before playing through the brief piece.

'It's pretty,' she commented, approvingly.

'Yeah; isn't it?' Leo said, taking the credit for it as if he were the composer. 'Combined with the strings, it'll make a nice little middle section. You played it beautifully, darling.' He had made no mention of the flute part, Leah noticed bitterly. Grace fluttered her mascara-thick eyelashes. 'Thanks, mister, er . . . '

'Leo,' Leo said, 'Call me Leo.'

' . . . Leo.'

'Right then,' Leo commanded, handing her headphones and gesticulating to Gary to begin recording, 'let's do a few takes. When you're ready.'

Grace donned the headpiece and Gary played her the existing instrumental track. She listened and said, 'Yeah, that's good. Love the flute,' casting a friendly smile at Leah.

As Gary restarted the piece she played the saxophone part then waited for him to play the mix to Leo. No-one had thought to give Leah headphones too so she had no idea what the final result sounded like. She remembered from the score that the flute part began four bars in and then was joined five bars later by the saxophone, the two instruments playing together for a further six and the strings then rounding off. But she still had her doubts about the instrument combination. The sax would surely drown her flute out. So much for all that nonsense of Leo's about being 'expressive.' Although Grace was good, she had to admit. She played with great delicacy. Maybe it wouldn't sound too bad, really.

Leo made Grace do her part nine times with varying degrees of forte and tweaks of phrasing until he was happy with the mix and the band members were too. Then he reached for his wallet again and gave her the same fee as she and the others had received, which seemed a little unfair to Leah as her part was only half the duration of the complete piece. But perhaps she was being churlish.

'Well, that was good, Grace,' he said, his beady little eyes twinkling, 'If I need a saxophonist again I know where to come. I'll keep your name in mind.'

'Thanks, Leo,' Grace simpered. 'You've made my day. You're very kind. I'll be only too delighted. Just give my agent a bell.'

Leo beamed. 'I will. I'll see you around then?'

Leah felt like throwing up as they left the studio. Dazzled by Grace's superior charms, Leo had completely ignored her again. Outside, they hovered, looking at each other before parting. Grace grinned. 'Well that was alright: a hundred pounds for less than an hour's work. Yeah, I'll definitely work for our Leonard again!'

Leah fought down irritation. 'Yes, you obviously pleased him. You're good though.'

Grace smiled a little condescendingly. 'Well I'm sure you are too, er, Leah, isn't it?'

Leah said wryly, 'Umm, my mom thinks so, at any rate. But the wider world has yet to discover me.'

Grace said, 'Look; have you got to be someplace right now? Have you got time for a coffee, or something?'

'Yeah, fine, sure. I'd like that. I've still got time to kill. Hubby won't be home for hours yet, as the City of London financial sector completely depends on him.'

Grace laughed. 'Ah, he's one of those indispensible high finance guys, is he?'

Leah nodded. 'Right. Let's go find a café then, shall we?'

They quickly found one, a quaint little place that did Italian cuisine too, and settled themselves at a red check tableclothed table with a cappuccino each and a plate of some sort of Mediterranean pastries. After a slightly awkward minuet of Who's Paying? Leah handed over the money for both of them. It was a relief to be inside, in the hot little room, out of the biting wind. They rid themselves of their coats. 'So,' Grace began, between enthusiastic mouthfuls (and looking as though she hadn't eaten properly for a week), 'how come you ended up in London, Leah?'

Leah did her wry smile again. 'Well, basically it was down to Shay – the other half – getting a high-powered job here. He's with one of the top investment banks. A case of following the money, I suppose.'

Grace grinned. 'Well, you could do worse, honey. Marrying someone like that; a good provider. Means you don't have to.'

'But I want to! I want to contribute my share! I don't want to be just the little women stuck at home, the passive little wife, with no other responsibility than housekeeping and cooking to entertain and feed his boring friends and clients. It's a waste of my expensive Juilliard education otherwise!'

Grace's eyes widened. 'Juilliard? Really? I *am* impressed!'

'Well, don't be. I wasn't exactly a star pupil. Only got a B grade diploma.'

'Still sounds pretty good to me. Should be the passport to big things, with the prestige and everything, shouldn't it?'

'Well, in theory, maybe. But to be anything top-ranking, like a soloist, you've got to be highest-level. And I'm not. I sometimes think my dad only paid for me to go there because of all the reflected glory that falls on him. Gives him great bragging rights at his dinner parties, sounding off about his talented daughter who went to the Juilliard.'

'God, what sort of circles does your dad move in? Sounds like he's loaded too.'

Leah laughed bitterly. 'Yeah, he is. He owns the Solomon Weisman chain stores. Heard of them?'

Grace looked astonished. 'He owns that? Ohmygod! Heard of them, sure, but they're a bit out of my league. A bit above the trailer-trash level.'

'What do you mean; trailer-trash?'

'Well that's how some people live, honey. Other side of the track, you know? My mom and dad split years ago. He left us, the bastard. Mom and us five kids. So I was brought up dirt-poor on a trailer park outside Beattyville, Kentucky.'

'Oh, I'm sorry. How come you got to learn to play sax so well then?'

Grace sighed. 'We may have been poor, but Mom made sure we got the most we could out of school. Not that I was very academic. In my case that meant learning music. It was the only thing I was really interested in. And I had an uncle, who played sax with a jazz band. He was pretty good; his band often played in New Orleans. So Uncle Clarence sort of took me under his wing and taught me all he knew. I'll always be grateful to him.'

'I envy you,' Leah said wistfully, 'having a mentor like that. I'm sure that's the best way to learn. I'm sure his enthusiasm would have rubbed off on you. Better than simply having an expensive musical education bought for you by a parent who's a complete Philistine musically.'

'Well, maybe,' but I still envy *you*, all the same, Leah. I'd have given anything for a chance like that.'

Leah shrugged dismissively. 'And so what brought *you* to England then?'

Grace laughed, but without humour. 'Same as you. A fella. Although not a high-powered one like yours. I joined a band – two guys on guitars, one on keyboards, one on drums and me on sax. It wasn't famous or anything; you won't have heard of them. Then one of them and me started a thing together. He was English. I was absolutely besotted with him. Then they decided they wanted to move to the UK for a while. They thought the musical climate for our sort of stuff was better; they might make a better go of things. I didn't agree, but I got outvoted. But I would have followed my guy – Joe – to the ends of the earth. I was a naïve idiot. So we all came over, on a year's visa, but then the band split up because we still weren't having any success, and Joe wanted to stay here but the others went back to the States. I stayed here with Joe. But then he ditches me, the bastard, and I'm currently working out the rest of my visa. I'm damned if I'm going to run back home to poverty-stricken Beattyville just because some low-life does the dirty on me. As you can tell, I'm no longer his adoring doormat! I'm gonna see a bit of the world before I go back.'

'Oh, I'm so sorry. That's tough. You must feel pretty disillusioned.'

'Yeah, well. That's guys for you, isn't it? Been the story of my life, really.'

'Yes, I suppose so,' Leah agreed. They aren't all Prince Charmings.'

That was how the rather unlikely friendship of two not very similar people began. Certainly, they were dissimilar as far as backgrounds went. They could hardly have been more different. There was a chasm of wealth inequality. Leah lived the high life, in more ways than one. In material terms, Shay and she wanted for nothing and lived luxuriously almost up in the clouds, in their Canary Wharf penthouse, with sweeping balcony views across the roofscape of London. Whereas the place Grace called home was a dingy bedsit in Camden: damp, crumbling, sordid bathroom-sharing and extortionately expensive. On low money-earning weeks, seventy five per-cent of her cash (and thankfully it was always cash) went straight to her rapacious landlord.

But it was no great surprise to Grace to find herself in such penury. It was par for her course, really; only what her and her brothers and sisters had grown up accustomed to. She stoutly, defiantly refused to countenance the idea of returning to America until she had to, but in truth she couldn't scrape the air fare together anyway, not when so much of her money fell straight into the insatiable pockets of landlord Stavros.

So when the expiry date of her visa arrived, Grace was in no position to leave and simply stayed: an illegal immigrant. She and Leah began to meet up regularly and occasionally played together in sessions. Grace found more work than she did though, Leah reflected, not a little jealously. Although she was good, it had to be admitted, quite apart from her other charms. And she needed the money for the rent.

As the year turned and January Two Thousand and Twelve came and went, replaced by an unseasonably mild February, on days when neither of them had work they sometimes met up and walked in the local parks and window-shopped and sat in cafés, drinking coffee that Leah still bought more often than not. And then, on days when mutually workless, Leah began inviting Grace to the penthouse. The first time she saw it, Grace simply stood open-mouthed. Finally she found words. 'Wow! And you can afford all this?'

Leah was embarrassed. She sometimes was by her wealth and good fortune. She hated to flaunt it. 'Well, yes. We can, on Shay's salary.'

Grace stared around at the white carpets and white leather sofas and stainless steel and ceiling-to-floor windows giving onto the balcony and tasteful minimalist décor. 'But personally, I'd be happier with some something less grand,' she quickly added. 'I'd really like a smaller place, maybe somewhere out in the country, like in Kent. But Shay says we need to live in Canary Wharf for his work. He doesn't like the idea of a long commute. I can see his point, I suppose. He'd be very late getting home at night.'

Grace looked at her, astonished. 'You are kidding me, right? You'd give this up?'

'Well, yes, I would. Money isn't everything.'

Grace snorted. 'Um; maybe you can afford to say that, honey, but from where I'm at, it certainly helps.'

'Yes, I can see that,' Leah apologetically agreed.

She showed her friend around the apartment, to many gasps of awe and murmurs of *Holy Cow!* Grace was particularly taken with the gleaming bathroom with its enormous tub. 'God, I envy you that,' she breathed. 'You should see the one I have to share. It's sordid. Well, I don't, actually. Can't bring myself to. I use the shower instead, which is slightly less ghastly.' She paused. 'Er, I don't suppose I could use it, could I?'

Leah laughed. 'Yeah, sure! Be my guest. There's plenty of hot water. I'll find you a bath towel.' She opened a closet and brought out the largest, whitest, plumpest towel Grace had ever seen. 'There you go. I'll put the espresso machine on while you're soaking.'

'Grace laughed. 'You've got one of those? I might have known!'

After that there was no keeping Grace away. You could forget about walks in the park or window shopping. She wanted a slice of luxury at every opportunity, even if it were only transitory. One late afternoon in March, Leah (as so often was still the case) was at home having a day of reluctant idleness. There had been no work offers for over two weeks now. The phone rang. Leah's heart missed a beat. It might be work! She looked at the display and groaned. It was only Grace and she knew what would be coming. The warmth of friendship with a compatriot and fellow-musician was beginning to cool just a little. Grace was beginning to take advantage.

'Hi. Lee! How ya doing?'

'Oh, hi, Grace. Good, thanks. You?'

'Yeah, great, apart from exhausted. Had a busy day. Another session with Leo, and you know what a slave-driver he can be!'

'Yes,' Leah agreed, through gritted teeth.

'So I was wondering,' Grace trilled, 'if you would be a sweetie and let me use your tub? I'm all wound up; need to have a good long soak in civilized surroundings; relax a bit.'

Leah did a rapid mental search for a plausible excuse for refusal, but couldn't find one. 'Er, yeah, sure. No problem.'

'Wonderful! See you in about half an hour. Thanks!'

The line went dead before Leah could say another word.

When Grace breezed into the apartment at five forty-five, after Leah had activated the outer door and then her own, her face was flushed and her eyes bright. She was clearly on a high.

'Good session?' Leah forced the words out, fighting down her jealousy.

'Yeah brilliant! Actually it was all instrumental, not just a filler piece. And predominantly sax. So I could really get my teeth into it. And Leo seemed very pleased with me.' Grace smirked then added, 'In more ways than one!'

'Sorry, how do you m . . . ' Leah began, before the penny dropped. Yes, she wasn't imagining it. There was the faint but unmistakable scent of stale sex about her.

'Right,' she said coldly, 'well go and take a bath then.'

It was lost on Grace though. She beamed. 'Don't know what I'd do without you, Lee!' She was already kicking off her shoes and undoing her clothes as she headed to the bathroom.

Irritated, Leah tried to reapply herself to her novel. But she couldn't suppress the dark thoughts. *Well, it's up to you whether you want to be Leo's floozy, Grace. But you've got a bit of a nerve coming here afterwards, taking advantage, sitting in my tub, washing the evidence away. The thought's revolting. I won't want to use it myself now. I really am going to have to put a stop to this. If I can just think of some reason to. But then, good old soft-hearted Leah, you won't be able to, will you? In case you hurt Grace's feelings.*

Her morose reverie continued. It really wasn't fair. Okay, Grace came from a deprived background. And her circumstances still weren't all that brilliant, although she was getting a lot more work than herself now. But now, Leah suspected, she knew why. Yes, she was a good musician; that was partly it. But her other good assets, as far as some men were concerned, seemed to be, well, lubricating her career progression.

She was brought out of her black thoughts by the apartment door opening. Shay strode into the living area, wearing a broad grin.

'Hi honey! What are you doing back so early?'

Shay beamed at her. 'Hi babe. Well I just closed a major deal that'll mean a few more grand on this year's bonus. So I thought I'd have an early one. Surprise the little wife with a celebratory evening out. How does that sound?'

'Oh, yes. Well done! Okay, fine.'

He winced. 'I'm dying for the bathroom. Must be all the excitement!'

Before Leah could say a word of warning he sprinted there, unzipping as he went. He disappeared through the open door. There was a scream. Then a pause. Then Leah heard him say, shocked, 'Oh God! Sorry! Sorry!'

He emerged, red in the face; came back to the sofa where Leah sat. 'What the hell's going on? Why's there a strange woman in our bathroom? Naked, in the tub?'

'Er, she's a friend of mine. Grace.'

'Okay. Right. And why is she taking a bath?'

'Erm, because she asked to.'

'Right. Why?'

'Well, she likes taking a bath here. It's better than her own place.'

'Oh, she does this regularly, does she?'

'Yes, quite often.'

'I see', Shay said, although he clearly didn't. He paused, staring at Leah. 'What do you mean, "friend"? What sort of friend?'

'Pardon?' Leah began then burst out laughing. 'No, not that sort of friend! Really! She's a fellow musician. We sometimes play together in sessions. She's American. From Kentucky. It's not what you think at all.'

A smile creased Shay's face. 'Oh. Right. I see. I think. Still don't see why she takes her baths here though.'

'Well, she lives in a pretty crummy apartment – well, bedsit. She asked me if she could use our bathroom once and I said okay. So now she does every so often. I think she appreciates being civilized occasionally.'

They were interrupted by the appearance of Grace, hair wet and awry, hurriedly dressed and looking mortified. 'Er, sorry about that.

Should have locked the door!'

'Yes, you should have,' Shay admonished, trying to keep his face straight. 'That was a bit of a surprise, to say the least.'

'Yeah. Sorry!'

Leah, feeling slightly ridiculous, felt she ought to make formal introductions. 'Er, Grace, this is my husband, Shay. Shay, Grace.'

Shay was still grinning. 'Yes, we, er, just met.'

Grace modestly studied her still-bare feet. They'd left a trail of wet footprints on the pristine carpet from the bathroom door. Shay said, 'So, you're a musician friend of Leah's then?' He'd completely forgotten his own need for the bathroom.

'Yeah, that's right. For my sins.' She managed a tiny smile.

Leah said, coldly, 'Well, don't let us keep you, Grace.'

'No,' Grace said. 'Right.' She recovered the shoes she'd kicked off fifteen minutes earlier. 'I'll just, um, tidy up a bit in the bathroom. If I may.'

'Hold on a minute. Me first.' Shay had finally remembered that he needed a pee, and made for the bathroom. Grace looked at Leah and grinned. 'Well, that was an unusual way to meet your hubby, and no mistake.'

'Yes, it certainly was,' Leah agreed, failing completely to see the funny side.

Chapter 4: 2013

'Well I don't see what the big deal is,' Shay said, after first sighing heavily to indicate exasperation. He always did that, infuriatingly, as if she wouldn't notice otherwise. 'It's not as if you aren't getting any work at all, is it?'

Yet again the subject had swung around to Leah's lack of work. She sighed too (two could play at that game), fighting down her own irritation. 'Shay, we've been through this so many times. I want a little more than the occasional session work. I want a proper, full-time job. Preferably with an orchestra, or at least with an ensemble. Okay; I know I'll never be a top-flight soloist or anything, but I trained for doing rather more than adding silly little frills to pop songs. Some of which are crap, musically, quite honestly.'

They were lying in bed, not touching, after the nightly dutiful (on her part, increasingly so, nowadays) lovemaking. He hadn't got home until very late, past ten-thirty, again, and he hated food kept warm and dried up; insisted on it being freshly cooked, whatever the lateness of the hour. So by the time she'd done that and they'd eaten it was pretty well bedtime, because Shay was never a night-owl, on account of rising with the lark to make an early start at the bank. Like as if the financial world would grind to a shuddering halt if he didn't and worked normal, reasonable hours.

So although she wasn't tired herself, she had no choice but to come to bed too, otherwise she'd never see him. Not that his lovemaking was all that enthusiastic either. Not like in their early days. He seemed distracted; it was going-through-the-motions-mechanical.

'Why, though?' Shay said. 'It's hardly as if we need another income is it? I'm making loads. More than enough to give you all this.' He waved an arm around in the dark to indicate the bedroom and metaphorically the entire apartment.

Leah sighed again. God, the man was obtuse, either genuinely or deliberately. 'You still don't see it, do you? It's not about the money. It's about my self-worth. I'd like to have some, surprisingly. Feel a bit valued for my talents. Feel I've got something to offer the world, to enrich it a little. Is that too much to ask?'

'No, not really, I suppose.' Shay's words lacked conviction though. 'But you don't want to get too involved with a musical career in England anyway, do you? We don't know where we'll be a few years down the line.'

'What do you mean?' Leah retorted. 'I thought you and my dad had it all planned. You're going to take over running his operation over here if it takes off, which it probably will, knowing him with his Midas touch, aren't you?'

'Well, yeah. Possibly. If it works out. But I'm watching it closely. I won't get involved if it doesn't. We could be back in the States in a couple of years.'

'Oh, are you going off the idea?'

'No, I'm not saying that. Just being prudent, is all.'

'Yes, well, it would have to be a sound "investment opportunity" for you of course, given your job, wouldn't it?' Leah could barely keep the sarcasm from her voice. 'Just wanting to be involved in my dad's business wouldn't be enough in itself then!'

If Shay noticed it, he let it pass. 'Well anyway; we'll see. But it's not just that. Don't you want to start a family?'

Leah turned to stare at him in the dark. 'No! Not particularly! Not just yet, at least. Honestly, Shay; it's as if you're just trying to find reasons why I shouldn't have a musical career!'

'No I'm not! But it's better to have kids early than wait for years, isn't it? And I want my kids to have a proper full-time mom, not palm them off on a nanny or something. I'm just saying that it's a consideration, what's wrong with that?'

'Well I'll tell you what's wrong with it, and what's wrong with all your little schemes, shall I?' She was really angry now.

'Yeah. Go on then.'

'Well it's this. I'll spell it out, slowly. None of them seem to involve my opinions, my feelings, *my* needs. You're as bad as my father, you are!'

'Oh come on, Lee. That's not true!'

'You don't think so? Well that's how it looks from here; that's how it feels!

'Oh for fuck's sake, don't be stupid,' Shay snarled. 'There's no talking to you when you're like this. I'm going to sleep. Got a busy day tomorrow.'

'Yes, I suppose you have,' Leah said, tiredly.

Grace called the following day. She sounded excited. 'Well things are looking up at last! I've got myself a decent apartment. It's considerably better than that other shithole!'

'Oh, that's great, Grace. I'm really pleased for you.' Leah tried to sound enthusiastic.

'Yeah, it's really good,' Grace babbled on. 'Got a proper bathroom, with a decent tub, and everything. Don't need to use yours any more. She chuckled lasciviously. 'I'm getting regular work now, so I can afford something civilised.'

'Well good for you,' Leah said, fighting down jealousy again.

'Come round and see it, if you aren't doing anything.'

Leah tried to think of a prior engagement that would rule it out but, as usual, there wasn't one. *'You* not working today then?'

'Nah, not today. Got one off, for a change.'

Yes, Leah reflected glumly, *good for you, Grace. Things are going well for you, aren't they? Plenty of work, although how much is that due to Leo? Or for services rendered to Leo? For that matter, is Leo paying the rent for your place? Well, perhaps not. Mustn't be cynical. Mustn't jump to conclusions. You are a good musician, after all. Better than me, it seems.*

Aloud she said, 'Okay then. This afternoon, perhaps?'

'Yeah, great. It's in Robert Street, near Regents Park. A big old house converted into apartments. I've got the ground floor. Take the subway – sorry, "Underground!" – to Great Portland Street station, then walk up Albany Street until you see Robert Street on the right. Then I'm on the left, a few hundred yards along, number twenty-seven. You can't miss it.'

'Okay, right; I'll look forward to it,' Leah said, almost meaning it. Well, it was a way to fill an afternoon.

And, she had to admit, when it came to it, it was quite pleasant, taking the (grey on the tubemap) Jubilee Line to Baker Street, then the Hammersmith and City (pink) to Great Portland Street, and strolling along Albany Street through the pleasantly warm, optimistically sunny April afternoon. The first dusting of lime-green was appearing on the plane trees and there was even a little tentative birdsong competing with the traffic noise. She found Robert Street and after a short distance Grace's really quite elegant Victorian (she supposed) four-storey white stucco house. She pressed the bell button with the name Miss G Eriksson next to it and waited. Yes, Grace's fortunes had certainly changed for the better. She shouldn't feel envy; after her poverty-stricken upbringing she deserved a break. And her sexual morality was her business. It wasn't for her, from her position of privilege, to judge.

Grace's voice crackled through the intercom. 'Hello?'

'Hey, Grace. It's me.'

The door clicked and opened a fraction. 'Hi Lee. Door's open. Make sure you close it after you. My door's on the right of the vestibule. Got my name on. Also open. Come on in.'

Leah entered. It was probably an impressive entrance hall when the house was complete, in its heyday, before it was chopped up into apartments. Now there was simply a small lobby with elaborate cornicing topping three walls and a clearly later-added bland fourth one that presumably shut off the staircase, with two doors: one straight ahead in the new wall bearing three tenants' names and one to the right. There was the ghost of another door on the left, but all that remained was an ornate architrave framing a bland featureless panel replacing a door.

She opened the right-hand door. It gave into what must have been a large elegant drawing room, once, in more genteel times. The ceiling was high and corniced again, with elaborate plasterwork encircling the light rose. There was a fine Adam-style fire surround although the fireplace had vanished, replaced with another stark infill panel in front of which stood a coal-effect electric fire. A tall sash window to her right was framed by maroon velveteen drapes. The furniture clearly wasn't new; a chunky old-fashioned three-piece suite with loose covers of pink repp was grouped around the fireplace and a set of dining table and four chairs of indeterminate age occupied a corner. Along the left-hand wall stood a pine bookshelf and storage unit containing no books but a CD player and many discs, and apart from a coffee table standing guard in front of the sofa, that was the full inventory of furniture.

Grace, looking decidedly better-heeled now in new blue jeans and a thigh-length shocking pink mohair jumper and glass bead necklace, was on her feet and moving towards her to embrace and air-kiss. Leah laughed. 'Gee, this is certainly a bit better than your last place, Grace!'

Grace beamed. 'Yeah, it's amazing what a difference a few pounds a week makes, isn't it?' She looked around proudly. 'This is the best pad I've ever had.'

Leah could believe it, judging by what she'd learned of Grace's childhood and having seen her squalid bedsit. It was still hardly luxurious and the sad décor did no justice to the faded elegant character of the house, but it must cost a fortune in rent. Surely (unless she were now earning a great deal of money) and even though she was working the black economy as an illegal immigrant overstaying her visa and not being troubled by inconveniences like paying tax, she couldn't afford it? But she nodded polite approval. It was Grace's business, not hers.

'Come on,' Grace said, 'I'll give you a guided tour.'

A new doorway seemed to have been created in the left-hand wall, judging by the plain architrave and panel-less door (presumably because the original hall had been stolen from the ground-floor apartment) to give access to the rooms at the rear. Stepping through, Leah found herself in a fitted kitchen with oak units in an incongruous country style, looking circa nineteen-eighties.

'Now isn't this cool?' Grace enthused. She opened a few cupboard doors. 'Look, all the appliances are concealed!'

'Yes. Lovely,' Leah agreed.

Another door led to a rear passage and off it, a bathroom. Leah poked her head inside. It looked a little in need of a makeover too.

'See?' Grace said from behind her, 'my very own tub! For my exclusive use. I won't have to use yours again!'

'Wonderful', Leah agreed again, meaning it.

Then there was a small bedroom with an awkward lobby carved out of it to access a larger one back at the front of the house, in what must have originally been a dining room. An expensive-looking king-size bed with satin sheets and flowery duvet dominated the room. Leah regarded it with amusement. *Oh yes; and did Leo provide this, I wonder? Possibly to share the use of it?*

They retraced steps to the country kitchen and Grace threw open the outside door. She proudly presented an overgrown area with rank grass and brambles and a few roses struggling for survival, surrounded by a sagging fence. 'And look; I've even got a yard! I might even get it sorted out in the summer!'

'Yes, you do that,' Leah smiled. It could be really nice.'

'Right, said Grace, let's have a drink, shall we? Tea or coffee? I've quite taken to the English way of drinking it with cream. Or milk, as they call it. It's a bit different from back home. Sorry I haven't got a fancy espresso, like you, for coffee. I can only do instant.'

'That's okay; don't worry,' Leah laughed, 'Instant is fine.'

She watched as Grace made the drinks and rummaged in a cupboard for cookies, chocolate covered ones, fanning them out on a plate. They repaired to the sitting room and Grace plonked down in an armchair. Leah sat adjacent on one end of the sofa.

'Well, I'm glad to see things are better for you now, accommodation-wise,' Leah said.

'Thanks. Me too. That bedsit was a hovel, but that Greek still wanted a lot of money for it. It was disgraceful, really. Just sheer exploitation. I was glad to see the back of it, and him, I can tell you!'

'And you're finding plenty of work now then?'

'Yeah, I am really. I often play with some jazz guys in a club in Soho, even though jazz isn't really my thing, in spite of being taught by a jazz player. Leo introduced me to them. But I just shut my eyes and improvise and hope for the best, and it comes out okay, most of the time. It's quite fun. They seem to like having me around, anyway. So yeah. It's all pretty good, really.'

'Well good for you,' Leah said, trying not to sound bitter. 'I'm pleased for you.'

'And what about you?' Grace asked. 'Are you doing much? Work, I mean.'

Leah sighed. 'No, not really. There doesn't seem to be a lot of demand for classically-trained flutists. Dammit. I'm still getting a bit of session work but it seems few songs call for flutes nowadays. Perhaps I chose the wrong instrument.'

Grace looked sympathetic. 'That's a shame, because you're good. You're wasting yourself. You ought to do something like that old Irish guy, what was his name? "The Man with the Golden flute". He's made a fortune.'

Leah laughed. 'Ah, James Galway. Yeah; he's had the luck of the Irish, all right.'

'Well there you go then. If he could do it, I'm sure you could. You're technically very good.'

'Yes, well. Perhaps it's just a matter of time, or getting established, or something. They never told us at Juilliard how hard it would be, finding work.'

'No; I suppose the training is only the half of it. Although I wouldn't know, not having had any – well, not properly, like you.'

'Well, I don't think you missed anything. I'm beginning to think that having formal training is neither here nor there, if you can achieve some success – earn a living anyway – without it,' Leah said ruefully.

'Mm; maybe. But yeah, it does seem unfair that I can find work but you can't.'

That remark gave Leah the lead-in to the question she wanted to ask. 'And how are things with you and Leo?'

Grace looked puzzled. 'How do you mean?'

'Well, are you still seeing each other?'

'No. we never were. Not like in the sense of dating.'

'Oh, I assumed you were.'

'No! Okay; we hit the sack together a few times, if that's what you mean. But there's nothing more than that.'

'Oh, right. Sorry.'

'It's okay. And since we're suddenly into probing questions, how about Shay and you?'

'What about us?'

'Everything's, like . . . okay, is it?'

'Yes, why shouldn't it be? Why would you think it isn't?'

Grace's expression was unreadable. 'Oh; no reason. Forget it.'

Leah stared at her, expecting explanation. None came. She sighed and changed the subject.

The afternoon wore on. Leah's mood lifted. Grace might be a bit of a rough diamond, and a bit enigmatic sometimes (like an hour ago) but she was fun to be around. A tonic, indeed. She made more coffee and they were surprised to find that they'd gone right through the plate of cookies between them.

Leah glanced at her watch. It was four forty-five. She clasped her hands to her knees, rising. 'Well I'd better be off. The rush hour will be starting soon and then the tube will be heaving. I hate it when it's like that.'

'Yeah,' Grace agreed. 'Me too.'

'Can I just ask a return favour and use your bathroom?'

Grace laughed. 'What, you mean use the tub?'

'No! Just spend a penny, as they quaintly say over here.'

'Yeah, sure. Help yourself.'

Leah went to the bathroom, locking the door. She didn't have Grace's casual attitude to privacy. She used the toilet and stood at the washbasin, washing her hands. Her reflection looked back from the mirrored wall tiles. The shabby surrounding tiles needed their grouting re-whitening. Her thin-nosed face needed a bit of rejuvenating too, she thought, sadly. It was pale and worry lines were creasing her brow and the corners of her eyes. Her hair lacked lustre. She looked demoralized. *God,* she thought, *I'm only twenty-three. Not forty-three. No wonder Grace wonders if there's anything wrong in my life. I really must pull myself together.*

Her eyes wandered down to the glass shelf with Grace's toiletries ranged along it. Something bright caught her eye, a flash of gold. It was half-hidden behind a bottle of shampoo; a cufflink. A monogrammed cufflink, like the ones she'd given Shay last Christmas. The second cursive initial was G. She pulled it out, looked at the entire monogram. She felt the blood drain from her brain. Her legs buckled; she sat down quickly on the toilet seat. It was YG. No! It couldn't possibly be! But it was: YG. It wasn't exactly a common combination of letters. It suggested an unusual name. A name like Yisayah Goldstein.

After an abrupt leave-taking of the surprised Grace, she somehow made the journey home. Although in a complete daze, very nearly going straight past her stop. She let herself into the apartment and ran straight to the bedroom, to Shay's drawer where he kept his jewellery and bits and pieces. *Please, there must be a rational explanation! Let me find the pair!* But it was as she feared. There was only the one. She rummaged through everything, desperately, throwing things on the floor in panic in case the pair had got separated, but its mate wasn't there. She took the one she'd purloined from Grace's bathroom and compared it with

Shay's single one. Yes, they were an exact match, as she knew they would be.

Shay was home unusually early; by his standards, anyway. It was still only six forty-three. Leah had made no attempt to prepare dinner, or even think of something and have the ingredients ready and waiting. She was sitting in the darkened room when he came in. He flicked the light switch and nearly fainted in surprise too to find her slumped on the large sofa.

'God, Lee, you gave me a start! What are you doing sitting in the dark?' He put down his briefcase and approached the sofa. He could see now that she'd been crying. 'Hey, honey, what's all this; what's wrong?'

Leah stared at him, this sudden stranger. She pulled the cufflink from her balled fist and held it up to him, taking a deep breath, trying to instill calm. 'I think you lost a cufflink, didn't you?'

He stared at her; at the link. 'Er, yeah; I think I did. Where did you find it?' He reached for it. She snatched it out of his reach.

'Well can you guess where that might have been?'

He looked puzzled. 'No?'

'Right. So let me help you. At Grace's!'

'Grace's? But . . . that's not possible. It can't be mine then.'

He opened and closed his mouth a few times, like a fish out of water. 'I don't know where she lives. You must be mistaken!'

Leah laughed; a humourless cackle. 'Oh no; I'm not. This one came from Grace's bathroom. It matches the one in your drawer exactly. I'm not mistaken! This one; this one I had engraved for you specially, must be pretty unique, don't you think?'

'Well I don't know how it got there then,' Shay blustered. 'She must have got in here and stolen it or something . . .'

'Don't be ridiculous! Why would she do that? There's only one way it could have got there, and that's if you left it there. Isn't it!' Her voice was rising, approaching hysteria.

He said nothing; stared at his shoes. Wearily he sank onto the other sofa.

'You've been there. Been to her apartment. Admit it!'

Still he said nothing.

'And there's only one reason why you would do that, that I can see,' Leah fumed. She paused; remembered something. 'After all, you had a sneak peek of our Grace and her undoubted charms last year, didn't you?'

Silence. If he was trying to conjure excuses, he was failing.

'Although I've no idea how you know where she lives,' she continued. 'I only learned myself this morning when she rang to tell me. How long's this been going on?' Her tears were flowing again now, hot and salty and blinding. 'How long? Talk to me, you bastard!'

'It was only the once. Last Friday evening. We went to a club, in Soho, a few of us from work. She was there playing her saxophone. We, er, went to her place afterwards. But it was only that one time. I had too much to drink. I must have left the link behind then. I'm sorry.' He looked at her for the first time, pleadingly. 'It was stupid. I'm so sorry.'

'And why should I believe that; that it was *only* once?' Leah retorted. 'How could you do it? With my friend?' How could you?' Her rage was subsiding a little but still a dull, lump-in-throat ache.

'Well please do, that's all I can say. Please, Lee! I've been a complete jerk. It'll never happen again. It didn't mean anything. Please forgive me. I love you!'

'Mm. Well you'll have to give me time with this. Let me get used to the idea.'

'Yes, I know.' Shay was full of contrition.

'And meanwhile, you can get your own dinner. I'm not doing for you. And I'll sleep in the spare room for a while, until I feel happier about things.'

'Yes, okay; that's fine.'

'Right then.' Leah got up from the sofa; walked wearily into the kitchen to make herself a sandwich. She was damned if she was going to make Shay one though.

Chapter 5

After a sleepless night and although it was the last thing she wanted to do, Leah forced herself to phone Grace the next day. If only to get the truth, or at least her friend's version of things, which wasn't necessarily the same thing.

Rather to her surprise, Grace picked up quickly. She would have realized who was calling from her phone's display of course. But perhaps she hadn't noticed that the incriminating evidence had vanished from her bathroom and was unaware that she and Shay had been rumbled.

'Hi, Lee.' Her voice sounded guarded though.

'Hi.' Leah made herself get straight to the point. 'Is it okay to talk right now? You aren't in the middle of work, or anything?'

'No, you're all right. Got a session at the jazz club this evening but I've nothing on at the moment.'

Leah felt a stab of resentment. *The jazz club. The bloody jazz club! Had it not been for that place, this wouldn't have happened!* She drew a deep breath; steeled herself. 'Okay. Right. Well you're probably wondering why I left in such a hurry yesterday.'

'Er . . . yes?'

'Well it was because of something I found in your bathroom.' She heard a sharp intake of breath on the other end of the line. She hurried on. 'You see what I'm saying?'

'Mm; no?'

'Oh come on Grace! I think you know perfectly well! That cufflink. There, I've spelled it out for you. My husband's cufflink!'

A pause. 'Oh right; yes, he left it here – '

'Yes, I know he bloody did!'

Silence.

Leah tried to keep her voice calm. 'Don't start trying to deny anything, or lie to me. He's confessed.'

'Oh . . .'

'So I want to hear your side of things, right?'

'Right. I'm sorry, Lee. I really am. It just happened. We love each other . . .'

'*What?*'

'Yes. I'm sorry you found out like that. He said he was going to talk to you about things, as you haven't been getting along lately. He was going to propose a separation – '

Leah felt the blood leave her cheeks. 'What? What are you talking about? He said it happened just the once. That's what he said!'

More silence.

'Grace? Talk to me, damn you!'

'Yes, that's what he said.' Grace's voice rose, tremulous. 'He said you two were finished, and he loved me. Oh Lee; I wouldn't have started anything with him otherwise. Really!'

'So he hasn't just betrayed me, but he was lying to me last night as well! Oh God, oh God! I don't believe this!'

Grace was sobbing now. 'I'm sorry. I'm so sorry!'

But a cold calm, like emotional anaesthetic, had taken hold of Leah.

'And how long has this been going on then?'

'Oh, I don't know. A couple of months. Something like that.'

'*A couple of months!* But I thought you'd only just got this place.'

'Well, I have. Only been here a few days. W . . . I moved in last weekend.'

The penny dropped for Leah. *Ah, last Saturday! When you were supposed to be working all day, so you said, and got home late. And me cooking you dinner at gone eleven o' clock, because I thought you actually had been. You deceiving bastard!*

She said coldly, 'So he was fucking you in that squalid little bedsit of yours to begin with, was he?'

Another silence.

'*Was he?*'

'Yes,' Grace sobbed.

'And now, all of a sudden, you can afford a much better place?'

'Yeah.'

Something else dawned. 'Ah! So this is why you were enquiring about how things were between my bloody husband and me yesterday, was it? You were fishing?'

'Yes.'

'And that's really why you invited me over. It wasn't to show me your wonderful apartment; it was to check on the lay of the land!'

'Well he did say you two would be breaking up. I wanted to see when that might be!'

'Yes, right, I get it. Well, he's welcome to you. Although I don't know what he sees in you, quite honestly, apart from a nice pair of tits. And you're welcome to *him*, the bastard.'

'I'm sorry,' Grace whimpered, yet again.

Somehow, Leah made it through the rest of that day, alternating between bitter racking tears and raging anger. Her world had imploded, to a black hole of despair. She went back to bed, crawling under the duvet of the bed in the spare room without undressing. Curled up foetally, pulling it over her head, shutting out the world. She sobbed until her throat ached. Her brain was a swirling maelstrom. It felt as though it might explode, that she might succumb to a massive cerebral bleed or something. Well that would be almost a relief; the oblivion a merciful release.

The desperate thoughts surged back and forth in a torrent. *You utter, utter betraying bastard! Why aren't I good enough for you? Aren't I beautiful enough? Pneumatic enough? Well I can't help that; can't help the genes I was born with. Blame my mother for that. Or not sexy enough, because I don't like doing the weird things you like, or don't orgasm enthusiastically enough? What is it? Is it that I'm not content to be your dutiful little housewife, always ready with meals on the table,* on demand, meekly keeping our apartment spotless? That I'm restless living in this city, at the top of this shiny tower, in the midst of these teeming masses but still feeling alone? Would rather live out in the country, where I can breathe? That I don't want to be your breeding machine, providing you with rosy-cheeked children, just yet?

Or is it that we aren't, after all, intellectual soul-mates; I don't share your aspirations to be even richer than we are? That I don't regard money as the be-all and end-all? I should have known I suppose that you weren't really interested in me for either my imperfect body or my rebellious mind. But I did think you were. Serves me right, I suppose, for being a naïve deluded fool. But that's what insecurity; poor self-image does for you, perhaps. I don't know; I really don't know.

And what happens now? Do you expect me to just forgive this little peccadillo, as you probably see it, and forget? Move on? Well no; I don't think so! You can't hurt me like this and then just carry on as if nothing's happened. I'm just not that forgiving. Not like my mother when my dad played around. You can just go to hell, Yishaya Goldstein, and preferably burn in it.

But what's to become of me? I can't go on living with you, not now, whether you keep seeing my so-called friend or not. Even if you get rid of her, discard her like some sex toy you're now bored with, things can never be the same with us. How could I ever trust you? But how can I leave? Where would I go? I can't support myself because I don't have a regular income. The only thing I could do is crawl back home; throw myself on the mercy of Mom and Dad.

The unhappy thoughts churned around and around. Eventually, emotionally spent, she drifted into troubled sleep haunted by terrible dreams: a surrealist kaleidoscope of Shay's face, puzzled, innocent; Grace's enormous seductive bed, the covers in disarray; a saxophone wailing like a banshee; and Grace's face too, invitingly licking lip-glossed lips.

Until finally, dreamless sleep came.

She awoke with a start to the sound of the apartment door opening;

groaned, looked at her watch. It was eight-fifteen. Shay's voice came. 'Lee? Lee, honey?' For a moment she fancied she was awakening from a nightmare. It wasn't true: there was no discovered incriminating cufflink at Grace's new place. She hadn't actually got one. Everything was fine. But it was only for a second or two. Then reality came brutally crashing in. She got up, wincing with a momentary muscle cramp, and wandered lethargically into the sitting room.

Shay was looking at her, concern furrowing his forehead. 'Ah, there you are. You okay?'

She snorted tiredly. 'Well what do you think?'

'Yeah. I know. Sorry.'

Leah sank onto a sofa. Stared listlessly at the white carpet. There were crumbs on it, presumably the residue of a solitary meal eaten by Shay.

He sat down too, across from her, not meeting her eye. 'Look, can we ta – '

She cut him off crossly. 'Talk? What's there to say?'

'So you can't forgive me?'

'She laughed bitterly. 'Forgive you? Why should I?'

'It'll never happen again.'

Leah ignored that. 'I suppose you've spoken with Grace today?'

'Well, yeah . . .'

'So she'll have told you that she came clean with me, no doubt. That she told me about you telling her about our "difficulties." About you telling her you loved her.'

He looked at her now, pleading. 'Yes, but I've been thinking about that. I realize now it's you I want. Not her. As I say, I've been a complete jerk. Can we try again? Please?'

'Ah, I get it! You're just a total, pathological liar, aren't you? You lied to me last night about it, about only having done it once, like some nasty little one-night stand. And you've been lying to Grace too, it seems, about us and about having feelings her, just so you can have her as a bit on the side for exciting sex, as well as good ole, dull ole, plain ole

Leah to keep house for you and give you kids. And then one day you step smoothly into owning the Weisman Empire. Having your cake and eating it, I'd call that, you bastard!'

'I know. I'm sorry. It was wrong. I can see that now. And I want to give us another shot.'

Leah's voice was rising shrilly. She glared at him. 'Really? Do you now? Well you know what? I just don't think I could trust you now; I really don't, you . . . you . . . with your inflated ego and sense of entitlement. You can go to hell!'

'Well we can't go on like this . . . .'

'Too right, we can't!'

'So what are we going to do? You can't just go. Where will you go *to?*'

'I'll go back home, to my mom and dad. Then you can have your little floozy all to yourself, can't you!'

Shay sighed. 'Okay then. If that's what you want.'

'Yes, it is. Just for a change, it is; it's what *I* want!'

There was no work on offer again the following day. Leah waited until the late afternoon before calling home. With New York five hours behind Greenwich Mean Time, her mother would have finished lunch by now. It wasn't the normal phoning day, and she would probably be settling down for her post-prandial nap, but it couldn't be helped. She couldn't wait any longer.

She could never get used to it that with transatlantic calls there was no audible ringing at the other end. Simply twenty second's silence and then her mother speaking: 'Hello?' Thankfully, there was little chance of her father picking up; he would be busy running his empire.

'Hi, Mom.'

'Oh, hi honey! This is a pleasant surprise!'

'You okay?'

'Yes, fine, thanks. You?'

'Yes.' Leah hesitated. *Might as well come straight to the point; get on with it.* 'Well, no, not really.'

'Oh dear!' Her mother was instantly anxious. 'What's wrong?'

'Well; I hate to spring this on you, but – '

'What is it?'

'Well, I'm afraid Shay and I are having some trouble.'

'What; you mean like personal problems?'

'Yes; afraid so.'

'What is it? Come on, tell your mom.'

Leah paused again, then plunged in. 'Well, he's been playing around with another woman.'

There was silence on the other end of the line, before Carmel recovered. 'No! I don't believe it! Not Yishayah. He's such a nice boy!'

'It's true, I'm afraid.'

'Oh, honey! But . . . how? I thought you two were so happy.'

'Yes, well. So did I. But he's been seeing a friend of mine. As they quaintly put it. A girl I know; another musician. From the States. Kentucky.'

'No!'

'Yes. I discovered it the day before yesterday. It's been going on for some time. About a couple of months, apparently.'

'Oh, Leah! And your friend, of all people! She doesn't sound much of a friend, if you ask me, to do that! With your husband! And is it still going on then?'

'Well, he says he's going to finish it with her, now he's been found out. Says he wants us to make a fresh start. But I don't believe him. How can I ever believe him?' Leah's lower lip was trembling; the words were difficult to form.

'Oh, poor you! But you mustn't let it get to you too much. If he says he's going to finish with the little trollop, I expect he means it.'

'Mom! Did you hear what I just said? I said I don't believe him! If he can do it once I expect he can again, but I'm not having it!'

'Ah, come on honey. It's not that bad you know. You know what men are like. Probably just needs to sow a few wild oats before he settles down. Look at your father.'

'Yes, exactly! Look at him! How many times did he "stray?" Three times at least, wasn't it?'

On her side of the Atlantic, Carmel sighed. 'Yes, three. That I know of, anyway. But none of them were serious. I never felt really threatened. He always came back to me. I know I was never what you call beautiful, but he was so handsome and strong and dashing in his younger days. He just had a big . . . appetite, I suppose.'

'Well that didn't give him the right to betray you, Mom, and repeatedly at that!'

'No, I know, honey. But that's just the way of the world. And he's been a wonderful husband in many other ways. I've never wanted for anything. He's been a marvelous provider. To both of us.'

'Bullshit, Mom! You're being pathetic! It's not all about that, about material stuff. If he'd really loved you, he wouldn't have played around with other women. And beauty doesn't come into it. He should have loved you for who you are, period. He must have really hurt you, and known that he was hurting you. Quite apart from the deceit. I really don't know why you stayed with him, quite honestly.'

'Well, when I was young, divorce just wasn't such an easy option. Not like it is nowadays. It's too easy for people to split up now, just because things get a little difficult. And when I married him, I took a vow for life. Marriage meant something back then. You had to work at it. There wasn't all this feminist nonsense.'

Leah laughed bitterly. 'Oh, come on! *You* may have had to "work at it" every time he treated you like dirt, but he obviously didn't. Otherwise he wouldn't have kept doing what he did. And attitudes are different now. More enlightened. Women are much less prepared to be doormats now, and quite rightly. And anyway, we're supposed to be talking about me; my situation. A little sympathy and understanding would be nice!'

Carmel's tone of voice hardened. 'Well okay then, young lady. Yes, I do feel sorry for you. I know how it hurts. So what are you going to do about it? Perhaps you and Shay could get councelling or something.'

Leah snorted. 'No, that's not what I want. And he'd never agree to it anyway. I'm not like you; I'm not prepared to just forgive and forget. I never should have bowed to pressure, to your expectations, and married him in the first place. We haven't got much in common, quite honestly. Apart from Jewishness. And that's no big deal. There has to be rather more than that. I want out.'

Carmel was shocked. 'Don't insult your religion like that! Oh come on now, honey! Don't be hasty. You'll get over this. I know you will. It's not the end of the world. Just give it time. He's a decent young man. I'm sure he'll see the error of his ways.'

'Oh yes? Like Dad did, you mean? Like I should show some "understanding"?' Leah didn't bother to hide her sarcasm. 'No; I've had it with him. I want to come home.'

Carmel ignored the barb. 'What do you mean, "come home"? You can't! You're not a little girl any more. You can't just run out on your marriage. You've barely been wed two years yet. You've got to give it a fair chance.'

'Don't tell me what I should or shouldn't do, Mom. I'm leaving him, and that's that!'

'Well I think you're being very stupid! Cutting off your nose to spite you're face!'

'Okay, fine, think that then! Thanks for nothing!' Leah slammed the phone down, furious.

September

At last Leah had found a reasonable amount of work. A good week's worth, at any rate. *Vagabond* were recording a new album, and because they were a folksy sort of band, very inclined towards instruments like accordion and fiddle and banjo, they usually needed several supporting session musicians. That meant traditional instrument players. And for this production it called for a flautist on eight of the ten tracks. Leah accepted the offer from her agent (who had almost given up on finding her any work) with alacrity. It would certainly take her out of herself. It might even lift her spirits a little.

It was a relief to be at work, in the same rather dingy recording studio where there'd been that ill-fated meeting with Grace. She thought about that now, sitting waiting for a track that called for her flute, looking through the scores of those that did. *Yes; if only I hadn't struck up a friendship with her, just because she was a fellow-American. That was all we had in common after all. Then she would never have tempted Shay away. Things might have still been okay. Well, perhaps. Or was it simply bringing forward the inevitable, which would have happened sooner or later? Really, we two had little to bind us either, apart from religion. What's the expression now? 'Marry in haste, repent at leisure? Yes; that was us, all right. A very quickly produced marriage proposal just two months after first meeting, eagerly accepted, followed by a three-month engagement. Talk about naïve!*

She was jolted out of her ruminations. The band had begun on track number two. There were five of them, all young guys, playing lead guitar, bass, mandolin (for this track) keyboards and drums. They made a nice sound, she had to admit: folksy but with a strong rock beat underneath. Like some of those groups from back in the seventies whose music she'd heard. There must be a bit of a revival of that sort of stuff going on, presumably. And thankfully, they weren't being directed by Leo. Seeing him there would have been hard to swallow.

The bass player shot her glances now and then as he didn't have to concentrate too much on his fingering and grinned a slightly wolfish grin. He looked your typical dark, smouldering-eyed, gypsy boy-type rock star, with black shoulder length curly hair (was it permed?) in contrast to the other band members, who were short haired and in one case (the drummer) smoothly head-shaven. A bush of dark hair sprouted from the vee of his open-necked floral patterned shirt. He looked thirty years out of date. She smiled back, shyly, feeling slightly, ridiculously, flattered. It made a change to be noticed.

They played six or seven takes until everyone was happy then stopped for a break. The producer called the supporting musicians, a fiddler, another percussionist and a double bassist, to play their parts. The band found themselves coffees from the percolator in the tiny scruffy kitchen next to the control room and wandered back into the studio, some lighting smokes, watching the session players.

Then when that was canned, the band squeezed into the control room for the mixing. Everyone ignored the supplementary players. Leah struck up a conversation with her three fellow underlings. Introductions were exchanged: Jim was the fiddler, Steph the player of the assortment of percussion and Brian the double bassist. She hadn't worked with any of them before. But then she hadn't worked all that much before, period. On every other occasion, almost, there had been different partners, apart from a couple of times when she'd worked with Maddy and Mel.

'It's a nice album they're doing,' Northern Irish Jim said. 'I do like some of the tracks.'

'Yeah,' Leah agreed. 'And there's a decent amount of flute playing – no disrespect to you guys. Better than turning up to play just five bars.'

'Okay, none taken. You been in England long?' Brian wondered. 'Haven't seen you around.'

'Couple of years, nearly. Well, I've not been all that busy, to tell the truth.'

'Ah.' Brian nodded sagely, as if understanding why.

'What sort of stuff do you usually play?' Steph wanted to know.

'Oh, this, really. General session work. I'd like to do orchestral really. Classical. But haven't found an orchestra worthy of bestowing my talents on yet.' The thin joke sounded hollow. Her listeners smiled politely.

'So you're classically trained then?' Steph asked. You could have cut her thick Lancashire accent with a knife.

'Yeah. Juilliard, for my sins.'

'Really? I'm impressed! Jim said, sounding as though he genuinely meant it.

'Mm; does sound pretty cool, I suppose,' Leah said sadly. 'But it's not a passport to instant success, I can tell you.'

'Know the feeling,' Brian agreed gloomily. 'Neither is the Guildhall. I did cello; was going to be the next Rostropovich. Instead I ended up playing bass fiddle for rock stars.'

'Or Manchester either', said Steph.

'Or my old man and the pubs of Belfast,' Jim grinned. 'But I'm not complaining.'

It was nice, enjoying some friendly banter with fellow musicians. Good to be out of the apartment and her gloomy introspection. They broke for lunch: sent-out-for-sandwiches and donuts via Daisy, the teenage general studio dogsbody who was only too willing to perform any duty (because it was such a thrill to be working for an actual recording studio and meeting bands) and struggled back with two stuffed-full carrier bags from the sandwich shop round the corner. Then the band made a start on track three. Leah and Brian would contribute to this one too, although he was teaming up with Keith, the band's drummer, for the rhythm part, leaving her to play the flute part solo before it was mixed with the other parts.

It took most of the afternoon to record the band's part to everyone's satisfaction. Ed the producer glanced at his schedule. He looked at Leah. 'You've been sitting here patiently all day with nothing to do, love. Shall we do the flute part next to give you a turn? Or do you want to leave it until tomorrow now?'

'Oh, yes, okay.' Leah said, slightly flustered. 'Let's do it now.' She was beginning to think she wouldn't be called upon at all today; would go home to the desolate apartment where she and a stranger led separate lives, not having played a note. And she was happy to stay as long as needed. There was nothing to rush home for.

She took out her flute, put on headphones and arranged the music on the stand. She felt nervous, being the centre of attention, as if at an audition. Her mouth tasted like a sewer. *Please God; don't let me mess up! Where has my self-confidence gone?* The band members and Jim, Steph and Brian were watching her keenly. She licked her lips, took several deep breaths and began to play a few scales, loosening her fingers, disciplining her breathing. Then waited, nodding to indicate that she was ready. The band's part came through her headset as she followed the music, beginning her part on cue. It sounded dreadful. She was so out of practice, not having done so for ages. Well, there'd been no point, and certainly no inclination to, in the last few miserable months.

She played through to the end. Through the glass (he preferred to be in the control room) Ed looked decidedly underwhelmed.

'Sorry,' she said, 'a little out of practice. Um . . . had 'flu recently.'

He sounded disappointed. 'Okay, let's go through it again.'

The track began again. She closed her eyes; tried to focus. *Forget everything else. Just the music. Come on, you're a trained musician. Nothing else matters.*

The second attempt was better. She finished and waited for Ed's reaction. His voice came through, more encouraging now, 'Yes, that's better, er, Leah, is it?'

'Yes. Thanks.'

'Right. Now let's try it again. You're a little tense. Just relax. Let it flow.' He was a lot kinder than Leo.

'Okay.' She began again. *Come on now! Do what the man says. Expressiveness!*

The third try was better again, and Ed told her so. After three more, when the producer seemed satisfied that she'd given her best, he seemed genuinely pleased.

'Yes, that's it, Leah. That'll do nicely. You're good you know. Well done!'

She could have wept with gratitude.

Chapter 6

The flames licked and curled around the logs in the fireplace, dancing tongues of yellow and orange, mesmerizing her. Leah could watch them for hours. She sighed happily. You really couldn't beat an open fire on a chilly December evening. And a nice red wine. There was a glass of burgundy in her hand and the rest of the bottle on the small table in front of the sofa. She would probably finish it before the night was out. Well, there was no one to share it with. Mick was with the rest of the band, jamming it in the music room. It was two rooms away but she could still hear them. It would be high-decibel in there, not that there was any danger of upsetting the neighbours with several acres of grounds and many more of lush Kent countryside surrounding the house.

He and the others would be on vodka, probably, and also probably other substances. Not that driving under the influence was an issue, really. They were all, Mark, Seb, Will and Keith and their various women (who were in with the boys too, having their eardrums assaulted) staying here this Christmas Eve night. They (the band and WAGs) had collectively decided that Mick's place was the best for spending Christmas. Seb's pad was up in the Midlands and Keith's in Yorkshire, both geographical outliers as far as most of the group were concerned, as the other three had places in the south-east. Will and Mark's were both in London though, and Mick's country pile had been voted number one for the get-together.

She was now virtually part of the band following the spectacular success of the new album, not to mention the single from it (currently number three in the Charts). It was one of those that featured her quite a lot, so she had to join them on stage nowadays for it and many of the other numbers from the album. But tonight she wanted to be alone, quietly with her thoughts, not carousing. It had all been a bit of a whirlwind, the last few weeks. She wanted to take stock.

Her thoughts fell back a couple of months, to the day she left Shay for her handsome gypsy-vagabond Mick. She remembered his face; the shock, the hypocrisy written large as his jaw fell open when she told him. As if it were perfectly fine to play around himself (and for all she knew, not that she really cared, he was probably still doing so after being found out) but an outrage, an affront to his male dignity that she should reciprocate the betrayal. She recalled his stony, 'Well, fine, if that's what you want to do. I'll file for divorce then.'

To which she'd replied. 'Good! Go for it then!' and stormed out of the apartment and taken the elevator down to the entrance foyer to put physical distance between them and called Mick to say she was packing her things, at least as much as she could cram into all the suitcases she and Shay jointly owned (and she had no intention of dividing the bloody things equally; she was the one who was moving out) and could he come to pick her up as soon as she could?

Mick had sounded just slightly put out at being given short notice (although he was as keen for her to move in with him as she was, he'd said), but she'd returned to the apartment to pack, and Shay had said right then, he'd leave her to it and she'd be hearing from his attorneys in due course, and himself disappeared, presumably so as to avoid meeting Mick. He had arrived two hours later and, he taking the two biggest suitcases and she the smaller ones, they'd loaded them into his Porsche and driven through the dark October night to Kent and her new life as Lady of the Manor.

Two weeks later a thick manila envelope had arrived through the post by registered delivery. She hadn't left Shay Mick's home address before leaving but clearly he'd discovered it, possibly through an expensive private detective. Money would have been no object to him. It was divorce papers of course. He'd wasted no time. Shay was proposing – no, he was demanding – a bilateral divorce as both of them were currently resident in the United Kingdom. It was suggested that it be a 'quickie' rather than the no fault two-years-apart routine that was common in British law. On the grounds of her adultery and desertion. She had read the cold legalistic words in disbelief. *Her* adultery? But *he* had started it! It was a travesty. And there was more. Because there was no property owned in common (the apartment was rented and Shay had never followed through with his intention of buying property in London) there was, ipso facto, no property to be divided between them.

And neither could she, as the offending party, make any claim upon her husband's earnings. If she attempted to do so, it would be vigorously defended. Mr Goldstein, on the other hand, as the aggrieved party, was prepared to waive any claim for compensation from her. Besides which, they understood from Mr Goldstein that she was a talented musician with the potential for a successful, high-earning career. Therefore, she would not be financially disadvantaged by divorce and would not be entitled to compensation. Should she decide to go to law on the matter, it might well prove very costly for her. His lawyers had therefore recommended agreement on a mutual non-compensation-seeking basis, with Mr Goldstein, in a spirit of good will, being prepared to meet his own legal costs himself.

She remembered how stunned she'd been. She was the innocent party but was being portrayed as the guilty one! Remembered how, incensed, she'd telephoned Shay to have it out with him, but he'd simply told her coldly that in these circumstances one party had to be depicted as guilty; that it was hardly a matter of them agreeing to part amicably, for the two year separation thing, was it? It was simply the way the law – the British law – worked. And besides, if she were now shacking up with a celebrity rock star, she was hardly likely to be short of money, was she? But if she wanted to make a legal fight of it, he'd willingly take her on. And make no mistake; he would win. He'd been absolutely implacable.

So that was it. There would be absolutely nothing coming from Shay. Well okay then; she really didn't want his money anyway. He was right at least in saying that it wasn't as if she needed it. Not now she had her lovely Mick. She had replied that she didn't intend to either defend or counter-sue.

And then of course there'd been the matter of telling her parents. She'd phoned her mother in great trepidation, knowing the probable reaction. It had been just as she'd feared. Her mother had hit the roof, calling her a little hussy, especially when she'd confessed, just a little embarrassed, that she'd left Shay for a rock musician, of all things. Good God, Carmel had shrieked, almost apoplectic, how could she do that; had she taken leave of her senses? Knowing what people like that were like, with their sex and drugs and everything?

She'd pointed out, trying to stay calm, that Shay, with his apparently insatiable 'appetite' that she herself couldn't satisfy had started it, started the adultery, so what about *his* behaviour? Her mom had rejoined icily that it wasn't the same thing at all. At least Shay was respectable and doing a proper job, and a highly paid one at that, not strutting about on a stage screeching, making a dreadful noise. And she presumed this Mick, or whatever his name was, wasn't a Jew, either?

No, she'd confirmed, angrily, but that was a total irrelevance. She loved him – well, was beginning to feel that way – for his character, not his religion. Which was far more important, surely? And she had far more in common with Mick than Shay, who cared only about money. Mick was a fellow musician. All right, not a classically trained one, but having had training in that was no big deal it seemed, judging by her lack of success in serious music-making so far. And apart from that, Mick was funny and caring and left wing-inclined; a bit of a rebel. She liked that about him. He was an idealist; in spite of his wealth he wanted a better society, which was more than could be said for Shay, who was concerned only to protect his privileged position at the top of the heap. Or close to the top, anyway.

Her mother had snorted and called her naïve and childish, having her head turned by someone like that. And besides, what about her and Shay inheriting the business? That was completely out the window now. Her father would hit the roof when he heard about it. He (Shay) would have been perfect for the role of president in time and the Solomon Weisman name would have stayed in the family. But now, when her father could no longer run it, it would have to go public and pass into God only knew whose hands. And as for being sniffy about her expensive music education, well, she was an ungrateful little madam.

At which she'd told her mother to spare her the crocodile tears; the company would sell for billions of dollars, probably, and Dad would be sure to employ a good tax accountant to minimize the tax take. They'd be even wealthier than they already were. And regarding her education: they needn't worry about that. Now that she'd be earning good money herself with her association with *Vagabond,* who were really going places, she'd be able to repay every last cent of the Juilliard fees. In fact she wanted to; she didn't want to be beholden to them.

After that the conversation had escalated into a full-blown slanging match, with Carmel shouting that she'd be hearing from her father, no two ways about it, before slamming the phone down.

And sure enough, later that night the phone had rung, Mick had picked up, listened, smiled wryly and handed her the instrument, saying it was her old man. He'd been absolutely ballistic and she'd held the phone away from her ear and let him rant. She was determined not to answer back and have another blazing row. Finally, realizing that she wasn't going react in any way, least of all apologetically, Solly had said coldly that she did realize, didn't she, that there'd be no inheritance for her now? Not now, not ever; even when the company was eventually sold. Not now that she'd thrown such a spanner into the works and ruined his plans.

'Yes Dad,' she'd said, equally icily, 'I do. But that's fine. I'm just glad I got out now rather than years down the line after a great deal more shit from Shay. Which there would have been.'

Her father had said, sorrowfully and wearily, 'So be it then. You've made your own bed, young lady. Now you must lie in it. But don't think you can come running back home if this madness doesn't work out.' And put the phone down.

Leah drained her glass and picked up the bottle to recharge it; settled back into the deep leather Chesterfield sofa. The flames in the fire were dying down, craving another log. She'd put one on shortly. She smiled to herself, her thoughts still swirling around in her brain.

Yes, I've certainly done that all right, haven't I? Made my own bed, although only in reaction to Shay's behaviour. I wouldn't have done it otherwise. Or to use another cliche, burnt my bridges. Well, there was no option, really. I couldn't have stayed with him. Not after that. I'm damned if I'm going to be the meek submissive forgiving little woman he would have liked. He can roast in hell, for all I care.

And the same goes for Mom and Dad. No, I don't mean they can go to hell. But I've burnt bridges with them too. Although what could I have done differently, really, other than acquiesce to their wishes? But I'm a grown woman, not their little girl to order around as they please. It's sad to be estranged, but there you go.

Oh well: c'est la vie. Let's think of the future. I've swapped fellas and got a much better situation. I'm making music regularly, even if it isn't classical. It's good to be with a real soul-mate as far as that's concerned – and others too. And have this wonderful old house to live in, far from the madding crowds, in the English countryside. It beats that cold clinical modern apartment, any day. Yes, I've really landed on my feet.

She got up to put another log on the fire. The wood must have been well seasoned and dry; it was immediately consumed in a flurry of sparks and greedy flame. She picked up the bottle again while she was up. There was one more glassful left. She drained her glass again and emptied the bottle into it, feeling decidedly woozy.

She fondly recalled the good parts of the last few weeks; that whirlwind falling for Mick. Remembered that first session recording the new album and her first nervous performance, although her nervousness had quickly dissipated with Ed's kindness and gentle encouragement. And Mick's too; how he'd been very flattering, complimenting her on her playing, fixing her with those chestnut-brown take-me-to-bed eyes of his. She recollected happily how on the second day he'd watched her steadily again, almost disconcertingly, but in a faintly thrilling sort of way. Enticingly, really. Like tempting with forbidden fruit. But then, why should she regard it as forbidden? The betrayal had begun on Shay's part.

She replayed the memories. At the end of the second day the band had repaired to the pub, joined by girlfriends Kate and Victoria (Mark and Will, reluctantly it seemed, having to make it a short one as they had to get home to their families). Jim, Steph and Brian had packed their instruments away and left, clearly with other places they needed to be. Mick, who apparently was currently unattached and hadn't failed to notice her lack of a wedding band (she'd removed it in disgust weeks earlier) had asked if she wanted to join them and she'd jumped at the invitation. She was in no hurry at all to get back to the apartment. Having some fun, some happiness for a change, and with a famous rock band at that, was infinitely preferable. At the pub they'd split into two groups: Seb, Kate, Mark and Will at one small rectangular table and Keith, Victoria, Mick and herself at another. With she and Mick side by side, shoulder to intimate shoulder. His magnetism had felt electric, breathtaking!

And the same thing had happened on day three, and again on day five, the final one of actual recording. All that would remain to do after that would be further mixing and tweaking and arguing amongst themselves and with Ed until the album was as perfect as they could get it. So day five was celebratory apart from anything else. The music was all committed to hard drive. Everyone was on a high, feeling it was their best album yet. It would surely do well. Mick had stopped asking if she wanted to join them; it had become an assumption that she would. And his interest in her had apparently increased by leaps and bounds. He was impressed by her music education credentials, although less so by her background. But then he didn't really hold with great wealth. Well, except for performers and creative people, anyway.

And then that final day a tipping point had been reached. A point of no return. He'd been telling her about his place down in Kent, quite near Ashford (wherever that was) but up on the North Downs (hills, apparently); how it was four hundred years old, a former manor house with a fascinating history. It had sounded absolutely wonderful. He'd brought up the tantalizing subject again that last day, and she'd said it must be gorgeous, and he'd said, well would you like to see it? And of course she'd said yes please, like a shot.

And half an hour later they were roaring out of London on the A20 in his silver Porsche, then hurtling along the M20, way over the speed limit (although he was keeping a sharp lookout for cops). Then turning off on a single-carriageway road, then off again onto a narrower one, then a narrower one still before, less than an hour after leaving London, they were waiting for a pair of high, security-controlled, ornate iron gates to open onto a long gravel drive. Of course it had been dark by then, so she couldn't see the house at all until the following day. He'd let them in through a wonderful wide iron-studded oak door, just like you would imagine, into what looked like a very big dining room (although it was a 'hall' in the old-fashioned sense, he'd informed).

A middle aged woman had appeared through an oak door set in an oak-panelled wall, like a character from some quaint British period movie (although she was dressed in modern garb) whom Mick had introduced as Pam, his housekeeper. Pam had smiled and said hello, a knowing look in her friendly eyes. He'd asked her if she was hungry and she'd said yes, famished. He'd asked what about some pasta? She'd said, yes, lovely, and Pam had withdrawn to prepare it.

While they were waiting he'd taken her on a tour of the house: the smaller drawing room with diamond-latticed windows, the library (but given over mainly to records, CDs and tapes) the music room and the kitchen. Then up a wide oaken staircase to the upper floor with its five, beamed bedrooms, a two-room flat for Jane and three bathrooms, one of them en suite to the master bedroom which boasted, wonder of wonders, a four-poster bed!

Then there'd been supper, a delicious mushroom and courgette cannelloni, eaten off trays on their knees by a blazing fire in the drawing room, with a nice bottle of Soave to wash it down. And then Mick had turned off all the lighting, joined her on the big Chesterfield and they'd finished off the wine. By now her head had been swimming. She'd felt utterly reckless. Then Mick's lips had found hers and she was greedily kissing him back, wanting to devour him, and he was tearing at her clothes and she his; and they were frantically wriggling out of their jeans, and he was laying her down on the sofa and spreading her legs and then quickly, urgently, entering and thrusting, thrusting until she thought she would explode. And all the while she was thinking, as the fire blazed like a metaphor for abandonment, rendering Mick's face a flickering vermillion satyr above her, and she climaxed and cried out in ecstasy, *Stuff you, Shay! Stuff you!*

The music had stopped. She glanced at the grandfather clock standing like a mahogany sentry on the wall over to her left. Ten past midnight, it Gothically informed. It was Christmas Day! The others trooped into the drawing room: Mick, Seb and Kate, Mark and Bel, Will and Janey, Keith and Victoria. Leah raised her glass in salute. 'Happy Christmas one and all!'

'What? Is it?' Mick's voice was a little slurred. He looked rather the worse for wear. But still ravishing, nonetheless. She pointed at the clock. 'Yes; look!'

'Bugger me, so it is; Happy Crimble, everyone!' he slumped onto the sofa beside her, wafting a cocktail of odours: vodka, whisky, cigarette smoke, weed and sweat, in her direction. Will and Janey plonked down beside him. Seb and Kate took the smaller sofa and Mark and Brian the armchairs; their women on their laps. Mick realized he had no drink in his hand. He turned to look at her, eyes not entirely focused. 'Fetch some beer from the kitchen, will you, Lee?'

Leah laughed. 'Right. Like I'm the maid around here, am I?'

He grinned mischievously. 'Yup! General dogsbody, flautist, sex slave, servant, you name it. Just get the beers, woman!'

She thumped him good-naturedly, knowing he was kidding. 'They didn't teach you a lot in charm school, Jones, did they?'

He laughed. 'No, only misogyny. Now get the booze, will you?'

She harrumphed theatrically, put her wine glass on the table and rose; left the room and made her slightly unsteady way along the passage to the beamed kitchen with its hand-made oak units and granite worktops and butcher slab island unit and enormous cooking range that, frankly, terrified her. It was a good thing that Mick employed Pam. The monster chest-type fridge in the adjoining utility room (once a dairy, apparently) was mainly given over to cans of beer and lager as most of the food was kept in the equally enormous American-style refrigerator in the kitchen. Poor Pam (although she was being paid handsomely for her trouble) would be cooking Christmas lunch for them all in a few hours time.

Leah opened the fridge and looked at the contents, bewildered. Now what did Mick mean, exactly? There were at least four different brands of beer and three of lager. She shrugged and picked up an eight-pack of beer and one of lager. The womenfolk hadn't been asked if they wanted anything else to drink, she suddenly realized. Well, that was up to them. They could sort it out among themselves. Re-entering the drawing room, the subject of conversation was still music. Well, it was never far away.

' . . . I think we should do another tour,' Seb was saying. He was usually the prime mover in the bright-ideas-for developing-the-band department. Sometimes he tended, although he tried not to, to use his public school background to lord it over the others a bit. They didn't have a leader-figure as such and no front man on vocals, but as keyboard player and the most competent musician he was the principal writer of their songs, with Mark and Will sometimes contributing lyrics.

'Yeah,' Keith agreed. 'The album's doing brilliantly, and the single too. We'd be fools not to follow up on it.'

'So what are you suggesting, another overseas one?' Mick wanted to know. 'It's only six months since we took the US by storm.'

Seb pondered a moment. 'No, not necessarily. We could do the UK; see how it goes. Then maybe do Europe later. What about that?'

'Sounds good to me,' Will said.

Leah dumped the two packs of drink on Mick's lap. He could sort out the distribution of them. 'Hey, that sounds fun. So . . . would I be involved?'

'Yeah, of course you would, as you're on most of the tracks,' Mick reassured. 'And we'd take the other three session guys too – what are their names now? If they're up for it. Wouldn't we?' He glanced around at the others. They nodded agreement.

'Jim, Steph and Brian,' Leah told him.

'I'm sure they would be,' Seb said.

Will's wife Janey was less thrilled about the proposal though. 'So you'd be buggering off again and leaving me with the kids!' she accused Will, as if he were the only proposer of another separation from her man. Will squirmed, embarrassed about his possessive wife. 'Well, like Keith says, we'd be daft not to do it. What do you think, Bel?' he said, looking for support to the other wife-and-mother-with-kids-at-school present.

'It's up to you lot,' the easy-going Bel grinned. 'It's all more money in the bank, isn't it?'

'Okay then, are we agreed?' Seb said, ignoring Janey's objection.

'Yeah, let's do it!' Will agreed.

The others added their concurrence.

'Right. So we'll get our poor overworked agent on the case after Christmas then?'

Mark laughed. 'Yeah; let's make him earn his ten-per-cent!'

Eventually, at well past three in the morning when the cans of booze were finished and another bottle of whisky had been shared around, the inebriated company decided it was bedtime. Mark and Bel and Will and Janeys' kids would be awake soon, eager to get at their presents. And dutiful Jane would be getting up early too, no doubt, for her mammoth culinary duties. Leah would have liked to have gone to bed hours earlier, while Mick was not too far gone, while he could still perform reasonably vigorously (not that she would be much better in her present state, but it was different for women). She was already getting to know him though. He wasn't the world's best self-disciplinarian. Well, it wasn't only him, to be fair. When the guys got into one of their sessions of Bacchanalia there was no stopping them; they simply egged each other on. She'd sometimes wondered how Bel and Janey put up with it, being wives and mothers. But perhaps they'd simply learned to accept it as part of the deal of having millionaire husbands. Perhaps she would too in that situation, if it came to it.

They stumbled up the staircase in a happy giggling gaggle, the couples dividing at the top to go right or left to their bedrooms. Leah felt too woolly-headed to wash or brush her teeth; she simply used the bathroom, undressed and climbed between the sheets. She could feel a headache starting already. It would be grim in a few hours' time. Mick did the same. He lay on his back, snorting and sighing. He would be similarly afflicted but even more so. She wouldn't like to be inside *his* brain in the morning. She turned towards him, nudging his arm to signal that she wanted it around her; snuggled in the crook of his shoulder with her fingers combing the thick mat of hair on his chest. Then, more in hope than expectation, moved her hand further south, beyond the even thicker mat. He was completely flaccid.

'Sorry,' he mumbled, the words thick and slurred, 'Just can't rise to the occasion at the moment.'

'That's okay, love,' she said, suppressing disappointment. 'Happy Christmas, anyway.'

'Yeah, Happy Crimble.'

A minute later he was snoring noisily.

Leah sighed and leaned across him to put out his bedside light, then extinguished her own.

Chapter 7: 2014

Leah had to secretly admit that she was glad when Christmas was over. When they weren't playing or gigging, the band were a hedonistic, carousing crew at the best of times, with their drinking and drug use, some of them, but the festive holiday had just been ridiculous. Their normal overindulgence had been multiplied several times over, much to Janey's (and her own) irritation. Only Janey and Bel (who had of course to keep fairly sensible to look after the children) and herself had stayed reasonably abstemious. For most of the boys it had been one long splurge of excess. And also, to her disappointment, other than a brief drunken bedtime groping, lovemaking between her and Mick had been a hopeless unfulfilled expectation.

If Will and Janey hadn't had to return to London on the fifth of January for their six-year-old to resume school, the increasingly bleary-eyed celebrations would have gone on and on.

The band stayed sober long enough in the New Year to get Scott their agent on the case to organize the tour though. He rang back after a couple of days, while they were still gathered in one place, with a provisional itinerary beginning in June: Croydon, Southhampton, Exeter, Bristol, Cardiff, Worcester, Birmingham, Liverpool, Chester, Lancaster, Carlisle, Glasgow and Aberdeen; then returning down the eastern side of Britain taking in Newcastle, York, Nottingham, Peterborough, Ipswich, Bedford and finishing climactically at the O2 Arena, London. Twenty venues. How did that sound?

They agreed that it sounded pretty good. And if it proved a sell-out, as it probably would, they could maybe think about a European tour to follow. And then after that, think about the next album. Seb already had some ideas about it. Scott said great; he'd work out details of dates and so on, trying to keep a sensible sequence of appearances that didn't involve too much backtracking travel-wise, and of course negotiate the money angle with the venues. He was first and foremost their agent, after all.

Jim, Steph and Brian were contacted to see how they felt about touring. All three of them jumped at it. Well, when you were a humble session player, twenty or more weeks' guaranteed work wasn't to be sneezed at. And so it was left in Scott's capable and enthusiastic, ten per cent commission-skimming hands to work out the nitty-gritty.

With the festive season now over, the band settled back into its normal routine. Scott arranged some stand-alone gigs too, in smaller venues in and around London, and an appearance on Jools Holland's new series of *Later.* And a promotional trip to the States to appear on the *Late Late Show.* And a similar one to Copenhagen to pimp themselves on Danish television. He had already, months earlier, negotiated appearances at Glastonbury and Leeds music festivals. But they wouldn't conflict with the tour; it could be arranged to begin after Glastonbury and could be interrupted by Leeds.

The single had peaked at number four in the Charts and was now sliding down, but the album continued to sell spectacularly well. It looked as though it would be their best seller to date. In between occasional performances and appearances, before the tour got under way, there would be days when they could develop some of Seb (and Mark and Will's) new song ideas. So there was a busy year in prospect.

With the annual binge of Christmas now over, Mick calmed down a little. He returned to his normal romantic, ravishing, Heathcliffian self; the self she found so irresistible. His lovemaking again carried her on a wild transport of delight. She had often felt uncomfortable with Shay, particularly when he demanded that she do unorthodox things and she demurred, and he sulkily said, well, she'd do it if she really loved him. With him she had increasingly felt a dearth of love; as little more than a sex object. Or a baby-making machine. And she ruefully understood why now. Shay had been finding most of his sexual needs satisfied in another's bed.

Whereas Mick was so different! He knew exactly how to arouse her passion; how to pique her desire; set her hormones coursing, her nerves jangling with need. All right, he didn't mention love. He was no Romantic poet, for all his sultry dangerous looks, but at least he was honest about things. She was under no illusions, knew exactly the limitations of what he was offering, and it was fine, just fine. She'd had enough of promises of rose gardens, as the song had it, for a while, thank you very much. But if in time love should grow from physical gratification, well that would be wonderful. But meanwhile she would keep expectations firmly in check.

January gave way to a wet blowy February, which in turn deferred to an equally wild March. And with March's lion-like entry, one day through the post came more divorce papers: the decree nisi, granted without too much delay because the judge had noted that it was uncontested and undefended. So now it really was a reality. It was all over, bar the shouting. And there wouldn't be any more of that. No more histrionics. Leah wouldn't give her husband of two short years that satisfaction. There was now just the decree absolute to follow in six weeks or so, and then that really would be it.

She had had no contact with her parents since the angry phone conversations last November and she had no desire for any more of them. If her mom had been content to be a doormat all her married life to a deceiving philandering husband in exchange for the glittery trappings of wealth, that was up to her. But she, Leah Sharon Weisman, was having none of it. Not bloody likely! And as for Dad, well, she saw no obligation to please or kowtow to him really, considering the way he'd treated Mom all these years. He didn't deserve her respect.

She would wait for the absolute to come through and then write them a letter, keeping it polite, informing them that she and Shay were no longer married. And as far as her father's plans for succession were concerned: well, it was just tough.

And sure enough the decree absolute papers arrived at the end of

April. She stared at the cold legalistic words; breathed a huge sigh of relief. There was a faint underlying sediment of sadness though, for what might have been. Irritated, she banished it. Away with you! There was no point in grieving for a future that wouldn't now be. She determinedly kept her thoughts positive: *well, this is it now. You really are rid of him. Already it feels like some bad dream, a brief interlude that never actually happened. Now you really are on your own. Free to live your own life. Travel wherever life takes you. Follow the Yellow Brick Road.*

She got onto Mick's computer and typed an email to her parents:

Dear Mom and Dad,

This is to let you know that the decree absolute for my divorce has now come through. Although it's been done through the British courts, it will be completely legally binding in the U.S., apparently. So that's it, I thought I should let you know.

I know you will be very disappointed in me, and I'm really sorry about that. But I have to live my own life. Things are different these days, Mom. Women don't have to be trapped in unhappy marriages and I certainly didn't intend to be. Marrying Shay was a silly mistake. I suppose we were too young to really know our own minds. So I think it's for the best that we've parted. I want to have another chance at happiness.

And I'm sorry my splitting from Shay has messed up your plans for succession of the business, Dad. But I have to put my own happiness first. I hope you will come to see that in time. I do appreciate your paying for me to go to Juilliard, and hopefully the education and your money will not have been wasted. I'm quite well established with the band, Vagabond, that I've become involved with and they (and therefore I) are doing very well with the latest album. So I am doing okay money-wise, I'm sure you'll be pleased to know, anyway. (I think you might like my boyfriend's house, it's a really old place, completely genuine, out in the country in Kent, not too far from London.)

But as you say Dad, I've made my own bed and now I must lay in it. That's fair enough, I'm a big girl now and I'm prepared to face the consequences of my actions.

Well that's about all I've got to say right now. Look after yourselves,

Love,

Leah

She read the letter through, sighed heavily and clicked Send.

It was May. The band was filling in time waiting for Glastonbury the following month. Then hot on the heels of that excitement and anticipation (she had yet to play before a really large audience) the tour would start. Congregated at Will's London pad, an elegant Georgian house in Berkeley Square (beneath which he'd had a basement music room built), *Vagabond* were trying out a new number, a slow one, Seb's latest creation. To Leah's slight chagrin it didn't involve any flute playing. But, she admonished herself, she couldn't expect every single one to include her, just because she was a band member now.

They played it through a few times, experimentally.

'Well I think,' Seb opined, 'it needs a nice slow sexy instrumental part in the middle, as it's basically a love song.'

'Yeah, I agree,' said Mark.

'Like a flute part?' Leah suggested hopefully.

'Nah, let's give that a rest for a bit,' Will said, sounding rather cuttingly dismissive. 'Fiddle and cello, perhaps?'

'No, I was thinking more in terms of something like a sax.' As usual, Seb knew exactly the sort of sound he wanted. 'I don't want it to be too gypsy. It needs a really smoochy feel to it.'

'I'd go for that', Mick agreed.

'Me too,' Keith said.

Mark grinned. 'Yeah, could be good.'

'Okay then; a sax it is. I'll see who we can get as a session player.' Also as usual, Seb had got his way.

'There's that woman who plays jazz and also does session work,' Mark suggested. 'She's very good. What's her name now? American, isn't she? On Laurie Morris's books, I think.'

'Oh, do you mean Grace? Grace Eriksson?' asked Mark.

'Yeah, that's the chick,' Will confirmed.

Mick looked at Leah, grinning. 'Isn't that the woman you were telling me about, the one your ex . . . ?' He left the question hanging.

'Yes,' Leah muttered through gritted teeth.

Two days later, back at Boughton Manor on an unusually lazy day with nothing very much to do, her phone rang, nearly giving her a heart attack. It was a rare occurrence, as she had so few friends and no spouse now. She looked at the display and groaned. Picked up. 'Hi, Grace.'

The voice on the other end sounded tight with embarrassment. 'Hi, Lee. How you doing?'

'Oh, well, you know. Quite busy now.'

'Yes, I'm sure. That's good . . . '

'So, what can I do for you?' Leah asked coldly.

'Well, I'm sorry about this, but I suppose you know. Your band wants a session musician and I've been approached. How do you feel about it?'

Leah snorted. 'You're concerned about *my* feelings, Grace?'

'Yes, well I'd understand if you didn't want me around . . . '

'That's very sensitive of you!' Leah couldn't keep the sarcasm from her voice.

Grace sounded utterly miserable. 'I know. Give me a hard time, that's okay. But I wanted you to know; there's nothing between him and me now.'

Leah repeated her snort. 'Well as if I care what's going on with either of you two now. We're divorced, so he can do what the hell he likes. He can fuck half of London for all I care!'

'Oh, right. I see. I'm so sorry, Lee.'

Leah sighed. 'Don't be. I think it would have happened sooner or later. Maybe it's a good thing it was sooner, really, before we'd had any kids. That would have really complicated things. At least this way it was a clean break.'

'Yeah, I suppose so. Well he did the dirty on both of us, anyway. Betraying and lying to you, and lying to me too. The bastard.'

'Yes, he's a complete asshole. So did he dump you then, or has he been playing away from home with you too?'

Grace sounded close to tears. 'I don't know really. He may have been. I think he only really wanted me for sex, in spite of all the things he said; I was just his bit on the side. Anyway, he's finished with me. It's been over for five months now. He just stopped coming to see me. Perhaps he's moved on to someone more in his league. I know I'm only a brainless little hick from Kentucky.'

'Okay, right.' Leah didn't know how to reply to that.

Grace continued, pleadingly now, 'So it's okay if I play with your band then, is it?'

Leah laughed mirthlessly. 'It's fine by me. You can't steal from me again.' She paused as a thought occurred. 'No Grace, you can't. You certainly won't, anyway. I take it you know I'm with Mick Jones from *Vagabond?*'

'Yes, I did know. Shay told me.'

'Right. Well here's a warning. Stay away from him if you value your health. If you so much as flutter your pretty little eyes at him once, I'll scratch the fuckers out. Okay?'

'Yes; of course not. I promise. Besides, I'm not hanging around. I can't. My visa's expired and the immigration people are on to me. They've served me a month's notice to leave the country, so I'm trying to make as much money as I can to buy an airline ticket. Otherwise I'll be arrested and put in a detention centre, or something, and then forcibly removed, they say.'

'Oh, I see . . . '

'Yeah, so you see I'm no threat. Honestly. And I do need this work; I must have the money.'

'Right then. Well I don't know whether I'll see you when the band next plays around with their new track. I don't know when they plan to actually record it properly; perhaps not until they've written all the stuff for another album. Maybe they'll record you separately and then add you to the mixing when they do it, if they like what you do. If you aren't going to be around in England much longer.'

'Yeah, maybe,' Grace said sadly.

There was a long awkward pause; there was nothing left to say.

'Okay; 'bye.'

'Right. See you.'

When he returned that evening, over a delicious coq au vin rustled up by Pam, Leah told Mick about Grace's breakup with Shay and upcoming expulsion from Britain. He seemed oddly unmoved; merely grunted acknowledgement of the news.

'So it seems if you want to use her, particularly, you'll have to do so pretty soon, before she goes back to America.'

'Okay, right. I'll tell Seb.' Mick seemed to be on a bit of a downer. Probably C-dust blues. Craving another line. He seemed to have the biggest drug habit of the five band members. In fact Mark and Will, being a little older and also perhaps because they had the responsibility of marriage and fatherhood, were clean now, according to their wives. Leah wished Mick could get off it too. Perhaps he would in time, now he had a good woman in his life.

She tried to jolly him up. 'Soon be Glastonbury now. Just four weeks. I can't wait!'

His face showed a glimmer of animation. Music talk always cheered him up. 'Yeah, it'll be good. And we're on the Pyramid Stage too; the main one. Not exactly headlining, but even so, it's the Pyramid. Let's hope the weather stays dry. They've had shocking weather down there some years. It's been a complete quagmire. I used to go there before we formed the band and it was terrible for mud sometimes.'

Leah laughed. 'Typical British weather then?'

He smiled too. 'Yeah, you could say that.'

'And are the other session guys signed up for it?'

'The fiddler is. The one we used on the album. What's his name now?' Not sure about anyone else. Well there's no point really. It's more a case of mega-decibels than great musical arrangement and all that. That's all the punters want.'

'Jim.'

'What? Oh, yeah. Right.'

'He'll be a bit lonely then, standing at the back by himself!'

Mick frowned. 'What do you mean? You'll be there with him.'

'Oh, won't I be at the front with you guys?'

'No, of course not! You're not a band member, really, are you?'

Leah felt the temperature drop a couple of degrees. 'Oh, I thought I was now . . . '

He sighed condescendingly. 'No, of course you aren't. You're a supporting musician, obviously. Anyway, we'll be doing a set that includes some stuff from our other albums too, and none of it includes flute.'

'Oh. What about royalties then?'

'What about them?'

'Well, er, I get a share, don't I? Only on the songs I contribute to, obviously.'

Mick stared at her. 'Of course you don't, if you're not an original band member. You're on a flat fee, like the other session musicians. Christ, woman, what do you expect? It's not like you're one of us: a founder member, who struggled to build the band up, is it? I thought you realized that.'

'Oh, I just assumed, as we're an item now . . . '

'Well don't assume! Even if I thought you should have a share, the others wouldn't agree to it.'

Mick's scowl relaxed into a smile. 'Ah, come on now Lee. It's not a bad fee you get for sessions, is it? It's a lot better than being on the minimum wage. And look at it this way: you're living here in luxury, full board, everything found, without it costing you a penny, aren't you? The dosh you get is like . . . pocket money really. You haven't got any expenses. You've got it easy. A lot of poor buggers have to get by on very little, really.'

'Oh, I see,' Leah said, deflated. Suddenly, she didn't feel terribly amorous.

Now it was Leah's turn for the blues. The situation, the relationship with the band seemed to have redefined itself. Or it had never been what she'd fondly imagined in the first place. She brooded over what Mick had said, and cursed herself for her naivety. Yes, he was right really, she thought glumly. What a fool to think she could just waltz right in and share their riches and success! The thought struck her now: she'd been so enthralled, living with beautiful Mick in his beautiful house in the country that she hadn't noticed the lack of money coming her way as the album had triumphed and the single sold in its many gratifying thousands. She'd just assumed that, somewhere, the band's accountants were setting aside a nest egg for her as her share of the earnings.

Although she supposed Mick did have a point. She didn't want for anything. She *did* live in luxury, as she'd done all her life. And he was right. She might have contributed to their latest creative effort in her small way, but she hadn't in any real measure to the burgeoning of their fame. She was really just Little Miss Spoiled Girl from New York, of unremarkable musical ability, like some eighteenth-century well-bred young lady doing it as a hobby, expecting everything for her upkeep to be provided, complacently assuming it would just land on her plate as of right. She hadn't worked for anything, strived for anything off her own bat, in her life. Not really. It was pretty depressing.

But at least there wasn't the awkwardness of meeting Grace again. A week later the band got together in the recording studio and she met them there so that they could record her part. Leah didn't go. She had no wish to. Apart from any antipathetic feelings she might have, there was no point in her being present as there was no flute playing involved. So she stayed at home and pottered about the house, strolling in the grounds, looking at movies on satellite and chatting to Pam; even helping her in the kitchen. It was good, a distraction, if only partial, to bury herself in practical tasks; it made her feel useful.

All the same, insecurity raised its unwelcome head and she worried. And when Mick returned that evening she scanned his face, anxiously searching for the slightest tell-tale sign of . . . what? Embarrassment on his part? Guilt? Eyes sliding quickly away, unwilling to meet her own? But there was nothing, as far as she could tell. And when they made love later, he was as enthusiastic as ever. She relaxed. There was nothing to worry about.

And her mood lifted when the America trip came around. It was good to be nostalgically visiting New York, going home, and doing her second TV appearance (the Jules Holland one had been the first, in April) although, obviously, she didn't take part in the interview on the *Late Late Show*, simply supported their performance of the single at the end of it. And then there was the Denmark visit, which was wonderful too. She was amazed at how fluently their considerate hosts spoke English; there was no language difficulty at all, as she'd imagined there might be. May had become a very busy month. Life was hectic and exciting.

June arrived and with it Glastonbury. It was thrilling too seeing some more of England, driving in the band's touring bus with Jim, camp-followers Kate and Victoria, Alvin the production manager, the flamboyantly tattooed roadies and all their equipment out to the west, past iconic Stonehenge to the county of Somerset with its famous and mysterious hill, Glastonbury Tor, rising like an island and topped by a ghostly romantic ruined tower out of the flat verdant landscape. She'd looked it up on the internet; learned that it was steeped in Pagan and Celtic legend; that it was claimed in later folklore to be the mythical

Avalon, final resting place of King Arthur, no less!. It sounded wonderful. She would have liked to have taken time out to visit it close up, not just see it poking up enticingly in the distance as they approached Worthy Farm outside Glastonbury town, where the festival was held. But the band was on a tight schedule: travel down on the Saturday afternoon, set up on Sunday morning for the afternoon performance (they were the first band on) and then dismantle and drive back home during the evening to prepare the next day for the tour. There was no time for the unnecessary distraction of sightseeing.

Thankfully (especially for the punters, who had camped in the fields surrounding the site), the weather had been kind. So far that weekend it had stayed dry – not blazingly hot, true, but at least it wasn't raining. There was no mud to have to wade through. And the performance was tremendous, if a little nerve-wracking in the anticipation, being up on stage before that huge sea of excited, expectant faces. She was quite relieved to be standing at back with Jim after all. The noise was extraordinary. There was no silent appreciation of the music they were making. The strobing, pulsating colours of the light show were a visual intoxication too.

She could see what Mick had meant about the performance not being very subtle, not being carefully crafted like a studio recording. She had a mic attached to her flute to amplify sound, but it still sounded a little puny. If she'd played completely off-key, she doubted whether the listeners would have either noticed or minded. When they started into a selection of the new album tracks, and particularly the single, the bobbing and waving audience went wild. It was exhilarating!

And then it was all over. Seb thanked the excited whistling and cheering multitude and they trooped off, paused and then went back on again to do an encore, which was also rapturously received. Still the crowd bayed for more, so they did another one, another hit from a previous album so there was no call for Leah to contribute, and then another one. And then it really was finally over. They stayed off stage and did a rapid exit to the performers' hospitality suite, dodging autograph hunters, flopping into chairs, looking around for celebratory booze. Mick looked wild-eyed; he was really on a high. But then he'd done a line half an hour before starting the set.

'Well that went very well guys!' Seb observed, grinning from ear to ear.

'Yeah, brilliant,' they all chorused.

'Yes, wonderful!' Leah agreed.

Chapter 8

They were back in London by nine-thirty on that still-sunny June evening, returning the bus to its secure lock-up garage (a small redundant warehouse, actually) a stone's throw from Connor the roadie foreman's house, where he could keep an eye on it. Mick, Seb, Keith, Victoria and Kate were all for finding a late-night eatery (and boozery, no doubt) but Mark and Will were anxious (and in Will's case, under strict orders) to get home to their wives.

Leah wasn't keen on seeking food and drink either. She felt a little queasy, as if she might be coming down with a bug or something. She said so; asked Mick if they could go home. He looked at her with barely concealed impatience and said, 'Okay, then, if that's what you want. I can get Pam to rustle something up for me, I suppose. Although it'll be a bit late at night to ask her.'

So the party divided. Jim, after casting Leah a sympathetic glance, thanked the band for the Glastonbury work and left to catch a bus out to Lewisham. Mark and Will collected their cars from the lock-up and departed too. Those craving sustenance piled into Seb's SUV and headed off, leaving Leah and Mick to their drive to Broughton Manor. Mick, as he always did, drove fast, staring straight ahead, stonily silent, clearly in a sulk.

'I'm sorry to be a pain honey,' Leah offered, wincing, trying to ignore her increasingly complaining stomach, hoping they'd make it back before she needed urgent use of a bathroom. 'Perhaps it's something a bit off that I ate back in Somerset.'

'Yeah, maybe,' Mick grumbled. 'Although I feel okay. Perhaps you haven't got used to English food yet.' His insensitivity was astonishing, Leah reflected. A little sympathy would have been nice.

They got home only just in time to avoid having to pull over somewhere. Leah was unbelted and out of the car almost before it had screeched to a halt on the gravel drive. She bolted to the nearest toilet, the downstairs one, threw herself down before the bowl, hastily lifted the lid and heaved and puked spectacularly, splattering it and the seat colourfully with the food and alcohol she'd had after the performance. She heaved and heaved until her stomach had nothing left but bile to offer then sagged, exhausted, propped on trembling elbows on the seat.

Footsteps sounded. An anxious voice asked, 'Are you all right, dear?'

But it wasn't Mick. It was Pam, bending down to her, a hand falling soft and solicitous between her shoulder blades.

Leah groaned. 'Just dying, is all. I think I ate something I shouldn't have a few hours ago.'

'Oh dear, poor you!'

Leah got unsteadily to her feet. 'Gee, I've made a mess of this seat.'

'Don't worry about that.' Pam pulled a generous length of toilet paper off the roll and quickly swabbed the seat, dropping it into the bowl and flushing. 'I'll clean it properly later.' Her kindness was touching, almost overwhelming. Leah could have cried; could have buried her face in Pam's ample bosom, had it not involved bending a long way down. She had a good nine inches of height over the housekeeper.

Pam became briskly practical. 'Right; now you wash your face and have a small drink of water, just to rinse your mouth. That'll make you feel a bit better. Don't eat anything though while you feel like this. You'll very likely only throw it up again and you need to purge yourself. Now get yourself off to bed, and I'll come and see you later. It's probably just a touch of food poisoning. If it doesn't clear up in a couple of days I'll get the doctor in to see you.'

'That's really very kind of you, Pam. Yes I will. Thank you.'

'Good girl. Well I hope Mick hasn't got it as well, whatever it is; I don't want to be looking after the both of you.' She sighed impatiently. 'I'd better go and get him something to eat now, before he starts complaining. I'll make sure he's feeling up to it before I do though.'

Leah managed a weak smile. 'Right. Bless you, Pam. You're a treasure.'

Pam waved a hand dismissively. 'Nonsense; go on with you!'

She must have fallen into a deep sleep because she was quite unaware of Pam checking or Mick sliding into bed beside her. The next thing she knew she was waking with a dull heavy stomach ache. But the queasiness had gone. That was something. She wasn't sure whether she felt hungry; it was difficult to tell when her stomach felt as though it had been rinsed out with bathroom cleaner. Wise Pam was right though: better not to risk food. Beside her, Mick stirred. He opened bleary eyes and squinted to focus on her. 'How are you feeling?'

She groaned for dramatic effect. 'Horrible! Feel as if I've been kicked in the stomach by an elephant! Not sick though; not at the moment, anyway.'

'Yeah, well take it easy. I take it you won't be coming with me today then?'

'Where are you going?'

'Well, we've got to sort things for the tour. Obviously. We've got the first gig on Friday, remember?'

Leah remembered. But wasn't it local, in Croydon? That was in Greater London. It didn't need four days to prepare for that, surely? And there was hardly any travelling involved. He just wanted to be with his mates, probably. It would have been nice to offer to stay at home and look after her. But she said, 'No, I'll give it a miss. You go. I'll be fine.'

He got out of bed, inviting her to admire his nakedness (of which she never tired) as he padded into the en-suite to shower. Then emerged, giving her a reprise, dressed, grinned and said 'See you then,' and was gone. Ten minutes later his Porsche roared out of the drive.

Leah continued to lie, debating whether to get up too. Or just play the poorly card and cosset herself. The door was rapped and Pam put her head around it. 'How are you this morning, dear?'

'Oh, not too bad, thanks, Pam. I think I'll live. Stomach hurts a bit but I don't feel sick.'

Pam came into the room and stood over the bed, her chubby sixty-something face soft with kindness. 'Yes, you were dead to the world when I checked last night. You got a good night's rest, did you?'

Leah stretched. 'Yes, I think I must have done. I went out like a light all right. I'll get up in a while, I think.'

'Yes, you do that, if you feel up to it. I wouldn't risk any breakfast though. Perhaps have a bit of toast or something later.'

Pam left her to it and she lay for a few more minutes, then gingerly got up, trying to ignore her protesting stomach, and went to stand under the shower. The hot water was soothing. She felt a little better already. She dressed and went downstairs to find Pam pottering around in the kitchen, wiping work surfaces that were already spotless. Pam smiled at her. 'Do you think you dare risk a cup of tea?' That would be tea British-style of course, with milk and (for most people) sugar, although Leah thought it tasted ghastly sweetened.

She smiled gratefully. 'Yes, I think so, thank you. Perhaps black though, and not too strong.'

'Yes, good idea.'

Leah took a chair at the big pine table. Pam flicked the switch of the kettle and waited for it to boil; poured water briefly over a tea bag in a mug and two-thirds filled it. She brought it to the table and sat down too. Leah could feel another cosy chat coming on. She enjoyed them; Pam, with her homespun motherly demeanour, was easy to talk to.

Pam began, 'I saw you on television yesterday.'

'Oh, really; did you? I didn't think rock music was your thing?'

'Well, a lot of it isn't, to tell you the truth. I'm too old for much of it. But some of the stuff Mick and his friends do is quite nice. Very melodic. Reminds me of my youth. *Pentangle, Steeleye Span, Dylan* and all those.' Leah nodded without having a clue who Pam was talking about, apart from Bob Dylan.

'And I liked what you were playing, although I couldn't hear it very well.'

Leah laughed. 'No; the sound balance wasn't all it could have been, although a quiet audience would have helped, I must admit. They're so . . . enthusiastic. I suppose I'll get used to that in time though.'

Pam smiled too. 'Yes, but you only really get that at festivals and big arenas. It's different with recording, or television work. Obviously.' She seemed to be talking with some authority.

'Yes, I suppose so.'

'You're very good. Seem a little wasted just doing session work though, if you don't mind my saying.'

'Thank you! Now at this point you're supposed to tell me I should aspire to be another James Galway. Everybody does!'

Pam looked briefly put out. 'Oh, sorry. Is that a sore point?'

'No, not really. It's just that everyone seems to have high expectations of me, that I should become a celebrity soloist, just because I went to Juilliard.'

'Juilliard! Really?'

'Yes, for my sins. A fat lot of good it's done me so far though.'

'Well I must say, I'm very impressed, all the same. Would you have liked to have done something like orchestral work then?'

'Oh yes; that was the dream.'

'"Was"?'

'Yes, well I seem to have taken a different fork in the road, now I'm with Mick.'

'Mm, I suppose so.' Pam sounded a little sad, almost disappointed. But then she brightened. 'So, what brought you to England?'

'Oh, don't ask! It was marriage, I'm afraid. My husband landed a plum job in London so we came here because of that.'

'Oh, I see. I didn't realize you were married.'

'I'm not now. It lasted less than two years. That was all it took for him to start playing around with other women. Well, one other woman at least. Another musician, as it happens. Also from the States, ironically.'

Pam looked sympathetic. 'Oh dear; I'm so sorry. And . . . it broke you up?'

'Yes, too right, it did! He promised he'd never do it again after he was found out, but I just didn't feel I could trust him after that.'

'Yes, they all say that.'

'Well, I just don't think we should put up with betrayal nowadays! Sorry to sound like a strident feminist. But it's not as if I had to stay married to him for financial support, or for the sake of children; I'm able to support myself – well, in theory, at least.'

'You're right; we shouldn't. It was different when I was young. Then it was very difficult being a single wage-earning woman living alone, unless you had a good job, anyway. There weren't so many of the benefits, housing and everything, there are now.'

Leah snorted. 'Well nothing much has changed, it seems. Even for someone supposedly well-educated like me. And with wealthy parents. I don't think I could be very autonomous.'

'How do you mean, wealthy? Do you mean really rich?'

'Yes, I suppose I do. My dad's a businessman. He owns chain stores in the States.'

'Oh. And you weren't able to go back home after you parted from your husband?'

Leah sighed. 'No. For a start, they disapproved of the divorce and told me I should have stuck with the marriage – you know: worked at it, as they always say. That's what my mom said, anyway. And we're Jews, and my ex was a "good Jewish boy".' She did the double finger-wagging punctuation signs. 'And highly suitable, not to mention making a huge salary as a banker. My dad really approved of him; he was the perfect match for his precious daughter, as he saw it.'

'You sound very bitter.'

'Yes, I suppose I am. Anyway, my dad's virtually disowned me, now there's no financial-wizard son-in-law with whom to inherit the Weisman empire one day. Not that I care, really. I'd rather have the freedom to be who I want to be, and he can keep his stupid money.'

'I'm sorry to hear about that, dear. You remind me so much of myself at your age.'

'Really? How's that?'

Pam smiled. 'Well, I was a child of the sixties. You know – well, no, you wouldn't of course – Flower Power, and all that. World peace. No possessions. "All you need is love"; that sort of thing. I was a bit of a rebel and a bit of an idealist. It was the first time a youth movement really kicked against the Establishment. I do rather admire some of the young ones today, the ones who feel passionately about things – perhaps that's why I like working for a rock star – but I was there doing it all forty-five years before them.'

Leah was all ears. 'What; do you mean you were a . . . hippy, Pam?'

'Yes, don't look so surprised! I wasn't always this wrinkled old crone! I was slender once, and beautiful, and wore long flowery skirts and flowers in my long permed hair and sandals and no bra, and sometimes, at the festivals, no top either.' Pam grinned mischievously. 'Well, I had a nice pair, although I say it myself. The boys thought so, anyway.' She sighed wistfully. 'Mm, *I* don't know; whatever happened to that girl over the years?'

'That's amazing, Pam! No, sorry, I don't mean it like that. I mean it must have been an amazing time. So inspirational and . . . *idealistic* and everything.'

'Yes, it was. We were going to sweep away all the corruption of our elders and build a Brave New World. Our parents knew nothing and were reactionary old stick-in-the-muds, as far as we were concerned. They were certainly heady times, with people like Dylan and Cohen and Baez to inspire us.'

'And what about, er, sexual morality. What did they call it, free love?'

'Aye, there was that too. Well, the old taboos about marrying as a virgin, and 'nice' girls not doing it before then, that were there in the fifties, went out of the window. Or perhaps there was suddenly just less hypocrisy about it; it was no longer hidden; sex by itself wasn't seen as such a big deal. Doing it before marriage stopped being thought a sin, unless you were very religious. And then of course, there was the Pill, which was liberating, although you were only supposed to be able to get if you were married and 'respectable'. You could only get it on prescription from a doctor and many wouldn't give it to you unless you were. Unless you went to a birth control clinic. But it took away a lot of the risk of unwanted pregnancy – at least, it was supposed to. There was less chance of having bastards, as they used to call them.'

'Mm, well my ex and I had sex before we married, obviously, but it was the *extra* marital stuff I couldn't cope with,' Leah said, a little irritated. 'I can't say I felt very liberal-minded when Shay took that attitude about it only being sex. But perhaps I'm just old-fashioned.'

'No no; you're right. I'm not saying it was a complete free-for-all for me. Well, not for very long, anyway. We were just kids after all; very immature and full of hormones. Although there was still jealousy and hurt and all the rest of it when we were cheated on. We still felt rejected and betrayed. Human nature doesn't change overnight. But I quite soon grew out of the free love thing and tried to form longer lasting, sensible relationships.' She paused. 'Well; tried.'

'Did you marry then, Pam?' Leah wondered.

Pam did her wistful smile again. 'Well, yes, but I didn't make a very good job of it. I don't know whether that was because of the promiscuousness beforehand, or what. I met my husband when I was twenty-two and he was twenty-one, at a music festival of all things, and, well, to be honest, we had to get married because I fell pregnant. So much for contraception! There was much less single parenthood then, in nineteen seventy-three. You pretty much had to marry. Certainly, as far as my parents were concerned I had to, anyway. But it was a mistake. We were far too young. And although I wanted to settle down and be the conventional, faithful wife, he still had a hippy outlook. So he played around, even during my pregnancy, and certainly in the later stages when sex was out of the question. He made no secret of it; said it was no big deal. But like you, I didn't see it that way. I felt as betrayed as you did.'

'Well I don't think you should blame yourself for it not working, Pam,' Leah retorted. It sounds as if your husband was like mine:

basically just a selfish bastard.'

'Mm; maybe so. But I suppose we tend to blame ourselves when relationships go wrong, don't we?'

'Yes, we do. I felt so inadequate, as if I just didn't measure up in some way. Although that didn't stop me being absolutely bloody furious with Shay and telling myself I just wouldn't put up with it. And then giving as good as I got and getting involved with Mick.'

'And how was he about that?'

'He was shocked; outraged. As if it was some sort of affront to his masculinity. In short, he was a complete hypocrite. And then he promptly slapped a divorce suit on me. Not that I was bothered about that; I welcomed it, and one of us had to do the suing, otherwise it would have meant a long drawn out, two-year, no-fault thing. I didn't want to wait for that; just wanted out. So we got a quickie divorce – had it done over here, because you can – and it was all over in a matter of three or four months. And I feel I'm well out of it, to be honest.'

Pam smiled sympathetically. 'Yes, maybe so, although it's not for me to pass judgment of course. And so how is it with you and Mick? – do you mind my asking?' An oddly anxious note had crept into her voice.

'No, that's fine. It's good to talk with someone who understands, actually. Well, I think it's pretty good. He doesn't do the love thing very much, but perhaps he doesn't like showing his feelings. Maybe that will come, in time. I think it will for me.'

'Mm.' Pam sounded uncertain. 'Well I hope so. I think you're good for him. You're sensible and obviously don't take any shit, which is good. Could give him a bit of stability, which he needs. He's rather a wild boy, still.'

'"Still"?'

'Well, you know; the old thing they say about rock stars? Sex, drugs and rock n' roll, and all that. His trouble is, his band's found fame very quickly, so now he's got more money than he knows what to do with and all this success, and he thinks he can buy anything and anyone, and have whatever his heart desires. He has trouble handling it all sometimes, I think. But he's a good boy at heart. Just needs a steadying influence.'

Leah laughed. 'Yes, well I'll try! I do wish he'd give up the drugs though – er, I suppose you know he does that?'

Pam grinned too. 'I'm not blind, dear! Of course I know. I wasn't born yesterday. But yes, you're right. He really ought to. Perhaps you'll get him off them, in time.' She laughed suddenly.

'What?'

'Well, when you were sick last night, I wondered for a moment whether you might be pregnant. Now that really would calm him down, having a child!'

'*Pregnant?* No, I don't think so. I'm on the Pill, anyway, so I shouldn't be. No; I don't want that. I don't think.'

Pam looked almost disappointed. 'No, I shouldn't think you are then. It's just a bit of food poisoning, more than likely.'

Leah said, 'Anyway, tell me more about yourself – if you want to, that is; I don't mean to pry.'

'That's all right.'

'You were telling me about your husband. Presumably you aren't married anymore?'

'God, no! It was like with you. I eventually thought: sod this for a game of soldiers and got myself another chap, and told Denis to get lost. I think I put it more strongly than that though. I lasted a bit longer than you: five years. Well, I suppose it was only three in effect. We parted company after then but did the two-years-separation sort of divorce. It was all fairly amicable in the end, so neither of us felt like blaming or suing the other. And neither of us had any money to speak of, so that didn't come into it.'

'And there was a child then? You said you had to get married?'

'Yes, Jade. I left Denis for Andy when she was two, taking her with me. She was the only child I had. There were none with Andy. He just wasn't interested in having any. I wouldn't have minded another one, a brother or sister for Jade, but it wasn't to be. A sibling would have been good for her, I've often thought. As it was, all she had was a stepfather – well, sort of; we never married – who did his best to relate to her, I suppose, but he wasn't what you might call a natural father. Otherwise he would have wanted kids of his own. He was like Mick, really: a charmer, but not too good in the responsibility department. Yes; talk about making the same mistake twice. Andy wasn't really very different from Denis. I just wasn't very good at choosing men, I'm afraid.'

'I take it you didn't stay with Andy then? Well, obviously not, if you're now working here.'

'No. It lasted for eleven years, until nineteen eighty-six. I inherited a few thousand pounds when my mother died and we set up a small business: a restaurant in Holsworthy, Devon. That's where I learned to cook. It was fine for a few years, our relationship, but then it gradually began to fizzle out. There was no big drama about it and no acrimonious divorce, obviously. And it wasn't a case of infidelity on either of our parts. Well certainly not on mine, anyway. I don't think it was with him, either. He just told me one day that he wanted out, and I could have the restaurant and the mortgage to go with it, and packed his bags and left. I didn't kick up a fuss because I didn't particularly care whether he stayed or went.'

'Oh, I'm sorry that it didn't work out for you, Pam.'

Pam sighed. 'Well, it's a long time in the past now. Feels like another life completely. Much water has flowed under the bridge, as they say.'

'Mm. And was that the end of you and men? – sorry, am I being too intrusive?'

'No, that's all right; don't worry. Yes, it was, pretty much. There were a couple of short-term . . . what's the word? Dalliances, is it? No one else came along who I really wanted to settle down with. It was enough trying to keep my head above water with the restaurant. It wasn't in a very good place, really, not on the coast at one of the seaside places, which would have been a lot better, being more touristy. But it was all we – I – could afford at the time.'

'That's a shame.'

'Well, it's just the way it goes, I suppose. Sometimes we don't have our dreams come true. I struggled on with the business until ninety-three but it was no good; I was just piling up debt and the place was getting more and more run down. So I decided to cut my losses and put it on the market. But it took a year to find a buyer and I had to take quite a reduction, so by the time I'd finished the money I got just about covered the outstanding mortgage and cleared my debts.'

'Poor Pam! So what did you do then?'

'I just had to move to a small rented house and go out to work for someone else, as a chef, which was a comedown after employing people myself. But there was no other option. It was that or go on benefit.'

'Well at least you were doing the thing you loved, cooking, weren't you? That was something, I suppose.'

Pam laughed, but there was a bitter edge to her voice. 'Ha! It was hardly cheffing really, churning out chicken or steak and bloody chips every night in a pub. Not exactly cordon bleu! And there was Jade to contend with. She was . . . quite difficult sometimes. Not that I blame her, really, poor kid. She didn't have a very stable family situation and I wasn't a particularly good role model, I don't think. I thought I was a bit rebellious as a teenager, but she . . .'

She stopped abruptly. Her eyes moistened; she bit down on her lower lip. There was a stricken pause, as she stared at the table top, seemingly miles away. She moved her chair back, its legs screeching on the ceramic floor. 'Well I've got work to do. Can't sit here all day gabbing. Now you just take it easy today dear. Let your stomach recover.'

Leah was taken aback by the sudden ending of the memoir. 'Er, yes, right. I will.'

Her expression unknowable, Pam picked up her mug and swept it as if it were an affront to tidiness to the deep white Belfast sink.

Leah heard car tyres crunching the gravel outside at twenty to eleven. And about time too! Poor old Pam (who was mysteriously upset about something; she'd been racking her brains ever since the morning's conversation to think what she might have said to offend her) would now have to start messing around at this late hour preparing food for the Lord And Master. It was inconsiderate of him, it really was. And he might have phoned to say he'd be late.

But Mick didn't burst through the outer door into the hall, with his usual swagger. Someone knocked on it. Pam was upstairs in her flat, so Leah got up from her book in the drawing room and walked through to answer it. Very strange; they hardly ever had visitors this late at night.

A policeman and policewoman wearing yellow hi-vis vests stood there when she opened the door, a dayglo yellow-and-blue Volvo estate car parked behind them, garish and incongruous against the mellow stone in the fading light. They removed their caps.

The policeman spoke. 'Good evening madam. We believe this is the residence of Mr Michael Jones?'

'Er . . . yes, it is.' The formal 'Michael' had briefly confused her.

'Fine. And are you related to Mr Jones?'

'Er, no, not really. Well, I'm his girlfriend – partner. What is this?'

'I see. And can I have your name, please?'

'Leah. Leah Weisman.'

'Right.' The policeman regarded her steadily. His colleague spoke. 'Would you mind if we came inside for a moment, please, Ms Weisman?'

Second Movement

Adagio – moderato

Chapter 9: August 2015

Benjamin Walters sat on the train clasping his precious instrument case in its concealing Tesco carrier bag tightly in his lap, the holdall containing his performance clothes on the seat beside him. Well you could never be too careful; there was always some opportunistic Johnny likely to snatch it just as the train pulled into a station then make a dash for it, and he was past the days of chasing after thieves. The instrument would be worth a great deal of money to a thief who had it valued by someone in the know, but that was hardly the point. It was heavily insured but to Benjamin it was priceless and irreplaceable.

He looked around cautiously, as he always did when carrying the case. He had always been a little paranoid since nearly having it stolen once (thankfully the attempt had been thwarted though by the intervention of a kind fellow-traveller), imagining that people would have x-ray eyes and still know what the bag contained. The carriage was barely a quarter full, but then the evening was still relatively young by London standards: only ten-fifteen, and no one looked suspicious. He relaxed. Increasingly nowadays, he liked to make as early an exit at the end of a performance as he could. His old bones liked to be in bed at a reasonably civilized hour. The others could linger drinking and chatting and winding down in the green room if they wanted to, but most of *them* weren't seventy-six years old.

Besides which, apart from feeling tired, he was anxious to get back home. Esther might have some good news.

It had been a good performance though. He'd thoroughly enjoyed it. They'd done one of his favourites: the Mozart First Flute Concerto in G. He'd been playing it (although not as a soloist of course, often just at home, as a practice exercise and for pleasure), all his working life and never tired of it. But then you would expect it to be high on his favourites list really, being a flautist himself. After all, it was one of the jewels of the flute repertoire. Even as First Flute with the Philharmonic orchestra he seldom got to play, highlighted by cameras if it was being filmed or televised, an extended sequence of bars by himself. No, he was no Jean-Pierre Rampal or Emmanuel Pahud. For the majority of the performance he was quite happy to contribute to the general orchestral sound or sit and listen to the soloist. He had come to terms many years ago that he would never attain the dizzy heights of celebrity himself.

But it did not matter. He had a good, fulfilling life; was fortunate enough to do the thing he most loved for a living, even if Esther kept pressurizing him recently to call it a day with the Philharmonic and retire. It was all right for her to say that though. She wasn't a musician. Although she tried, she could not really know what an all-consuming passion in his life it was, how much a part of his very essence, his DNA, how ingrained under his old liver-spotted skin, for all that they'd been married nearly forty-seven years.

He glanced idly at the advertisements above the seats opposite. There was one advertising the summer season at the Wigmore Hall, which he'd just left, funnily enough. Tonight's had been the seventh concert and there were thirteen to go. Perhaps after that they might take a bit of a holiday; maybe have a few days down in Cornwall, by the sea. Perranporth, perhaps, if Mrs Woods at the guest house had any vacancies. Yes, that would be nice.

The advertisement to its left was for Barnardo's. It had a heart strings-plucking picture of a boy and girl: the boy about five years old and his elder sister possibly eight or nine, standing holding hands, posing and looking beseechingly at the camera. Above it a bold headline invited, *Please help us give Sophie and Max a bright future.* Benjamin smiled at it. It struck another sort of chord apart from the obvious one of compassion. A very personal one.

Yes, he thought, *a future indeed. Every child deserves a future. A future lived in peace. It should be an entitlement. Wherever in the world they are. How ironic that Aliza and I might not have had one at all, had we not been rescued, but I've spent my working life often playing the sublime music of the German masters.*

It triggered memories of long ago: of his own childhood. Himself and elder sister Aliza, living in Suffolk near Aldeburgh by a European sea, just down the road (appropriately as it would turn out) from another Benjamin, composer Benjamin Britten's, Snape Maltings concert hall.

Although it had been a serendipitous deliverance that had landed the two of them on the east coast of England in nineteen thirty-nine. They might so very easily have missed the British government's final rescue of Jewish children from the clutches of the Nazis: the very last *Kindertransport* from Berlin on the first of September, the day that Germany marched into Poland and Britain and France declared war.

Of course he couldn't remember that far back; he was only one year old at the time and in the nominal care of Aliza, who was a small child too: only six (although there were, apparently, adult supervisors and carers on the train and then the boat across the North Sea to Harwich). She could remember it vaguely, she informed him years later when he was old enough to understand what he was being told; the alarm of separation from their tearful parents and the seemingly never-ending journey, and the arrival in a strange place where all the people including the gently-but-indecipherably speaking lady who met them used a language she didn't understand.

Later again, when he had been considered old enough to handle the full implications of it, he had had the full story from the woman whom he'd assumed at first in a very confused sort of one-year-old way was also his proper mother, as if somehow he had two: kind Maisie Walters. Maisie and her husband Douglas had been touched by the plight of the ever more oppressed Jews in Germany and volunteered their services as foster parents for the refugee resettlement scheme. And big brother Gerald two years older than Aliza) was not their blood brother either but the natural son of Maisie and Douglas. As for their real parents, Maisie had gently told him, her eyes brimming with tears at the thought and the horror of it, they had almost certainly perished in one of the concentration camps. Otherwise, after the war they would surely have tried to locate their children.

It seemed that one of the conditions of the government's scheme (he had found out still later when researching the *Kindertransport* as a young man) was that, apart from bringing with them a financial bond for their maintenance, the refugee children were expected to return to their country of origin when the war was over. Some had done so, or gone to other European countries, and others had moved on to the United States. But many of the ten thousand refugees from tyranny had stayed. As Benjamin and his sister had. By nineteen forty-five he and Aliza were as much a part of the family and as dearly loved as Gerald, and after the Foreign Office had tried to trace Samuel and Golda Wolfewitz, their parents, in the chaos of post-war ruined Europe and failed, Maisie and Douglas had applied for permission to legally adopt their charges.

And so Maisie and Douglas had become Mum and Dad and his life as a British subject, a middle class Englishman, had been ordained. His Jewish heritage had been effectively extinguished, not that his mother and father had deliberately wanted it so. They were not anti-Semites. But with no Judaic influences in the adoptees' lives now, what was the point, really, in identifying two of their children as Jews? Although if Benny or Liza wanted to resume that identity when they grew up, it was up to them. Aliza had quickly learned English (although it would be a few years before she finally dropped all traces of a German accent) and they had become as English as all their friends in the neighbourhood. And Benjamin's childhood, growing up in the austere post-war years in Aldeburgh by the windswept haunting North Sea, had been everything a child could wish for.

Sitting on the Tube that August evening, clutching his shrouded instrument case, Benjamin's memory rewound to those far-off days.

It had not been long, he mused, a nostalgic smile raising the corners of his mouth, before music had entered his soul. Well, Dad had been an amateur musician after all, a clarinetist and friend of the local and much acclaimed composer Benjamin Britten. And certainly a role model. Aged nine and anxious to please him, he had begun piano lessons with the stern and redoubtable Miss Spencer who was also his father's friend and a music teacher at the grammar school in Ipswich. She also gave extracurricular music lessons and had taken him under her disciplinarian wing for an hour every Friday evening. A second-hand upright piano had been obtained when he was ten, as a combined Christmas and birthday present that year (well, in straightened nineteen forty-eight it was quite an expensive item) as he had quickly begun to show Miss Spencer some promise and certainly plenty of enthusiasm (Aliza and Gerald showed no musical inclinations whatsoever).

And with the opportunity now for endless practice, with unlimited hours at the piano when the other two were being typical young teenagers and interested only in popular music and the opposite sex, he had quickly become proficient. Three years later, now at the grammar school and one of Miss Spencer's chosen few star pupils, he had begun to seriously think that he wanted to make music for a living. He had discussed it with Dad, Miss Spencer and also Mr Britten. They had all encouraged him, although Miss Spencer had cautioned that he stood a better chance of realizing his dream if he played some other instrument. After all (at least if he wanted to do classical music), being a pianist almost by definition meant being a soloist. That was a very high ambition to realise. Whereas, with any other instrument the bar could be a little lower. There were always opportunities for working orchestral musicians.

Benjamin remembered how deflated he had felt at that dose of realistic advice. With the arrogance of youth he had seen no reason why he should not become a soloist. It just required a lot of application and a lot of ambition, and he had plenty of that. And they were always telling him that he had the technical expertise.

But then he had come around to the idea that perhaps his advisors were right. Perhaps he *should* take up another instrument, if only as something to fall back on, as a plan B if the Grand Concert Pianist Plan came to nothing. Which one though? He had not been particularly interested in any of the strings, or the brass. And certainly not percussion. So that left woodwind. He had flirted for a while with the idea of following Dad and going for the clarinet, until one evening he had heard on a gramophone record Mr Britten's Sea Interludes from his opera *Peter Grimes*, which had been such a success at Sadler's Wells. The first one of those had featured flute (to suggest the cry of seagulls, presumably) and he had been bowled over by it. It was a gorgeous, haunting sound. He had decided there and then that his second musical string, so to speak, would be the flute.

Benjamin was lost in his reverie, back in his childhood past, back at Christmas nineteen fifty-one, excitedly unwrapping his first instrument. It had not exactly been top-of-the range, but it was all his parents could either afford or were prepared to risk. It would be quite adequate for learning on.

And then memory fast-forwarded five years, to his acceptance at the music department of Norwich University. He remembered the astonishingly kind gift of a better flute from Mr Britten because he had proved himself worthy of one, a semi-antique, professional-standard instrument that produced the most exquisite, mellow sound. Well, it had been a joint gift from him and his parents really, who had paid Mr Britten (who had no children, musical or otherwise, to gift it to) some of the value of it, as a matter of principle. It was a beautiful instrument; a Rudall Carte built in eighteen ninety-two by Moujard, with silver keys but with a new later body of jet black cocus wood, exquisitely fashioned in nineteen thirty to modern pitch. Dad had been very envious. But then he had not risen above the level of reasonably proficient amateur. Architecture was his trade. He did not begrudge his adopted son, who was far a better musician than he, a fine instrument.

It was the self-same flute that Benjamin cradled in his lap so protectively now.

What a faithful friend it had been to him over the last fifty-eight years! He had never wanted another. It had collaborated with him in perfect harmony to make music in countless concerts all over the world.

It had borne witness to all the major events in his life, not least meeting, romancing and marrying his dear Esther.

Benjamin thought about that now, memory advancing again to nineteen sixty-three and one of the first overseas tours he had gone on after joining the Philharmonic – and to West Germany of all places. Playing in the principle cities: Bonn, Düsseldorf, Cologne, Frankfurt, Stuttgart, Munich. It had been a slightly uncomfortable feeling, visiting his country of birth twenty-six years after fleeing it. Although in fact it had not been this western, Federal Republic of Germany where he had originated (he knew that from his adoptive parents) but Berlin, still trapped then behind the Iron Curtain in the communist Democratic Republic east.

He remembered his apprehension before going, not having any idea of what to expect, and his pleasant surprise. There were still melancholy echoes of the war; still vacant gaps between buildings, like missing teeth, which must have been bomb sites waiting for redevelopment and the German recovery and economic boom to come. But there was an air of optimism, and the people were friendly and hospitable. If any were still harbouring grudges about their defeat, occupation and humiliation only eighteen years previously, they did not show it. The tour had been a great success, with enthusiastic and appreciative audiences, and the social intercourse between performances genuinely warm. It was impossible to feel any animosity to their welcoming hosts, not that he had the faintest recollection of the Third Reich of course.

It had happened, that chance meeting that would change his life, in Frankfurt in that far-off nineteen sixty-three. There had been a reception following their concert there (playing Brahms, Mozart and Elgar, he remembered) attended by local newspaper journalists. One of them, he could not fail to notice, was a tall, elegant young woman with sloe-black hair, still in her twenties. Notebook in hand, in which she was scribbling notes, she was quizzing John Bartholomew, the conductor. She was alone; there was no other person with her acting as translator (although possibly, for all he knew, John could speak German). It looked as though she might be taking more than a casual interest in him too, judging by the way her glance returned to his direction periodically after first noticing him.

She had concluded her interview of Bartholomew, thanked him (he had distinctly heard her say *danke shoen*), the conductor had nodded and she had moved across the room towards him. Benjamin smiled at the memory as if it were only yesterday, not over fifty years ago. He could picture her now; recall his panic that she might engage him in conversation when he had no German at all (well, there had been no point in learning it, obviously) and he would appear an utter fool. So he had been astonished when she stopped before him, looked down slightly as she had at least two inches over him in her high-heeled shoes, and spoke a confident, only moderately accented 'Hello.'

He remembered his surprised, grateful, mumbled 'Oh, hello,' in reply and his inane follow-up, 'er, do you speak English? Her smile, just slightly condescending, revealing astonishingly white and perfect teeth. Remembered her first words; the first she ever spoke to him. 'Yes, although not perfectly I am afraid. Do you speak German?'

To which he had had to admit, feeling an idiot after all, that no, he didn't, which was rather shameful as he was actually German by birth.

She had looked at him quizzically and he had hurriedly explained that he had left Germany as a baby in nineteen thirty-nine. She had asked him why that was, and he had said he and his sister were refugees, and she, her beautiful brown eyes rounding in surprise had said, 'Do you mean that you were on the *Kindertransport*? And he had said, blushing a little as if it was some sort of embarrassing confession, yes, and he and Aliza had been adopted by an English couple, which was why he spoke no German.

And she had exclaimed, 'Well that is astonishing! So was I! A year earlier than you, in nineteen thirty-eight, but also a baby, one year old, with my two older brothers.' She had paused, eying him steadily. 'So . . . are you a Jew?'

To which he had said, 'Yes, well, born of Jewish parents at least, but my adoptive parents are Christian, so I suppose I am too, now. And you are Jewish then, I presume?'

She had smiled, sadly. 'Yes. And did your . . . natural parents, er, go to the camps?'

He had replied, 'Yes; Auschwitz, it seems. I found that out a few years ago, researching them. Neither of them survived.'

She had said, 'I am so sorry. It was a terrible time, wasn't it?'

He had agreed and asked about her and her parents and she had told him a story quite similar to his own. How she and her brothers, Karl and Herman (who had deliberately not been given Jewish forenames so that they would not stand out), had also been fostered in England, although not as happily, and at the war's end the British Foreign Office had located her father, who had clung desperately onto life in the hell of Bergen-Belsen before being liberated by the British army in April nineteen forty-five. But her mother Ruth had perished, along with thousands of other poor souls, from typhus. After being nursed back to relative health her father, who spoke English, had worked for the occupying forces as an interpreter. When he was well enough and had somewhere to call his own in which to live, Esther – that was the young woman's name – and her brothers had been returned to ravaged Germany and tearfully reunited with their haunted-eyed father, and they had eventually settled in Frankfurt.

But the horrific experience of Bergen-Belsen and other camps before it had taken its physical and emotional toll on Isaac Adelstein, Esther had told him, and he had died in nineteen fifty-four, leaving twenty-three year old Karl, twenty-five year old Herman and the teenaged Esther to fend for themselves. Esther had found a job with a Frankfurt newspaper and risen to the impressive heights of assistant to the music critic, which was why she was here now.

They had chatted avidly, oblivious to the socializing people around them, until the tour manager had let it be known that the reception was ending and then, impulsively, he had asked whether he might write to her, and without a moment's hesitation she had said yes, and written her full name and address in her notebook, torn out the page and given it to him, and he had borrowed her book and pen and done the same.

Benjamin smiled, remembering those many airmail missives winging their way across the North Sea: politely formal and carefully not too often at first but steadily increasing in emotiveness and frequency as he found friendship and then love for her growing. Because it was not simply their common heritage and their remarkably similar experience of rescue from probable death that bound them, but a deep natural rapport: a profound meeting of minds. They were kindred spirits. Not to mention the physical attraction, of course.

And then that holiday during the break between seasons five months later: the trip full of nervousness and anticipation to Germany where Esther had naughtily booked a room in an inexpensive hotel on Karlstrasse for a week in the name of 'Herr und Frau Adelstein', doing all the talking to the hotel proprietors so as not to give the game away, although they probably knew perfectly well what was going on. And the wonderful rapturous discovery of each others' bodies, and his throat-tight, unstoppable, blurted out proposal of marriage in bed together on the last night of his stay.

Eight months later in the autumn of nineteen sixty-four they had been married, in England, at Ipswich, because Esther had given up her job at the newspaper and applied for residency in Britain as his fiancée. It had been a simple, quiet, register-office affair (Esther had not insisted on a Jewish ceremony) with the only guests Karl and Herman, Aliza and Gerald and Mum and Dad.

And then, almost before they had had time to catch breath, it seemed, Esther was giving birth to their beautiful daughter, whom they had named Ruth for her cruelly-lost maternal grandmother. And two years on again, the birth of their son, who was to be Sam in honour of Samuel Wolfewitz. Mum and Dad had been completely understanding about that. In fact Mum, very moved and wiping away a few tears, had thought it a lovely idea.

Benjamin sighed, letting the memories wash over him, flicking through the years like a symbolic time-advancing desk calendar in an old movie. On he went, another twenty-three years to nineteen ninety, and saw in his mind's eye Ruth offering for his delighted inspection their first grandchild, Daisy, who would be followed in due course by Simon and Rose. And then, seemingly in the blink of an eye (how time seemed to have telescoped in the last few years!) to last year and Daisy being suddenly grown up too, and taking up with her handsome dark-haired boyfriend Hassam.

He smiled, remembering the slight awkwardness – and perhaps a touch of chin-jutting defiance on fiercely idealistic Daisy's part – when he had been introduced, although there had been no need for it at all. Did she really imagine that Esther and he would disapprove? He was a very personable young man: quiet, rather shy and a medical student. And a born-in-London British subject. Both he and Esther liked him a lot. It seemed his parents and their five children had fled the Palestine West Bank in nineteen eighty-nine during the first intifada, able to gain acceptance and sanctuary in Britain because the father, Ahmad, partly, probably, wasn't a poverty-stricken asylum seeker but a qualified engineer and therefore a wealth-contributor to the host country.

No, Benjamin reflected, it really was not a problem. There was too much hate and intolerance and ignorance in the world, still, in the supposedly civilized twenty-first century; still terrible wars, often if not usually because of religious and cultural differences. That and resources. He had so nearly been a victim of it himself, after all. That was what he so liked about Daniel Barenboim and Edward Said's East-West Divan Orchestra with its mixture of young Jewish and Arab musicians, united by music in equality and untainted by hate. They were an inspiration; a beacon of hope. Why couldn't the world coexist in harmony and create beauty like they did, rather than inflict cruelty and death?

Benjamin was jolted abruptly out of his reverie. The train had stopped and the doors were sliding open. He was at Bushey, his station; lost in thought, he had nearly gone straight past. Gathering his bags, he got up as quickly as his old bones allowed, before the doors closed again. He didn't want to have to go on to Watford Junction, wait and come back. It would not have meant a long delay, but he was tired. He wanted to get home to Esther.

Chapter 10

It was only a twelve minute walk from the railway station to his Edwardian villa in Prospect Street, but that was quite enough these days, Benjamin thought, as he stood, slightly out of breath although he'd taken it steadily, fitting his Yale key into the lock and opening the front door. Oddly, he also felt slightly light-headed. That had happened more than once recently. He placed his carrier bag on the hall barley twist-legged table and dropped the holdall on the floor. Esther would take his evening suit out and hang it up in a bit, and if necessary iron it to banish any creases in the morning.

He took off his light anorak and hung it on the hook rail; walked through into the sitting room. Esther was reclining on the sofa, long legs curled up beside her like a twenty year-old, watching *Newsnight*. Her hair might now be nearly lint-white in the much-loved words of Rabbie Burns (he was one of their favourite poets) but she was still remarkably lithe, for a septuagenarian. She moved her feet onto the floor to allow him to sink down beside her and smiled affectionately; asked the same question she always asked when she didn't accompany him to his concerts. 'Good performance?'

Benjamin smiled too, tired but content. He knew that she knew that Mozart One was one of his favourites. Her enquiry was just a formality. 'Yes, wonderful. Wunderbar. The soloist was very good. An exceptionally gifted young man. I could have listened to him all night. They certainly train them well in Korea.' He paused, gazing at Kirsty Wark interrupting a politician as usual on the television screen. 'No news then, I take it?'

'No; I would have told you the moment you walked in if there were. Obviously. You men, honestly! You're far worse than us women in situations like this!'

'Yes, that's probably true. Sometimes I really do think you women are the stronger sex. Emotionally, at any rate. It's just the waiting I can't handle very well.'

'Don't worry, it'll be fine. I'm sure she's in very safe hands.' The topic had changed on *Newsnight*. Something about bank interest rates still staying the same; boring! Esther heaved herself up to go and make coffee (and hang his dress clothes up). Benjamin let his head loll back against the cushions of the sofa; closed his eyes. Thought about that soloist. He was only a young whippersnapper, as Dad used to say. Still in his twenties with what would doubtless be a glittering life of celebrity and success ahead of him. But fine; he deserved it, with his talent. He didn't feel jealous in the slightest. Good luck to him . . .

He drifted away.

To be awakened by Esther sitting back down beside him. She looked at him, concern clouding her face. 'You do look very tired again, Benny.'

He forced another smile. 'Now who's worrying? I'm fine, really. Pass the biscuits, there's a love.' She handed him the packet of plain chocolate Hobnobs. He took two: his ration. Although he was still relatively thin, apart from a distinct paunch, Esther allowed him only two.

'Well someone has to; you won't look after yourself!'

Benjamin bit into his first biscuit; prepared himself for The Lecture. Again. It had become quite a regular thing lately. He emptied his mouth and tried a joke. 'And that's what I've got you for, my sweet. That's what wives do, you know.'

She snorted. 'Be serious! For goodness sake; you should be retiring. It's not as though you've got to carry on until you drop because we need the money. We don't! We've got the old age pension and you could take your private one as well. It must be worth quite a bit as an annuity because you've delayed taking it for eleven years already. That plus state pension would give us plenty to live on, wouldn't it?'

Benjamin finished his first biscuit as Esther eyed him crossly. 'Yes, I suppose it would. I haven't checked how much the private one would give per month lately, to be honest.'

'Well do so! Talk to the pension people! If you delay taking it for much longer, we'll never get back what you've paid in.'

'I don't think it quite works like that, Essie –'

'Benny; you're just prevaricating!'

'But it's not a matter of money, anyway. You know how much music means to me. It's my life. The thing I get up for each morning –'

'Fiddlesticks!' Esther retorted. The television programme was signing off and the credits rolling. She found the controller and angrily turned the set off; resumed, 'You know I'm not suggesting you just give it up completely! Just retire from the orchestra, when the season's finished. Vacate your place. Let one of the other flautists move up to First Flute, which would leave a vacancy. There must be lots of young musicians who'd love to work for the Philharmonic.'

'Well, I don't know . . .'

Esther pressed on. 'You could still do it as a hobby, at an amateur level –'

'What do you mean, "amateur"?'

'Well *I* don't know! Join a local music society or something. There must be one around here. One that does playing I mean; not just an appreciation society. There must be lots of them in London.'

Esther hastily corrected herself. 'Er, no, you don't want to be travelling miles away, or you'd be no better off than if you stayed with the orchestra. No; just something local, that plays once a week in the afternoons; something like that.'

Benjamin chewed his second biscuit as his wife watched, sipping her coffee. 'Oh, you mean like visiting retirement homes to play for the poor old dears, most of whom are asleep with their mouths open, dribbling down their cardigans? That sort of thing? No thanks! I'm used to playing to an appreciative audience!

'No, no, I didn't mean that, not if you didn't want to.' Esther said persuasively, 'Something like a quartet or quintet, where maybe you could play something you could really get your teeth into, like chamber music for the flute, sort of thing. Then it'd be almost like being a soloist, instead of a small cog in a very big wheel.'

'Mm, well perhaps there's something local like that; I've never looked into it . . .'

'Oh come on, Benny, at least think about it; you can't go on like this forever. And I really don't think you should do another foreign tour. You know how taxing they are. There's Germany and Australia scheduled for next year, you know.'

Benjamin smiled, reaching for his coffee mug. 'Yes, I know. Germany was the very first tour I did, all those years ago; do you remember? I was thinking about that on the train coming home. And look what that resulted in.'

Esther smiled too, placing a mottled hand on her husband's knee. 'Yes, of course I remember. Such a long time ago now, isn't it? And yet it seems only yesterday. Just think: if I hadn't gone to that reception that night, standing in for Johann Erhardt because he was ill, I would never have met you, and then what would I have done?'

'You would have met someone else: some fine young Teutonic German chap, and had lots of fair-haired children with him, and lived in luxury, instead of being saddled with a dreamy, work-obsessed, short-sighted, fifth-rate musician like me.'

She shook his knee mock-crossly. 'Don't joke about it, Benjamin Walters! You're not fifth-rate! And I wouldn't have wanted anyone except you! I think God was smiling on me that evening. He must have been.'

'Well he was on me too then. It was like in that song: *Some Enchanted Evening*. What's it from now? *South Pacific*, is it?' He crooned softly, 'Some enchanted evening, you may see a stranger. You may see a stranger, across a crowded room.'

Esther sighed nostalgically. 'Ah, yes. You old softy! Love at first sight then, was it?'

Benjamin sighed too. 'No, of course not. But it was certainly attraction at first sight.'

'Yes, and me too. There was just something about you, standing there, looking a little bit lost, a bit vulnerable, casting furtive glances in my direction now and then. Something made me gravitate towards you.'

'I can't think why, really. I can't see that the little-boy-lost look is particularly appealing. I bet you don't remember the first thing I said to you!'

She frowned, racking her brains. 'Er . . . Oh, yes. You asked me if I spoke English, because I'd said hello to you.'

'That's right! And you said, 'Yes, but not perfectly, I am afraid,' and asked if I spoke German, which made me feel a complete fool because of course I didn't.'

'I suppose you were just beginning to pick a few words up, well, baby words, but then lost them again when you were with your foster parents.'

'Mm, I suppose so. Although Liza would have had quite a good vocabulary, being six. But I suppose it was harder for her, in a way, because there were no adults around to keep her German language alive, only English speakers, so she lost it and had to start again from scratch with English instead. And of course as I grew up it became the only language I've ever really known.'

'Yes, the old thing about "use it or lose it", I suppose,' Esther said. 'Although it was different for me. Having to learn English as I did, I could also have lost all the German I'd got as a one year old when I came over, but my siblings were relatively older than yours. Karl was six years older than me and Herman eight years older; in thirty-eight they'd have been, er, let's see, Karl seven and Herman nine. So they'd have had a good command of German, and had each other to talk to in their mother tongue, so of course when we kids were alone, away from the foster parents, that's what we did.

'So as a small child I grew up completely bi-lingual. Besides, we always saw ourselves as Germans first and foremost and expected that one day we'd return to Germany. But I didn't lose my English when we did go back, because Papa spoke it and he thought it important that we three keep it up. He used to say America would become the dominant force in the world, so he encouraged us to.'

She sighed again. 'Poor Papa, surviving that dreadful camp but then living only another nine years! And poor Mama too of course: not even having that.'

'Yes, and mine. Neither of them saw Liza and me again. They would have had no idea what became of us. It must have been unbelievably terrible, mustn't it?'

'It certainly must.' Esther shook the knee she was still fondly holding. They were silent for a moment, each wrapped in their own thoughts.

Then she said, 'Anyway, I think it's bedtime, don't you? You need your beauty sleep.'

Benjamin grinned. 'Well, I don't know about that. Lost cause as far as that's concerned. But I'm ready for bed, certainly.' He drained his mug. 'Right; take me to bed, wicked woman!'

They lay in bed, Esther's head in the crook of Benjamin's shoulder, as they had done every night without fail for fifty-one years (except, of course, when Benjamin had been away touring and Esther had not gone too). There were always a few more words to sleepily murmur in the intimacy of their bed to fill the minutes before sleep took one or the other of them.

She said, 'What set you off thinking about our meeting then?'

He smiled in the dark. 'It was an advert on the Tube. For Bernardos, showing a little boy and his big sister, I suppose she was meant to be. The words said something like, "Help us give them a bright future". Something like that. It just made me think of Liza and me, throwing ourselves on the mercy of kind people all those years ago. I tried to recall my earliest memories. Couldn't remember Germany, obviously. The first thing I can remember is when I was, oh, about three, I suppose, being somewhere with Dad, and picking up his clarinet and trying to play it, but not succeeding. Well, not making a proper sound because I wasn't articulating the notes or anything; just blowing and making a terrible racket. And Dad taking it off me and laughing.'

Esther laughed too. 'Typical! It *would* be a music-associated thing, wouldn't it!'

'Yes, well, I got the bug very young, I suppose. What about yours then? What's the first thing you can remember?'

She pondered. 'Er, well just faintly the coming over to England with Karl and Herman, but they aren't really memories, as I was only two; just sort of vague impressions, like half-memories. I can remember those five years with Mr and Mrs Jarman, our foster parents, fairly well in the latter stages of the war. They were all right I suppose, and of course we should have been grateful to them for taking us on. We must have been a bit of a handful for them, the three of us, as they had no children of their own, so had no experience of them. Let alone looking after children who weren't their own. Karl used to say, later when we were back in Germany, that they seemed more like a rather distant uncle and aunt than parents, really.'

'Yes, that's a shame. But yes; at least you were safe – after the danger of invasion had passed, anyway.'

'Mm. Thank God it never happened; that Hitler didn't strike when he had the opportunity. Europe would have been entirely different if he'd conquered Britain too.'

'Yes, true, although perhaps America would still have got involved in the war in Europe after Pearl Harbor, and beaten Germany on its own by sheer force of numbers and resources.' Benjamin chuckled. 'Then it really would have been just like Hollywood's always portrayed it, as America winning the war virtually single-handed, not the Allies.'

Esther laughed too. 'They'd have never let us forget it! Except of course it would still not have been a case of that. There might still have been the Soviets attacking from the East.'

'Mm. That might have been interesting: Berlin might have been carved up between just America and the USSR. There could have been even more of a political dichotomy in Europe.'

'Yes, perhaps so.'

'Well, anyway, what's your first really definite memory? Do you have one?'

'Oh, yes. Erm . . . I think it was when I was about five. Yes, I must have been. So that would be nineteen forty-two. It was my first day at school. Karl was already there of course, in the top class, although Herman would have moved on to the senior school. I can remember being taken into a classroom – the infant's classroom – with little miniature desks, none of the modern sitting-around-tables that you see now, and a very tall one at the front of the room, by the blackboard, and the school mistress, who seemed very tall and stern and alarming and sometimes used words I didn't understand, although I think I'd probably picked up English pretty well by then. And I remember something called "optional" on Friday afternoons that really just meant a play session and being able to choose between various toys like Steiff teddy bears to play with. Hence the term "optional". For years I thought it meant "playtime" though!' Esther giggled at the thought.

Benjamin did too. 'But you can't have known they were Steiff bears specifically!'

'Well, no. But I'd like to think they were German-made ones.'

'But remember the times you're talking about. Wartime. I shouldn't imagine any German product would have been popular in Britain, even a toy. They would probably have been *verboten*.' Benjamin tittered at his own witticism.

'Very droll! Alright then. So maybe they were from that American company that started them too. What's the name now? Michton. But then I wouldn't have thought the British could afford such luxuries as American toys during the war.'

Benjamin laughed. 'Talk about my first memory being typical; it seems yours was too!' he teased.

'How do you mean?'

'Well, yours was about learning, wasn't it? The start of your journey to the brainbox you became!'

'I'm not! Not really! Being a journalist isn't all that brainy. All I do – used to do – is string words together into reasonably coherent sentences. Anyone with a half-decent education can do that. Although I must admit: I've seen some terribly-expressed writing by supposedly well-educated people in my time. No; you're the clever one, with your music making; producing beautiful sounds like you do. And the way you can just look at sheet music and know exactly how to read it, and how it will sound when all those notes and chords and rhythms and keys and things, which are complete double-Dutch to me, are played.' Esther laughed. 'Really, my dear, you're the brainy one in this family.'

She paused. 'Anyway; I wonder if we'll hear anything tonight.'

He did not reply. His breathing had slowed and he was snoring softly, surrendered to sleep. She had been talking to herself. Esther sighed; disentangled herself from his encircling arm, kissed him softly on the cheek, said Night Night, turned onto her side away from him and settled to sleep. She fell into oblivion almost as quickly as Benjamin.

To be awoken only moments later, it seemed, by her mobile ringing insistently on the bedside table. She did not normally have it switched on but tonight, with an important call expected, she had made an exception. She reached to switch the table lamp on; snatched up the phone. Looked anxiously at the display. Yes, it was Ruth.

'Hello?'

'Hi Mum, it's me.' Ruth always stated the blindingly obvious. If Esther didn't know her own daughter's voice by now, she never would.

'Yes?' Her heart was suddenly pounding nineteen to the dozen.

'It's okay. All's well. Congratulations; you're a great-granny!'

Benjamin had awoken too, turning towards her, blinking in the lamp light, also anxious.

'Oh. Thank God! And she's all right?'

'Which one?'

'Oh, the baby, of course! And Daisy too!'

'Yes, both fine, after all that anxiety. They had to do a caesarian in the end because Daisy was taking so long and they thought the baby was getting a little distressed. I didn't see it myself, unfortunately; had to wait outside. Although I'm not sure I *would* have wanted to see an operation. But Hassam was there. He's just come out of theatre. He's as pleased as Punch. Actually hugged me, he did! Well, I hugged him, really. He looked in need of it. Quite overwhelmed, he was.'

'Well of course he is, poor lad! So would your dad have been. You know what men are like in these situations.'

'Yeah; tell me about it!'

'And have you seen the baby yet?'

'Give us a chance, Mum! It only happened five minutes ago! She's two weeks premature of course and Hassam said they put her straight in an incubator, but they assured him she's fine. So I'll have to see her in the intensive care place I suppose. But I'm not leaving this hospital until I have done, no way. I've not waited eight and a half months with all the worry not to see my granddaughter at the end of it!'

'Oh, I see. Well take a picture, won't you?'

'Mum!' Of *course* I will! Many pictures, probably. And I'll email them to you, don't worry.'

'Good. And they really are all right, are they?'

'Yes, so Hassam says. Look, when I've seen them I'll call you again, okay?'

'Yes, do. Doesn't matter how late. I'll let you get off the phone now then darling.'

'Okay. Speak later. Bye!'

The line went dead before Esther had a chance to reply. Eyes moist, she looked at Benjamin. 'Did you get the gist of that?'

'Well, only your side of the conversation, of course.'

'You're a great-granddad, Benny!'

'Yes, I gathered that. And I take it they're both all right then?'

'Yes, thank God. Ruth didn't see the birth because it was a last minute emergency caesarian but Hassam was there, apparently.' Esther's moist eyes became liquid. 'Oh, what a relief, after that tricky pregnancy!'

'It certainly is. Trust our Daisy not to do things the easy way though. And what were you saying to Ruth about me?'

Esther put her phone down and switched off her light; laughed. 'Oh, nothing much. Ruth was saying how Hassam was a bit overwhelmed by it all and she had to give him a hug.'

'Well naturally; he would have been. Especially as it was a bit – traumatic. Us men don't have hearts of stone, you know!'

'Yes, that's what I said to Ruth. More or less, anyway.'

'Mm.'

'I remember how you were with Ruth when she was born. Very tearful, if I recall correctly. And her birth was perfectly uncomplicated.'

Benjamin chuckled. 'Was I? I don't remember. But you did take ages over the labour; I remember that!'

'Yes, you were. And first pregnancies often take longer than subsequent ones.'

'Well, I suppose I was then. But I remember thinking what an especial miracle Ruth was, because of her parentage. If either you or I hadn't escaped from Germany when we did, we probably wouldn't have survived, and then she wouldn't have come into being.'

Esther found his hand and squeezed it. 'Yes; that's certainly true.'

Benjamin closed his eyes. His lids were heavy. The excitement had tired him again.

'Get some sleep,' Esther said. 'I ought to as well, but I won't sleep now until Ruth phones again.'

Benjamin did not hear the phone when it rang a second time. But Esther was already awake waiting for him to surface in the morning. She switched her phone on and handed it to him. A picture was already selected. He fumbled his reading glasses on. It showed a tiny red wrinkled person wearing a woolly hat and oversized nappy and nothing else, lying on its back, arms spread, in an incubator. There were no tubes attached, which he took to be a good sign.

'There she is,' Esther cooed. 'Isn't she gorgeous?'

Benjamin was not too sure about that, although he knew she would be, given a few weeks. But he said, 'Yes, she certainly is. When did Ruth ring then? I was completely out; I missed it.'

'It was about three quarters of an hour after she rang the first time: at twenty to two. She spent some time with Daisy first, and then demanded to be allowed to see the baby, so the staff let her. Then she took a few pictures, although they all look the same, to be honest. She rang before she left the hospital. I didn't wake you as you were sound asleep. You don't mind, do you?'

'No, that's all right. It was something nice to wake up to. What was the name they chose for her again now?'

Esther laughed. The last I heard from Ruth, it was Amira. It's Arabic for Princess, apparently. Isn't that beautiful?'

Benjamin grinned agreement. 'Yes, it certainly is.'

'I can't wait to see her. But I suppose it'll be a few days before the hospital allows her out, as she's a little premature.'

'Yes, well just be patient, Great-granny Esther,' Benjamin smiled. 'There's plenty of time.'

Chapter 11

Two and a half weeks later they were invited to visit Daisy, Hassam and their little arrival. She had been discharged three days earlier when the hospital was satisfied with her progress. Now, having settled in at home (a rather unprepossessing flat in Edmonton, a stone's throw from the incessantly noisy North Circular – but it was all they could afford, and that, barely) she was available for visits and admiration. Benjamin and Esther did not run a car. It was not worth it, for the tiny amount of travelling around that they did nowadays. For holidays they went by train or hired one.

There was no simple sideways bus route to Daisy's though, that did not involve tiresome changes and waits. Edmonton, to the east, was on another of the northward-creeping tentacles of the Greater London public transport system, which was an octopus, not a spider's web. So there had to be a rather long dog-leg of a journey that sunny September afternoon on one of Benjamin's non-performing or rehearsing days: southwards towards the centre of London by over-ground train to pick up the Underground Bakerloo line to Piccadilly Circus, then crossing platforms to turn back northwards again on the Piccadilly line.

So it was two-thirty before they were ringing the bell, peeling-labelled with the identifier Hassam and Daisy Ahmed, beside the scruffy blue outer door of their weary-looking flat in Victoria Avenue. Hassam, swarthy, raven-stubbled, tall and slender, shirtless and black chest-hair from a light mustard sweater, opened it to them. He smiled shyly. 'Hello, come in. Er, Daisy's feeding the baby at the moment . . .'

Esther, assuming he was saying that which she thought he was saying, said, 'Oh, we don't mind that. We've seen it all before.'

Hassam looked a little uncertain but led them up the grubby-carpeted staircase to their first floor flat. Daisy was occupying the only comfortable seating, an orange repp-covered sofa (the only other thing to sit on was a fraying peacock chair) with her checked shirt open and a tiny white bundle clamped onto her left breast. 'Hi!' she greeted.

'Hello darling,' Esther said, making a bee-line towards her. Benjamin, old-fashioned and gentlemanly in his sense of propriety, did not know where to look.

Esther peered at the baby, although it was difficult to make out very much with her face single-mindedly buried in Daisy's engorged breast. There seemed to be a lot of black hair in evidence though. 'Hello, little girl,' Esther cooed. 'How are you, then?' Daisy laughed. 'She can't talk at the minute, Great-granny; she's busy!'

'Yes, so I see. It looks as though she's got Hassam's hair, anyway.'

Hassam grinned, flattered. 'I'll make some tea then.' He looked questioningly at the guests in turn. 'Or would you rather have coffee?'

'Tea's fine, if that's what you're making.' Esther replied for both of them. 'Milk, no sugar, for either of us, please.'

Hassam nodded. 'No problem. And tea for you, Daze?'

'Please; need to recharge a bit after this little madam's been at me,' Daisy said, nodding her blonde head. She mock-grimaced at her grandmother. 'Agh, I don't know how you two can drink it without sugar. Still, I need to top up on the carbohydrates. That's my excuse, anyway.'

Hassam retreated through the plastic screen to the kitchen area to put the kettle on.

Esther returned her attention to the baby, sinking down beside Daisy. Benjamin settled himself beside his wife. He was ready for a sit down after the walk from the station. 'Yes, that's an amazing amount of hair for one so tiny. And so dark! Although I had jet-black hair in my youth too, so I suppose this little one's very likely to inherit it one way or another.'

'Yeah, I suppose so. It obviously doesn't come from me.' Daisy lowered her voice conspiratorially. 'But I have to say that it definitely comes from Hassam, to keep him and his folks happy.'

Esther was a little shocked. 'Oh; is he being, er . . . like that about it?' She bit back the word 'misogynistic' just in time.

'No; just joking! But I think his dad's convinced it's Hassam's genes at work. Although personally I don't care where they come from.'

'That's right; it really doesn't matter, does it?' Benjamin finally managed to get a word in.

'And what do Hassam's parents think of their new granddaughter then?' Esther asked fighting down the rogue thought, *think about having a mixed-race grandchild, and of another faith too? Or, knowing our Daisy, of no faith at all?*

Daisy's reply surprised her. 'Yes, I know what you're really asking, Gran. Mr and Mrs Ahmed are really fine about it. They think Amira's lovely and haven't got a problem about her having a white mother. They aren't like the usual stupid stereotype of Muslims: backward-thinking and super-conservative, at all.'

'Oh; that's good. And, er, what about you and Hassam not being married?'

'Gran! What you mean, "not married"? Why should it be a problem?'

Esther laughed. Benjamin chuckled too. 'Well, not everyone, not all societies, are as liberal-minded as us in the West, you know, darling! Not that some Westerners are, particularly, either. I'm not saying that's a good or a bad thing; just that people have different attitudes. It's only in the last few decades that having partners as opposed to spouses really became acceptable in the West, after all. It didn't happen in your granddads and my day.'

Daisy tittered. 'Yeah; perhaps not. But then there was a lot of racism and sexism and homophobia back in your day too, wasn't there? We're a lot more enlightened now!'

'Yes, we are. Thank goodness. But what about Hassam's parents? How do they feel about you two living together? Do you know?'

'Well, as far as I know they're absolutely fine about it. Hassam hasn't said otherwise, anyway.'

'Really? Well that's good! It could be really difficult if they were opposed to it. Especially from Hassam's point of view.'

Hassam chose that moment to reappear bearing a tray of drinks and a plate of heaped chocolate biscuits (Daisy still had the voracious appetite she had had during pregnancy). 'What's all this? What are you saying about me?'

Daisy giggled. 'Ears burning, were they? My gran was just asking how your parents were about us two living in sin!'

Hassam's face fell. He stared at Daisy, horrified. '"Living in sin"? What do you mean?' He put the tray of drinks on the coffee table.

She grinned. 'Haven't you heard that expression? They used to say unmarried people living together were "living in sin" back in Gran and Granddad's day, because that's how the religious establishment saw sex outside marriage.'

'Well, that wasn't the universal view darling, believe me,' Esther put in. 'Not for us agnostic types anyway. It certainly wasn't for your granddad and me. And I doubt whether it was for your mum and dad either.'

Now it was Daisy's turn to stare, as Benjamin shifted uncomfortably. 'Really, Gran? You don't mean you and granddad . . .' She blushed; could not finish the sentence.

'Oh, no; we didn't live together. But that was partly because we were living in different countries: me in Germany and your granddad over here, so we couldn't, obviously. But that doesn't mean we didn't, ah, get to know each other, erm, completely before we married. In fact, it happened at just our second meeting.'

Daisy grinned. 'No!'

'Well, it wasn't quite like it sounds. We weren't that forward! No, we met at a concert your granddad's orchestra gave in Frankfurt in nineteen sixty-three. After that we started writing to each other, and gradually we fell in love. And then after a few months your granddad took a short holiday in Germany, just a few days, and we stayed in a hotel, and I suppose we could have had separate rooms, but we didn't want to . . .' The anecdote petered out.

'Ah yes,' Benjamin piped up, surprising them both. His voice was soft with nostalgia. 'That hotel. In – where was it now, Essie?'

'Karlstrasse.'

'Yes, that's right. I remember. And you'd booked us in as Mr and Mrs Adelstein, for the sake of respectability. Or Herr and Frau Adelstein, to be precise. I'm embarrassed to remember all those letters I wrote to you, like some lovesick teenage poet!'

'You shouldn't be, Benny! They were lovely. Anyway, I was just as bad, and I was a professional writer, or aspiring to be. I had certain standards to maintain!'

Benjamin smiled. 'Well, yours were much better expressed than mine. You wrote such beautiful prose, whereas I just blurted out my feelings.'

Daisy listened, entranced. 'Oh, that's wonderful! It's so romantic. Just like in an old movie!'

Esther laughed. Yes, I suppose it was. And do you know; your granddad proposed to me on our last night, and of course I said yes.'

'Ah, wonderful!' Daisy repeated.

'So then we got formally engaged, and I applied for residency in Britain because I was your granddad's fiancée, and a few months later we were married in England. And that's how we got together. So you see: your generation didn't exactly invent sex before marriage, young lady.'

'No, right. I suppose us young people can never imagine you older ones, er, doing it. And so there wasn't any inhibition about it because of your religion?'

'Good grief no! Well, I wasn't a practicing Jew and your granddad had stopped being one altogether, being adopted into a Christian family.' Esther glanced at Hassam, trying to gauge his reaction but there was none as far as she could tell; certainly not a hostile one, simply polite interest.

The baby seemed to have finished feeding. Daisy handed her into the eager arms of Esther and sorted her clothing out. Benjamin relaxed, visibly relieved. As Daisy reached for her mug of tea, her grandmother took in baby Amira properly for the first time. The baby returned her gaze, wincing a little, probably needing winding.

'Oh, she really is beautiful! Look at those eyes. They're nearly black, like little glossy beads. She's lovely. Isn't she, Benny?'

'Yes, she certainly is,' Benjamin agreed.

'And is she up to a reasonable weight now, Daisy?'

Daisy was in mid-biscuit. She swallowed the current mouthful. 'Well, yes, I suppose so; otherwise the hospital wouldn't have been happy to let us bring her home. She was two-point-seven kilos when I weighed her yesterday.'

'Oh, I can't do modern weights! What's that in pounds and ounces?'

'Don't ask me, I haven't a clue! I only look at the metric on the scales.'

'Just under six pounds, I think,' Benjamin said. He had always been better at metric-imperial conversions than Esther.

'Oh, well that's quite respectable, considering how tiny she was when she was born.'

Esther stared at her great-grandchild, rapt, but directed her words towards Daisy. 'And you feel perfectly alright now, do you, darling?'

'Yes, pretty much,' she mumbled, her mouth half-full again, spraying biscuit crumbs. 'The scar's still a bit itchy, but otherwise I'm fine.'

'Good! Yes, it's amazing how quickly the body recovers, really. And you didn't exactly have a straightforward pregnancy, so your mum says.'

Daisy laughed. 'Don't remind me!' She grinned fondly at Hassam. 'It was a good job I had my own personal trainee doctor to look after me!

Hassam smiled modestly. 'Well, I'm a long way from graduating still. But we have done a little about obstetrics, just the basics, so I know a little bit. Enough to know when to call an ambulance when things don't look too good, at least!'

Daisy finished her tea in a single long swallow; said, 'I quite fancy a walk, as it's such a nice day. Shall we do that? Perhaps go to the park?'

'Yes, that would be nice,' Esther agreed. 'But have you got a pram for

Amira? I can't see one.'

'No, but I've got a sling. They're much easier really, especially when you're shopping and haven't got a car. She should be alright in that – well so Mum says, anyway. It's not as if she's got to be swaddled in blankets or anything. She shouldn't get cold.'

'Oh, right. The things they have, nowadays! There was none of this when I had your mum and Uncle Samuel.'

Daisy grinned. 'Well, things move on. Right; I'll just change her nappy then, and we'll be off.'

'Er, I think I'll give it a miss,' Benjamin said, looking a little anxious. 'Is it all right if I stay here?'

Esther looked at him sharply. 'Are you feeling tired again?'

Benjamin smiled weakly. 'Just a little. I'll be fine though. Just need a little rest. You go and enjoy the sunshine though.'

'I'll stay behind too; keep you company,' Hassam offered.

'Right; that's settled then,' Daisy said, 'We'll divide along gender lines.'

'Yes, nothing changes, does it?' Esther quipped, wryly.

Hassam offered to make another cup of tea after the three generations of females had left them. Benjamin relaxed, letting his head loll against the high sofa back. This was only his fourth meeting with Daisy's young man, but he was coming to like him a lot.

Hassam brought in his recharged mug and set it down before him and, hospitable to a fault, the packet of remaining biscuits to refill the plate. The two men looked at each other for an awkward moment, each mentally searching for a small talk topic

Benjamin felt he ought to keep the subject on the little one, at least offer the opportunity of it, if only out of politeness. 'So how are you finding fatherhood then, Hassam?'

His host grinned, showing very white teeth. 'Oh, it's good. It really is. It wasn't quite what we'd intended, but there you go. We'd meant to wait a while with Daisy still in her job, as I'm not able to earn very much just working a few evenings in the coffee shop.'

'Yes, well, things don't always turn out quite according to plan. That's life. But I hope you can keep at your studies, even if things are tight financially now. The country needs all the doctors it can get.'

'Oh yes, I mean to! Three years in, I don't intend to waste all that effort so far and pack it in.'

'But it must be very difficult for you now, all the same. I know there'll be child benefit for the little one, but you've still got the rent to find, haven't you?'

Hassam smiled. 'Well, it's not too bad. We might have been able to get housing benefit too, Daisy says, as I'm a student, but my parents are helping us out with that, as a matter of fact. They're proud people. They'd rather help come from within the family as much as possible and as little as possible from the state. They don't want . . .'

He trailed off, embarrassed.

'Don't want what?'

'Well, you know; don't want to give ammunition to those people who slag off immigrants for coming over here just to claim benefits.'

Benjamin took a sip of his tea. 'Oh, that's a silly, ignorant attitude! Just plain racist much of the time. You always get a proportion of lazy freeloaders, whatever the ethnicity. Most of the ethnic minority people I know – which isn't a lot, admittedly – work damned hard. Like the Indians and Pakistanis you see running corner shops, working all hours, for instance.'

Hassam nodded sadly. 'Yes, that's true. But there are always some people who'd rather just follow their own agenda: believe what they want to believe; take their attitudes and opinions from the tabloid press, aren't there? But I'll say that for this part of London: it may not be very posh, but because it's very multiracial there's mostly a good level of tolerance. People generally get along well together. Things are better than they used to be. I don't often find prejudice now, and if people saw beyond my appearance and knew I wasn't a potential terrorist or something but a medical student who'll be giving them medical care in a few years' time, hopefully, I'm sure there'd be even less.'

'I think you're right. It's funny how concerns about race and ethnicity mostly disappear when people are ill in hospital, because the NHS relies so heavily on so many people of all colours and creeds.'

'Yeah.'

Benjamin continued, warming to his theme, (he enjoyed a good putting-the-world-to-rights discussion), 'I suppose it was different when your parents came over in, when was it again: in the late eighties?'

'Eighty-nine. Before I was born.'

'Right. Obviously you couldn't possibly be able to remember that far back, then, but I imagine there was much more rampant racism in the nineties. I know there was in the Metropolitan Police, at least, and I suppose they only reflected the general attitudes in society at large at the time. Sadly.'

'Yes, I think there probably was. There was certainly some of it when I was at school, and I know my brother and sisters got some too, because Mum wore the hijab outdoors. Some kids would take the micky out of us because of that.'

'Do any of your sisters wear it?'

'No; they're all thoroughly Westernised. Well, two of them, like me, were born in England anyway. Apart from at home, they've never known Palestinian culture.'

Benjamin finished his tea before continuing. 'And – do you mind if I ask – how are your parents about that; about their daughters not following their traditions?'

'Fine, pretty much. My mum has no problem with it at all, although she *is* slightly less conservative than my dad. He was a little worried about it at first but Mum talked him round, I think. She often wears the trousers in our house, contrary to the usual stereotype of Muslims!'

Benjamin laughed. 'Tell me about it! And what about religion: do they go to the mosque?'

'No, they don't. So there's no teaching from the Qu'ran or anything like that. They're fairly secular, really. Well, they really want to integrate and be British, and want us kids to be too. Of course three of us technically are, anyway, being born here. We're Londoners through and through! And I'm a complete atheist, to tell the truth, which isn't something you'd hear most Palestinians admit to, probably.'

'Well good for you, Hassam! I think you prove by what you say and what you want to do for a career that you don't lack kindness or humanity at all. When you think of all the divisiveness and hatred and cruelty that's still being caused by some fundamentalist believers in religion, even now in the twenty-first century, especially in the Middle East, you rather wonder whether we'd be better off without it. After all, it's played little part in the lives of most Europeans for decades now, and we seem to get along all right without it. We've certainly stopped having European wars, anyway.'

Hassam nodded enthusiastic agreement.

'It's slightly ironic really, isn't it,' Benjamin continued, well into his stride now, 'that you and I are sitting here like this agreeing with each other, when we originate from tribes who are today often such implacable enemies. Well, there are exceptions of course, but you know what I mean; the ring wingers in Israel and Hammas don't look as though they'll ever reach an accommodation. They seem poles apart and an uneasy peace is only maintained because of Israel's overwhelming United States-backed strength. And meanwhile fighting flares up on a regular basis and the innocent civilians, mostly Palestinians, continue to die. It's such a tragedy.'

'Yes it is.' Hassam paused. 'And you know all about being a refugee too, don't you, Mr Walters? So Daisy tells me.'

Benjamin sighed. 'Well, in a way. Although I can't remember any of it, being a baby at the time. Esther has a slight recollection of those terrible times, being over a year older than me. But yes, we were both very lucky indeed, unlike both our parents. I presume she told you what happened to them? And please, call me Benny.'

'Yes, she did – Benny. It certainly was dreadful; utterly evil.'

'Indeed. Although by no means the only evil collective act that's ever been committed in the often inglorious history of the human race, usually by governments calling themselves religious, and often Christian, for that matter. Except perhaps it's particularly horrific because of its sheer scale. But even there, other genocides have run it close, like Biafra in Africa. Although killing a thousand people just because of their religion or ethnicity is just as bad for the victims concerned as six million. I know I should be, and am, eternally grateful to Britain, but the Allies indulged in slaughter of innocents too towards the end of the War. Look at Dresden. It was such a beautiful city, apart from all the human suffering. And the people in Hiroshima and Nagasaki, of course. But the Allies justified it by saying that it shortened the war by months – the brutal means justifying the end. Perhaps it did; perhaps not. I'm not wise or expert enough to have a certain opinion about it. But that's war for you, I'm afraid. By its very nature, it involves killing and suffering and destruction, whatever the scale.'

The conversation wore pleasantly on. The subject lightened and returned to the baby, and practicalities. Hassam's mother had offered, in a year or so, to babysit Amira for a few hours per day so that Daisy could get a part time job. That would give them back a measure of independence. And then, four or five years in the future, there was her education to consider. Benjamin asked if they would want to put her in a faith school, although he suspected he already knew the answer to that. Hassam confirmed it. No, absolutely not, he said, surprisingly vehemently. And Daisy would never hear of it, either.

Voices drifting up the stairs announced the return of the females. They came into the living room, Daisy a little red in her plump face from climbing the stairs. Hassam moved to help her divest herself of the sleeping baby.

'Did you have a nice walk then?' Benjamin asked.

Esther smiled. 'Yes, very nice. And a little, er, stimulating at one point.'

'How do you mean?'

'Oh, well, your outspoken crusading granddaughter here got a bit, shall we say, enthusiastic talking to someone in a café. I thought we were only going in for a nice quiet cup of tea!'

Relieved of Amira, Daisy shed the sling, rotating her shoulders, glad to be rid of the weight. 'Well,' she snorted, her forehead wrinkling into a frown, 'the man was a complete pillock!'

'Oh, what happened?'

'There was a little, er, difference of opinion between Daisy and a customer sitting at the next table,' Esther said, grinning at her granddaughter. 'A man started going on about the refugees from Syria and Iraq and so on, crossing the Mediterranean to Europe, saying they were all chancers just coming here for a better life. That they should all be kept out and we should look after our own; we had enough problems here in the West without being swamped by migrants competing for jobs and housing and services. And, naturally, that set Daisy off. She told him he should just try imagining what it must be like living in a war situation with bombs falling and rockets and bullets flying and people, women and children and old people, being blown apart all around him, and ask himself whether he wouldn't want to take his family out of that horror.

'To which the man said that it was all very sad but was no concern of us in the West; that it was up to the Arabs to sort their own problems out, and some of them were probably terrorists trying to sneak into Europe anyway, because they hated us; then Daisy accused him of being callous and uncaring and talking bollocks, excuse the language, and he called her a stupid little leftie who had no idea what she was talking about. And it just escalated from there, and Daisy said she was proud the father of her child was Palestinian and the son of a refugee, which made the man even more angry and contemptuous, and he suggested he should piss off back there then. And she said that Hassam was as British as he was, and a far better man, and by now they were shouting at each other, and the other people in the café were staring and looking embarrassed, and Amira was getting frightened and starting to cry, and the lady behind the counter shouted to us to shut it, or we'd have to leave, and then the man and his friends stormed out anyway. Then it took me quite a while to calm you down, young lady, didn't it?'

'Daisy scowled. 'Yeah, well I was bloody furious. He was a stupid racist bigot! And a moron.'

They stayed for another hour, until five-thirty. Daisy and Hassam offered them a meal (Hassam, it seemed, was a quite an accomplished cook, at least according to Daisy). But Esther was keen to start heading home. It would be a fairly taxing journey for Benjamin: five minutes' walk to the tube station, then the changing at Piccadilly Circus for the Bakerloo line, then the change again to surface rail to Bushey and finally another ten minute trek home after that. So they declined the offer with thanks, Esther had a final cuddle of the baby and then they left.

And they were in bed by nine-fifteen, because Benjamin expressed himself ready for it, although Esther was far from tired. Lying there in the twilight of the shortening September evening, she tackled him. 'That's worn you out, hasn't it, Benny?'

He sighed. 'Yes; a little. Not as young as I was. It was a lovely visit though, wasn't it? The baby's beautiful. Hassam and I had a good old chinwag while you were out with Daisy. He really is a very nice young man. I do hope they stay together.'

'Yes, she is; a little sweetie. And yes, I like Hassam too. And I hope they do too. But I was talking about you, Benny. I'm concerned about you. You really should see the doctor. You shouldn't be getting as tired as this. I'm going to make an appointment for you, whether you like it or not.'

Benjamin sighed again, theatrically this time. 'Yes, all right, love. You win.'

'Right; and you will retire at the end of the season?'

'Yes, I will.'

'Promise?'

'I promise.'

Chapter 12

Esther had almost forgotten that she had invited Patrick for dinner. It was to be the day after tomorrow. The poor man had seemed a bit down the last time they had seen him, when he had gone with them to one of Benjamin's performances the previous month. It was a marital problem, he had confessed, as if she were some sort of amalgam of confidante, sympathetic mother-figure and agony aunt over coffee after driving them back home later.

She thought about him now, rather surprising herself by the warm glow of affection that triggered. Yes, he did in a curious way tend to bring out her maternal instincts, for all that he was forty-four years old (although he did not look it, with his rufous curls skirting his bald pate, beard, freckles and roguish Irish grin; given a pointed cap and green outfit, she'd mischievously thought the first time they met, he would have been the perfect stereotypical – albeit rather oversized - leprechaun). You could have taken him for a man ten years younger. But apart from his charm, it was possibly his troubled history and faint air of vulnerability that provoked tender feelings or at least sympathy anyway. That and the fact that, although he could have been taken for a folk musician, an Irish uilleann piper perhaps, he shared their interest in classical music.

Also, like them (well, more so really; she and Benny were legally British after all) he was a foreigner, a migrant in Britain, being as he was from the Republic of Ireland, not Ulster. So he was a bit of a fellow-traveller, in a way. He had not had the happiest of childhoods, so he had told them once in one of their surprisingly frequent intimate chats: growing up in a large dysfunctional family in Sligo, his mother harassed, embittered and finally abandoned by his alcoholic, abusive father, although they were all glad to see the back of him. But along with some of his many siblings, Maeve and Julie being just two of them, apparently, he had escaped to England and in his case to comparative affluence and a career as a newspaper journalist with one of the quality broadsheets. So apart from anything else, he and she had something – careers – in common.

In fact it had been his work that had introduced him to her and Benny, when he had interviewed them, along with Benny's sister Liza, before she died, for a piece he was writing about the *Kindertransport*. They had taken an instant liking to each other then, and the friendship had stuck. Now they almost regarded him as a surrogate son, as his mother had died a few years earlier, and his absent father probably too, from excess, for all he knew.

But no; he hadn't been radiating a lot of cheerfulness the last time they saw him. He had clearly wanted to unburden when he dropped them back home (they'd driven to the concert in his car), so, after Benny had excused himself and gone up to bed, she had sat and listened to his recounted woes: how he had had the divorce papers through at last, after the messy, acrimonious ending of his marriage to Catarina and the not-very-satisfactory arrangements for access to his daughter Bella, Catarina having returned to her native Italy and taken Bella with her, as she had been legally deemed to be the primary guardian of her. That was fair enough, he had conceded ruefully, but now he really missed his daughter. She had sympathized. Yes; it seemed rather unfortunate, although no doubt Catarina was perfectly within her rights to return to Palermo with nothing to keep her in Britain now.

He had sighed and admitted that, yes, it was fair enough. It was just a bugger, he had supposed, that he had chosen a foreign person to marry. This would always have been a possible consequence if things did not work out. Then he had got a little self-pitying (although she had not minded that) and said that he never seemed to get it right with relationships, that he had two failed marriages to his credit (or was it debit?) now, although at least the first one had been childless, so it had been a clean break. Poor Patrick. It did seem such a shame. Yes, he seemed to be unlucky in love. Well, anyway, perhaps a nice meal and sympathy might cheer him up.

And then he had phoned back and said that he had a friend, whom he had asked if he might bring too, if that was all right? Yes, she had said, of course it was.

The soonest Esther could get an appointment with the doctor was in ten working days' time. So there were two more performances scheduled before then. But one of them involved little flute work and the following one even less. And he felt as though he were starting a cold after the first one, so Benjamin rang in sick. It was not a problem. Henry the orchestra manager had a zero tolerance of coughs and colds amongst the players; they could so easily spread like wildfire and could seriously affect the wind and woodwind players' ability to play, particularly, and impair a performance. Besides, the other flautists could easily cover for him.

Benjamin hated going to the doctor. It was not something he had done very much in his largely ailment-and-accident-free life. Even when he had had the flu the previous winter, he had stoically (Esther, disapproving, had said 'masochistically') refrained from going. A few days in bed, paracetamol and lemon drinks had seen it off. He had never broken a limb or even so much as sprained an ankle, so had never visited A and E in his life. His only appointment with his GP in recent times had been (at Esther's insistence) with that persistent cough in the spring, which had gone on for several weeks and which, fair enough, he had had to get sorted out before the summer season began. Because, obviously, he could hardly risk being unexpectedly taken with a coughing fit during a performance, whether he was playing at the time or not. That time, the doctor had prescribed a course of antibiotics (which Esther had insisted he complete, even though it had gone away before it was finished) and it had certainly done the trick.

Yes, he hated going; hated the feeling that he was wasting the busy doctor's valuable time; hated the feeling of being a hypochondriac, feeling sure he was being a pest.

But if the doctor, a very pleasant middle aged woman with a sympathetic manner thought so, she certainly did not show it. She coaxed a description of his symptoms out of him: his increasing tiredness; breathlessness after even the most moderate exertion; occasional (but also rather increasing) light-headedness. Then she seemed to go off on an irrelevant tangent when she noticed a bruise on the back of his hand: how had he come by that? Had he banged it hard? No, he said, it was just a silly little thing; he had fumbled his instrument case and it had fallen on his hand. But he had fumbled again and caught it, preventing it from falling to the floor. That was the main thing. She asked him, oddly, about his gums. Were they prone to bleeding at all? Well, he said, just a little, but he always brushed his teeth quite vigorously. But they had been a bit more prone to bleeding lately. She asked if she might take a look and raised his upper lip to see for herself, nodded and made no comment.

She asked him to take his shirt off and sounded his chest, and examined the lymph glands in his armpits and throat. She donned gloves, unwrapped a hypodermic and extracted a blood sample from his left arm and labeled it, saying she would send it away to Watford General Hospital for testing. She said there was the slight possibility that it might be leukaemia, but it wasn't all that common; it was a matter of eliminating possibilities. It could be any one of a number of things. She mentioned a few ailments with obscure names that he had never heard of, so it was rather pointless, and said not to worry.

But Benjamin did brood and worry as he walked slowly home. Well, at least it might not be a matter of time-wasting this time. A fatalistic part of him almost welcomed it, as if it that made it somehow worthwhile. But he must not burden Esther with worry. Not yet, at least. He would share any burden there might be to share if or when it arose. So after he reached home and sat for a few minutes at the kitchen table with a mug of tea to regain his breath, he told a small white lie.

'She thinks I've probably got a bit of a chest infection again, and she's taken a blood sample for testing.'

Esther was instantly suspicious. 'Oh? What was that all about? Why would they want to do that?'

'I don't know, love. She didn't say.'

She was exasperated. 'Oh, Benny! For crying out loud! You really are useless! I knew I should have come with you. You don't know how to ask the right questions!'

'It's all right,' Benjamin reassured. 'I expect it's just routine. Nothing to worry about.'

But of course Esther was not fooled, and she did worry, too. Today was Friday so there was the weekend to get through. She very much doubted whether the hospital laboratory worked at weekends, apart from for pressing emergencies happening in A and E. And the doctor's, other than the out-of-hours locum service, did not anyway. They would just have to try and put anxiety on hold and wait.

So Esther forced herself to do so, until the Tuesday afternoon. Then she rang the surgery. To be told that, no, the results were not back yet. They should be on Thursday, if she could wait until then. Esther was on the phone at eight-forty-five in the morning two days later, joining a lengthy telephone queue. After holding for what felt like an eternity, an impeccably polite receptionist finally answered. Esther repeated her anxious enquiry. There was a pause as the receptionist presumably checked her computer screen. She came back on. 'Yes, they're back now. Doctor Lewis would like to see Mr Walters as soon as possible?' The upward inflexion of the final word turned the statement into a question.

'Oh, right. Yes. When can we come in?'

Another lengthy pause. Perhaps the receptionist was consulting Dr Lewis. Then her voice again, brisk, efficient. 'I can fit you in tomorrow afternoon. Four-thirty?'

Now the doctor could see Benjamin quickly, it seemed. 'Yes, fine. Thank you.' Esther said, 'We'll see you tomorrow then.'

Doctor Lewis brought up a second chair for Esther to sit down alongside Benjamin. She looked at her computer screen, angling it, Esther did not fail to notice, slightly further out of their line of vision. They waited, tense, for her to begin. Her expression was kind but she did not prevaricate, presumably knowing from long experience that it was better, less brutal, to deliver unwelcome and worrying news immediately than leave patients hanging in anxiety.

'Well the test shows an excessively high white blood cell count. The problem with that is, they're often abnormal and don't work properly to fight infection. And there's also a low red cell count, which explains your tiredness and breathlessness, and also giddiness. The platelet count is low too, which would tend to cause too-easy bleeding or bruising. That's why I was interested in your gums and the bruise on your hand.'

Esther took a deep breath. 'So what does all this suggest; do you think?'

The doctor looked steadily at Benjamin. 'Well, I'm afraid it does look increasingly like leukaemia, Mr Walters. I may be wrong – I'm not a haematologist – and it could still be other things. I want you to see Mr Wilkinson at the Watford General. He's one of the top people in the field. Writes in the *Lancet*. I've read him. He's very good. Leave it with me and I'll try and get you an appointment as soon as I can.'

So now there was another anxious wait. Esther tried to maintain an air of cheerful optimism. Tried to reassure Benjamin that he would be in good hands. Had not Dr Lewis said so? The consultant was one of the best. And she had said herself: it still might not be leukaemia. It could be something else. Something quite benign and easily treatable.

As for Benjamin, he seemed to retreat into himself, behind an uncommunicative wall of – what? Denial? Worry? Acceptance? Esther supposed that he was assailed by a cocktail of emotions. It was impossible to know how he was feeling, much as she tried to encourage him to share his thoughts. But no, it wasn't impossible; not entirely

There had been that worrying period years ago, not long after she had given birth to Sam, when she had had that breast cancer scare from a possibly over-zealous (but better that than be negligent) mobile screening radiographer who had referred her to her GP, who had diagnosed mastitis and prescribed diethylstilbestrol, which had cleared it up satisfactorily.

Yes, that had been very worrying for a few days, and the worry had not completely abated until the lumpiness had fully cleared up. She had remembered thinking dismally how ultimately lonely a position it was, being faced with the possibility of no longer existing. Her residual religion had been no comfort or reassurance at all; the panic had blotted out everything. She didn't want to go to some other mystical place promised by the scriptures, which she personally doubted the existence of. Not yet; not at the age of thirty-two. She wanted to stay on earth, in the imperfect but real world, with Benny and the children. Of course Benny had tried his hardest to be understanding and loving and encouraging and supportive, but he could only do so much. Ultimately, she was on her own. So Benny was probably thinking all this too.

Fifteen days later a letter came from the hospital, from the haematology department, saying that an appointment had been made at eleven-thirty in the morning for Benjamin to see Mr Wilkinson. Esther ordered a taxi to take them to Watford rather than trust to the vagaries of public transport. It would be less taxing for Benjamin, too. After following the signs, slowly, to Haematology and announcing their arrival at the reception desk they sat nervously in the waiting area, in the company of fifteen or so other people of all ages, although most were elderly. There were four couples, some clutching slips of paper which were presumably test results for the perusal of Mr Jenkins, some of them holding hands, all of them either morosely studying the floor or glancing anxiously around. A middle-aged couple sat with a thin, pale, bald-headed little girl of around ten. Clearly she was having chemotherapy. A younger woman with a female companion, possibly her mother, by her side, nursed a lethargic toddler.

They had positioned themselves facing a wall clock, ultra modern and minimalist with light sans serif numbers and stick-thin hands, marking time in almost imperceptible, tiny jerks. They had arrived in plenty of time to allow for Benjamin's slow progress, so the clock presently informed eleven-ten. Esther hoped to goodness that the appointments were running to time, although she knew it was probably a forlorn hope. The clock's hands crawled to eleven-fifteen. A nurse emerged from the consultant's inner sanctum and called a name which was not Benjamin's. One of the other elderly couples, an emaciated lady and presumably supporting husband, got up and slowly followed the nurse. At eleven twenty-five they reappeared and were led away looking dazed by another nurse. Five minutes passed and the first nurse reappeared. Esther looked up expectantly, heart thumping. The nurse called another name and the couple with the young girl got up.

They were in with Mr Wilkinson for over ten minutes too. His minion summoned the next patient and it was the couple with the toddler. Then at gone eleven forty-five it was another of the elderly couples; the man looking as if he were the patient. And then finally, at three minutes past twelve, their hearts collectively missed a beat as the nurse called Benjamin's name.

The tall, rather sad-eyed consultant (he must have been involved in this scenario so many times before) rose to shake their hands and bade them sit opposite him. There was another doctor in the room too, a young Indian woman in her twenties, presumably an assistant. It looked as though he had already been reading Benjamin's details, doubtless provided by Dr Lewis, on his computer screen. He asked the same questions again, and some new ones, and nodded sympathetically, unsurprised, at the answers. He too looked at Benjamin's gums and the unhealed bruise on his hand and listened to his chest.

He asked questions about Benjamin's parents' medical history, to which, of course, he could give no answers. They held their breaths waiting for his expert opinion. But he simply confirmed what Dr Lewis had thought, without fully committing himself to a firm diagnosis because, he said gravely, it would depend ultimately on the results of further tests, which they would do now. He shook their hands again in dismissal and said that he would see them again when the results were through. He gave his assistant some instructions and asked them to go with her into an adjoining treatment room for them: a bone marrow biopsy, an MRI scan and the extraction of more blood. The young doctor introduced herself as Meera and asked Benjamin to please not worry, did the uncomfortable biopsy and the blood-drawing herself, found a porter and wheelchair for Benjamin as he felt a little fragile after the biopsy needle, and then led them to the radiology department for scanning.

By the time Benjamin had recovered from the various testing the day had gone. It was late afternoon before they were back home, Benjamin was slightly painfully ensconced on the sofa and Esther was making him a nice cup of tea.

Six days later, back from a second anxious visit to see Mr Wilkinson. Benjamin sat in his conservatory, gazing unseeing over a garden bathed in early September sun. The dahlias were still making their exuberant Mexican carnival display, although the grass could do with a mowing. A breeze stirred the leaves of the flowering cherry at the far end, by the chestnut brown-stained fence. Smokey-grey nimbus clouds were stealing in from the west, threatening the sun. It looked as though there would be rain before long.

It might as well have been raining already though. Because now Benjamin had the diagnosis, firm and unequivocal from Mr Wilkinson, albeit delivered as gently as he could. It was indeed cancer running amok in his bloodstream, sending his white blood cell count spinning malignantly out of control and depressing production of the red corpuscles and platelets. And the results confirmed the haemotologist's suspicions about his tiredness, increasing light-headedness, and tendency to bleed. Yes, it was acute myeloid leukaemia that was spreading its malevolence throughout his body and had already established a vanguard in his liver and also, slightly, in his spleen.

And the initial treatment, the induction chemotherapy, was to begin in two to three weeks time. Esther, loyally annoyed, had wondered why it could not start immediately. Mr Wilkinson had sighed, looked apologetic and said that, sadly, it was a matter of priorities and limited resources. Of course he appreciated that waiting would be an anxious time for them, and in an ideal world with double the number of hospitals and double the staff to run them, it would be possible to begin treatment much more quickly. And possibly, if they had a fully comprehensive private healthcare plan, Benjamin would be able to opt out and begin chemotherapy within a few days, although he did not believe that speedier service offered by the private sector produced significantly better outcomes.

Well, Benjamin thought dismally, it was academic anyway. Esther and he did not have private healthcare. They didn't really hold with it. With their political outlooks and being lifelong Labour voters of the Tony Benn persuasion, they had always placed their trust in the NHS. He stared at the patio slabs outside the conservatory door; Rogue weeds were sprouting through the grouting here and there. The garden was beginning to look decidedly shabby. He and Esther usually kept it so spick and span. Especially Esther, now she was retired and had time on her hands.

Yes, retirement. That was a point. He had reluctantly promised Esther he would retire himself at the end of the season. But that was still over two months away. And the coming weeks were uncertain, to say the least. He would never be able keep his mind on the job with the prospect of cancer treatment hovering like a sinister black crow over things. It would mean giving no notice at all, but it would have to be done now. They would understand though. After all, he could hardly have a better reason for bringing down the final curtain on his career. And there were other talented flautists in the orchestra who could move up to first flute, like Marion Barber, who usually stood in for him when he was indisposed. Yes, there should be no problem there. He would ring Henry the manager in the morning and put him in the picture. The next performance was due in two evenings' time and he really did not feel up to it physically, never mind anything else.

Not now. The significance of the situation was beginning to sink in. He had been in a state of denial about recent events, been suppressing his fears, he supposed. But he had always felt so hale and hearty, making a conscious effort to keep in trim because he was aware of having such a sedentary occupation and the health problems it could bring. He had thought he was invincible; had always walked briskly to and from the railway station, always made a point of taking the stairs rather than the lift when away touring and Esther and he had usually spent time at weekends walking locally in Bushey Heath or further afield in the Chiltern Hills, or in the evenings if the weather was fine and he was not working, in Epping Forest, And they had had lovely walking holidays.

Yes, they had had some grand times. He suddenly realized where his thoughts were leading. 'Had some'. Past tense. As if life was already over. He felt his throat tighten and suddenly the held-back tears of panic and fear and despair and why-me? anger came, and he brought his hands to his face and sobbed.

Third Movement

Andante – accelerando, crescendo

Chapter 13: July

I decided at the weekend to start walking to work. Sure it's only a mile or two, and I really ought to get some exercise. My sedentary job, too-frequent visits to the pub at lunchtimes (and increasingly after work too, nowadays) and a diet of ready meals now that I'm alone are all conspiring to pile on the pounds. It was catalyzed because I caught sight of myself sideways-on in the bathroom mirror and it wasn't a pretty sight. I'm getting quite a beer belly. I must cut down on the drinking and junk food too. And the comfort eating snacks. I wonder why it is that sweet food lifts your mood (well, a little, anyway) when you're feeling low? Perhaps it's something to do with stimulating pleasure centres in the brain. A hit of transient pleasure as a balm for sadness, or something like that. I suppose it's a bit like taking a drug to make yourself temporarily high, but without the addiction or sleaziness or possible catastrophic damage to health.

Well, there *is* damage to health of course with too much sugar, albeit a little more insidiously: the possibility of diabetes. So all in all, I'm probably being a death-wishing eejit; risking a coronary from lack of exercise, sclerosis of the liver from too much booze and diabetes from too much sugar. So it's time I pulled my socks up.

After all, things aren't that bad. I know I got a bit maudlin and self-pitying at Benny and Esther's the other night, but there was no excuse for it. I really shouldn't inflict my troubles on them. Although Esther was very sweet and understanding, bless her, letting me ramble on about being free of the oppression of marriage to Catarina now but missing Bella.

But I do feel an enormous sense of relief, now it's finally all over after all that unseemly and bitter bickering over money and custody and I have the decree absolute in my hands. And now she's away back to Italy and out of my life and I'm many thousands of pounds poorer, I've downsized to a less salubrious dwelling (a flat in Canning Town) and the BMW coupe has been exchanged for a three-year-old Ford Focus.

Sure it was a big mistake, that marriage, if ever there was one. Talk about mistaking lust for love; being bowled over in my stupid male way by her dark beauty and vivaciousness. And if I'm honest, I suppose, voluptuousness. I thought at the time that she was a dream come true: over here in England on holiday for three weeks before starting a course in economics as a somewhat mature student (well, twenty-nine, anyway) at Turin University. We were introduced to each other at the beginning of her stay, by matchmaker Beryl from work, who was a friend of her aunt, so there was enough time for a heady, passionate affair to germinate and take hold. And enough time for us to be a little too casual about contraception and for the germ of Bella to be planted in her so soft, so irresistible belly.

And then when, back in Italy, she found herself pregnant, there was no question but that we would marry. Abortion would have been unthinkable; in her case because of religious constraint (and traditionally-minded parents) and in mine because I really wanted us to be together and have the child. So that put paid to her plans for a career in financial services. She had to exchange them for relocation in England and marriage to her red-haired Irish Danny Boy and motherhood. Possibly that was the fatal flaw in our marriage, that Hobson's choice: the constant irritant, the slowly festering sore of resentment. She was less seduced by dreams of domestic family bliss than I; rather, she saw it as a loss of self-determination.

As far as I was concerned my want of her certainly wasn't just pathetic male attraction to the physical, though. Or because she'd given me a child; she did seem to satisfy an emotional need too. Looking back on it now, I can see that it was probably a rebound thing because I had had such a miserable experience with Melanie. Yes, my cheating first wife certainly gave me a hard time. But at the time, Catarina really did bring love and light and hope back into my fragile, unhappy life. Well, no fool like an old fool, I suppose.

And now here I am, alone again. I don't feel the loss of Catarina. We were married ten years but the love went out of it long ago. We spent the last three or four years doggedly staying together trying to make it work largely for the sake of Bella, before finally mutually accepting that it was a hopeless cause and we'd both be better off free, with another chance of finding happiness.

But I do miss Bella! I can appreciate that she's better off living with her mother, but because they're now in Italy it does make access to her difficult. I would gladly pay for air tickets two or three times a year for her to come here to visit, but Catarina and her lawyers have got things nicely sewn up in her favour on that front. They magnanimously say I can visit my daughter as often as I like (generous of them!) but sending her over here to see me is quite out of the question. Because, they say, there's the possibility that I wouldn't put her on a flight back again. As if I would do that! So all I can do is take holidays over there, finding a hotel in Palermo, and have Bella with me on a day-at-a-time basis, dutifully returning her to Catarina at the end of each one. Just because she won't trust me. It's far from ideal, although, admittedly, I can speak to her regularly on Skype. But it's the best that can be done.

So, to return to the subject of walking to work. It meant getting up a bit earlier of course, and on the first day I allowed a full hour because I didn't know how long it would take. But I walked briskly, because that's the point after all – it's supposed to be exercise – and did it in thirty-three minutes. So I was conscientiously early, almost the first in. The office cleaners had barely cleaned up the chaos of the previous Saturday. Journalists are a messy lot. I was a little out of breath, admittedly, but I was quite pleased with myself. And I added to the virtuousness of it by not going to the pub at lunchtime either, to the astonishment of my drinking buddies Tony and Alistair; simply went out for sandwiches and a coffee and brought them back to consume at my desk. The thing to do now is keep it up. That'll be the hard part, probably. It's fine on a nice dry sunny summer day, but will I have the dedication (or masochism) to still be doing it in the middle of winter when it's raining cats and dogs and blowing a gale? Well I must try. A little physical discomfort is character-building, sure it is.

Of course, strictly speaking, I don't necessarily have to go in to the office every day. It's not as if I'm working in the newsroom as part of the news team and need to be under the watchful eye of the editor. I could write my articles and opinion pieces and editorials from home perfectly well and email my copy in. But I like the companionship of the others. It would be a bit dreary and, quite honestly, lonely being stuck at home in my untidy flat, with no one to talk to, like some insular monkish novelist.

It's surprising how much more of the world you notice when on foot though. I was walking along Brewery Street, not far from the office, and there was a busker sitting on the pavement, back against a wall, long legs taking up half of its width so that people had to funnel around her. A young woman, of rather unkempt appearance, wearing grubby jeans with holey knees, an equally scruffy embroidered smock thing and a multicoloured wooly hat. Her long dark straggly hair looked as though it would benefit from hot water, shampoo and a brush. Her dark, heavy-framed glasses did nothing to improve her appearance either.

She was playing a flute, quite an expensive instrument by the look of things, and giving quite a good rendition of that tune of John Denver's from years ago. What is it now? Oh yes; *Annie's Song*. Perhaps she fancied herself as a bit of a James Galway, or something. Didn't he popularize it? Well it made a change from the ubiquitous guitar and reedy indifferent singing voice of most buskers, anyway. She had her instrument case open on the pavement in front of her, with a small scattering of coins in it, only three or four of them pounds. Although it was still early morning of course, and most people hurrying to their daily grind full of their own concerns probably wouldn't pause to throw a coin into her case.

I do wonder why these people do that. Busk, I mean. When they've got obvious talent, as that woman had. It seems a bit of a waste to me.

But I reached into my jacket pocket for change, found I had a couple of pound coins and dropped them into her case. She gave me a nod of her multicoloured head in lieu of a thank you.

There was something to look forward to in the evening though, so again I didn't linger at the pub after work. The weekly Skype to Bella. I'd gone an entire working day without a drop of alcohol passing my lips.

I was home by ten to seven, which was nice timing because our regular slot is seven o'clock, eight European time, which gives us half an hour or so before she has to get ready for bed at eight-thirty. Her mother's a stickler for strict, not-too-late bedtimes. That used to be one of the problems between Catarina and me: parenting. We didn't always see eye to eye. She was quite disciplinarian in some ways whereas I tended to spoil our daughter. I was a bit inclined to be overly permissive, I suppose; a soft touch. Bella quickly learned as a small child that if she wanted something, it was better to ask me first. Or preferably, ask only me. She only had to look up at me and fix me with those nut-brown eyes and raise her eyebrows imploringly and I was conquered. Especially towards the end of the marriage as things became increasingly fraught and I could see divorce and separation from her looming.

I suppose that in my reluctance to deny her anything I was desperately trying not to alienate her. Terrified of her taking sides with her mother and against me. Trying to be the Good Parent; the innocent party in the schism that was coming. Trying to tell her clumsily that just because her mum and I were not happy together, that didn't apply to her. That nothing had changed in that regard. It was a bit pathetic, I suppose. But it happens. It's happened to a couple of my colleagues; they've got divorced and gone completely out of their children's lives. Well I don't want it to happen in my case. I really don't. If it's a choice between that and spoil her a bit, then so be it.

There was just time to make myself a mug of tea and settle down on the sofa, laptop on my knees, and boot up. I waited a minute or so and then there she was, her face filling the screen, a little soft-focus, but no matter. I've no idea how far up the model range Catarina's computer is, how many megapixels the camera boasts.

My chest did its usual squeeze. 'Hello sweetheart! How are you?'

Bella grinned. 'Hi, daddy. Good, thank you.' We've always taught her good manners. Sorry; I mean "we'd." Past tense now. But I'm absurdly pleased that I'm still "daddy"; haven't yet morphed into grown-up "dad".

'Good. Have you had a good day?'

'Yeah, pretty good.'

'How has school been?'

'Okay.'

It was always like this at the beginning of conversations: groping for subjects on my part; succinct replies on hers. Until we got going, and then she was away, talking nineteen to the dozen, so that it was difficult to get a word in. Not that I mind that in the slightest. I'm happy just to listen to her chattering happily away about her eleven-year-old life, easy in my long-distance company.

'You've settled in alright? How do you find speaking Italian all the time?'

'Well, I'm getting used to it. It's a good thing I can speak it fluently, otherwise it might be a bit difficult, I suppose. And we speak it at home all the time now. Well there's no point in speaking English any more, is there?'

'No, I suppose not.' I felt a twinge of resentment. My daughter was going to gradually become more and more Italian, less and less Irish. It felt like a sort of abandonment. But I said, 'And you're making lots of friends at school, are you?'

Bella grinned. 'Yes, one or two. Mirabel is nice. And Adriana. They think I'm quite cool because I'm half Irish, I think!'

I laughed too. 'Well I suppose you are, love. You're an unusual mixture, sure.'

'Mm, I suppose so.' Bella didn't expand on that.

I searched for another topic. A sideways one, at least. 'Of course, it must be quite a change for you at school anyway because you've not just changed country but are also at a big school now . . . er, is that the way it works in Italy?'

'Yes, I think it's just the same as in England. Primary school and then secondary. Well, lower secondary, actually, until you're fourteen. Then I think you go on to upper secondary. You start at eleven, just like over there.'

Over there. There it was again: a simple, innocent little remark with profound meaning. You're over there, I'm over here. We might as well be a world apart.

'Mm. And do you still like doing maths? I know it used to be one of your favourite subjects, didn't it.'

'Yes, it's okay. I'd still like to go into computers, I think.'

'Good! So you'll be able to sort me out when my computer crashes and runs slow then!' The phrase slipped out before I could restrain it. *Idiot! How can that happen, now!*

Silence.

I changed the subject again. 'And what about your music? Are you still doing that?' She had begun piano lessons at age eight, showing reasonable promise, and we had bought her a fairly decent second hand Yamaha upright for the last Christmas before the marriage finally fell apart. Perhaps I thought that in us both encouraging Bella in her passion, it would somehow hold it together. It didn't though. The piano went to Italy with Catarina's agreed share of our divided possessions.

She sounded a little embarrassed; looked down at the keyboard of her computer. 'Well, a little. But not as much as I used to, really.' She paused then said awkwardly, 'It's not the same now.'

'How do you mean, love? How is it not the same?'

I waited. She was still avoiding my eyes. 'Well, mum doesn't encourage me so much. Not like you used to. Doesn't seem to care whether I practice or not.'

I silently cursed Catarina. *You miserable, unsupportive bitch!* But I said, 'Ah, that's a pity! But you must do what you want, not what your mammy or I want you to. Perhaps I was a bit too pushy before . . . Before. If I was, I'm sorry, Bella.'

She looked at me then. 'No, you weren't, daddy. Not at all. I'm glad you got me interested in music. Proper music I mean; not just rock and pop and all that.'

My throat tightened. 'Yes, well, it was only because you seemed keen to play an instrument in the first place.'

'Yeah.'

'Well, anyway, you keep it up if you want to. Never mind about your mammy and me. Okay?'

'Yes, okay.'

End of subject, it seemed. I searched again. 'So . . . what else have you been doing with yourself?'

She brightened. 'We went to the funfair last Saturday afternoon. Had a great time. With Mum's friend and Antonio.'

'Antonio?'

'Yeah; he's the son of Mum's, er, friend.'

'Right. And what's her name?' Stupidly, I didn't see the answer coming.

'Er, it's a "he", actually. Luigi.' Bella cast her eyes down again, embarrassed. She was probably aware of straying into dangerous territory. She's very intelligent and sensitive, my Bella.

'Oh.' I felt an irrational stab of jealousy. Completely irrational. What the hell business of mine was it what Catarina did with the rest of her life now she was rid of me? Or was it something else: fear? Of a possible stepfather looming, who would be Bella's new father figure, a competitor for her affections? Her love, even. It would be so much easier for him, being there, nudging his insidious way into her life. Stealing her from me.

But I forced myself to say, 'Oh, right. And how long has your mum known, er, Luigi?'

'Erm, not long. He's just a friend, that's all. From work.'

'Oh, she's working now?'

'Yeah. In an insurance office, or something.'

'So what do you do when you've finished school? You don't go home to an empty house, I hope!'

'Oh, no! I go to Grandma and Grandpa's house. Then Mum picks me up from there later, when she's finished work.'

'Right,' I said impotently. And a bit irritated, but with myself. Catarina seemed to have her new life, her life without me, all sorted out, for both her and Bella. My daughter. I suddenly felt very peripheral; stripped of any influence in her life. As if she was slipping from me, drifting away on a merciless ocean to total separation. Emotion welled up. I wanted to sulkily end this conversation with its hurtful jealousy-piquing revelations. I didn't want to be talking to an electronic image of her, hearing her electronic voice, listening to stuff about her new life; I wanted her here with me.

Our time was nearly up anyway. Catarina would be calling her to finish and get ready for bed in a minute. Well sod that. I wouldn't allow her the satisfaction. I would pre-empt it. I said, my voice strangled, 'Well it's nearly your bedtime, sweetie.'

She looked at me again; said in a tiny voice. 'Yes, I suppose so.'

I blurted out, 'I do love you, Bella. And I do so miss you. And I'm so sorry things have come to this. I'm just so bloody useless as a parent. I'm sorry!'

Bella said, far more in control and far more mature than me, 'Yes, and I love you too, Daddy. And I miss you. Don't worry. It's not your fault. It'll soon be December. I'll see you then, when you come over.'

I couldn't go on. I could only manage a croaking, 'Yes, that'll be nice. Okay then; night night.'

She gave me her knockout smile. ''Night night, Daddy.'

The next morning, now that I knew how long the walk to work took, I allowed myself just forty minutes. It was promising another nice day; the sky was already an unbroken azure and the temperature already in the mid-twenties, it felt like. It would be hot by midday.

She was there again, in Brewery Street. The busker. Occupying the same place, proprietorially, as if it was her undisputed pitch. Wearing the same scruffy clothes, even the hat. Wasn't she hot in it? And she was playing the same damn tune again. But she was certainly a good musician. I found a couple of pound coins and dropped them into her case (which looked a little fuller today, but then it was twenty minutes later than yesterday) then stood, looking down at her, until she'd finished.

'Very nice. But is it the only piece you know?'

She scowled. 'No, of course it isn't!' I couldn't quite place her accent; it wasn't English. I'm usually pretty good at accents and dialects: Irish (obviously, since I come from the Gaeltacht of County Sligo), Scots, Welsh and the British and some of the foreign variants of English.

'Okay, sorry. But you were playing it yesterday when I came past.'

'Yes, well it's the sort of stuff the punters like. I get more bread playing this than Mozart, or whatever.'

'Oh, you play classical too?'

She sighed. 'Yes! But there's not a lot of call for it, busking on the streets of London. I doubt whether the typical British Joe would be very familiar with that side of my repertoire.'

I grinned, amused by her feistiness. And the penny had dropped now; she was American of course, from in or around New York, for a guess. North-eastern seaboard, anyway. But well-educated; middle-class. That was what had thrown me.

'Well, you never know. You don't necessarily have to know the name or provenance of a piece to know whether you like it or not.'

The busker snorted. 'You've got to be kidding me! I've tried a bit of culture, believe me, but it doesn't translate into coins, let alone notes, dropped into my case.'

'Well, I said,' determined not to be beaten in this little game of banter, 'It seems a shame, if you can play the good stuff, not to do it.'

'Yeah, I'm sure you're right,' she said, and there was an edge of bitterness in her voice now, 'but the cookie doesn't always crumble the way you'd like it to.'

Of course I didn't know how to answer that. So I simply muttered, 'Mm; well I've got to get to work. Nice to talk to you.'

'Yeah, and you have a nice day too.' She didn't bother to hide her sarcasm. She picked up her flute, placed the mouthpiece below her lower lip, arranged her fingers and launched into another transcription of some pop song or other. I left her to it.

Chapter 14

The busker was also there on Wednesday, playing the same damn thing again. I'd been thinking about her, vaguely, the previous day. There was something slightly familiar about her. Not so much in terms of her scruffy appearance but . . . something. Perhaps her voice. I'd been racking my brains for a while on Tuesday night, briefly, without being able to dredge anything from memory, before giving up. It didn't matter, anyway.

She must have been glancing to her left and noticed my approach, because she suddenly stopped dead in her tracks, seemed to ponder for a few seconds, and then began again. My own steps were arrested too. I recognized the opening bars instantly: Fauré's *Pavane.* Wonderful! That gorgeous, stately, elegiac melody. Obviously, she was playing a transcription for solo flute; doing all the parts herself. Never mind; the lack of strings didn't detract at all from the lovely crystal-clear, liquid sound she was making. I resumed walking, slowly, towards her, and when I drew close stopped again. She turned her eyes back to mine and now there was a light in them that wasn't there before. She seemed to be transported too.

I knew how long the piece was from hearing it so often in the past, so I waited for her to play right through it. Being a few minutes late for work wouldn't really matter. Besides, I'd started early on Monday; I was owed. The slightly melancholic, haunting phrases washed over me as I stood there on the pavement of Brewery Street, serenaded by this ragamuffin flautist abandoned to her music. Whoever she was, she really was very good. She reached the end and held the final fragile note perfectly. I was already reaching into my pocket for my wallet. This was definitely worth a fiver. I bent to place it in her case rather than toss it in. It seemed more respectful. 'Bravo! That was beautiful!'

The plaudit sounded inadequate. I searched for a better superlative. 'Bravissimo, even!'

She grinned. 'Thanks! And thanks for that money. I don't get many of the green paper sort.'

'No problem,' I said. 'It was worth it. And congratulations on the diversification.'

She scowled at that, not appreciating the joke. 'Yeah, well I said I could do serious stuff too!'

I laughed. 'Peace! You really are very good, you know.'

The smile left her face. 'Mm; I don't know about that. I've always been criticized for lack of expressiveness.'

'Well to musical ignoramuses like me it sounded pretty good, believe me.'

The clumsy, rather dubious flattery seemed to go over her head. She snorted rather bitterly. 'Okay; thanks again. But to people whose opinions matter I don't come up to scratch, for sure. Otherwise I'd be playing in an orchestra somewhere, not sitting here with an aching ass busking in the street.'

I didn't know how to answer that. I said, 'Well, anyway, you played one of my all-time favourite flute pieces. Thank you!'

She brightened again. 'Yeah, well it's very popular in the flute repertoire. I remember it being one of my test pieces at music school. You know it then?'

'Yes, Fauré's *Pavane*. I heard it just recently, actually. At a concert at the Wigmore Hall. A friend of mine plays in the Philharmonic. He's also a flautist, funnily enough.'

'Oh really?' she said, a slight edge of bitterness in her voice.

I quickly changed the subject. It seemed to be a little touchy. 'I sometimes tend to confuse Fauré's thing with that other pavane: the Ravel one. You know; I imagine the tune of one in my head and it tends to drown out the other.'

'Ah, "Pavane for a Dead Princess"? Yes, they're very similar melodies. Not many notes different. And the same rhythm, pretty much. Well, they would be, obviously, both being pavanes.'

'Yes, another gorgeous tune. Except the Ravel's a bit more poignant. Because of its title I suppose.'

'Yes, I suppose so,' my scruffy companion agreed, suddenly looking at me intently, as if puzzling over something, from behind her schoolmarmish glasses.

I could have stayed there all morning talking to her about our shared passion but I had work to do, an article that needed a fair amount of research to write by the end of the day. So I wished her a faintly embarrassed nice day and left her. As she launched into another transcription of a pop song.

That evening after dinner (not a ready-meal: a healthy risotto with seafood, mushrooms and flaked almonds in a cook-in sauce, concocted by my own fair hand, followed by a Conference pear) I decided to give Benny and Esther a ring. It would more than likely be Esther, as she usually answered the phone. And I really did enjoy talking to her. Well, I liked them both enormously; they were both very good friends. But I seemed to have an extra special rapport with Esther, for some reason. I think I subconsciously regarded her as a mother-substitute; the mother I never had. Well, that and confidante. After all, my own poor old mammy back in Ireland, dead these twelve years now, rest her sad, embittered soul, hadn't been much of one. I could never have told my troubles to her. And our Julie certainly couldn't have told hers, poor kid. Not that I blamed Mammy, really. She had had a very hard life, trying to bring us all up after Da walked out on us, swapping poor old Mammy for a younger model. Although we had been well rid of the drunken, violent, abusive brute, really.

The pretext for ringing my friends was to say how much I'd enjoyed the concert (although I thought Benny looked rather exhausted at the end of it; I wondered if he was coming down with something) but I also wanted to thank Esther for her kindness and understanding, listening to my woes. Although I was feeling slightly less sorry for myself now, after that conversation with the busker that morning.

After all, apart from the frustration of having little physical contact with my daughter now, I had little to complain about really. Not compared with the busker-lady. I was less well off in asset terms now, but I still had my rewarding job, doing what I really loved. I had done pretty well, although I say it myself, to rise from humble disadvantaged beginnings to a middle-ranking (but senior in terms of length employment) writer on a quality broadsheet paper. I might not be the world's greatest journalist, but the minor literary masterpieces I produced weekly were generally well received (apart from the occasional troll) in the comments threads and the editor was more than happy with my work. Well, he must be, I imagined, as he seemed keen to hang onto me. When the *Independent* threatened to poach me last year he was quick to offer me a significant salary rise, although I would probably have stayed anyway, regardless of the money.

But, I reflected as I washed up my solitary plate and mug and the saucepans after eating, that flautist woman, who seemed very talented in spite of her apparent low self-esteem, must surely be terribly unfulfilled. And, I suspected, unhappy. What on earth was she doing busking on the streets, anyway? Surely she could get a proper job, with her talent? It seemed such a waste. And what was she doing over here, apparently drifting? Although she didn't sound like a stupid or inadequate or deprived person, who couldn't earn a living, by any means. It was very strange.

Sure enough, it was Esther who picked up the phone. Her opening words were predictably warm. 'Hello, Paddy. How are you then?'

'I'm fine, thanks, Esther. You and Benny?'

There was a brief but distinct pause before she answered. 'Yes, we're both all right. Benny's looking a little tired at the moment. I keep trying to persuade him to retire, but you know what he's like. Just can't give up his music!'

I laughed sympathetically. 'Yes, I know. He's a typical performer. It's the same with actors, isn't it? They just go on and on, working until they drop. They don't seem to understand the concept of retirement at all.'

'Yes, you're right. He's at it now; in the dining room, playing some Vivaldi, by the sound of things. Says he's got to practise. Practise indeed! At his age! If practice makes perfect, he must have attained perfection long ago!'

'Mm, I should imagine so. I don't really know, of course, not being a musician myself, but I would have thought that once you achieve a certain standard of excellence, you don't need to be playing every single waking hour to maintain it. I know it's not quite the same thing, but I don't need to be constantly writing to keep my modest talents up to scratch.'

Esther laughed too. 'Right, that's what I used to find. But perhaps it *is* different for people with a physical skill. Which is what it is, of course, apart from the expressive and emotional aspect, when you come down to it. Like being a sportsman. Sorry, we're supposed to say "sportsperson" nowadays, aren't we?'

'Yes, got to be politically correct, Esther! Anyway, I was just ringing to say thanks for the concert the other evening. I loved it. Nice varied programme, wasn't it? Funnily enough, I heard that Fauré piece again this morning, being played by a busker in the street.'

'Really? Odd how things sometimes come in twos, isn't it? Yes, it was a nice concert. There were several of Benny's favourites in it, like the Bach.'

'I also wanted to say thanks for listening to my troubles, Esther. I was feeling a bit low, I'm afraid; although the concert did cheer me up a bit.'

'Oh, that's all right. Any time. Think nothing of it. I can see that it must be pretty awful for you, with your daughter. I couldn't imagine being separated from our two kids when they were little. Quite honestly, and I know it's nothing to do with me, but I think your ex wife's being most unreasonable about access. Why on earth she can't send the child over to see you two or three times a year too, so you share the cost of air fares, I really don't know. Then you'd see her a bit more often, at any rate.'

'Yes, well she's a very litigious woman. We had some angry words before the divorce when she said she'd be returning to Italy. That's fair enough of course, thinking about it now; she's a free agent, but at the time all I was thinking was that it would make access to Bella difficult. So now she thinks that if she sent Bella to see me, I wouldn't give her back.'

'Well that's just nonsense! Of course you would. I know you hear of tug-of-love cases, but for Heaven's sake. Oh dear, Paddy, poor you!'

'Thanks for your understanding Esther.' I was touched by her empathy. Dear Esther; she was so understanding and supportive. I was tempted to pour out my heart again and tell her about the previous Monday's Skype to Bella; about my fears of gradually losing her as she settled into her new life without me in the daily picture. And of what I suspected was a new man in Catarina's life to whom she might transfer her affection. But I resisted it. She'd had quite enough of my self-pity, although she would have patiently listened again. I changed the subject. 'So how's your granddaughter doing? Did you tell me she was having a rather difficult pregnancy?'

'Yes, she is, poor love. I'm not sure what the problem is; something about her perhaps not being able to carry to full term. She might have to be induced before then, when they're confident the baby will be sufficiently viable.'

'Ah, well I hope she goes on all right. It seems a long time now since I was the proud father of a baby.'

'Come now,' Esther teased, it's only been, what, ten or eleven years, hasn't it? Our two are both in their forties now. We've got five grandchildren: Daisy's brother and sister and our son Sam's two boys as well. When they all start reproducing, goodness knows how many great-grandchildren we'll finish up with!'

I laughed. 'Yes, there'll be quite a tribe, quite a dynasty of the Walters before you know where you are, so there will.'

Esther giggled too. 'Well, tribe yes, but I don't know about dynasty.

None of our family has been really remarkable in any field. We're just a very average lot really. Yes, I know Sam has done well at the estate agents, but I don't know how much further up the tree he'll climb. He doesn't seem terribly ambitious. He says he's quite happy to be an employee; doesn't particularly want to become a partner in the firm. And Ruth seems content with her basic teacher status. I don't see her becoming a Head or anything. And the grandchildren are still too young to have made their mark too.'

'None of them want to emulate their granddad and be a musician then?'

'No! Certainly not in serious music anyway. I gather that Sam's Harry has vague aspirations to become a rock star, but he's only fourteen and you know what they're like at that age.'

'Yes, didn't we all!'

'Well I didn't, Paddy, speak for yourself!' Esther laughed, then continued, 'And is your daughter still keen on her piano playing now she's living in Italy, do you know?'

I sighed, more heavily than I'd really intended, but it slipped out, unchecked. The conversation had returned to Bella after all. 'I really don't know whether she'll persist with it now. She was telling me on the computer on Monday that Catarina doesn't pressurize her to practise – coming back to what we were saying about Benny practising – like I used to. Well, I hope it was encouragement, not coercing her to do it. But she seems to be less keen to do it now that I'm not in her life.'

'Oh, that's a pity. Was she showing some promise, do you know?'

'Well, yes, I think so, not that I'm a great judge of these things. But her music teacher used to say that she was becoming pretty adept. I would certainly have continued encouraging her, provided she wanted it, anyway. But now that's gone: my influence, Esther. It really bugs me, that does.'

'Mm; poor old Paddy. I can see your problem! Do you feel she's slipping out of your orbit? Or rather, her orbit of you, I mean.'

'Yes, that's exactly it! I don't mean that I want to be controlling; jus having some influence on her in her formative years, without being a bully or overly pushy. That's not unreasonable, is it?'

'No, of course it isn't. I mean, obviously, she would still have become her own person as she grew up if you hadn't had this enforced estrangement now, but part of a parent's responsibility is to encourage their child in any passion they might have, isn't it?'

'Yes, I suppose it is,' I agreed ruefully. But doing that with Bella isn't so easy now.'

'Oh, don't be too despondent, Paddy. You're maintaining contact as much as you can with your weekly chats, aren't you? It's not as if you're disappearing from her life completely, as so often happens with fathers after divorce. I'm sure you are still quite an influence, and I'm sure she wants you to be. I expect she likes to please you and values your opinion of her. It sounds as though you two have a pretty close relationship; am I right?'

'Yes, we have. I've always thought so, anyway. I've always thought that I was closer to her than her mother is, quite honestly. That's why it grates so much that Catarina has custody of her and all I have is infrequent access because she's now so far away. It doesn't seem fair.'

'Well,' Esther said gently, 'That's just how it has to be, sadly, when parents of a child split up. One or the other has to have legal custody, and I suppose your ex wife feels just as strongly that she's the closer parent, and argued it in court, and the judge had to decide between you and awarded custody to her by default. I don't know much about law, but I think mothers are usually adjudged to be the more appropriate custodian on balance where there's dispute and both parents are seeking maintenance. Is that what happened?'

I scowled, remembering the miserable family court proceedings; my expensive but useless barrister trying to character-assassinate Catarina and persuade the judge that I, with my good income, and my assurances under cross-examination that my relationship with my daughter was close and loving, would be the better guardian. Except for the unavoidable fact that, as her ladyship the judge pointed out in her lengthy judgment, I couldn't, practically speaking, be simultaneously a successful newspaper journalist and a stay-at-home parent adequately caring for a child.

'Yes,' I said crossly, 'that's just what happened.'

'Mm, I do sympathise. But I suppose those of us who are lucky to be blessed with good, enduring marriages just can't really know the trauma and heartache of divorce, especially when there's a squabble over children.'

'No, perhaps not.' I said, resignedly, 'Well anyway, thanks for your understanding. I'm sorry to load you with my troubles again. I didn't mean to do it. I was really just phoning to thank you for your sympathetic ear last time.'

'Oh, fiddlesticks,' Esther reassured. 'That's no problem at all. I'm here for you whenever you need a friend to unburden to. You know that.'

We chatted some more, about generalities, and Esther asked if I wanted to talk to Benny. I said yes, as long as he didn't mind being interrupted in his practice. Esther snorted and said well he just wouldn't *have* to mind, and took the phone through to him. So we had a nice little conversation too. He still sounded a little tired, I thought, but genuinely pleased to speak to me, as if I was some errant neglectful son ringing up from the other side of the world. Here's a correction to what I said before: *both* of my elderly friends are like surrogate parents really. Finally I wound up the conversation, urging Benny to take it easy. He told me not to fuss, saying he thought he might be coming down with a bug or something, which would be a nuisance as he hated missing performances; always felt he was letting the others down when he did. I told him to take care all the same and wished him goodnight.

I flicked through the television listing magazine, searching for something interesting or entertaining to watch, but there was nothing that appealed. So I put a CD on the music system instead, a little Tchaikovsky: the *Pathétique* symphony. It was another of my all-time favourites, especially the tripping, trilling, dancing second movement that so contrasted with the pathos and ultimate despair of the rest of it. It evoked youthful love perfectly. Old Peter Ilych certainly knew how to craft a ravishing melody and trowel on the emotiveness and romanticism, I've always thought.

Relaxing on the sofa with the music washing over me, gazing at the faux-woodstove (actually gas-fired) in the fireplace opening, my thoughts returned to the conversation about Bella; my frustration that I was no longer a mentor in her life. Well at least she had some sort of positive parental influence, even if mine, hampered now by distance, was in danger of evaporating away if I wasn't careful. She had a damn sight more encouragement than her old man had had as a kid.

Thinking that, my memory skipped back across the years, forty or more of them, to the humble little terraced house in Connelly Street, Sligo that was the Brennan family home. I remembered how cramped it was: all my sisters squeezed into one bedroom and we boys in the other; how even more impossibly claustrophobic it was when we all packed into the living room, although we didn't do so all that very often. I preferred to be upstairs in the boys' bedroom with my borrowed books from the library (I never owned any of my own; there wasn't the money to buy them with or the inclination –or money again – on my parent's part to gift me any) reading avidly, lost in the wonder of literature and words until my younger brothers were sent up to bed, destroying my solitude.

No, there had certainly been no encouragement from *my* parents when I was a boy. Well, Da was never there, always in the pub, drinking away his scant wages, leaving precious little for Mammy to buy food to feed us all. We regarded it as normal at the time – we certainly weren't the only poor family in the street, or the only one with a drunkard husband and father, for that matter. My school friend Connor, had an alcoholic dad for one, although I can't remember whether he said he was a wife beater too, like ours. But if he was, perhaps my friend was too ashamed to admit it.

And as for Mammy, well, I think she was too broken down and

embittered by the constant struggle to feed us, and by Da's brutality, to have any such fine emotion left over to expend encouraging any of us in our aspirations or dreams. Let alone any affection, for that matter. It had been beaten out of her. And it didn't get very much easier for her when Da left for his young floozy, because then she had to find such work as she could, although I think she was relieved when he went. At least there'd be no more violence – or any more new mouths to feed. But it must still have been a struggle for her to put bread on the table.

Although she might have welcomed our earning power and contributions to the family finances, she was relieved too, I think, when we began to leave school and leave home: first Maeve who as soon as she could left for England, then my other big sister, the second-born, Julie, who followed her over the water, and then me, to a job as office boy-cum-cub reporter with the *Sligo Champion* local newspaper. Mammy did have the benefit of a slice of my wages for three years or so, but then I too was tempted to seek my fortune in England.

But no, there was certainly no encouragement for me or any of my siblings from doting, involved parents, I reflected sadly, as the melancholy fourth movement of Tchaikovsky's sixth symphony came to its anguished close.

Chapter 15

The following Monday morning the weather had broken, sunshine displaced by a steady drizzle. According to the forecasters it would only get worse. A deep depression from the south-west was bringing a huge blanket of grey cloud to London, apparently, and rain looked to be set in for the day. It was my first taste of less-than-perfect weather for walking to work and for a moment my good intentions wavered. I nearly mentally said Sod it and stayed abed for another twenty minutes. I could always hop on the bus.

But self-discipline won out and I got up, showered, breakfasted, donned my waterproof, pulled the hood over my head, hoisted my rucksack and set off. And once I was walking I felt a little smug and superior, actually, striding in hearty manly fashion through the light rain as the other whey-faced commuters, most of them probably disgustingly unhealthy, passed in cars or peered vacantly through the steamy windows of red London buses.

As I walked along Brewery Street the busker was there again, surprisingly, sitting on the already wet pavement on some sort of rubber mat, like those you used to have beside a bath. She was wearing a bright orange cagoule that ended mid thigh and the dirty blue jeans which emerged from it were already mottled dark with wetness. She hadn't pulled the hood up and the black hair beneath her multicoloured hat looked damp and even lanker than usual. I wondered whether the light rain would be damaging her flute, but it seemed to be working all right, judging by the sound it was making: yet another transcribed pop song or other. *Rather you than me*, I thought. Surely she didn't sit out there trying to earn a pittance from her playing in all weathers?

She didn't notice my approach and so didn't this time switch to another piece for my benefit. As I drew level I found a couple of pound coins again and dropped them into her case. There weren't many in it: perhaps three or four pounds, a similar amount of silver and even a few coppers. Some people were disgracefully parsimonious, I thought. I didn't stop to chat. Well, there was nothing to talk about really. She gave me her usual curt nod of thanks for the money without interrupting her playing and I carried on to work.

Mondays are always light days on the paper, because it's a Sunday rather than a daily. It's mostly spent in editorial meetings which in my case, because I'm a features writer as opposed to a news hack, mean brainstorming ideas for articles or pieces in response to current happenings either UK-based or in the wider world. Then there are hours sitting at my desk thinking and doodling on paper ideas, approaches, and angles for the pieces agreed with Ken Pascoe, our redoubtable editor.

And all right, hands up, I admit it, I did succumb to the temptation of a liquid lunch as the tempo of the day was slow. But it was the first one since my Damascus-road conversion to a healthy lifestyle. And I'd walked to work in spite of the inclement weather, so I didn't feel too guilty about it. I reckoned I'd earned it, in fact. Tony and Alastair were pleased to welcome me back into their company of course, as if I'd seen the error of my ways and was returning rueful and contrite to the fold. No, I told them, joshing, it wasn't a question of that; I was simply settling to a position of reasonable compromise. They grinned at me before exchanging smirking, o*h, yeah?* glances.

Most of us journos left work on time at five-thirty on Mondays as it was the least-pressured day, and I did too. Well, it was Bella night anyway; I couldn't be too late home. As I stepped out into the July evening the rain was still falling steadily. Head down, I walked back along Brewery Street. And nearly tripped over the legs of the busker. She was still there, looking soaked to the skin, still stubbornly playing her music. This time I stopped. She ceased playing and looked up at me, dejected and miserable.

'What are you doing, still here?' I asked, the question escaping automatically, 'haven't you got a home to go to?'

She ignored my crass question. 'I haven't made enough bread yet.'

I looked at the pavement. Her instrument case was missing. There were still only a few coins between her feet.

'Not had a good day then, by the look of things.'

She looked as though she might burst into tears. 'Well, it would have been okay if some thieving asshole hadn't run off with my takings. I'm trying to make up!'

I felt a surge of pity for her. She looked so forlorn. 'Oh dear. I'm sorry to hear that. How did that happen?' The question sounded inane as soon as I'd asked it.

She looked at me as if I were stupid. 'Well, how do you think? This guy came along, about an hour ago, just as I was about to call it a day, bent down, grabbed my case and ran off. I suppose he needed the dough for his habit. By the time I'd gotten to my feet to chase after him, he was way out in front. I shouted after him but there were very few people around, and the one or two who were just stood there looking. No one tried to intervene or anything. Nice public-spirited people you have here in England!'

I didn't begin to explain that I wasn't English; it didn't seem the right moment. But I knew what she meant. 'How much have you lost?'

'Oh, I don't know. I hadn't counted it. It'll take a while to make it back though. And I've lost my case now, too!'

I looked down at her for a moment. She looked beaten, sitting there soaking wet. I reached for my wallet and took out a twenty pound note; offered it. 'Will this cover it?'

She eyed it greedily, trying to mask her want, her need. And probably her instinct to grab. 'Well, yeah. But hell, no; I couldn't take all that from you. I haven't earned it.'

'Why not? Come on, it doesn't matter about that. Take it, please.'

She relented; smiled gratefully. 'Okay, thanks. That's restored my faith in humanity a bit.'

'You're welcome.'

And then my mouth ran away with me a little. She looked so wet and pale-faced; looked half-starved. There was a café at the end of Brewery Street. 'Er, look, Can I buy you a cup of tea and something to eat; save you breaking into that money?'

The busker stared at me, a medley of expressions flitting across her face, as if trying to fight the temptation of the offer. 'Hey, is this a pick up, or something?'

I grinned. 'No . . . it really isn't! But you look as though you need a bit of a warm up, if you've been out here all day.'

She smiled again, wanly. 'Okay then. Thanks. It's very kind of you.' She scrambled to her feet; picked up the sodden mat she'd been sitting on and rolled it into a cylinder. Pondered uncertainly for a moment and then lifted her drenched cagoule, stuffed her flute down the waistband of her now-soaked jeans and lowered the waterproof again. Then bent to pick up the handful of coins, to stuff them into a pocket.

I did a quick mental calculation. There wouldn't be time to walk home now and be in time for the call to Bella. But I could take the bus, and as long as we didn't spend too long in the café . . . Well, as long as *I* didn't. I could leave her there to spend as long as she wanted. We walked to the café. Chandras' Café, the flamboyant, cursive lettering of its sign announced with casual disregard for punctuation rules. It looked as though it might be one of those that stayed open all hours. There was just one other customer in the small room with its plastic tablecloth-covered tables and painted bentwood chairs of many hues, when we entered. An old grizzle-bearded man wearing a scruffy raincoat sat in the middle of the room in splendid isolation, his hands wrapped around a large white mug of tea. We took seats. My wet companion pulled her flute out of her jeans and separated it into its component parts, shaking each in an attempt to dry it. I still thought being wet like that couldn't be doing it any good.

We took seats, across a small table from each other. She removed her hat and placed it between us, like a sodden woolen tea cosy. I took her in properly for the first time: long jet-black hair in wet rat's tails matched by eyes behind her glasses that were almost as Stygian. Narrow, slightly aquiline nose above a wide mouth; slightly buck teeth showing when she did her sad smile. Certainly not a pretty face but, well, characterful.

'This is my local eatery,' she said, and there was more than a hint of sarcasm in her voice. 'I bring all my friends here.'

'Oh, right,' I said, uncertain how to respond to that. 'What can I get you to drink?' She glanced at the old man then looked at me, managing a third faint smile. 'I'd love a nice big mug of your hot sweet English tea.'

'Done. And to eat?'

There was a rather dog-eared, plastic-laminated menu on the table but she ignored it. 'I could kill a toasted cheese and tomato sandwich, please. If that's okay.'

I went to the counter, which had the gastronomic delights on offer reiterated in multicoloured chalk on a blackboard above it, and placed the order, including a tea for myself. The plump Asian lady proprietor produced the mugs of tea, one large, one small, from her noisy urn immediately, and I left her to prepare the sandwich. Back at our table the busker grabbed the larger tea, wrapping her hands around it, grateful for its warmth. 'Thank you!'

She raised it to her lips, still two-handed, and sipped.

I searched for something to say. 'So do you do this, play in the street I mean, all the time?'

'Yeah; afraid so. Otherwise I'd starve.'

'In all weathers; even in winter?'

'Yup. Well, I haven't done a complete winter yet.' She smiled, but with her mouth only. There was a bitter edge, no happiness in it. 'But I'm just filling in time until my prince comes along, you understand.'

'Oh.' I joked, weakly, not really knowing how to reply to that either 'You're a damsel in distress, are you?'

That sad smile yet again. More like a grimace, really. 'I suppose you could say that. Things have certainly been better, that's for sure.'

She didn't try to hide her self-pity. But then for all I knew, she perhaps had good reason for it.

It was the inquisitive journalist's instinct operating I suppose, but I couldn't help asking, 'So what's a smart talented American lady like you doing over here busking on the streets of London?' Then I remembered my manners. 'Er, if you don't mind my asking?'

We were interrupted by the Indian subcontinental lady bringing the sandwich. Well, I'd asked her to do two, double-deckered in a pile on a single plate. She smiled at my companion. 'Hello dear. How are you doing today?'

'Well, it's not been the best day of my life, Chandra, to tell the truth; I had my takings stolen'.

Chandra looked suitably shocked. 'Oh, that's terrible. I'm so sorry! I don't know what the world's coming to, I really don't, when even people like you get stolen from.'

People like you? What did she mean by that? I was intrigued and slightly amused by the irony: Asian immigrant condescends to apparently down-at-heel Westerner. Sighing and tutting for the decadent world, Chandra placed the plate in the centre of the table and returned to her station behind the counter. I pushed the plate towards the smart talented American lady, who didn't question the quantity and fell on them hungrily. I watched her eat. She looked famished. If she wanted to tell me her human interest story, fine; if not, that was up to her of course. She finished and took a long pull at her mug of tea.

'You look as though you were ready for that.'

'Yeah, I was. Thanks so much.' An awkward hesitation. 'I haven't eaten all day. To be honest, I wasn't sure how long I'd have to sit out in that fucking rain making enough for a drink and something to eat, after that bastard ran off with my takings.'

'Yes, that was rotten. So why do you do it; a talented musician like you?'

'Do what?'

'Busk.'

Once again there was the smile, more relaxed now. And somehow vaguely familiar. 'Oh, you don't want to ask. It's a long, sorry story.'

But saying that was like a red flag to the proverbial bovine. It simply piqued my interest further. 'But you surely don't earn enough doing that to keep a roof over your head in London, do you?'

The smile vanished. 'No, I don't,' she said tartly.

A sudden realization hit me. 'Er . . . excuse my asking, but are you saying you're homeless?'

She stared at her mug, nodding, silent; probably embarrassed. It was empty. I hadn't touched mine. I pushed it across to her. 'Do you want this? I haven't drunk from it.'

The busker looked up, her eyes suddenly glistening slightly. 'Thanks. You really are very kind.'

'It's nothing. So are you saying you sleep outside, in all weathers? And you did through last winter?' I'd forgotten exactly what she'd said.

'Well just the last bit of it.'

'Jesus!'

I stared at her. I'd never really spoken to a homeless person before. Well, not like this, eyeball-to-eyeball, anyway. 'Where are your possessions – sleeping bag and so on – then?'

'I've got them stashed away in a safe place; in Chandra's store room, actually, where no thieving bastard can run off with them. It saves having to cart them all around in this weather. Not that I've got many, now. They've mostly been sold. I'm left with just a change of jeans, a couple of tops and some underwear, which get washed occasionally when I make enough money to afford a trip to the launderette.'

'Poor you,' I said. The words tumbled out automatically. 'It sounds a pretty miserable existence.'

She smile-grimaced again. 'It's not a lot of fun, for sure.'

'And you really have no alternative to this?' My question was impertinent of course, but as I say, it was the journalist talking. I could begin to see glimmerings of an article here about homelessness in the richest city in the world in the twenty-first century. Ken would almost certainly go for it.

'Well, there's one, I suppose. A reverse-charge phone call to New York, to my father, and a grovelling apology for being so pig-headed and wrong and wanting to do my own thing and going against his wishes. And followed by throwing myself on my parents' mercy and asking them to take me back.' She looked utterly desolate.

'You sound as though that isn't really an option.'

'It isn't. It would just be so humiliating. There'd be the I-told-you-so-looks, as if I'm a stupid reckless child finally seeing the error of my ways. The last time I spoke with my mom it ended with her slamming the phone down on me and the last time I spoke with my dad he told me I couldn't expect to go running home to him if things didn't work out right. I really am like the prodigal daughter as far as they're concerned now, except that there isn't any forgiveness on their part.'

'I'm so sorry,' I murmured. There really was the smell of a good story here now. But it wasn't just that. The poor girl had been through, well, eventful times, to put it mildly, by the sound of things and now, for some reason, she was really down on her luck. I did feel genuinely sorry for her too.

'Thanks,' she said, woefully. 'Yeah, life certainly is pretty shitty at the moment.'

'So what are you going to do then,' I wondered, still much too nosey and rather impertinent, really, 'stay here in Britain living on the streets? It's not much of an existence.'

'No!' Her eyes blazed briefly. 'But I'm damned if I'm going to crawl back to my parents. I'm trying to save up the cost of an air fare, so I can at least crawl back to the States on my own terms, having failed so miserably over here. It'll probably take me years to do it at this rate, but I'll do it!'

'Well good for you. You go for it.'

I suppressed a smile; thought, *That's more like it. You certainly have a feisty, independent streak. I like it. It sounds as though you have a mountain to climb though.*

My left eye caught sight of the clock on the wall of the rainbow café. Six twenty-two, it informed the now-nearly empty room. The old man had risen, screeching his chair against the laminate floor to the frowning disapproval of the watching Chandra behind the counter, and ambled slowly out, leaving just us two. Time had flown sitting here listening to this fascinating, mysterious woman. I really must be making tracks, or I'd miss Bella.

'Er, well I do hope things work out for you in the future. You sound as though you deserve some good luck.' The words sounded hopelessly inadequate but I didn't know what else to say. It was like trying to find appropriate and kind words for the bereaved.

'Thanks,' she said dully. The animation in her pale face had died as quickly as it had flared. 'So do I.'

I rose. 'Well, nice to talk to you but I really must go. Got a phone call to make to my daughter.'

'Okay.' She stared at the second empty mug. 'Well, thanks for the food and drink. I really appreciate it.'

'No problem.' I nearly found myself saying, ridiculously, 'Any time.'

'Right then,' I muttered, feeling absurdly guilty that at least I had a nice comfortable flat to return to, in spite of my trials on the Bella front. 'So I expect I'll see you tomorrow.'

'Yeah, I suppose so.'

I got up. Paused, looking down at her. She looked so forlorn. And then I said it. The words just came out, unbidden; crazy, impulsive words.

'Er, look. I hate to leave you here like this. You're still wet through. Would you like to come home with me and get dry? You could give me a private recital; earn that twenty pounds!' The weak joke sounded almost sleazy. I instantly regretted it.

She looked up at me sharply. *'What?'*

'Well, I just thought . . .'

'Now that really does sound like a pick up! Get out of here!'

'No, no, really, it isn't! I didn't mean it to sound like that. I'm completely respectable, honestly. A hard-working journalist and married man. I'm no rapist or anything . . .'

I bit my tongue, cursing myself for my stupid careless Irish tongue. It was digging me a deeper and deeper hole.

'Well it sure sounds a bit suspicious to me!' She searched my face, as if my true intentions could be found displayed transparently there if she looked hard enough.

'I'm sorry. So sorry. I really didn't mean to alarm you. My intentions really are entirely honourable, so they are. Believe me.'

Her determination to resist seemed to falter a fraction. 'Well . . .'

'Please?'

'Well okay then. But no funny business. Or I'll scream your place down and bring the neighbours running.'

She got up, gathering the pieces of her flute uncertainly, not quite knowing what to do with them now that they'd lost their box, it seemed.

'Let me put them in my bag,' I offered, 'Stop them getting any wetter.'

'Okay,' she said, 'thanks.'

I put them in my small rucksack (everyone in London with a cool persona to cultivate who walks or cycles to work has rucksacks), keeping the pieces separated so that they didn't knock against each other. She called 'Bye, Chandra, see you later' to our café-keeper and we left, turning into Carver Street towards the next bus stop on my route home. It was a main east-west transport artery and we didn't have long to wait. We spoke little, sitting close together rubbing shoulders (in a really rather pleasant intimacy, I found, in spite of her appearance) on the Routemaster bus as it trundled sedately westwards. There were many questions I was impatient to ask, if she would open up to me.

It seemed impolite not to introduce myself formally though, so I did.

'I'm Paddy, by the way. Patrick. Patrick Brennan, from County Sligo in the Emerald Isle. At your service.'

She chuckled beside me.

'What?'

'I love the formality. It's cute. Very British . . . oh, no, sorry; you aren't British, are you? European then. And that's a bit of an obvious Irish stereotype, your name isn't it?'

I groaned theatrically. 'Yeah, don't remind me! But we don't choose our own names, do we?'

'No, we don't, unfortunately. And I'm Leah. Leah Weisman, with an equally stereotypical Jewish name, from Connecticut, US of A.'

Fifteen minutes later I was fitting my key into the lock of my dark blue, less-than-immaculate front door in Coronation Street, Canning Town, Leah Weisman waiting patiently behind me.

Chapter 16

The flat felt chilly and not particularly welcoming as I opened the right-hand inner door into the gloomy hall; what was left of it. The probably once-elegant staircase had disappeared behind a bland plasterboard partition demarcating my ground-floor flat from the first-floor one above. It was finished with beige-painted woodchip wallpaper, circa 1980s, and left a dark, claustrophobic passage that turned a dogleg at the end, the symmetry of the house having been ruined by the brutal carving up into flats, presumably done back then. It and the rest of the hall really ought to be painted a nice light white sometime; that would be much better.

I led the way along the passage and into my sitting room with its high Victorian bay window and ornate fireplace. Well, the grate was replaced by my pretend-woodstove but the surround was still present. Unaffected by the house's rapacious alteration, at least this room had mainly retained its original spaciousness and charm, as had the master bedroom, which was the other front room. Ms Weisman followed me cautiously in. She probably didn't entirely trust me and I didn't really blame her for that.

I glanced at the time display on the stereo. 6.57. We'd made it back just in time. She glanced around the untidy room. I felt an irrational prick of embarrassment. Well, I hadn't really been expecting a female visitor.

'Shall I turn the fire on for you?' I offered.

She nodded. 'That would be nice. Thanks.'

I dropped my rucksack gently onto the sofa, mindful of what it contained; turned the knob of the fire. With a soft pop it flared into life 'If you'll excuse me, I must go on the computer to my daughter. We have a regular Skype session on Monday evenings. She lives in Italy now,' I added, as if that explained everything.

'Yes, fine. Please don't mind me.'

'If you'd like to make yourself a drink, the kitchen's through there, the door on the right.' I pointed back out of the room.

'Okay, thanks. Er . . .' she hesitated, as if weighing up whether it was wise to ask it. 'I'd quite like to get out of these wet jeans, if you have anything I could put on?'

I kept my expression firmly sober. A smile could have been misinterpreted. 'Yes, of course. I'll get you something.' I walked out of the room and across the passage into my bedroom; found a clean pair of my jeans. She was nearly as tall as me although decidedly slimmer (quite skinny, in fact), so allowing for her wider hips, they should be a reasonably good fit. I found a belt too. When I came back into the sitting room she'd taken her flute out of my rucksack and arranged the parts in a fan around the fire and was kneeling in front of it, warming her hands.

'Here you are; these should fit, I think.'

She looked up at me and smiled. 'Thanks. You're very kind, er, Patrick.'

'Right,' I said, picking up my laptop, 'I'll leave you to it for a while and go and Skype Bella. If you need the bathroom it's next to the kitchen.'

I took the computer into my bedroom and logged on. I was slightly late now and she was already online waiting for me. We chatted about her day at school (starting to learn calculus in maths, apparently, and liking it) and her week since last we'd spoken. There was no mention of her mammy's boyfriend, if that was what he was, not that it was any business of mine of course. And I found I didn't really care now anyway, apart from the slight nagging worry that Bella might see him as a replacement for me. And she said that she'd been doing some piano practice, so that pleased me.

Although, I must admit my thoughts kept straying to the fascinating young woman with the mysterious past and possibly an intriguing story to tell across the hall in my sitting room. The conversation with Bella began to flag a little by twenty-five past because I was slightly distracted, so I wound it up, Bella didn't seem to mind though. *A dopo,* she said brightly, and her image faded from the screen.

When I returned to the sitting room my impromptu guest was wearing my jeans, sitting cross-legged in front of the fire, as if loading up with warmth to see her through the chill night sleeping outside to come. She'd taken her cagoule off and hung it dripping in the hall, I'd noticed on my way back, and was wearing just a t-shirt on top, which only served to accentuate her thinness. Her hair was dry now, although it still hung in rat's tails. It looked as though she'd borrowed a hand towel from the bathroom to also dry her flute, which was reassembled and lying on the sofa. She'd pulled a dining chair close to the fire and her jeans were draped across the back of it.

'Okay,' I said, 'I'm going to get myself some dinner now. Will I get you some too?'

She looked up quickly, her face a confusion of emotions. 'Oh no; I couldn't impose on you anymore. You've already bought me food . . .'

'Nonsense,' I quipped, 'that was just a starter.' I stopped quickly, teetering on the edge of a self-dug pit again. *Shut up, you eejit! You're making it sound like a dastardly seduction plot.*

I continued, trying to sound offhand. 'But really, I can't eat alone. That'd be seriously bad manners. Join me, please.'

Her internal battle resolved itself. 'Okay then. Thank you. I'll extend the musical performance to cover it.'

'Done! Right; I was going to do a risotto. How does that sound?'

'Wonderful!' She smiled. And with her eyes too, this time. Ms Weisman looked so much nicer when she smiled than when her forehead was creased in her usual unhappy frown.

'Right, I'll leave you to it again then. Go and find my chef's hat.'

She scrambled long-leggedly to her feet. My jeans looked considerably better on hers than mine, I found myself musing, before quickly banishing the thought. 'Oh no; Let me help, please.'

'It's no problem. I can manage, really.'

My new friend looked disappointed.

'Well, since you feel you owe me more music now, you could serenade me while I cook. No one's ever done that for me before. How would that be?'

Her smile became a wide grin. 'Okay, deal!' For the first time in our brief acquaintance she looked positively happy.

I walked to the kitchen, a mean little room at the rear of the house resulting from the partitioning to create a ground-floor bathroom. It was reasonably well appointed though. Sufficient for me, at any rate. She picked up her flute and followed me in. I looked out rice, oil, a courgette, a red pepper, plum tomatoes, onion, chicken breasts and, because I'm only a passable cook, a packet of Bolognese cook-in sauce.

'How about a Mediterranean chicken risotto then?' I asked, feeling unaccountably light-hearted myself.

Her grin was still in place. 'Sounds good! And how about for you, chef; a bit of twentieth-century: a little Martinu, perhaps?

'Yes, that sounds pretty good too. What is it?'

'Sonata Number One for Flute and Piano. But minus the piano part, obviously. The thing still works pretty well just leaving it out; you don't need to transcribe it for the flute. I know it all the way through. It was one of the pieces we did in music school. Do you know it?'

'Erm, no, but I'm looking forward to hearing it. I don't know that much of the flute repertoire, to be honest.'

My guest lolled against the work surface, rested her flute below her lower lip waggled her fingers a little and began playing. Her instrument was clearly none the worse for getting wet. Its lovely liquid sound filled the miniscule kitchen. The acoustics were probably terrible but it didn't matter. I busied myself preparing the meal, trying to remember to double all quantities, soon transported by her music. The second movement was slow, languorous; the third chirrupy, like birdsong. It was wonderful.

The meal didn't take long to prepare and my personal minstrel finished with a long, perfectly held, high-register note just as I gave the pan a final stir and assessed the risotto ready. 'Bravo!' I enthused, 'You played that beautifully.'

'Thank you,' she said, looking at me a little oddly, as if there were a question trembling on her lips not quite brave enough to ask itself.

I took cutlery from the drawer and two table mats and rushed into the sitting room to clear papers and other accumulated detritus from the small table (it was never used for dining normally; an undisciplined philistine, I usually ate off my lap on the sofa). Then I found two clean plates from a wall cupboard, mentally kicking myself for forgetting to previously warm them, and decanted equal amounts onto each. Well, she looked as though she needed fattening up. And she certainly didn't protest that I'd given her too much.

I carried the plates through to the table and we sat down, opposite each other. 'I'm sorry there's no wine,' I joked, stupidly. 'A nice crisp Italian white would have been nice, I know, but this entertaining was a little unexpected.' And then immediately mentally berated myself for my crassness.

She didn't seem offended though and tucked in as if still ravenous. I wondered if she actually ate regular meals at all, if she were trying to save up for an airline ticket from her meagre earnings from busking.

'So,' she asked politely, between mouthfuls, 'Is your daughter on vacation or something then?'

'No,' I replied, without thinking. 'She lives there now. In Italy,' I added, forgetting I'd already told her that.

Ms Weisman looked at me sharply, a forkful of food halted halfway to her mouth. 'Oh. And your wife?'

'. . . She does too.'

Her tone cooled several degrees. 'Working over there, or something, is she?'

'Erm . . .'

She laid her fork down. Frowned. The lines were back on her forehead. 'O-kay. And you're now going to tell me that you're separated and she doesn't understand you, right?'

'No!' I squirmed.

I hesitated. 'All right; I'm sorry. I'll come clean. I'm actually divorced. My wife – my ex-wife – went back to Italy a few months ago, when the decree absolute came through. And took our daughter with her. She was granted custody of her. I'm not happy about the situation, but that's the way it's turned out.'

'I see. So why did you tell me you were married? No, let me guess. It makes you sound more respectable. In fact, you used that very word, didn't you, "respectable", when you were trying to persuade me to come home with you. I'm getting a very bad feeling about this, all of a sudden.'

'Yes, I know. I'm sorry. Well, it seemed such an impertinent thing to suggest and I was just trying to persuade you to come in out of the rain for a while. That's all, really. I know how it must look.'

'Yes, well you did that. You persuaded me to go to the café with you. Although I would have gone there later anyway. But that wasn't enough. You inveigled me to come home with you too. Why?' She stared at me; repeated, 'Why?'

'Just because . . . I didn't like the thought of you going back out into the rain, with nowhere to shelter. I felt sorry for you. I'm a bit of an old softy when it comes to . . . things like that.'

'Mm.' The woman grunted, not sounding entirely convinced. 'And tell me; that thing about being a journalist. Was that made up, to make you sound respectable and trustworthy, too? Or am I being too cynical now?'

I rushed to reassure her. 'No! I mean I didn't make it up. I'm with the *Clarion*. A features writer. You'll have seen my name if you've read it.'

She snorted; laughed humourlessly. 'Yeah, right, like I can afford to buy a quality broadsheet every Sunday!'

'Oh, no, of course not. Sorry. But I do. Work there, I mean. I've been with them fourteen years now, for my sins.'

'Right. Okay then.' She picked up her fork and conveyed the delayed parcel of food to her mouth; munched. I relaxed tentatively, equilibrium restored until I put my foot in it again.

'So I presume your wife – your ex-wife – was Italian, then?'

'Yes, from Palermo. That was part of the problem, I think. She never really felt happy living in England. And I didn't want to relocate to Italy. Perhaps I was selfish. But I had a better job that I loved, here in London, than I would probably have got in Italy. It's much easier to work in another English-speaking country than one that isn't, I guess. Well, there isn't the language problem, obviously.'

'Mm, maybe so. She gave me that odd, searching look again.' My prickly guest seemed to be unfreezing again, judging by the way she made short work of the rest of her meal. She put her fork down and sighed. Favoured me with a smile, for which I felt ridiculously grateful. 'Mm, that was very nice. My compliments to your cook.'

I risked a smile too. 'I'll pass them on. Er, would you like some fruit to finish with? Banana? Apple? Pear?'

'I'd love a banana. Haven't had one for, oh, over a year, it must be. Come to think of it, I haven't had a real square meal for ages, either,' she added, wistfully.

I finished my own, got up and gathered the plates. 'And some coffee? The proper sort, not instant?'

'Ooh yes please. And then I'll play something else, if you like.'

And she did. She sat on my sofa and I sat in my one armchair and watched and listened, rapt, as she played Bach's Flute Sonata in B Minor, then some Schubert variations, then the Reissiger (whom I'd never heard of, let alone any of his music) Concertino in D Major, and then some Vivaldi. And some lighter pieces, transcriptions of popular music tunes, just for variety. I could have listened to her all night. She really was remarkably good as far as I could tell, with my limited knowledge of music and zero ability to play anything, anyway. And she had a remarkably extensive repertoire too, it seemed, if she knew all this from memory and wasn't even a professional musician. I wondered again about her mysterious past. Why on earth, with her obvious talent, wasn't she at least playing in an orchestra somewhere, not busking on the streets of London with no roof over her head? It was a puzzle.

And she was clearly as lost in her music as I. Her eyes closed, she seemed utterly absorbed; away in another place. Completely absorbed in her private world. I could only stand on the outside, looking in. I glanced at the time on the sound system again and was astonished to find it was past midnight. She chose just that moment to look at me and follow my gaze, and her eyes widened in surprise too. She stopped dead. 'Oh, look at the time! I'd got really carried away. I'm sorry. You'll be wanting to get to bed.'

But the fact of the matter was; I didn't want to. She could have carried on and on, as far as I was concerned. And besides, I would have felt guilty going to my comfortable bed knowing what her sleeping arrangements were going to be. I suppose it was the Irish in me, so it was (hearts worn on sleeves and all that) that led me to blurt out again, impulsively, 'I hate to think of you sleeping outside on a night like this.'

She forced a smile. 'Well, I won't literally be out in the rain. I've got one or two favourite doorways that are quite sheltered.' Her smile faded. The hostile defensiveness was back. 'And besides, if you're suggesting what I think you might be suggesting, forget it, okay?'

Which of course forced *me* back onto the defensive. And it riled me, rather. 'No, of course I wasn't suggesting that, you stupid distrustful woman! Jesus!

She was clearly taken aback by my vehemence. 'Oh, all right then. Cool it.'

I took a couple of deep breaths to calm down. And then I risked another crazy suggestion. 'Okay. But I was thinking. If you wanted to, you could become my lodger. Have the spare bedroom. Then you wouldn't have to be sleeping on the streets, at least.'

'But I couldn't do that! I'd have to pay you for my board, and if I did that, I couldn't save the few crumbs I earn for an airfare, could I?'

That threw me. She had a point. She might be down and almost out but she clearly had her pride, judging by the short shrift she'd given me when she suspected I might be set on exploiting her vulnerability for my own evil ends. I thought quickly, of my original motivation for bringing her home (which had rather got forgotten about in the last few hours). But dare I suggest it? She'd probably jump down my throat again.

'Well what about this then? I did have another reason for inviting you back here. It wasn't only feeling sorry for you – and it certainly wasn't to get inside your pants, I hasten to add.'

Her eyes narrowed suspiciously. 'Go on?'

'Well, back in the café, when you first told me you were homeless, and implied that you might have an interesting story to tell – the events that led to your homelessness and so on – I thought I'd very much like to hear it, and do a piece for the paper about homelessness, as it's so on the increase now in these austere times. I know my editor would go for it, as we often deal with issues like that.'

'Mm; I don't know about that. It's a pretty sorry story of stupidity and naivety. I think I'd be too embarrassed to tell it. And besides; what's that got to do with paying you rent?'

'Ah, well, newspapers generally pay the subjects of the stories they publish a fee, you know. I'm not saying it would necessarily run to megabucks. We aren't like the rich high-circulation tabloids with loads of money to splash around. But it could still be a tidy sum. Enough to pay rent and board for a few months, especially if it that was quite moderate. Which it would be. And it would leave your busking money free to salt away for a ticket. I'm sure Ken, my editor, would go for the idea.'

She still looked doubtful. 'Well, I don't know, really. I'm not sure I'd want my name and dirty linen washing spread across a British newspaper. And it would be bound to come out to my father, who'd probably play hell about it. He's quite a powerful man. And couldn't I lay myself open to law suits for slander or something?'

'No, there'd be no danger of that. Not unless you really dished the dirt on someone. We always take legal advice before we publish anything that might be litigious, and anyway, we could anonymize you if you wanted, and you wouldn't have to name any actual names.'

She frowned then said doubtfully, 'Mm, I don't know. I'd have to think about it. This is all a bit sudden.'

I stifled a sigh of disappointment. But obviously, it was up to her. 'Okay then. Well it's just a thought. I expect I'll see you again, so if you change your mind . . .'

'Yeah, sure. Thanks for the offer, anyway.'

'And I can't offer you a bed for the night? You won't get a bus back to Brewery Street now; they'll have stopped running.'

She shook her head. 'You never give up, do you? No; it's all right. I can walk. You do, after all.'

'Yes, okay. Well, thanks very much for the music. I really enjoyed it.'

A wry, weary smile reappeared. 'But you paid for it, remember?'

'No I didn't,' I said foolishly. 'Not adequately, anyway. It was priceless.'

Her eyes glistened. 'That's so nice of you to say so, Patrick. It really is.'

Our eyes locked for a long moment, before she blinked first and shook her head again. 'Well I must be off.' She made to walk out of the room to fetch her waterproof and then stopped. 'Oh, I can't walk out wearing your jeans!'

My guest picked up her own from the chair back and crumpled them to check for dampness. 'They're pretty well dry. Can I use your bathroom to change?'

'Of course.'

She left me and reappeared two minutes later, wearing her own attire and cagoule, picking up her flute to stuff it down her jeans again.

'Well, thank you very much for the food and good company.'

'You're welcome. It was my pleasure.'

I escorted her to the flat door and then opened the outer one. It was still raining steadily. 'You're going to get wet, I said.

She grimaced. 'Yeah. Story of my life. Well I suppose I'll see you tomorrow.'

'Yes, I expect so.'

'Goodnight then.'

'Goodnight, Leah.'

With a final uncertain parting smile she turned to trudge along the shiny pavement. I watched her departing back for a minute or so as it faded into the gloom, hoping she would make it back before the street lights went out, before going back inside.

I turned off the fire, went into the bathroom to wash my face and brush my teeth. My jeans were draped across the edge of the bath, like an accusation. Only then did I remember that I was still in my office clothes. I hadn't thought to change into casuals. Not that it mattered, really. It hadn't been a looking-cool occasion. Not a date. Just helping out a scruffy damsel in distress. But it had been very enjoyable. I turned out the sitting room lights, walked into the bedroom, undressed and fell into bed, feeling immediately guilty, thinking of the poor woman who'd just left me, walking through the darkness and rain back to her own wretched sleeping quarters, wherever they were; her own dismal reality. Whatever had caused her fall into destitution, I mused, it was so, so unfair that she was reduced to such a miserable situation, along with so many others all over London, the poor, helpless, hopeless souls, whilst I had so much. All right, I'd lost a daughter's immediate presence from my life, and had had to downsize from the family home in West Ham to this less-salubrious dwelling, but so what? I was still very lucky, comparatively speaking.

But the only thing Ms Weisman seemed to have, the only glimmer of hope to cling to and avoid the desperation of begging, was her music. I remembered her face when she was playing; it was so alive, so suffused with joy. She was so lost in it. Yes, her normally-sad face, which had briefly seemed rescued from care . . .

I was abruptly shaken back to wakefulness by the doorbell ringing. Who the hell could that be? Thankfully it only rang inside my flat so Spanish Miriam upstairs wouldn't be disturbed by it, hopefully. Cursing, I groped to switch on the bedside light, swung legs out of bed, pulled on the shirt I'd only discarded ten minutes ago (it seemed). Buttoned enough buttons for decency and pulled the recently removed trousers back on. Fumbled feet into slippers and stumbled blinking to open the outer door.

It was still raining.

Leah Weisman stood there. She was soaked again.

'I'm sorry, Patrick,' she mumbled, eyes downcast, embarrassed, 'could I take you up on that offer of a bed after all?'

Chapter 17

I stepped aside to let her pass. 'Yes, of course you can. Come in.'

'Thank you.'

Closing and locking the door behind her, I led the way into the sitting room. 'Did you think better of it?'

She managed a wry downcast smile. 'Yeah. Well, I got about halfway back before I realized I wouldn't be able to get my sleeping gear out of Chandra's storeroom, not without knocking on her door and getting her up. And I must admit your offer of a bed was tempting. Just for a night. Sorry.'

'No problem. You're soaked again.'

'Yeah,' she ruefully agreed.

'Er, would you like a hot bath or shower? Warm you up a bit?'

She looked at me for the first time, desolate, as if near to tears. 'Oh, that would be lovely. Yes please. I'd love a nice soak.'

But saying that seemed to inexplicably alter her mood, She sniggered, although somewhat sourly.

'What?'

'Oh, nothing. Just a not-very-happy memory.'

I waited for her to elaborate but she didn't. 'Okay, I'll find a clean towel for you.' I went into the pokey bathroom, to the miniscule airing cupboard, and to my relief found there actually was a bath towel clean. Knowing my lackadaisical attitude to laundry, there could well not have been. I draped it over the edge of the bath and found a clean shirt to go with the jeans she'd borrowed, so that she had a complete change of dry and clean clothing, before returning to the sitting room. She was still standing where I'd left her. 'Right, it's all yours. There's a towel over the bath and one of my shirts. Will I make some coffee?'

'Thank you Patrick, you're very kind.' She smiled gratitude and peeled off her dripping cagoule, took it into the hall and hung it where it had hung before, over the pool of water it had gifted me the first time. Then took her flute out of her waistband again, removed her boots and padded in her socks into the bathroom. I went to find bedding for the bed in the spare room (the bed that had been Bella's in another life) and set more coffee beans percolating.

Fifteen minutes later she emerged barefoot from the bathroom, my casual check shirt worn smock-like on her slender frame. I suppressed a double-take. She was transformed. Her cheeks were pink and glowing. She'd had the bath or shower water very hot, by the look of things. Scrubbed up clean and without her spectacles she was actually fairly pretty in a thin-nosed, porcelain-faced sort of way. Almost elegant. She must have used my shampoo to wash her hair because she'd wrapped the bath towel around her head in an oversized turban and was massaging it dry.

Having now buttoned myself up properly, I'd been sitting in the armchair waiting. 'Does that feel better then?'

Leah Weisman smiled radiantly. 'Oh yes, wonderful, thanks!'

'You'll need to dry your own things again now, I expect.'

'Yes please. Sorry I'm being such a nuisance.'

'That's all right.' I moved to switch the fire back on. 'I'm getting a strong feeling of déjà vu about all this, you know.'

'She laughed. 'Me too.'

She returned to the bathroom to fetch them and I got my clothes horse from the kitchen. Then I went back to pour the coffee. I glanced at the display on the microwave. One thirty-five, its emerald digits told me. It was going to be a very late night by the time my guest had got her hair dry enough to lay her head on a pillow. Oh well; it didn't matter. I was feeling peckish and she doubtless was too, so I took the half-empty packet of chocolate digestives (which I now firmly rationed myself to two of at bedtime) from its cupboard and tucked it under my arm. It didn't matter about plates.

She had her head bowed in front of the fire, still towelling the long black hair cascading over her face, when I returned to the sitting room. I placed the mugs on the coffee table; waved the biscuits in front of her face. She stopped what she was doing and took one.

'Thanks. I love chocolate cookies. Sorry, "biscuits". I'm sorry I'm keeping you up.'

'Don't worry about it. I won't feel guilty about you being out in the rain when I get back to bed now.'

That wry half-smile again, with her mouth full of biscuit, weary, quite devoid of humour. 'No.'

I studied her. She seemed to oscillate so quickly between moods: one minute vibrant and alive, especially when immersed in her music; the next teetering on the edge of depression.

And then the realization suddenly hit me. I'd been struggling to recall something ever since I first saw her sitting in the street. Well, since she first spoke to me really. It was voice rather than physiognomy that had seemed vaguely familiar. Neurons fired. A light bulb switched on somewhere in a dark recess of my brain and a memory came.

I remembered where I'd seen my guest before.

I couldn't help myself; I blurted, 'Jesus, yes, of course!'

She looked up at me sharply. 'What?'

'Well we were talking about déjà vu a moment ago, weren't we?'

'Yes? So?'

'Well I think we've met before!'

Leah Weisman stared. 'What are you talking about?'

'How long have you been in the UK?'

She considered for a moment. 'Since twenty-eleven. Four years. Why?'

'Right. And did you ever take a holiday in North Wales? About four years ago?'

'Er, yes. Well, it was a honeymoon actually.'

'In Llangollen?'

'Yes . . .'

I could hear wheels begin to revolve in *her* brain now.

'Right. And you went on a canal boat trip. Over a high aqueduct?'

'Yes!'

'And there was a little girl who was afraid of the height, because there was no guard-rail, and had a bit of a panic attack, and you sang to her to calm her down?'

She laughed, her wide mouth fully agape. Properly, with humour. Grinning ear-to-ear, crow's feet radiating from the corners of her bead-black eyes.

'Yes! And there was this know-all guy who gave me a lesson in pronouncing those impossible Welsh words . . .'

'That's right!'

'That was you? And Bella? And your wife?'

'Sure it was.'

'Oh my God! I've been thinking there's something familiar about you too, but I couldn't put my finger on it.'

'Yes, well I've changed quite a lot in the last four years, so I have. Including physically. I've put on weight; lost hair. From on top, anyway. And it's a lot greyer now. More silver threads among the red. And I keep it shorter at the sides than I did then. And I didn't have this bushy rufous beard then either. I look like some Irish fiddler from a pub in Dublin now, or something. Catarina never liked beards so I didn't grow one, to keep the peace.'

'Oh, well I like it. It's . . . exuberant. Indicates strong character. In a good way, I mean.' Leah Weisman blushed a little; passed quickly on. 'Yes, you do look very different from what I remember. But it was your voice, your nice soft Irish brogue that rang a faint bell. And your eyes, I suppose. They haven't changed, now I think about it.' She stopped, possibly embarrassed by the sudden intimacy.

'Yes,' I said, picking up my mug and offering the biscuits again, 'and it was your voice that I found familiar too, rather than your physical appearance. Has it changed too? I can't remember.'

She took another biscuit. 'Thanks. Yeah, I suppose it has. I've probably lost weight recently – not that I ever had a great deal of it in the first place. I take after my mom. We're both like rakes. And my hair's different. I used to have it short and styled; now I just let it grow. I can't be bothered with it. And I didn't wear specs back then. Contacts instead. I wanted to be as attractive as possible to my husband, just because he was a handsome hunk. So yeah, I suppose I do look very different now. Not that it really matters now, anyway.'

Leah Weisman looked melancholy again, ate her biscuit and went back to rubbing her hair. I would have to lend her my comb to disentangle it shortly, I thought. I wondered whether I dare ask any questions about her past, as she hadn't agreed to my pay-you-for-your-story suggestion. 'Are you still married then, can I ask?'

She snorted. 'God, no! It lasted barely two years. Big mistake. But I was very young and there was a lot of parental pressure to "marry well". And I was used to having plenty of money – my dad's filthy-rich; a business man – and Shay was a high-earner too. He was in finance. Wall Street. And look at me now. How the mighty have fallen!'

I didn't know how to answer that. But clearly there was an interesting back story there. Possibly a cautionary one. I could have stayed up all night (or the rest of the early morning) listening to her, but I must get some sleep.

'Mm, I'm sorry. You really seem to have fallen on bad times.' I glanced at the stereo system display. It was twenty past two now. I finished my coffee and sat forward. 'Well I really should get to bed. Need my beauty sleep, although I'm probably a lost cause as far as that goes now.' She didn't respond to my little witticism. 'Right, I'll leave you to finish drying your hair. See you in the morning then. Or rather, later this morning.'

'Yeah. Okay then.' She managed only a tired little smile this time 'Goodnight, Patrick. And thanks again.'

'No problem,' I said. 'Night, Leah.'

The alarm woke me at seven-thirty. It felt as though I hadn't slept at all and I probably hadn't very much, having lain awake for ages thinking about that young woman lying in Bella's old bed in the room at the back of the house; that ship who'd passed me in the night four years ago. In Longfellow's immortal words, 'on the ocean of life we'd passed and spoken, only a look and a voice, then darkness again and a silence.'

I climbed out of bed, went to the bathroom and showered, being noisy to let Ms Weisman know that my working day was beginning and she must rise too, and be out of my flat in three quarters of an hour's time, remembering not to walk between bathroom and bedroom naked, as I usually did. Her encountering me like that would have been decidedly embarrassing and completely undermined my assurances of innocent intentions.

She joined me in the kitchen as I was taking toast from the toaster, wearing her own scruffy clothes again, presumably having stayed up until she got them dry too. She looked a little downcast again when I asked brightly whether she'd slept well and replied with a non-committal 'Yes.' I finished my breakfast, made more toast for her to go with the large bowl of cereal she quickly demolished, as if stocking up in a time of plenty against a future time of famine, and because there was time, we walked companionably back to Brewery Street together. The rain had passed and a sunny day promised, judging by the almost cloudless sky. Well, the walk wasn't entirely companionable. She spoke little and I struggled for conversation, steering clear of the lodging subject. There would be no point in trying to pressure her about it. What she did to achieve her goal of buying a plane ticket out of the UK – and out of my life – was entirely up to her, I reflected, in slight, irrational irritation.

We reached her usual pitch and I hesitated; hovered uncertainly.

'Well,' she said, 'Thanks very much again for rescuing me last night.' She looked as though she wanted to say more, but didn't, simply studied her boots again.

'That's okay,' I said, adding inanely, 'Any time. And I loved your playing. It was definitely worth a meal and a bed.'

'And a bath, don't forget,' she said, with a tiny smile.

'Definitely. Well, I must get to work. Er . . . see you around then.'

'Yeah. See you around.' She was already taking out her flute and sinking to the pavement.

I had the day's and indeed the rest of the week's writing agreed with Ken (and for that matter the next three weeks, in general outline, too) but I tackled him as soon as he had five minutes of his valuable time to spare me to discuss my new pet project. Even though my new, too-proud-for-her-own-good American friend had rejected my offer of a regular roof over her head, I could still help her get her air ticket as soon as possible. Then at least she'd be on her way back to the USA to rebuild her life, and off the streets of London. And apart from that, it did sound as if her story would make a good feature in a few weeks' time. There would be kudos; I'd be doing myself a favour too.

As I knew he would, he liked the idea. I've known our editor for seven years or so now, ever since he rose to that exalted position, so I know the sort of story he goes for. I told him about Leah Weisman and what she had told me; that she seemed to have had a particularly spectacular fall from a position of some privilege and luxury to destitution and homelessness. But that she had a real musical talent, which made her present parlous state all the more perplexing. She wasn't at all the stereotypical homeless no-hoper. That wasn't to disparage such people of course or suggest their disasters were in any way less worthy of sympathetic airing in the media (Ken agreed) but her story with its apparent polar extremes of privileged good fortune and down-and-out ill would surely appeal to our readership. Whilst at the same time shine a light on the scandal of homelessness in general (Ken agreed again).

'All right,' he said, peering at me over his half-moon glasses, 'when you see this woman again, try and persuade her; tell her we'd be very interested in doing her story, in about a month's time. I could agree a fee of, oh, around a thousand, which ought to cover her return to the

States, if that's what she wants to do. Mind you, it sounds as if she might be here illegally now – no proper job and no longer a spouse – so she's probably got to go before she's pushed, anyway.'

I could have hugged Ken. 'Right, yes, I will. And meanwhile I'll try and get more of her story out of her, so we know what we've got.'

Ken beamed. 'Yes, you do that Paddy. I look forward to hearing what she says.' And then he went on to discuss my current project: a piece about the government's declining interest in renewable energy versus their enthusiasm for fracking, dropping hints that I ought to be applying my fine journalistic talents to that subject at the moment. I returned to my desk and did so. But it wasn't easy with my mind elsewhere. My drinking friends succeeded in persuading me to the pub at lunch time but I didn't linger there too long. Then, trying to banish other distracting thoughts, I got a good solid three hours of writing done and pretty well had my piece in the can by five-fifteen. I could edit it tomorrow after a run-through with Ken (although he rarely blue pencilled me) and then go on to the next journalistic gem.

I really didn't expect to see her still there when I walked back along Brewery Street. She'd certainly put in long day, but then the weather had been considerably better than yesterday, having reverted to British type: restrained, understated sunshine. It seemed she'd been looking out for me, because she spotted me while I was still twenty paces away. She stopped playing and scrambled to her feet; waited for me to draw near. There was a bashful smile on her face. 'Hi, Patrick.'

'Hello there; not still at it, are you?'

'Got to earn a crust, you know.'

'Of course. Had a profitable day?'

She glanced down. Her multicoloured hat had taken over as a collecting dish. There was a reasonably decent assortment of coinage in it, although not too many of the high-denomination variety. 'Well, not too bad. I've got a couple of fivers in my pocket too.'

'Good. Well done.'

She looked embarrassed again. Hesitated, before blurting out, 'Er, Patrick. I've been thinking about your kind offer. Of lodgings. I was wondering; could I take you up on it then?' Her eyes met mine, full of anxiety.

I was wrong-footed; I hadn't really seen that one coming. 'Oh, yes, fine.'

'Is it still okay?'

'Yes, absolutely.'

She breathed a blatant sigh of relief. 'I'll pay you whatever I can, of course.'

'But then, as we discussed before, you couldn't both pay me for your board and save for a ticket, could you?'

'No, not really.' She said in a small voice, frowning. 'Well, I'll just have to pay you whatever you think is acceptable and put the rest towards the ticket, however long it takes.'

'Right. But actually, I was talking to my editor today. About you; I hope you don't mind. He is very keen to do a story about homelessness and thinks like me that you'd have something interesting to tell, and he says he could pay a thousand pounds for it. Which would pretty well buy a ticket, I reckon. Then you could give the greater part of what you earn to me for board and could be winging your way back to the States in a few weeks' time.'

Her eyes widened. 'Really? He would pay that much?'

'Yup. That's what he said.'

'Oh my God!'

'So will you do it, tell me your story so I can write it?'

'Erm, yeah. That would solve my problem, I guess. And I wouldn' have to be so much in your debt.'

'Good! There you go then. So you're coming home with me now then, are you?'

Her face lit up. 'Right, yes. Er, I'd better pick up my stuff from Chandra first though. My vast wardrobe of clothes and everything.'

'Okay then,' I said, feeling absurdly pleased about the turn of events 'let's go.'

We walked along Brewery Street to Chandra's colourful café. She was doing a little more trade this evening, possibly because the weather had brightened up. The old man was there again, nursing another mug of tea, and there were several other customers, a microcosm of society: a middle-aged couple sitting by the window sipping tea and giving serious attention to a plate of assorted cakes and scones; a group of teenage schoolchildren giggling over Cokes and their mobiles in a corner; another couple, young and Chinese-looking (tourists, for a guess) gaping in amused wonderment at the natives as they sucked fizzy drinks through straws; and incongruously, against stereotype, a turbaned Indian youth (possibly a relative of Chandra) at the table nearest to the counter, working his way through a mountainous plate of fish and chips. Presumably, Chandra was adept in both Indian and British cuisine.

We made our way to the counter. The proprietor greeted Leah and nodded a smile to me. 'Hi Chandra,' Leah said, 'I need to get my stuff out of your storeroom now, please.'

Chandra glanced at me again, a little too knowingly. Whatever she was thinking, she was wrong. 'Right, my dear. Moving on, are you?'

Leah lowered her voice. 'Well, I'm getting a roof over my head for a while. I'm going to lodge with my friend.'

Chandra beamed; conspiratorially dropped hers too. 'That's nice for you. You want somewhere out of the elements to stay. Going far away, are you?'

'Canning Town,' I said.

'But I'll probably still busk around here, as I've got my regular clientele to keep happy,' Leah finished.

'That's nice,' Chandra repeated. 'Well, go through and pick your things up. Then let yourselves out the back door.' It seemed that Chandra had to keep up appearances.

Leah led the way through a curtain of beads of many colours behind the counter, past the foot of a narrow staircase and into a tiny back room chock-a-bloc with a large chest freezer and cartons, boxes, drums and catering-size bottles of oil. I had wondered why, if Chandra was kind enough to let Leah stash her stuff in her store room, she couldn't have let her doss down in it too. But I could see why now. There was barely room to lie down, and besides, Chandra had standards to maintain. Leah rummaged behind a wall of boxes and brought forth a grubby rolled-up sleeping bag, a none-too-clean holdall and a bulging black refuse sack.

She smiled wryly. 'This is it: the sum total of my worldly goods.'

Once more she had me stumped for a sensible, sensitive answer. All I could think of saying was, 'Well you're on your way back up again now, that's the main thing.'

She said nothing to that; opened the door that led out into the back alley with its rank of colour-coded wheelie bins. I picked up the sack, she the sleeping bag and holdall and I pulled the door closed behind us. We emerged into Brewery Street and set off home – my home at least – through the late afternoon sunshine. It was a more cheerful journey than the morning one had been. Then, she had been lost in her own thoughts and not wanting to intrude, I'd left her to them. But now she was much brighter. Quite chatty, in fact. She admitted that she'd been thinking about the selling-her-story idea but hadn't wanted to bring it up again. It had surely been too good to be true and she didn't want to push her luck. Whereas checking me out about lodging, as to whether I really meant it, and getting off the streets, was the first priority.

'So, she said, as we strode along, 'when do you want me to start telling you my pathetic story?'

I laughed. 'Just as soon as you like. It wouldn't appear for a few weeks as the paper has other things scheduled for the immediate future, and so the payment wouldn't come through before then, but you can tell me and I can write it in the meantime. And to be honest, I'm intrigued about it, from what you've said so far.'

'Mm, well you might think me a stupid, naïve little girl when you hear it.'

'No, I'm sure I won't. Anyway, to move on to more important issues: I'm wondering what I can rustle up for us both to eat when we get back. I hadn't anticipated having a guest again otherwise I would have bought supplies at lunch time. I'm not very good at meal planning, being a mere man.'

She laughed too (it was nice to hear it) and exclaimed in mock-penitence, 'Oh no; I'm eating you out of house and home already!'

'Ah, that's okay,' I joshed, 'I'll adjust for it, so I will. And besides, you can earn your bread by playing for me some more as well – or have you exhausted your repertoire on me already?'

'No!' She giggled. 'Okay, it's a deal. And don't worry about not having much food in. I don't expect cordon bleu. Whatever you've got will be just fine.'

'Well I've got some eggs, I know that. What about good old British egg and chips?'

She looked at me aghast. 'What?' And then roared with laughter. 'Oh, I see what you mean. Egg and *fries*! I thought you meant egg and what you call "crisps" over here!

'No, of course I didn't mean that! That wouldn't be much of a meal would it? Egg and *chips*. We inhabitants of the British Isles swear by them; they're staple diet. So how does it sound?'

She sighed happily. It sounds wonderful.'

Chapter 18

Leah Weisman attacked my egg, chips and frozen peas with the same gusto she had my risotto the previous evening. When in, traditional British style, I offered supplementary bread and butter (well, low-fat spread) to go with it to augment the stomach-filling carbohydrate quotient, she cheerfully accepted that too. Looking at her slender frame bent over my dining table enthusiastically forking food into her mouth, it was difficult to imagine where she was putting it. And here was I, trying to moderate my own calorie intake. She would be a bad influence, this unexpected lodger, I thought a little ruefully. She would get me back into bad habits.

We finished with fruit again: an apple for her and an orange for me. Then she insisted on doing the washing up while I set the coffee beans percolating and changed into casual clothes. She asked if she could borrow my shirt and jeans again so that she could put all her clothes (which didn't amount to many; barely more than a load) in my washing machine. This could quickly become a comfortable routine, I thought, happily humming to myself as I changed; her presence in my flat filled a void I hadn't known was there.

Then, with her ensconced, bare feet curled up under her, on the sofa and nursing her mug of coffee, we got down to discussing practicalities. She was all for giving me everything she earned from busking rather than a set sum, because the amount varied so much. Sometimes it could be as much as thirty pounds on a good day but on others, as little as five. 'No,' I countered, 'whatever you earn, keep a little, a couple of pounds per day, for yourself. You need a little pocket money.' So we agreed on that. Even with her elephantine appetite, that ought to cover her keep. Having her as a guest living in my flat would cost me little else extra. As a probably now-illegal resident of Britain, I could hardly declare her as living under my roof for council tax-paying purposes. Besides, she would be gone in a couple of months, probably; back to America and out of my life.

It was time for her to start telling her story. I silently cursed that I hadn't got the means to record her, except on my phone. I must remember to bring a portable recorder from work tomorrow.

'So, I began, 'can you give me a little background then? Whereabouts in the States do you come from?'

She smiled, although I wasn't sure whether it was in fond reminiscence or not. 'Middlesex County, Connecticut. Funny, that, isn't it? You've got a county of Middlesex here too. A little town called Deep River. On the Connecticut River, as the name implies. My dad opened a store there when I was a little girl, and it thrived. He has great business acumen, my dad. Then he borrowed and bought a bigger store in Hartford. That's the State capital. So we moved there. Then he did well with it too and bought a department store from a firm that was going bankrupt, so he got it at a knock-down price. And he built it up – he had a knack of knowing just what sort of merchandise to sell – and after that he just went from strength to strength. When I was fourteen we moved to New York, when he opened a high-end store there, and he then opened another three along the eastern seaboard and then moved west. Now he's got at least one in every state, except Alaska, and sometimes more than that. I've no idea how many he's got now. And the last I heard, he was looking to open places in Europe too. He probably has done by now.'

'Mm, quite the entrepreneur.'

'Sure is. He's the typical stereotype of your billionaire Jewish businessman.'

A penny dropped in my brain. 'Oh, of course. You're Jewish. I should have realized that, with a surname like yours. Or is that your married name?'

'God, no! I reverted to my single name after my divorce. Although my husband was Jewish too, so either way I had Jewish surname.'

'Oh, I see. And what brought you to Britain? Oh, hang on; I think you told me. Husband getting a job here, wasn't it?'

'Yeah. Well Shay worked on Wall Street, doing something high-powered and high-paying. I never really understood exactly what he did. My dad – well, both my parents – thoroughly approved of him as being someone who could keep their precious daughter in the style to which she'd become accustomed. And he was the Right Religion, so it was a no-brainer, really. So yeah, he got an even more high-powered job with an investment bank in the City of London and we moved over here, a few months before we got married. We got a very smart apartment in Canary Wharf; a penthouse. Dad had offered him the job of running his European operation when he expanded over here, further down the line. And then eventually, as he'd no male heir and I wasn't interested in inheriting the Weisman empire because I only really cared about my music, he – we – would have got all of that too when Dad retired. If he ever does.'

'So; and that time I saw you in North Wales, you were on your honeymoon, you said?'

'Yeah. Shay was sulking for most of the time though because it wasn't luxurious or exotic enough for his taste. We'd agreed to split the honeymoon, doing half what he wanted, which was sun and sand, and half what I did. He wasn't good at compromise though. Warning bells should have begun ringing right back then. But I was just so thrilled to have landed such a hunk of a man, such a catch for silly little plain-Jane me. I was blinded. I was a stupid, naïve fool really.'

'Ah, don't be too hard on yourself. I didn't do too brilliantly with either of my marriages either; otherwise I wouldn't be alone now.'

She smiled sadly. 'No, relationships aren't exactly an exact science, are they?'

'They certainly aren't. So; clearly, your marriage didn't work out?'

'No. He cheated on me. With my friend. Well, she wasn't a huge friend; more just a fellow-musician and American really – and she certainly wasn't a friend after I found out about it!'

'Ah, Jesus, that's bad. So there was no chance of reconciliation then?'

Her smile became a frown. 'No, absolutely not! Perhaps I'm just not the forgiving type. But I figured I'd just never be able to entirely trust him after that. And it seemed like all he really wanted me for was as an entrée into the Weisman empire and in order to give him kids. And be the dutiful, compliant little wife at home, the domestic goddess impressively whipping up meals for his fancy business friends. It was as though he thought he could get his other needs, like ass, elsewhere with cuter models, like Grace – like my dad did, more than once. But I just wasn't prepared to stand for it, not like my mom did. She's no raving beauty either. I take after her: thin as a rake and not exactly God's gift to men. But I wasn't going to stand for it; be his doormat, the bastard!'

I was a little taken aback by her vehemence. 'No, er, right. I don't blame you. So did you divorce him then?'

Leah reverted to the sardonic smile; sipped her coffee. I waited for her to resume. 'No. I reciprocated, in kind.'

'How do you mean?'

'Well, things were pretty bad between us. He continued to play around with my friend in spite of promising to end things with her and I withheld conjugal rights, as they say. And apart from that, I was really frustrated because I couldn't get any work, classical anyway, so I'd lowered my sights a bit and had been doing some session playing with rock bands. Yes, I know. It wasn't really my bag, but at least it was work. That was how I got to know Grace, my husband-stealing so-called friend. Anyway, one of the bands was *Vagabond*. Do you know them?'

'Er, no; sorry. Not really my thing. Well, not the current ones, at least. I'm a bit of an old fogey, I'm afraid.'

She didn't offer an opinion on that. 'Okay. Well I was doing quite a bit of work with them on a new album they were recording. Their stuff is quite folksy and a lot of the tracks called for flute. But none of them played it. So enter Yours Truly. And there was this one guy, their bass player, who was currently unattached and quite a looker, in a

Heathcliffian sort of way: dark and smouldering; you know? He made a pass at me and I responded, partly just to spite Shay. Plus, I was quite flattered that someone at least fancied me. I felt so unconfident, having been rejected. We quickly got into a relationship and Shay found out, and he promptly filed divorce papers on me. It was pure hypocrisy. Okay for him to play around, but if I did it, it was unforgiveable. That was okay by me though; I wanted out of the marriage anyway. But my dad hit the roof, because it affected his plans for expansion and handing on the empire. That was all he cared about, not my happiness. He thought I should have stuck with Shay, like my mom had stuck with him, and was outraged that I was taking up with a common rock musician, as he saw it. So we had a major bust up, my folks and me, and that's why I refuse to go crawling back to them now with my tail between my legs, apologizing for my stupidity.'

'So you want to go back to the States but not home to them?'

'That's right.' She stared at her coffee mug, adding defiantly, 'I'm going to make my own way in the world, not be a wouldn't-say-boo-to-a-goose, poor little rich girl anymore.'

'Well good for you. That's what I had to do, although I came from a hugely different background from yours.'

A silence. I prompted gently, 'Do you want to continue your story?'

The sad little smile again. 'Yeah. Well Mick – Mick Jones, the bass player – had a splendid old house in Kent and I moved in with him there. It was a really nice place, genuinely old; a manor house. And I really thought I had feelings for Mick. He was a breath of fresh air, and a bit of a rebel, after Shay. But it was probably more of a rebound thing than anything else. So I became a member of the band – at least I thought I did, but really I was a bit peripheral, just one of the backing musicians; little more than the girlfriend of one of the members.'

I interrupted. She was racing along with her story, the words tumbling out in a torrent as if she were baring her soul to a therapist or priest or somebody.

'So at this point you were still married to Shay?'

'Yeah, although he'd filed the divorce papers via an expensive attorney, who made it appear to be a case of me being at fault for desertion, so that he wouldn't have to make a financial settlement. I had little money of my own so I couldn't hire my own defence team to fight it. But as I say, I didn't really care. I just wanted out; I thought another door had opened, with Mick.'

I couldn't see how her story so far had led to her homelessness, but I would have to wait, let her to tell me in her own good time. Well, journalists are supposed to be good listeners, if nothing else. I prompted again. 'But presumably things went wrong with Mick?'

There was a faraway look in her eyes now, betraying mixed emotions of, it seemed – what? Nostalgia? Sadness? Loss?

'Yeah, and how! The divorce came through quite quickly because I hadn't contested it, and then I was a free agent. It was good at first. We – the band, I mean – did some local gigs in London, and some promotional trips for the album: appeared on Jules Holland's show, then on Danish TV and then the Late Late Show in New York. It was a little weird going back there. I don't know whether my parents would have seen it; if they did, they wouldn't have approved. Then in the summer of 2014 we played Glastonbury. That was quite an experience. It was the nearest I came to being famous. By association, at least.'

She sighed. 'Or ever will, probably. That was going to be the start of a British tour, with possibly a European one to follow. But I picked up a stomach bug at Glastonbury and it quite possibly saved my life, as it turned out.'

'How so?'

'Well, we drove straight back to London after the gig and I was as sick as a dog when we got there, and still felt fragile the following day, so I stayed at home. But Mick drove up to London to arrange things with the others for the tour. And on the way back that evening he had a horrendous smash on the motorway. The police told me he'd been speeding, way over the limit –he always did – and had lost control and run off the motorway, up an embankment and into the side of a concrete bridge. They said he might simply have nodded off. He must have veered right across all the lanes. Thankfully, by a miracle he didn't hit any other vehicles, or it could have been complete carnage, but he was killed outright, apparently.'

'Oh, no!'

'Yeah. They did a post-mortem and he was not only pissed out of his brain but high on crack-cocaine too. He had a serious drug habit. I'd hoped I might get him off it, but I probably wouldn't have succeeded. He wasn't the type to take advice or recognise that he had a problem.'

'That's terrible.'

'Yes, it was. But I found myself being angry with him more than grieving, really. He was an idiot. The band was really starting to take off because the album I'd been playing on went to the top of the charts, so he really didn't need to play Russian roulette with his life like that. I would have helped him try to kick his habits if he'd let me.'

'Well, it can be really difficult to help people with addiction if they don't want to help themselves.'

'Mm, I suppose so. And I suppose, selfishly speaking, I thought of myself as a loser because of his death too. Obviously, I couldn't then stay on at Broughton Manor. It wasn't as if I was his spouse or even long-term partner, and he hadn't willed me anything. I was really just his latest chick, I realize now. So, for a second time, I'd lived with a man in the luxury to which I'd become accustomed only to lose it.'

'That's a shame. You went from having all that to virtual destitution. How did that happen?'

'Yes, it's ridiculous, isn't it? Well, I left the manor of course, and the band, although I was never really with them, except as Mick's girlfriend. Now that he'd gone, they didn't want me as part of their scene any more. So I came back to London with a thousand pounds in my pocket, which the band in their infinite generosity deemed a fair golden goodbye, although they made it plain that I couldn't expect a slice of ongoing royalties as I was never actually a band member. A lot of the money went on a bond and a month's advance rent on the cheapest furnished apartment I could find, in a dingy side street off Brewery Street. It was a bit of a comedown, to put it mildly. And I had to find some work, of course. There were no jobs going in orchestral or ensemble work so I had to go back to session work again. But there wasn't a great deal of that either. Not enough to give me a full, regular weekly wage.

'So within three months I had to leave the apartment because I just couldn't keep up with the weekly rent. It took virtually everything I made. I'd often find myself literally having to choose between eating and finding money for rent and the electricity and gas meters. And when I left there was neither the advance rent money to come back, because it had been used to pay for my last month there, nor the bond. The landlord maintained that he was entitled to keep it against damage done, which was ridiculous; I hadn't caused any. But he knew my situation. I'd foolishly told him my business: that I was probably living in Britain without a visa now that I was divorced. When I tried to demand my bond back he told me to get lost. Or words to that effect. Ruder words actually. He said he'd report me to the Home Office if I didn't just go forth and multiply. He said he preferred benefits claimants as tenants really, so his rent payments were guaranteed, not people who shouldn't be here.'

She paused, suddenly looking concerned. 'Oh, you won't print that, will you? Am I dropping myself in it?'

I smiled reassurance. 'No, don't worry. As I said before, we don't have to identify you exactly. No one's going to send the police around to cart you off to a detention centre or anything. You haven't got an official address anyway, so they can't. You're pretty invisible to the authorities.'

'Okay. That's a relief. Now where was I?'

'You were being evicted from your flat.'

'Oh yes. So then I began to think that all I could really do was go back to America. But on my own terms, not crawl back to my parents. There was no future for me in Britain, as far as I could see. I'd save up for a ticket. But I needed somewhere to lay my head. I'd become quite friendly with one of the session players I sometimes worked with, Brian – in fact he was another backing musician on the new *Vagabond* album and was going to tour with us, until Mick died and the tour was called off – and he and his wife let me sleep on their couch. So that was nice of them, and I thought it wouldn't be for too long.

'But then the session work began to really dry up. I was getting quite depressed. No one was arranging stuff and calling for a flute, it seemed. I had quite a nice Christmas though. Brian and Jill spent the day with her parents in Essex and I was invited along too. It was a bit less of a binge than the previous one at Mick's place had been, but it was good, spending it with kind, ordinary people.

'And then Brian and Jill suddenly got accommodation problems too. Their apartment was pretty crappy, not a whole lot better than mine had been, and they got problems with the roof. Water began coming through their bedroom ceiling. They mentioned it to their landlord, who said he'd do something about it, but didn't. They kept pestering him and things came to a head, and he evicted them. Well, he terminated their contract, refused to give them another one and put them on notice to leave, so it came to the same thing. And then when they threatened to take legal action he did the same as my landlord had done: back in February he told them to quit immediately or they would be evicted. They were nearly as hard-up as me, because Jill had lost her job as a teaching assistant due to public spending cuts, and couldn't find a bond or advance rent on another place. Housing for the people at the bottom of the pile in London is shocking; the well-off have no idea. So they moved in with her parents; it was all they could do. And obviously, I couldn't go too.

'So I was homeless.' She sighed heavily, hollow-eyed, as if reminding herself of the burden of troubles she carried. 'And that's pretty much it, Patrick. This is how I came to be a pauper on the streets of London. Pathetic really, isn't it?'

The desolate look was back on her thin face. She stared morosely at the empty mug she was still holding. I wanted to go to her, sit down beside her; put a comforting arm around her skinny shoulders and tell her that I understood; that things might seem bleak but they would get better. That the world wasn't entirely a bad place. That all men weren't irresponsible idiots who got themselves killed, or betraying bastards. That she would soon be able to fly back to America and begin rebuilding her life. Wasn't this a first step? At least she no longer had to sleep on the cold hard streets.

But I didn't. Journalistic distance must rule. I mustn't get too involved. And she was clearly in quite a delicate emotional state; had taken a battering from the winds of misfortune. I didn't want her to misconstrue my motives, think I was coming on to her.

So I simply said, 'Thanks for telling me that. You've certainly had a rough time.'

'Yeah, you can say that again.'

I tried diversion. 'Will I make us some more coffee?'

She managed a small smile. 'That would be good.'

'Okay, and you can serenade me while I do it.'

Her smile widened. 'It's a deal.'

So she got her flute and as I set fresh beans to percolate she stood in the kitchen and played for me the beautiful, melancholy Ravel's *Pavane for a Dead Princess,* the piece we'd discussed so recently in the street, before I got so impulsively involved with her. She knew this stately pavane by heart too.

She finished the piece and I poured coffee, and as we returned to the sitting room carrying our mugs the telephone rang. It was a familiar number on the display. I picked up. 'Hello Esther.'

'Hello Paddy. How are you?'

'Fine, thanks. And yourself? And Benny?'

'Oh, I'm as fit as a fiddle, as always. Benny's all right, although a little tired. I do wish he'd retire, but you know what he's like.'

I laughed. 'Tell me about it. I think he'll go on playing until he drops!'

She didn't respond to that. I mentally kicked myself. *Eejit! That might be a sore subject!*

'I was just ringing to see if you'd like to come to supper on Friday. Benny isn't playing and it's been a while since we fed you.'

'Oh yes, love to, thanks, Esther.'

'Good,' she said, briskly. 'About eight o' clock, shall we say?'

'Yes, fine, thank you.'

The conversation drifted to other things as Leah sat there trying to look as though she weren't present, trying not to impinge upon my privacy. Then Esther drew it to a close. I always waited for her to do that; it seemed only polite. And besides, I tended to regard her and Benny almost like parents; the parents I never had. But wished I'd had.

I replaced the handset in its dock. 'That was someone you'd find interesting,' I said, by way of explanation. 'Well, her husband, Benjamin, actually. He's a flautist.'

Leah looked up quickly from perusing her mug, immediately interested. 'Oh, really?'

'Yes, he plays with the Philharmonic; First Flute. Been with them for years.'

'Lucky him,' she said, and there was just an edge of bitterness in her voice. I kicked myself again. *Jesus, Brennan, shut up!*

'Er, yes. Would you like to meet him? I'm sure he'd be interested in you too. He's a very nice old chap. Well, they both are; him and Esther.'

'Well, yes . . .' Leah said uncertainly.

I plunged on. 'That call was an invite to dinner. I'm sure they'd include you. Shall I phone Esther back and sound her out?'

She sounded doubtful. 'Oh, I don't know. That's a bit presumptuous, isn't it? It's for them to do the inviting, really.'

'No, they'd be fine about it, they really would.'

'But I haven't got any decent clothes to wear, and I could hardly go wearing yours!'

She had a point. I thought quickly. 'Yes, well you're going to be earning money for your story soon. I could give you an advance on that. Call it a loan. Just enough to buy you a respectable outfit: say some new jeans, a top, maybe some footwear. That's all you'd need, this weather.'

Leah thought about that. I could tell that she was tempted. 'Well, are you sure?'

'Sure I'm sure!'

A smile lit up her face. 'It would be very nice . . .'

'Right then. I'll call Esther back.'

Leah watched me intently as I picked up the phone again. As I knew she would be, dear Esther was absolutely fine about it when I asked if I could bring a friend to supper. 'But of course you can, my dear. Do bring him or her.'

'Well it's a her, actually, love. A flautist. Classically trained.'

'Oh really? I'm sure Benny would find her very interesting. They'd probably spend all the time talking shop, but you and I can talk about journalism or current affairs or something to keep them in check!'

'Ah, thanks, Esther.' I breathed a sigh of relief. 'Great. So we'll see you on Friday then.'

Chapter 19

Yes, it was already becoming a comfortable routine, to be sure. The following morning was dry and bright again as we walked companionably in the direction of my work. At a cash machine we passed I withdrew fifty pounds to give Leah as a loan for clothes buying, adding thirty more I already had my wallet to do a food shop, leaving it to her to choose what to buy. I sensed that she would appreciate my delegating that responsibility to her and judging by the way her eyes lit up when I suggested it, it looked as though my surmise was right. It probably increased her sense of self-worth and usefulness. She needed lifting as far as that went, I reflected, as I left her in Brewery Street, saying I'd meet her there later, and continued on to the *Clarion*.

At five-thirty sharp, rather to Ken's surprise (this was the third evening in a row I hadn't lingered over a piece of writing in progress) I left the office and strolled back to Leah's usual pitch. She was sitting there playing incongruously surrounded by a palisade of new plastic bags, two of them of the supermarket variety. She must have been keeping an eye out for me because as I approached she looked in my direction, stopped playing *Annie's Song*, grinned and switched to something classical.

'I smiled back. 'Hey, you look as though you've been busy!'

She beamed. 'Yeah; it's been a while since I did any retail therapy. really enjoyed myself. Even the food shopping!'

'Good. Be careful; I'll be putting you to work in the kitchen next!'

A peal of laughter this time. 'You misogynist, you! But that's okay Seems a fair deal to me. I never would have said that two years ag though.' She scrambled to her feet, picking up her hat, transferring th contents into her pocket and tucking the flute down the front of he jeans, which for some reason I now found vaguely erotic. Possibl because there was a momentary glimpse of naked midriff and navel. I picked up the two food bags and, gallantly, one of the others, leaving her to carry the remaining two. We set off. 'So; you've had a good day then, it seems. Did you have enough money?'

'Yeah. I'm not a big spender anymore. That's something this experience has taught me; to be frugal. I got some trainers, a pair of jeans, some new socks and a jumper for forty-seven pounds ninety-seven. Oh, and some underwear. I really needed a new bra. I forgot that.'

'Good, well done,' I said (rather wishing she hadn't mentioned the underwear), congratulating her on her thriftiness, like an approving parent, without quite knowing why I did it.

'And I still had time after I'd been to the food store too to make a little bit playing. So it's been a pretty good day. Brilliant, in fact.' Her almost childish, suddenly-discovered joie de vivre was quite touching.

'That's great,' I enthused in sympathy.

She became serious. 'I really do appreciate what you're doing, Patrick. Thank you. It restores some of my faith in men – well, humankind generally, for that matter.'

I brushed it off jocularly. 'Yes, well we aren't all selfish, cruel brutes, you know. And you don't have to keep being so formal. I'm "Paddy" to my friends.'

She glanced at me. 'No; you're certainly the exception . . . Paddy.'

Back home, like an excited little girl, she couldn't wait to show me her purchases: white chunky-soled trainers with red tongues, bright red socks, blue jeans and a pink, skinny-rib, turtleneck jumper which she held up against herself for my appraisal. And which I perhaps gave a little too enthusiastically; I found myself idly musing that it would be very figure-hugging.

'Yes, very nice. Suits you'.

Her eyes lit up. 'Do you think so?' I almost thought she was going to embarrass me by peeling off her clean-but-unflattering smock of a top and putting it on for confirmation there and then.

'Oh yes, and before I forget.' She laid the jumper over the back of the sofa and rummaged in her jeans pockets; brought out two crumpled five pound notes and the loose change she'd earned, picking out the three pound coins from the assorted copper and silver. Thrust the thirteen pounds at me. 'There you go; my first contribution to the household budget!'

I began to decline them but changed my mind. Paying her way, no matter how slenderly, was probably important. And it was the deal, after all. 'Ah, right. Thank you, minstrel lady.'

After supper: pasta with mushrooms, garlic, cauliflower, herbs, chicken again, in a white sauce topped with cheese (Leah had bought ingredients with this in mind), and after fruit and coffee, she took a bath and changed into her new gear, apart from the shoes. She seemed to like padding around my flat barefoot. And now she was further transformed. Gone was the formless androgynous look when she wore my clothes; now she was a willowy, pert-breasted, elegant young woman, really quite attractive, rubbing her wet hair in a towel-turban as she'd done that first evening. She'd rolled the top of her jumper down to keep it away from her hair and getting wet. I tried not to stare. She sank a little proprietorially (but that was fine) into her usual place on the sofa. 'What shall we do now, then?'

'Will I play *you* some music for a change?'

'Right, yes, that would be good.'

I moved to the music system on the shelf behind the sofa. Leah smelled wonderfully clean and subtly perfumed as I passed, as only women straight from the bath can. She seemed to have bought herself some toiletries today too. So that was what was also in the bag she'd coyly taken into the bathroom then.

I glanced back at her, sitting feet-up on my sofa, hands raised to rub her hair, looking for all the world like a subject from an impressionist painting. The pale naked sliver of the back of her slender neck between towel and jumper was almost painfully appealing (it's one of my favourite parts of the female anatomy); made me feel an uncouth, overweight, hirsute, middle-aged slob by comparison. I dragged my attention back to music. The Tchaikovsky I'd played a week ago was still in the player. 'Something symphonic perhaps? Tchaikovsky's *Pathétique?*'

'Ooh yes; wonderful. I love that. It's so . . . melancholy, isn't it?'

The surprising rapport was back again. I set the CD to play, but softly. 'Yes, poor old Peter Ilyich. Sure he was a tortured soul, all right. Wrote some gorgeous tunes though.'

'Mm; sure did,' she agreed.

Returning to my armchair (although I would far rather have sat beside her) I cast about for conversation. 'Er, do you want to dry your hair? I'm sorry I haven't got a hair dryer. Will I put the heater on?'

She laughed, thoroughly at ease. 'No, don't do that. It's too warm a night to have heating on. I don't have to get it dry quickly; I'm not going anywhere.'

'No,' I said, and knowing that, I suddenly realized, was actually a very nice feeling.

'So do you want to know any more about me, for your article?'

'No, it's all right; not at the moment. You can fill me in with more detail when I write it. You can sit beside me at the computer. It can be a sort of joint enterprise.'

'Okay. That'll be fun. I've never seen a journalist at work before. Let alone collaborated with one.'

I relaxed; sighed contentedly, catlike, in the warm ambience of the situation. 'Well I've never met a talented American lady-flautist before, either. So touché.'

She smiled modestly. 'So tell me something about yourself, Patrick – Paddy. What brought you to the UK? Or am I being too nosy?'

'No, you aren't at all. Fair's fair; you've told me your story so I'll tell you mine. Well, my background could hardly have been more different from yours. There was no wealth or privilege to it, to be sure. It was quite the opposite: poverty and deprivation. My mother – she's dead now, rest her soul – brought the eight of us kids up single-handed after my father walked out after my youngest brother Seamus was born. Apparently he took up with a younger woman. My mammy was well rid of him though, because apart from pissing much of his wages away on drink, he used to knock her about, the brute. The only thing was; he then left her without any income at all, apart from assistance from the government, which I don't think was a great deal in those days, back in the late seventies, early eighties. Ireland was a pretty poor country back then. That was why so many of us emigrated; often to America of course.

'So she had to take any work she could get. Anything that could be done at home, at any rate. She couldn't go out to work because of looking after my youngest siblings. So she took in ironing, working late into the night to get it done to earn a pittance to supplement the benefit. At least after Da went there couldn't be any more mouths for poor old Mammy to feed, but it really was a struggle for her, I remember. There was never any spare cash in the house. And she had very little time for us, which I used to resent at the time, but I can understand why now. She became a very embittered woman. Life didn't treat her well, one way and another.'

Leah stared. 'Good God, Paddy; that's grim. Your poor mother! No you didn't have it easy, at all, did you?'

'No, not really. Things should have got a little easier for my mother financially when my two elder sisters, Maeve and Julie, left school. There should have been their incomes coming into the house when they began work, although the benefit Mammy got for their support would have ceased. So she might not have been all that much better off anyway. But first Maeve – she's the eldest – came over to England to find greener grass and then Julie followed her, to promptly get herself into a spot of trouble, but that's another story I could tell you some time.

'Then I left school – I'm the third eldest – and got a job on the local paper in Sligo. It was only as an office boy to start with, but I'd always liked reading and writing little essays and stories at school, and they began to let me do little pieces for the paper – reporting the really boring local events that the other hacks didn't want to do. But I loved it. So I really did start right at the bottom, you might say. And it was a good grounding, really. Anyway, that went on for three years, but then I got the wanderlust too – well, I was getting a bit bored with the *Sligo Champion,* to be honest – and came over the water as well, to Wales, to work for another local paper, the *North Wales Chronicle* as a fully fledged reporter. That's how I came to pick up a bit of knowledge of the Welsh language. I felt a rapport with the Welsh, to an extent, coming from a non-English speaking part of Ireland myself.'

'Ah, that explains that time on that canal boat.'

'Yes. Well then in nineteen ninety-five I applied for a job with a bigger local paper, the *Birmingham Mail,* which suited my left-wing views, so it meant upping sticks again to move there. It was quite a culture-shock after sleepy Ireland and Wales. I met Melanie – she was another journo on the paper – and we started going out. I was twenty-six; she was a couple of years older and my first proper girlfriend. It's pathetic really. But I was a young, naïve, overawed Irishman in the big metropolis of England's Second City. It was more a case of her chasing me and deflowering me than the other way round. I fell for her hook line and sinker because she was my first actual lover, and we shacked up together. After eighteen months of that I wanted marriage. She seemed to too, and so we got hitched, in ninety-seven. It was fine with her at first, for the first two or three years, except that she was more interested in her career – she was a brilliant journo – than wanting babies and domesticity. But I thought that was fair enough; she was good at her job and just didn't want to give up work, or even put it on hold.

'Mind you, I was pretty ambitious back then too. After five years in Birmingham, in two thousand, with the new millennium, I wanted to make my next big career move. I applied for another job, with the *Clarion* in London. Or rather, we both got itchy feet, and both applied for jobs here. Significantly better-paid ones. Melanie got one too, although with another paper. Well, London was the Centre of the Newspaper Universe as far as the British Isles went, and as far as I was concerned, a quantum-leap from backwoods Sligo. So then I had it all: money, nice pad in Barking, beautiful wife, sporty car, the lot.

'But then things began to go wrong. It wasn't just a case of greener, more lucrative grass for Melanie but fresh faces too. And faces more attractive than my freckled red-haired one, and wittier, and more charming; more urbane. I think that I, with my Celtic passion, my sentimentality, my naïve idealism, just couldn't compete with that. The almost-inevitable happened and she started an affair with a photographer colleague a few years her junior. She kept it secret for a while but then came right out and said that she wanted us to part. Well I was devastated; I hadn't seen it coming at all. But perhaps a lot of it was hurt male pride. And there'd increasingly been the thing about her not wanting a family. We didn't really have the same aspirations as far as that was concerned.'

I paused, memory back in an unhappy past. Leah murmured, 'Ah, yeah; tell me about it. I know how you feel about being rejected.'

'Yes, it wasn't good. But these things never are, are they? So that was in oh-two. And then a few months later, Catarina came into my life, courtesy of match-making Beryl at work.'

'This is your Italian wife? Sorry, ex-wife?'

'Yes. Talk about a case of jumping from frying pan into fire!'

I told Leah about my first acrimonious – although, admittedly, not expensive – divorce and about the thrill of a new love, then the joy of finding myself a father (albeit an unintended one); about the early, good years, the heavily-mortgaged country place out in Essex; before Catarina too became dissatisfied with me, and restless, and wanted to go back home to Palermo; and the second bitter parting of the ways (which *was* expensive) and the tug-of-love over Bella. And how much I missed my child now. I confess I was getting quite emotional by now. But like Esther, Leah, it seemed, could look into my soul, the dark troubled corners of it, could empathise and feel my pain. Almost as if we were natural kindred spirits.

And of course the melancholy music playing quietly in the background didn't help. It had begun Tchaikovsky's despairing final movement, the one traditionally reckoned to signify death. I finished my account. With eyes suddenly soft and a gentle half-smile of sympathy on her face, she looked at me, totally understanding.

'Poor Paddy,' she said.

No other words were needed. We listened to the diminuendo end of the symphony in complete communion. The music was unbearably sad, but we shared it; it was a good sadness, in a way. A silly fantasy crept into my brain, like a tempting little devil. How good would it be to lie naked in bed with this woman, cocooned in the dark, so that the vision sense was switched off, leaving just touch and sound, with sublime music like this lapping against our single united consciousness?

I imagined it. Drifting off to sleep . . .

'Paddy?'

I was jolted out of my reverie. Or perhaps I'd actually nodded off. She was grinning at me. 'My, you were off with the fairies then!'

I smiled too, sheepishly. 'Sorry, were you saying something?'

'Just how nice it is to listen to music with someone who loves it as much as you. And commenting on our Russian friend. Saying what a tortured soul he was, and how it so comes across in his later music.'

'Yes, it does, doesn't it? I stretched. 'Right. Is it time for more coffee, do you think?'

'Sounds good to me,' she said, unwinding her legs, 'But you sit still. I'll make it.'

Friday evening came. I decided to get the car from the lock-up garage where I kept it for the visit to Benny and Esther. It was a fair distance to Bushey Heath and would be quite a tortuous journey by public transport. Besides, like a spotty teenager, I found myself wanting to impress Leah. My vehicle was only a mundane, entry-level, three-year-old Ford Focus now, but chauffeuring her there would be cooler than going by bus or train.

Leah had not worn her new outfit again in order to keep it clean for her evening out. She'd taken her bath as soon as we'd got home from our respective money earning, and spent time crouched in front of the heater again getting it dry. She wore no makeup (but then that had hardly been a priority for her recently and she probably hadn't got any) and her face looked scrubbed-clean and glowing. It might have been my imagination, but she looked a little less gaunt, both facially and generally, too.

We were there, ringing the bell on my friends' front door, at just before eight. Leah stood nervously beside me, looking as though she didn't know what to do with her empty hands. She had no sort of bag that she could have brought, anyway. I glanced at her and our eyes met.

'All right?' I asked.

Her hand came up to clasp my bicep. It felt very nice. 'Mm; a bit nervous. Do I look okay?'

I bit back the urge to tell her she looked wonderful; modified it to, 'Very nice. You'll be fine. They're lovely people.'

Of course I'd told her about Benny and Esther's backgrounds and their deliverances from probable death. That they were Jews, albeit naturalized British now; Benny particularly. She'd found that fascinating and, as she'd put it, 'kinda romantic in a way, like they were characters from an old black-and-white movie or something', and remarked that she and Benjamin probably had a special affinity then one way and another. I'd agreed, having thought the same thing.

The door opened and Esther stood there, flowery pinafore over sapphire-blue dress, friendly welcoming smile immediately in place. Her eyes quickly flitted from me to Leah, who dropped her hand from my arm.

'Hello Esther.'

'Paddy; lovely to see you!' She beamed at Leah again. 'Hello, er . . .'

'Esther, this is my friend Leah.' I completed the formality. 'Leah

Esther.' The women said hi and hello to each other.

Esther's eyes returned to mine. There was surprise, the obvious question in them and a slight, amused curl of the lip. She would give me a grilling at the first opportunity we were alone together, I knew she would. She stepped aside to let us enter; closed the door behind us against the sunny late-July evening sky. 'Come through,' she said, unnecessarily, leading the way into the sitting room. Benny arose slowly, politely, from his armchair to greet us, a smile on his face too. I felt a slight stab of shock. He looked pale and tired, markedly more so than three weeks previously.

I repeated the introductions. Benny shook Leah's hand in gentlemanly fashion, saying with impeccable politeness, 'Very pleased to meet you,' before sinking gratefully back into his armchair. Leah murmured 'And you too, Mr Walters. Paddy's been telling me all about you.'

Benny smiled tiredly. 'That's why my ears have been burning! And please, it's Benny.'

Esther hovered. 'Well, sit down everyone. It's nearly ready.' It certainly smelled as though it was, judging by the wonderful smells of roast beef drifting through from the kitchen. I sank onto the Chesterfield sofa. Leah, gratifyingly, sat down beside me, our shoulders almost touching.

'Would you like an aperitif; a sherry or something, while you wait?' Esther asked. She looked at Leah. 'Or a beer, perhaps, for you, my dear? I'm not very *au fait* with what you young people drink nowadays, I'm afraid.' Esther was apparently taking over drinks duties from Benny.

I said yes please and Leah echoed me, possibly out of politeness too. 'No, sherry's fine, thank you . . . Esther.'

Esther smiled benevolently and fetched a bottle and three lead crystal glasses from the Welsh dresser on the wall by the door, plonking them on the coffee table. 'You be mother, will you, Paddy? I'll go and dish up.' She scurried away in the direction of the cooking odours.

I poured the drinks. We clinked glasses, toasting no one in particular.

Leah took a tiny, slightly apprehensive sip of hers. We each waited, smiling, for someone to initiate small talk. After a slightly strained silence began to threaten awkwardness I thought I'd better take the initiative.

'Er, did Esther tell you, Benny? Leah is a flautist.'

He looked at her, his face showing a flicker of animation for the first time. 'Oh, yes; she did. I'm sorry; I'd forgotten. What sort of things do you play?'

Leah shifted awkwardly. 'Well, anything really. I trained in classical flute though. And piano.'

'Oh? Are you with an orchestra, or an ensemble?'

'Er, no.' Her voice faltered. 'Not at the moment. . . .'

I silently cursed myself again. *Eejit, blundering in! You might have known this would happen!* I attempted rescue. 'Leah's American. She trained at Juilliard. She'll be returning there soon. To the US, I mean, not Juilliard.'

Now Benny was *very* interested. 'Did you, by God? That's very impressive!'

Leah began to speak 'Well, I don't know about that – '

I cut across her. She'd get into her usual silly self-deprecation if she wasn't checked. 'Yes, that's what I thought. And she's actually very good, in my opinion.'

'And so you haven't found a position yet? Are you over here on holiday, or taking a sabbatical, then?'

I could sense Leah blushing beside me

'Er . . .'

The poor girl was really embarrassed. I grasped for another escape route for her. 'Erm, well . . .'

But then we were saved by the bell as Esther reappeared to tell us that supper was served in the dining room.

Chapter 20

Esther's dinner turned out to be wonderful, as usual. She didn't do exotic foreign cuisine, just simple, superbly cooked traditional British fare, which was pretty much the same as traditional Irish in most ways. Her roast, followed by apple crumble and custard, must have been designed to undermine my efforts at temperate eating, I thought, wryly. Leah tucked in to it too, clearly with relish. The two of us came back for seconds to finish off the pudding. The only bow to sophistication was the accompanying bottle of Burgundy, which I managed to discipline myself to just one glass of, as I'd already had sherry and would be driving us home later.

Esther served coffee back in the sitting room. She and Benny had made typical polite conversation of the just-getting-to-know-you variety during the meal but Esther was clearly dying to know more – including whether we were some type of item. Esther, bless her, knew I'd been through the emotional wringer over the last twelve months and in her motherly way treated my mental wellbeing as very much her own concern. Rather than risk another faux pas I decided to keep my mouth shut and leave it to Leah to tell as little or as much about her business in response to Esther's friendly inquisitiveness as she wanted to. The degree of her divulgence was entirely up to her, after all.

Leah told our hosts about her Jewish background and her entrepreneurial father with his plans to conquer the world. They made polite noises of interest although it was fairly plain that they regarded her cultural background and experience as wholly different from theirs. As of course it was. She told them about coming here in twenty-eleven as a hopeful young bride with her big-shot husband, and about her later divorce. But she said nothing about her wild rock-musician fella or the circumstances leading to her homelessness. Perhaps she was embarrassed about relating that part of her story. I didn't blame her if she was, although my kind friends would have fully understood. But she left it that now, with her divorce finalized, she saw no point, no future in staying in Britain and would be returning to America in a few weeks' time. There was nothing about how she, a young American musician, and I, a world-weary old newspaper hack, had met, and what sort of relationship we had, if any.

I stole occasional glances at Esther. The look on her face when she sensed I was looking and returned it made it plain that she knew she wasn't getting the whole story. And that she was intrigued. I tried a diversionary tactic, asking Benny how his season was going; what pieces the orchestra had been playing; what plans there were for after the season finished. Where was the next tour going to? Esther gave me an if-looks-could-kill stare, as if I'd put my foot in it again. Benjamin said that in all probability he would be retiring at the end of the season, adding jocularly that it was due to instructions from on high.

It took me a few seconds to realize that he was talking about Esther, not God. Well, she had a point. He must be getting into the second half of his seventies, and he did look tired. He surely didn't need to keep on working for financial reasons? With whatever private pension he'd made provision for added to the state pension (was he taking it yet?) they'd surely be reasonably comfortable.

Esther recharged our coffee cups and, as Benjamin's work seemed to be a slightly touchy subject with her, I changed the topic again to some of the stories I'd written recently (which she'd read; she'd been a *Clarion* reader for years, she'd once told me). I said nothing about the plan to tell Leah's story though.

After coffee we divided along gender lines as Leah insisted on helping Esther clear away and load the dishwasher, in spite of her insistence that she should, as guest, stay with Benny and me. But I could hear as I chatted to Benny with one of my ears cocked in the direction of the kitchen that they were having a fine old conversation. I found this strangely pleasing, as if my surrogate mother was somehow conferring approval on a girlfriend, which really wasn't the situation at all.

The women rejoined us. Benny said, 'Before you sit down, Essie, will you get my flute, please?'

Esther walked through into the dining room and returned with a worn leather-covered instrument case; placed it on Benjamin's lap. He undid the clasp, opened it and took out his pride and joy, assembled and offered it to Leah. 'Have you seen an instrument like this before, Leah?'

Leah sat forward beside me, instantly fascinated. She took it gingerly, as if it might be some fragile artifact. 'Ooh; an antique, is it?'

Benjamin smiled. 'Yes, well partially, anyway. It's a Rudall Carte, made in eighteen ninety-two by Moujard.'

'Really? It's beautiful!' Leah was agog.

'Mm, isn't it? Well some of the parts are original, at least. The keys are. They're silver. It was rebuilt with a new cocus wood body in nineteen-thirty, to modern pitch.'

'Wow! Well that's still seriously old.' Leah turned it this way and that, examining it from every angle. 'How long have you had it?'

'Fifty-eight years, now. Most of my career. I never wanted another.'

'I should think not, Benny; it's just . . . *fabulous!*'

'Yes, it is. And it has a very fine provenance.'

'How do you mean?'

'It was given to me – well, part-given; my father part-bought it to jointly give to me – by Benjamin Britten, no less.'

'Really? That's just amazing! Did you know him then?'

Benjamin smiled nostalgically. 'Yes. We lived near him in Suffolk. In Snape. My father and he were good friends, because Dad was a bit of a musician too. Clarinet, although not classical, and he was never more than a good amateur. Anyway, Benjamin Britten seemed to think I had some promise as a teenager, and he had no children to leave the flute to, being gay, so he gave it to me and Dad paid him some of the value of it. I really was a most extraordinarily fortunate young man.'

Leah was entranced. 'That's just *incredible*. (I smiled; she was in serious danger of running out of superlatives.) What a *wonderful* gift!

And what a man to have as a mentor!'

'Yes, isn't it? It has a beautiful tone. Wonderfully mellow. It's been a very good friend to me. And yes; I was blessed to have known Benjamin Britten. He was a fine composer and a very nice man.'

'Yes, what an honour to have known a famous composer like that, never mind being given this beautiful thing!'

'Indeed. In fact it was a piece of his music that started my love of the flute, really. Do you know his Sea Interludes, the first one, from *Peter Grimes*?'

Leah beamed. 'Do I know it? I learned it at music school! It was one of the first things we did. The allusion to seagulls and everything!'

'Really?' Benjamin was animated too. His eyes shone. 'Yes, it was hearing that on an old gramophone record that made me want to switch from piano.'

'You began with piano as well? Another co-incidence! And both of us Jewish too!'

I glanced sideways at Leah. Her face was flushed with excitement.

'Would you like to try the flute out?' Benjamin asked.

'Oh, I really couldn't . . .'

'Yes you could! Can you play that Interlude without music? Did you commit it to memory?'

'Leah knows a lot of pieces by heart,' I interjected, feeling oddly proud of the fact and slightly proprietorial.

She said, 'Well, I think I remember it. The flute part isn't all that long of course.'

'Give us a little recital then,' I encouraged. 'Go on!'

'Well, all right . . .'

She placed her fingers, lifted the instrument to her lower lip and experimentally played a scale. The sound was a little hesitant, but then it was probably very different from the instrument she was used to. Benny watched patiently. But then confidence came as she became accustomed to the keys and the body's pitch and timbre. Benny was right; it really did make a gorgeous sound, or so it seemed to my uneducated ear, at least.

Leah finished tuning, waggled her fingers in that endearing way she had, took a deep composing-herself breath and began. I'd heard the piece although it wasn't in the instant-recall department of my brain, but as the atmospheric, haunting melody came, I remembered it. It was so, so evocative of a wild Suffolk beach. Leah made one or two mistakes, but then she perhaps didn't carry it note-for-note in memory, quite apart from probably being nervous and self-conscious, playing in front of a professional.

She petered out. 'That's all I remember of it, without having the music, I'm afraid. Sorry, that wasn't very good, I know. And it misses a lot without the harp part, I think. We used to include that too at Juilliard; playing it like a duet.'

Benjamin smiled. 'Yes, it's a necessary component of the orchestration, really. But that was nice, Leah. You've got very good articulation. Don't worry about fluffing it a little; it's not an audition! Will you play something else for us?'

'Oh, thank you,' Leah said, blushing a little. 'Er, yes, if you'd like me to.'

'What about the Pavane,' I suggested. 'The Fauré one?'

'Yes, okay.' She raised the beautiful dark-wood instrument and out came the exquisite sound again, now measured and stately, in formal dance-time. And this time, more confident now, she made no mistakes. Benjamin closed his eyes and listened, the smile still playing on his lips. She played it right through. Waited for Benny's reaction. There was a lengthy pause; I began to think he'd nodded off. But then his eyes opened and he clapped languidly a few times. 'Bravo! That was quite charming!'

'Yes,' Esther agreed, 'Absolutely lovely.'

'She's very good, Benny, don't you think?' I said, like some doting parent, careless of Leah's embarrassment.

'Yes,' Benjamin agreed, looking Leah directly in the eye, 'You certainly are.'

'Thank you; that's very kind,' Leah said, still pink-faced. She looked radiantly happy.

There was no stopping the two of them now. They began a lengthy animated conversation about flute playing, comparing notes and exchanging experience: hers limited by youth of course and his vast from a lifetime of playing; like student and mentor. Benjamin's face was alive. He talked of music from the flute repertoire that Leah had never heard of and of course I hadn't. She listed to him, utterly rapt. Esther and I simply sat and listened to both of them. It would have seemed crass to impinge, to rudely invade their special world. Leah played some more pieces as Benjamin listened and smiled.

Ten o'clock came, according to the antique clock on the mantlepiece, and Esther rather pointedly suggested more coffee as a preliminary to our leaving, although I think that both of us would have happily stayed there all night. Benjamin was looking decidedly droopy now though; doubtless Esther wanted to get him to his bed before much longer. I took the hint and we were saying our goodnights by twenty-five to eleven. Benjamin didn't see us to the door. Esther said she hoped they might see Leah again before she returned to America. Leah suddenly looked sad and bit her lower lip and said yes, she hoped so too.

We drove home, through streets of London outside the car windows that looked far from ready for bed.

'Well,' I asked, 'Did you enjoy your evening out?'

I sensed her looking at me. 'Oh, yes! That was wonderful. What a lovely old couple they are! I haven't had such a nice time since . . . oh forever, really.' She stopped abruptly, as if afraid of having said too much. 'Well, for a very long time, certainly.'

'Good.' I wanted to follow on with, 'I'm really pleased for you,' but thought better of it. Instead I said, 'Yes; they're certainly very dear friends. Almost like the parents I never had.'

'Yes.' She sounded wistful. 'I know what you mean.'

'Mm.'

We were silent for a while, each of us probably considering that idea. Well I certainly was, anyway.

She spoke, puncturing the silence. 'It's kinda funny; I feel slightly guilty that I wasn't entirely honest with them.'

'How do you mean?'

'Well, I told only a carefully edited version of my life story.'

I chuckled. 'That's understandable. Anyway, you weren't actually dishonest. Well only by omission, anyway.'

'Mm; maybe.'

'It sounded as though you and Esther were having a good old chinwag in the kitchen though.'

Now she laughed too. 'Yes, she was certainly digging. Trying to find out if we had a thing going, I think. But I still held back. Embarrassed to admit too much, I suppose. I said that I was lodging with you, because she asked where I was living, which perhaps sent her imagination into overdrive a little!'

'Ha! So how did you explain that?'

'Vaguely. I just said I'd had an accommodation problem after the divorce came through and I'd had to leave Canary Wharf, and I got to know you through a mutual friend who worked on your paper. Yes, okay, that was a little porkie, but I had to say something!'

'You'll never go to Heaven now,' I joshed. 'But seriously; there's nothing you could tell them about your recent past that would shock them, any more than it did me, honestly. They're very understanding and enlightened people. I've certainly told all my troubles to dear old Esther. She's a complete confidante, like a Samaritan. Well, they both are. So if you feel you want to give them the full unexpurgated version, warts and all, you could. Or I'll tell Esther for you, if you like. She really won't think any the less of you. And you've got a fan in Benny, anyway.'

She sighed. 'Really? He said such very nice things about my playing. Like you do. It means so much.'

'Well I'm sure he meant them. Like I do.'

'Mm. Thanks, Paddy. It's very sweet of you. It means a lot.'

She lapsed into silence, as if hugging that precious knowledge to herself.

The following evening, while Leah was taking her bath, I rang Esther, mainly just to thank her for dinner. Predictably, she was dismissive.

'Oh, think nothing of it, Paddy. It was our pleasure. It was most enjoyable. And I do like your young lady. A definite improvement on your last woman, if I might be so bold.'

'Esther, she isn't my "young lady"!'

A wicked chuckle. 'Yes, well, howsoever you want to define her. She did strike me as being very fond of you when we were girl-talking in the kitchen though.'

Ridiculously, I felt myself blushing slightly, even though we weren't speaking face-to-face.

A pause. 'Oh; is she there with you now, within earshot? Should we be discussing her?'

'No, she's in the bath.'

'How do you know that, you rascal?'

'Er, I mean she's in the bathroom, doing something or other. I'm not her keeper!'

'Yes, right. And Benny was very impressed by her playing. He thinks she's very talented. You can tell her that if you like.'

'Yes, I will. That's quite an accolade if Benny thinks so.'

I paused. 'Erm, actually, Esther, Leah feels a tiny bit guilty about not being entirely straight with you last night – although she has understandable reasons for doing so.'

'Ooh, what's this; has she been a bit of a naughty girl?'

'No!' I lowered my voice, deleting the outrage. 'I mean no. Not at all. Just badly used and very unlucky, that's all.'

'Mm. Should you be the one spilling the beans about her, Paddy?'

'It's all right. I have her blessing to. She'd be a bit embarrassed telling you some of the things.'

The teasing tone had left Esther's voice. 'All right. You tell me then.'

So I did. I told Esther about what a bastard her husband had been, and what poor role-models her parents seemed to be. I told about her rebound-fling with her wild rock star fella and the tragic end of the affair. Esther listened without interrupting as I related Leah's rapid slide down the social ladder to miserable bottom-end renting; her finding insufficient work to afford decent accommodation; her sleeping on her friends' sofa and her final fall to absolute rock-bottom: the London streets.

I told Esther about our co-incidental first meeting in North Wales. About encountering her again in the street just because I'd decided to walk to work. About feeling sorry for her that first time in the rain and how one thing impulsively lead to another. And about telling her story in the paper, which would enable her to return to America. Although I didn't disclose my mixed feelings about that.

I finished Leah's sad tale. There was silence on the other end as Esther digested it all. Finally she spoke. 'Well, that's a sorry story and no mistake. Poor girl! It's such a shame she hasn't been able to find enough suitable work, or work in any sphere of music, for that matter. Then she wouldn't have found herself homeless, would she?'

'No, that's right. But London's such a terrible place for housing; the wickedly high cost of it, for people in the bottom stratum. Perhaps in some ways it's not quite so bad for those on housing benefit, because at least they get their rent paid, although it's a shocking indictment of society, especially in London, that people on low wages can't afford to live here except by subsidy from benefits.'

'Yes indeed,' Esther agreed. 'Of course back in the old days, before the nineteen-eighty Housing Act, there were rent controls. But now landlords can charge just whatever they feel like and because there's such a chronic shortage of housing, it's a seller's market, so to speak. It's all wrong, in my opinion.'

'I quite agree, Esther. Perhaps slapping on controls wouldn't work now, because they'd simply drive a lot of landlords out of the market, making the shortage of renting property even worse. It seems to me the only real answer is for local authorities and housing associations to build far more houses to rent at affordable rates. Reducing demand would tilt the balance back in favour of tenants a bit. And look at all the employment that would create, apart from anything else.'

'Yes, that's right. Honestly, Paddy, those of us who are fortunate to be comparatively affluent have no idea what it must be like at the bottom of the heap, have we?'

'No, we certainly haven't. Although I suppose I'm more aware of the problem than some, being a journo on a liberal paper. We run stories on the topic quite often. Well, that's what made me think of telling Leah's story, really, apart from the fact that it helps her in practical terms. It's certainly topical, and hers has a certain extra dimension of human interest.'

Esther chuckled.

'What?'

'Listen to yourself, Paddy! It has extra "human interest" because you've let yourself get involved. What about journalistic distance and objectivity?'

'No I haven't! She's just my lodger. I offered her a roof over her head because I'd got the spare accommodation. Unfortunately. I'm just helping her out and shining a light on an important social issue at the same time, that's all!'

Another chuckle. 'Yes, all right, you soft-hearted Irishman. I'll leave you to your little crusade. But good luck with it. And . . .' She trailed off.

'And what?'

'Well, young Leah couldn't have found a nicer person to land on her feet with.'

'Mm. Well I was just helping. To change the subject; I thought Benn looked very tired last night. Although he perked up when the two of them started talking music. Is he alright? Looks as though he might be sickening for something.'

Her tone changed. 'Yes, I've been thinking that for some time. The trouble is; he won't go to the doctor. Typical man! So I've made an appointment for him, for tomorrow. And I've made him promise to retire at the end of the season, as he told you. It's only a few weeks away now. The orchestra will just have to find another first flute, that's all.'

'Yes, quite right too, Esther. Just because you see all these ancient actor types going on and on until they drop, as if they couldn't easily afford to retire, that's no reason for Benny to think he should.'

Esther chuckled again, but there was no mirth in it this time. 'Well I wish you'd have a word with him about slowing down, dear. Perhaps he'd listen to you.'

I was interrupted by the appearance of Leah, wearing her towel turban, new jeans and skinny jumper.

'Yes, I will, next time we talk, Esther. I'll just bring it up casually, so he doesn't think we're ganging up on him. Ah; the subject of our conversation has just arrived.'

I offered the receiver to her; mouthed 'Want a word?'

She grinned, nodded, took it from me and settled on the sofa, bare feet up on the cushions.

'Hi Esther'

. . .

'Loved it too. Thanks very much again.'

. . .

'Yes; it's beautiful. I'm very envious.'

. . .

'Yes, I'm glad he's told you. All a bit pathetic really, isn't it?'

. . .

'Well thanks for being so understanding. Paddy said you would be.'

. . .

She looked at me, her eyes glistening a little. 'Yes, I'm thinking that too.'

Chapter 21: September

We sat close together, shoulders pleasantly rubbing, at the small dining table. We'd spent two evenings like this, jointly writing my homelessness piece for the paper; her supplying information, I typing into my laptop. This second session was the refining part: Leah going over the content again, adding or subtracting personal information; I polishing my prose.

I typed the final revised sentence. We studied our end result. 'Okay then? Happy with that?'

She smiled, although it was one of her sad sort. 'Yes, I think so. That tells it how it happened, pretty well. It's a rather pathetic story though. I'm glad you're calling me "Lucy", I must admit.' It's not a story I particularly want to claim credit for.'

'Yes, well, don't be hard on yourself. It's not as if you were ridiculously stupid, or anything. It was just the way things panned out. It could have happened to anyone.'

She stretched her new-smelling bottle-green shirted arms (she'd had another session of retail therapy yesterday) above her head, the one nearest to me falling to rest across the back of my chair. 'Mm; it's sweet of you to say that, Paddy. I suppose, five years from now, my London interlude will just be a bad, embarrassing memory.'

'Yeah; you'll be famous by then. This will all be in the dustbin of your history. Sorry, "trashcan".'

Another wry smile. 'Yes, I suppose so. Not sure about the "famous" bit though.'

'Well Benny thinks you're pretty good. And I'm sure he's not saying it just because we're friends. He knows talent when he sees it.'

'Mm. Well anyway, it hasn't been a complete unmitigated disaster this last four years. The last few weeks have been . . . well, they've mad up for some of the other crap. I've met some really nice people, just on the point of going back.'

'Good! I hope you'll stay in touch.' I wondered if my remark sounded as wistful as I felt.

She looked at me, twisting her neck right around to face me full-on, her hand shifting onto my shoulder. 'Yes, of course I will! That goes without saying!'

'Promise?' The silly teenager-plea slipped out before I could hold it back.

'Only if you promise to too!'

'Right,' I said, trying to sound brighter than I felt. 'I do. It's a deal.'

There was a small but undeniable lump forming in my throat. I banished it. It was stupid.

'Right; I'll send this now and the piece will be in the paper at the weekend.' I went into email, called up the *Clarion*'s account, wrote a heading, attached the file and hit Send.

'There,' I said, 'Done. You should get the fee next week. It can be in cash if you prefer; I don't know whether you've still got a British bank account. Then you can buy your ticket.'

'Yeah,' she said, not sounding overly-enthusiastic. 'Cash would be best, I suppose. I haven't used a bank account since I got divorced. Well, since I drained the settlement funds before the last move to the streets, at least. I want to close it down anyway, if it hasn't already lapsed due to non-use, or something.'

'Okay; I'll tell Ken that.' An awkward, almost accusatory silence fell, although there was actually no call for accusation, on either part. She seemed to be waiting for me to speak first.

I quipped, 'You'd probably better high-tail it back to the States pretty soon now, anyway, before the British Border Agency realizes you've no longer got a valid visa and kicks you out!' But my pathetic joke sounded distinctly flat.

Presumably she found it so too, because she certainly didn't smile. 'Yeah; I suppose so.'

I ploughed on. 'So where will you go, if you don't want to crawl back to your parents? You don't want to end up sleeping on the streets of New York. Sure I'd be very cross if I thought you were going to be doing that.'

Leah sighed heavily. I was acutely conscious that she hadn't moved her hand from my shoulder. 'Oh, I've got friends over there. Like Judy. We were at Juilliard together. I'm sure she'd let me sleep in her spare bedroom, or even her couch if it isn't spare any more. Just until I find some work and get myself an apartment. Don't worry about me. I'll never sink as low as I was recently.'

'No,' I said, 'I'm sure you won't.'

'Anyway,' she said, determinedly brightening up. 'We haven't had any music tonight yet. What shall I play for you?'

'Anything you like,' I said, a little sulkily, feeling slightly, irrationally peeved at her cheerfulness. It seemed a bit of an affront to my childish despondency.

She removed her hand and pulled her chair back; got up. 'Okay. I think you've heard all my repertoire now, so I'll have to repeat myself. Shall we go back to the beginning? I'll play you what I played that first night you brought me back here, doing your damsel-rescuing thing. That seems ages ago now, doesn't it?'

I forced a smile. 'Yes, it does. It's only, what, seven, eight weeks though.'

'God; is it really only that? It seems much longer.'

'Yeah. Do you remember what it was you played then?'

She grinned. 'Oh, yes! It's engraved on my memory. First I played the Martinu flute concerto, the number one, then a Bach sonata. Then there was some Schubert and some Vivaldi, I seem to remember. And I played some pop stuff too.'

'You've got a good memory. Much better than mine.'

Her grin vanished. 'Yes, well, memories of some events in life just kinda stay with you, you know.' She paused. 'Like when people show great kindness.'

'Well, anyone would have done the same.'

She looked down at me, steadily. 'No, Paddy. Anyone wouldn't. Believe me. There are some uncaring bastards in the world, as I've found to my cost. You've no idea how much I've appreciated your kindness, these last few weeks. And introducing me to your lovely friends Esther and Benny. I'll never forget it. Never.'

Her bottom lip began to quiver. She looked as though she might burst into tears. Things might become emotional and embarrassing and I wasn't altogether sure how well I might handle that. I changed the subject. 'It was nothing, really. Which reminds me, talking about memory, and Benny. I'd forgotten; I must ring Esther; see how he got on about his test results. They were waiting to hear about them.'

'Oh yes, do that! Let's hope it isn't what they fear it might be.'

'Right. I'd better do it now, before it gets any later. They might be wanting to get to bed.'

'Yes, do. We can have some music later. Shall I make some coffee?'

'Yes, lovely,' I said.

It was some time before Esther picked up. I was glad it was her doing it. Had Benny done so, it might have been an awkward conversation. I'm not good at delicate situations like this, being a typical blundering not-knowing-what-to-say male. Her voice sounded flat, tired. 'Hello, Paddy. You just caught me as I was going to bed.'

'Hello Esther. Ah, I'm glad I didn't get you out of it. Sorry to phone so late.'

'That's all right, dear.'

'Erm, is Benny within earshot?'

'No, he's already gone up. That's why I'm going to bed too. I don't like him lying there alone, with his thoughts. I can be a little comfort if I'm there with him, hopefully.'

The tone of her voice told me all I needed to know. But I still had to ask the question. 'We were just wondering if he'd had his test results through.'

I could almost hear her sigh. 'Yes, we went back to the hospital on Monday. It's not good, I'm afraid. The oncologist confirmed his provisional diagnosis. It *is* leukaemia. Acute myeloid.'

A cold hand gripped my heart. 'Oh no! Oh Esther. I'm so sorry.'

Silence. I began to think that the line had disconnected. Then: 'Thank you, Paddy. Yes, well, we half-suspected it, really. Well I did, to be honest, although I've never said as much to Benny. You have to try and appear positive and encouraging, don't you? After all, at his age, the probability of it being so would be pretty high, I should think. Perhaps he was thinking the same thing, but if so, he didn't say. I suppose we both shied away from saying the unsayable.'

I struggled for something sensible or sympathetic to say. 'Yes, I suppose so. Poor Benny though. Poor man.'

'Yes.'

'How is he? I mean . . . you know. How's he taking it?' I cursed myself as soon as I'd asked the inane question. *Well how do you think he's taking it, you eejit? How would you?*

'Oh, pretty well, as far as I can tell. But it's such an utterly private, inner thing after all, isn't it? The ultimate personal battle. People's thoughts are unknowable, really. Obviously. He's very quiet. I'm trying to take my cue from him. If he wants to talk, about anything, of course I'll listen. If he doesn't, well, I'll just be there. It's all you can do, isn't it?'

'Yes, it is, love.'

'Anyway, the oncologist is recommending chemotherapy. So we aren't giving up just yet. He's going to start inductive treatment in a couple of weeks' time and we'll see how he gets on with it.'

'Oh, right. Well the consultant evidently thinks that's the way to go so that must be good, I should imagine.'

'Well, yes.' Esther sounded doubtful, as if she were humouring me in my clumsy positivity. 'Unfortunately it's metastacised to some extent. It's in his liver and also slightly in his spleen. I blame myself really. I should have made him go to the doctor before, when he first began to feel tired. But he's a typical man; it was the devil's own job to get him there. And now it may be too late.'

'Oh, don't say that, Esther. They may catch it before it spreads further. People do survive it more often these days than they used to.' I couldn't bring myself to use the c-word.

Esther was no fool though. She could see straight through my bumbling reassurance. She wound the conversation down to a finish. 'Yes, I expect you're right, Paddy. Nil desperandum and all that. Well, I must go up to Benny. Thanks for ringing. I'll tell him you rang. Oh, how's your young lady? Still with you or gone back to America yet?'

'Still here. Goes in a few days time. My piece about her is in the paper next Sunday.'

'Good! I'll look forward to reading it. Well wish her luck from us, when she goes, won't you?'

'Yes I will, Esther,' I said, my throat constricting a little again. Goodnight then; I hope it goes well for Benny. Give him my love. Speak again soon.'

'Goodnight Paddy,' Esther said sadly, her voice faltering a little. 'Yes I will. Thank you.'

Leah had returned with the coffee, placing my mug on the coffee table and curling herself onto the sofa.

'Did you get the gist of that?' I asked.

'Yes. Not good, by the sound of things.'

'I heaved a long sigh. My eyes were smarting. 'No, not good at all. It's spread, to his liver. So I don't think the prognosis is good. Poor bugger.'

'Oh, poor Benny.'

'Yeah.'

I don't know what triggered the reaction, although I was already feeling a bit down before the phone call, but suddenly hot salty tears erupted, streaming down my cheeks and, soaking into my beard, I cupped my hands to my face, embarrassed by my sorrow.

'Oh, Paddy!'

She got up, placed her mug on the table; came across and sat on my lap. A hand burrowed behind my shoulders and the other cupped the back of my head, pulling my face into her breast, holding it there as I sobbed and shook. 'Come on, love. Just let it all out. It's okay. It's okay.'

My hands went around her, one grasping a shoulder blade of her thin back, the other the nape of her slender neck, clinging desperately; craving comfort. She rocked me, soothing, repeating, 'Okay. Okay.'

We stayed like that for a long time, until I was spent. I became aware that the top of my head was wet. She must have been weeping too, in sympathy.

'Come on,' she said, her voice a little croaky, 'let's move to the couch. This is getting uncomfortable.'

She pulled away from me, shiny-eyed. Her shirt was wet, green-black now where my face had been. 'Jaysus', I said. 'Sorry about that. You're wet through!'

'It's okay; don't worry about it. It's only tears.' Leah gave a fragile little laugh. 'Your pate's all wet too. I'm just as lachrymose!'

She got off me and returned to the sofa. I followed, after picking up the box of tissues from the shelving unit, sinking down with a hair' breadth of separation between us. I didn't fully trust myself to be any closer, much as I would have liked to have been. I blew my nose, hard and she did too. She laid a slender hand over one of my thick-hairy fingered ones. 'You really do think the world of those old folks, don' you?'

I sighed; snuffled. 'Yes, I do. They're like family. Like the parents never had. Well, my mammy was all right, I suppose. She did her best in a God-awful, poverty-stricken situation really. But I never got clos to her. She didn't allow it. None of us did, except perhaps my siste Sorcha, to some extent. She looked after her in her final few years. No; was upset when she died, of course, but it was mainly feeling sorry fc her rather than any feeling of loss. The poor old girl.'

Leah patted my hand absent-mindedly. 'Yes, I suppose that's how regard my mom. As someone to be pitied rather than actually like Except that she didn't have anything like as bad a time as your mor obviously. Just had to suffer a philandering husband. And like you, I've little time for my dad, although he gave me everything I wanted materially.'

'Yeah. We have that in common, I suppose. But Esther and Benny; I warmed to them the first time I met them. They're just so thoroughly *nice.* And good-hearted and generous of spirit. So are their offspring: Sam and Ruth. I've met them a couple of times. Haven't met their grandchildren though, although one of them, Daisy, sounds like my sort of person: a bit of an idealist. Esther thinks she ought to be an investigative journalist, like her and me. She was telling me: a few weeks ago, soon after Daisy's baby was born, they were in a café and she got into a spectacular slanging match with some idiot about refugees, and nearly got them thrown out of the place. I would have loved to have been a fly on the wall that day.'

Leah smiled wanly. 'Yeah, she does sound like you. Another one trying to put the world to rights.'

'Well, I don't know about that. I try to expose some of its cruelties from time to time, that's all. It's my job. I did a piece about refugees last year, actually. Well, not the Middle East war refugees, but a gay chap trying to claim asylum in Britain from persecution in Uganda.'

'Mm.' Leah brought me back to the subject. 'Getting back to Benny; so what happens now then? He's going to have treatment, chemotherapy or whatever, is he?'

'Yes. But it doesn't look too hopeful, I don't think. But I suppose they have to do whatever they can.'

'Yes, true.'

I stretched forward to retrieve our coffee mugs; sipped at mine. It was almost cold. It seemed appropriate, somehow. It matched my dismal mood.

We looked at my homelessness piece on the online version of the *Clarion* on the following Sunday morning. Leah seemed curiously unbothered about seeing her story in virtual print – although I wasn't enthusiastic either, as its author. I felt completely uninterested. There was no picture of her as the article was anonymised; simply a stock library image of some homeless unfortunate (although it might have been a model) trussed up in a sleeping bag, huddled in a shop doorway.

'Well, there you are,' I said, grasping for something to say about it and finding only a weak joke, 'fame at last. Of a sort, anyway.'

She didn't smile. 'Yeah. Of a sort.'

'You should get the money through in a day or two. The paper's usually pretty good at paying the fees, I think.'

'Yeah. Right.' She really was morose.

'What are you going to do with yourself today?'

She pouted. 'Dunno, really.'

'We could go for a nice walk after lunch,' I offered. 'Or something really exciting, like food shopping.'

'No. I think I'll go and do some playing. It's what I'm supposed to do, after all.'

'Or you could play for me. At home in comfort. It's looking as though it might rain out there.'

She got up. 'No; then I won't make any money, will I?'

'You don't need to though, do you?'

'Yes I do, Paddy! You've only had eight pounds from me in the last four days!'

'That doesn't matter, not now . . .'

'Yes it does!' Her voice was like a whiplash; shocking in its vehemence. 'I'll see you later, okay?'

'Right. Okay . . .'

Two days later, at work, Janice from accounts placed a manila envelope on my desk. 'It's the fee for that woman you did your homelessness piece for.'

Something inside my brain, a tightly-coiled spring of tension, semi unraveled. 'What do you mean, "That woman"?' I snapped. 'She's a human being, for fuck's sake!'

Janice jumped back like a startled antelope, flushing vermillion. 'Oh, sorry, Paddy! *Do* excuse me!'

Leah was already home that evening. Lately, since having her own key so that she could come and go from the flat as she pleased, she was sometimes back before me, making a start on dinner preparation. It also meant that, no longer having to meet up with her, I could revert to old habits and linger late at my desk if I found myself engrossed in writing and didn't want to interrupt the literary flow. Although that didn't happen often, knowing that there was Leah's quiet companionship to go home to.

I took the envelope from my rucksack and presented it to her. She seemed unexcited again. 'Right. I'll go to the travel agents tomorrow and see about a ticket then.'

I could have suggested going online to check out flight possibilities. But I didn't want to spend one of our few remaining evenings doing that. Instead I just said, lamely, 'Yes, right-oh then.'

She contemplated the wad of fifty-pound notes; peeled three of them off and handed them to me. 'I owe you this though, for those loans I've had.'

Which was the case; she'd had that first fifty pounds for the buying of an outfit for the dinner party, then another, at my insistence, to enlarge her wardrobe beyond one pair of jeans and a top. And then another a few days ago to buy things for her trip, like luggage and a cheap mobile phone, with which to re-enter the modern world of telecommunication when she was back stateside.

I pushed it back at her. 'No, you keep it for now. You don't know how much the ticket will be, at this time of the year. They might still be holiday-season prices. And there might be one or two more things you need that you haven't thought of. If there's still any left over after you've bought everything, you can give me that, okay?'

She didn't argue or stand on dignity; just said, listlessly, not meeting my eyes, 'Yes, okay then. Thanks.'

The following evening I was back home first. It was another three quarters of an hour before Leah showed. She still looked dejected as she pulled her flute out of her waistband, gifting the usual exquisite glimpse of flesh again, and dropped it carelessly onto the sofa.

'Did you get your ticket then?' I asked.

She sighed, as if carrying the entire troubles of the world upon her thin shoulders. 'Yeah. Heathrow to John F. Kennedy. Eight forty-five a.m. the day after tomorrow. There was just one seat left on the flight. I was lucky.'

She didn't look as though she felt lucky.

'Right, I said. I'll drive you to Heathrow. Make sure you don't miss the flight.'

'Oh, you don't have to do that . . .'

'Yes I do!' I said, a little too forcefully. 'Yes, I do.'

'Okay then. Thanks, Paddy.' She still would not meet my eyes.

'Well,' I said, struggling for cheerfulness, 'we'll have a nice meal tomorrow night. To celebrate your return to the normal world! I'll take you out somewhere.'

Then she did look at me, suddenly, her eyes wide in alarm. 'No! No, I don't want to go out. Please. Let's just have a last night here together, in your lovely home. That's all I want. Please.'

'Well only if you promise to play for me,' I quipped, feeling no remotely like quipping.

Her eyes moistened. 'Okay. It's a deal.'

I carried on preparing the meal, leaving her to go for her bath. It was difficult to concentrate though. I simply went through the motions entirely on autopilot. *The day after tomorrow! Holy Mother; a indecently soon as that?* I felt an odd queasiness starting; the lump in the throat again. I tried to pull myself together. *Jaysus, man, get a grip!*

It was probably the worst meal I've ever cooked, although Leah fragrant with essences of shampoo and bath oil and femininity, bu looking empty-eyed, seemed not to notice. As she'd done every evenin since my piece had appeared in the paper, she toyed with her foo moving it listlessly around the plate.

Afterwards, after clearing away, washing up and making coffee, she didn't offer to play. I didn't press her. I didn't really feel in the mood for it either. I switched the television on and we sat together on the sofa listlessly watching some documentary or other, although I struggle to remember what it was now. She was wearing the green shirt again (not that she still had much of a wardrobe, so it was that, the sweater or her old tops) and had carelessly forgotten to do up the last three buttons. When I glanced at her at one point as she leaned forward, it gaped. There was no cleavage to be seen but a glimpse of the soft white margin, the first three centimetres, of un-cupped breast curving beneath her shirt. I tried to ignore it.

The documentary finished. I switched channels for the ten o'clock news. And then half an hour later switched again for *Newsnight*. And then it finished too. By mutual agreement I switched off. Leah got up to make coffee, her shirt gaping again as she rose. She brought our refilled mugs and a packet of chocolate biscuits to the sofa and sank down again. I could think of nothing to talk about. Childishly, I didn't want to discuss her plans when she was back in America. She seemed lost in private thought too. We drank our coffee and munched biscuits in silence. I didn't restrict myself to the normal two. Neither did Leah.

'Well,' I said, as there seemed to be little prospect of conversation. 'I'm ready for my bed.'

She spoke at last, quietly but again without eye contact. 'Yes, I'm ready for it too.'

Dense eejit that I am, the penny didn't drop. Or I simply misheard her. She repeated, as if to make sure I'd understood. 'I'm ready for your bed too.'

She looked at me now, almost pleading.

I stared, now comprehending what she was saying. I wanted her desperately, the comfort of her, but couldn't risk it. I couldn't let her into my bed. If I did so, I would never let her go.

'No!' I said, my heart banging in my chest. 'No, for Christ's sake.

Leave me be. Please!'

She recoiled; looked stricken. 'Oh, Paddy! I've fucked up again. I'm so sorry!'

'No, that's all right,' I managed. 'Not your fault. I'll see you in the morning.'

Breakfast was an ordeal by embarrassment. She spoke hardly at all and I simply didn't know what to say. Perhaps sensing that our usual walk to work together, our last one, would be fraught, she announced that she was going in the other direction, westwards to The City, to get a few things for her journey. Relieved, I set off eastwards alone.

The day didn't improve. For all the use I was, it was a waste of time going in. My brain was in turmoil. Giving up on the article I was writing, I tried to apply it to thinking about food for the final supper. There was no inspiration forthcoming there either. I indolently settled on steak and went out and bought it and wine and some yogurt desserts at lunchtime, putting the meat in the office fridge to keep it chilled during the afternoon.

The prospect of the evening loomed like a threatening grey storm cloud. I found myself almost wishing that she'd left for good that morning. It would have been a sad but at least a clean, clinical break. This way, we were simply prolonging the agony. And what if she tried coming on to me again? I would probably, weakly, succumb a second time. Which would then make parting infinitely worse.

But she couldn't stay with me. We were ill-matched. She was a young woman with her life ahead of her. I was a middle-aged, hopelessly sentimental Irishman; a complete eejit with women, as I'd proved more than once in my chequered romantic career. Yes, last night I'd managed, suffering for it with a sleepless, tossing and turning aftermath, to be strong for both of us, but I didn't trust myself to be as disciplined a second time.

Five-thirty came but I lingered, reluctant to go home, deciding to take the bus rather than walk and have yet more time alone with my oppressive thoughts. It was a quarter past six when I fitted my key into the front door. Leah would probably be back by now. I resolved to be positive and cheerful on our last night, regardless of whatever mood she might be in. After all, I had the advantage of years; of greater maturity. I wasn't a silly teenager. It was up to me to be sensible for both our sakes.

I heard the noise as soon as I entered the hall, before I'd opened the flat door. The Tchaikovsky Sixth, the second movement, blaring at high volume. It was a good job Mirium upstairs worked late, or she'd certainly be down, complaining, and quite rightly. What the hell was Leah doing? A wall of decibels hit me as I walked into the sitting room. Annoyed, I quickly crossed to the sound system to lower the volume. Leah was nowhere to be seen. I walked back into the hall and towards the kitchen.

'Leah?'

She wasn't in the kitchen either. Or in her bedroom.

The bathroom door was wide open and she clearly wasn't in there.

That only left my bedroom, but why would she be in there? Its door was also ajar, not how I remembered leaving it. I poked my head through the doorway. She was in my bed, naked, propped semi-prone against pillows leaning vertical against the headboard, legs bent and splayed tenting the duvet that lapped against small dark nipples; her head lolling. A tumbler was held loosely askew in her left hand, dribbling contents onto the bed linen. In the crater of the duvet were a three-quarters empty, quarter bottle of vodka and a large bottle of Coca-Cola.

And two opened cartons of paracetamol and their mostly empty inner blister-packs.

I stared at her. 'Leah! What the hell are you doing?'

Chapter 22

And then the realisation hit me. 'Oh no! God! No! Oh fuck! Leah! No!' I stumbled into the bedroom, over her clothes in a disordered heap on the floor, crossing to the bed; lifted her chin, turning her face towards me. She regarded me, bleary-eyed. 'Hi, Paddy.'

'What have you done?' It was a ridiculous, inane question. It was starkly obvious.

She didn't speak; simply smiled a despairing, utterly desolate smile.

'How many have you taken?' I could see for myself though. I grabbed the two packs. One had all sixteen of its blisters burst and empty; there were eight or so remaining tablets in the other. Still she didn't speak.

'How many, for fuck's sake!?'

Finally she spoke; her voice thick and slurred. 'All of one pack and about half the other.'

'Jesus! Why?'

She didn't answer that. 'Will you get into bed with me? Hold me?'

'No, of course I won't!'

I grabbed the phone from the bedside table. Fumblingly dialed 999. It seemed an age before a calm female voice answered. 'Emergency, which service do you require?'

'Ambulance! Quickly!'

The voice said, calmly, 'Okay. Tell me what's happened, please.'

'My friend's attempted suicide. Overdosed. Hurry, please!'

The voice, unperturbed, said, 'Try and stay calm. On what; do you know?'

'Paracetamol!'

'Right, I see,' the calm voice said, her phrases punctuated by pauses. She was probably typing details into her computer. 'And the address is'

I gave it, being asked to repeat it as I stumbled over my words, and enduring another silence as she recorded it.

The voice came back on. 'Okay, sir. Ambulance is on its way. Now; do you know how many tablets he's taken?'

'It's a she.'

'Sorry, she. How many tablets?'

I did a frantic mental calculation. 'Er, about twenty-four, I think,' I said, my voice shaky. Shock was probably catching up with me.

'Right,' the voice said. 'She's conscious then?'

'Yes!' I said. 'And she's been drinking too. Vodka.' I could feel panic welling up again.

'Okay. And have you just discovered her then, is that it?'

'Yes! I've just got in from work. I've not been sitting here watching her popping pills, for Christ's sake!'

'No sir,' the voice said, soothing, infinitely patient. 'Of course not. Now give me your phone number, please, in case I need to phone you back, and then I'll ring off. The ambulance will be there very soon.'

And so she left me, tossing the bottles and pills angrily onto the floor, making Leah lie down and pulling the duvet over her to cover her pitiful nakedness as if keeping her warm would somehow help, lying down on top of the covers, embracing her, stroking her hair, telling her everything would be all right, it would, but terrified, not knowing actually whether it would, until twenty minutes later, the ambulance arrived with its blaring forewarning siren to disturb the early evening of my street.

The next twelve hours were almost anti-climactic, apart from her throwing up violently in the ambulance on the way to hospital (which was a good thing though, the watchful paramedic at her side assured me, as he held a bowl to catch her vomit containing two or three unbroken capsules). The doctors in A and E were efficient and almost annoyingly relaxed, it seemed to me, once they'd heard from the ambulance crew (who had questioned Leah) as to how long she had been swallowing the capsules for, which was about twenty minutes before I found her, although she had begun drinking to give herself Dutch courage for over an hour beforehand; and how many she'd swallowed. In their unflappable professional way they'd noted how many tablets were left in the packs. Satisfied that she wasn't critical, the staff ruled out brutal stomach pumping and fed a charcoal solution through a tube up her nose instead, as she screwed up her face in discomfort. That was to mop up as much of the paracetamol as possible and reduce absorption into the bloodstream, they told me calmly.

With Leah drip-attached and looking reasonably stabilized and comfortable en route to a ward, the casualty registrar, Dr Singh, a portly blue-turbaned Indian, took me aside. 'So, Mr Brennan, tell me again; you say you got home at around six-fifteen, and discovered Miss Weisman in the process of overdosing. And she says that she began about twenty minutes before then?'

'Yes. Well that probably figures,' I said miserably. 'When I got in there was a symphony playing on the stereo. She presumably put it on before she began to take the pills. And it was about halfway through the second movement. If that's what she did, it would have been about twenty minutes before I arrived.'

He nodded thoughtfully. 'I see. So then she would have begun swallowing pills at around six o'clock, possibly. Interesting. Almost as if she'd timed it for your imminent arrival home.'

'Well possibly. But I really don't know why she would have begun a suicide attempt knowing she was likely to be discovered.'

Singh smiled sympathetically, showing very white teeth below his thick black moustache. 'It could be cry-for-help-syndrome. It often is with suicides. Could the young lady be having emotional problems? But anyway, that's not my area of expertise. I can get one of our psychiatrists to have a look at that aspect of things. Knowing she probably began overdosing at around six o' clock gives us the beginning of a timeline. At ten o'clock I'll do some bloods to ascertain the amount of absorbed paracetamol and other levels. Then we'll know whether we need to use another intervention too: acetylcysteine. That's basically a antidote, if you will, that pretty well removes the risk of liver failure if given soon enough after ingestion.'

'Oh, I see.'

He continued, warming to his theme. 'Yes, that's the greatest danger with paracetamol poisoning. An overdose – and it doesn't even have to be all that great; it can be just as a result of exceeding safe dosage over a period – inevitably leads to that if untreated. People think that it's an easy, relatively painless way to commit suicide, just because the tablets are easy to obtain, but believe me, it isn't. It certainly isn't a case of drifting gently off into oblivion, as your friend has found. There are very few symptoms to show immediately after ingestion, so it was very fortunate that you caught Miss Weisman in the act, as it were. If you hadn't have done and she'd assumed that her attempt had failed and kept it secret, it would have been a few days before she began to feel seriously ill, by which time it would have been much more difficult to treat, if not impossible. If it's not caught in time, preferably very early, you're talking about either a liver transplant or a very painful death. So I think the prognosis here should be good, with no lasting damage.'

I breathed a long sigh of relief, feeling the familiar tightening in my throat again. 'Really? Thank God for that!'

'Indeed.' Doctor Singh smiled again. 'And thank fate, or whatever, that you intervened in time. But I think you must help her to address whatever emotional problems she has, if you can.'

'Yes, doctor,' said I grimly, 'I really must.'

Of course I stayed the rest of that evening, sitting by Leah's bedside, holding her limp, delicate hand. Her face looked ashen; her eyes empty. And judging by the way she frequently furrowed her brow, a hangover was probably kicking in. Although any more analgesic for a headache was the very last thing her body needed. We spoke little. I didn't castigate her for her silliness. She was paying for it enough now, in discomfort. I wanted to ask her why she'd done such a desperate thing, but this was neither the time nor place. There would be time enough for that when I got her home and could look after her.

At ten-thirty Doctor Singh appeared, with the results of the blood tests for which Leah had recently given samples. He rested one buttock on the edge of Leah's bed; smiled kindly down at her. He looked tired. I wondered how many hours he'd been on duty now. 'Well,' he said, 'the results show paracetamol on the median line of the graph, so that indicates that we should give you a course of NAC.'

'Of what?' I asked. He transferred his gaze to me. 'The antidote I told you about. N-acetylcysteine. Just to be on the safe side. He looked back at Leah. 'We'll give you an intravenous infusion now, another in four hours, then a final one four hours after that. Then we'll check the levels again. If you're below median then, you'll be able to go home tomorrow at some point. Provided you feel well enough, of course. And perhaps after having a little chat with our psychiatrist. All right?'

'Yes, okay,' Leah said, dully.

There was no point in my staying overnight at the hospital though, as Leah was in no danger, so after Doctor Singh had left us, I did too. She looked as though she didn't want me to go, judging by the way her eyes welled with tears when I got up from my bedside chair, took her hand again and bent to kiss the top of her head.

'You really did give me a fright there, you know,' I gently admonished.

She tilted her face up to me, tears now squeezing out onto pale cheeks. 'Yes, I know, Paddy. Fucked up yet again, didn't I? I couldn't even get topping myself right.'

'Shush,' I said, the thumb of my free hand rubbing away a tear. 'It's okay. We'll talk about it when you're back home.'

'Home?' she said tiredly.

'Yes, well . . . okay, I'll see you tomorrow, anyway. I'll ring to see what the situation is; whether they're going to discharge you. All right?'

'Yes, okay,' she said, in a tiny voice.

I telephoned Ken in the morning to say I couldn't make it into the office for a few days, but I'd work from home and deliver the planned pieces for the week all right, no problem. I didn't elaborate as to the reason. Remembering what Doctor Singh had said about the schedule of the antidote treatment, I left it until ten o'clock the next morning to ring. But Leah beat me to it and telephoned me at a quarter to. Her voice sounded a little stronger. Not happy, true, but a bit less shaky. She'd been seen by a junior doctor on Doctor Singh's team, been retested and the analgesic level was down to acceptable levels. And she'd had an audience with the psychiatrist, whom she'd assured she wouldn't contemplate such a thing again, and satisfied him that she would be discharged into my responsible care. So that was it. Could I come and collect her, please? And could I bring her some clothes? She'd arrived at hospital the previous evening clad only in an ambulance service blanket.

An hour and a half later, having disinterred the car from the lock-up garage to save her the dubious delights of travelling home on London public transport, she was sitting looking not a little sheepish on my sofa.

'Here you are then,' I murmured, the words sounding ridiculously inadequate.

'Yeah. Here I am. I was supposed to be winging my way back to the States today, wasn't I? I've wasted the airplane money now.' She smiled a bitter smile. 'Perhaps you can do another piece on me – "stupid pathetic American woman tries and fails in suicide attempt" or something, so I can earn some more.'

She looked on the point of tears. I sat down beside her, my arm going around her thin shoulder. 'Hey, it's okay. Don't talk like that. We'll work something out.' Although I couldn't for the life of me think what.

I changed the subject. 'How are you feeling now then?'

'How do you mean: physically?'

'Yes.'

She grimaced. 'Bloody awful. Head hurts like hell and so does my stomach.'

I tried a little levity. 'Sounds like a hangover. But then it probably is, judging by how much vodka you put away yesterday, apart from anything else. Well, a hangover-plus. Your poor system's really taken a battering, love.'

'Yeah. Too right.'

'Would you like anything to drink? A nice cup of tea perhaps? The standard British answer to all ills?'

She almost smiled. 'You're not British. Neither am I.'

'"Neither".' I corrected her pronunciation.

'"Let's call the whole thing off". Do you remember that?'

I gave her a squeeze. 'Of course! Llangollen; twenty-eleven. Engraved on my memory, so it is. Anyway, will I get you some tea, or something?'

'Mm; yes please. Nice and sweet. I'll give it a try, anyway.'

I got up and went to the kitchen to make a sweet milky tea for her and a coffee for myself. When I got back she'd kicked off her trainers (she still had no proper shoes) and was lying curled up, foetally. She looked so, so vulnerable, like a poorly child.

'Sit up a minute and drink your tea.'

She uncurled and sat. I handed her her mug, the one with fluff-ball cartoon chickens she always claimed as her own, and sat back down beside her. She tried a sip of tea, wrapping both hands around the mug. I watched her as she gazed at a point that might have been two feet away or equally ten thousand miles. Her expression was unreadable. She drank half of her tea and set the mug down. 'That's all I can manage, sorry.'

'That's okay. You've done well. Perhaps you'll manage a little something to eat later.'

'Mm; don't know about that.'

'Well, see how you feel.'

She twisted around and put her legs back up, lying down to face me, her head in my lap, one arm snaking around my waist,. Closed her eyes. I took a pull at the coffee I was holding, set the mug down and cupped her head with one hand, the other falling on her shoulder blade.

She sighed. 'Mm; this is nice. Even if I do feel lousy.'

'Are you tired? Did you sleep at all last night?'

'No, not a wink. I was thinking of what I'd done. Or tried to. And I had a splitting head. And besides, a doctor came in at some point in the middle of the night to put a second lot of that stuff into me.'

I shifted my hand to stroke her forehead. 'Poor you. Why don't you go and lie down?'

'I *am* lying down. Where I want to be.' She opened her eyes; looked up at me. 'Don't send me away, Paddy, please! Not again.'

'Okay, okay,' I said, throat choking once more, 'I'm not going to. Stay here then.'

She closed her eyes again as I continued the stroking. I said no more; she needed to sleep. Eventually she did drop off, her mouth falling ajar, and began to snore softly. I couldn't reach to retrieve my coffee mug, so I left it. I sat there for hours, nursing her, watching her, as the clock on the stereo announced one o'clock, then two, then three, then four.

She wasn't the only one who'd had a sleepless night. I'd not got back from the hospital until nearly midnight and then there was the bedroom to sort out: my rucksack to pick up from the floor where I'd roughly shrugged it off in urgency; the food and wine transferred to the fridge; the vodka and coke bottles taken into the kitchen and their remaining contents angrily poured away; the painkiller packs, even the one still containing pills, dealt with equally summarily. I didn't want any of it in the flat. I'd gone beyond hunger and simply undressed and crawled into bed and lain there, brain racing, thinking of Leah lying in a hospital bed, and before that for some inexplicable reason lying naked in this one, with the stereo belting out Tchaikovsky, surrendered totally to despair, trying to end her life.

But why?

I hadn't found an answer the previous night and I was still no wiser now. She would tell me when she was ready though. I was getting achy, risking cramp, sitting for so long trying not to disturb her and I needed the loo, apart from the fact that hunger was finally beginning to catch up. I glanced at the clock again. It said ten to six now and I hadn't eaten since breakfast time. I lifted her head as she murmured and twitched in her sleep and wriggled out from under her, laying her head carefully down again. But the action woke her. Her head lifted again and she addressed the sofa back, alarmed. 'Paddy?'

I was still perched on the edge of the sofa. I put a reassuring hand on her shoulder. 'It's okay. I'm still here.'

She turned onto her back and swung her head towards me and smiled. An inexpressible tenderness welled up from somewhere deep inside. I gently palmed the side of her face. 'You've been asleep for hours. Do you feel a bit better?'

Leah stretched a hand up to mine and clasped it, although not strongly. 'Mm, yes, I do now.'

'Still got a headache?'

'It's not so bad.'

'Do you fancy anything to eat now? Something not too demanding?'

'Yeah, I think so. Just a little something.'

'I did buy some steaks for our dinner last night, but events sort of intervened and they're still in the fridge. Would that be too much?'

'Yes, it would really. But you go ahead and have it yourself.'

'No, it's okay. I'll wait until we can both have it. What about some toast? Perhaps with scrambled egg. And I've got some wicked yogurt puddings that were supposed to be for last night. That's sort of invalid food, I think.'

She still had hold of my hand. She squeezed it, limply. 'That sound lovely.'

I got up. 'Right. Your wish is my command, Ma'am.'

So I made that for both of us. I would have felt guilty eating a big meal myself. We sat side by side on the sofa, eating from plates in our laps. It was the first time I'd seen her not attack food with gusto. Doubtless her stomach still felt fragile. She managed half of her eggs and toast before giving up. 'Sorry; that's all I can manage. Do you want the rest?'

I finished mine and then took her plate and did so, and the doing of that felt oddly intimate, like a sort of act of communion. I offered her a dessert, which she did manage. Then I made milky invalidy coffee, not too strong, and she was able to deal with that too without feeling nauseous. I cleared the crockery away and washed up. When I came back into the living room she was stretched out on the sofa again. I perched on the edge, regarding her. She gazed back at me, looking certainly better for having eaten something. Her expression was soft, although sad. 'I think it's time I told you about yesterday, Paddy,' she said, her eyes searching mine as if requesting permission to divulge.

'I know, don't I?' I said, slightly alarmed by her earnestness.

'No, not all of it. Or why.'

'Why?'

'Why I did that stupid thing.' Her bottom lip began to quiver.

I tousled her hair. 'Don't get upset. Tell me then.'

She hesitated. 'Well I want to ask you something, but I'm afraid you'll say no.'

'Try me,' I offered.

Leah paused again. 'Well . . . could we get into your bed? Not for sex, obviously. But it would be easier told lying down, like lying on a therapist's couch. And it would be . . . nice. Please?'

She looked so pleading, it was impossible to refuse. Not that I wanted to refuse. 'Well, yes,' I said, but you're not to take all your clothes off again, otherwise I can't guarantee to behave responsibly.'

She smiled, infinitely sadly. 'Okay, my lovely Paddy. And you mustn't either, for the same reason.'

'"Either",' I corrected.

So, although it was still only seven-fifteen on that gloaming September evening, we went to my bed. She simply slipped off her jeans and socks, leaving her green shirt on, and I removed my socks and trousers too. There were only two pillows on the bed, double-deckered on the side on which I slept, so I redistributed them. We stood looking at each other across the bed, uncertainly, me on my habitual side, her on the other, each waiting for the other to make a move. I broke the ice, pulled back the duvet and got in. She followed suit.

We lay like duplicate waiting dental patients, nervous, not quite touching, but then she shuffled down a little and turned towards me, bare knees against my bare shins, and lifted my arm so that she could nestle her head into my shoulder, her hair against my jaw. My hand came to rest against the swell of her buttock, on the knicker-ridge. I quickly shifted it higher, into safer, clothed territory. Her hand fell across my chest, the fingers probing my shirt. I wondered anxiously if she could detect my accelerating heartbeat. I spoke first. 'Is this comfy enough?'

She sighed, almost sounding happy. 'Yes, it's lovely. Much nicer than last evening.'

'I should hope so too. So tell me what you want to tell me. When you're ready.'

A pregnant silence. I began to fear she wasn't going to speak; that this was simply a get-you-to-bed ploy. Then, in a small, unhappy voice came the words, 'I've lost my flute.'

'What? How?'

'Well I was going to lie and say that I had it stolen, but that's not what happened.'

'So what did?' I gently coaxed.

Another pause. 'Well, I took it out with me to have one final day of busking. Just a few hours, anyway, for old times' sake, or something. So I walked west, towards the city. I suppose I thought I wanted to do some sightseeing too, because I might never see London again. I wanted something to remember. Something else to remember . . .' Her words petered out.

'Go on,' I nudged.

She resumed. 'I stopped and did a bit of playing, but the music just wouldn't come. I had no heart for it. I was already feeling dismal and it just made it worse, somehow. So then I just walked, aimlessly, blindly.

got to Tower Green, and it was such a nice sunny day yesterday, wasn't it? And there were all those happy people there, strolling around, enjoying the sunshine, with no troubles. And couples, lying on the grass, lost in each other. But here was I: alone and unloved.

'Something seemed to snap inside. I walked around the Tower of London and onto the bridge, and I thought, "stupid instrument, it's brought me no success or happiness". I wasn't thinking clearly, because I was so unhappy. And then I walked to the railings and took it out and flung the thing as far away from me as I could, out into the river.'

I brought my free hand across to cup the side of her face. It was wet again. 'Oh, Leah! Sweetheart!'

'I know. Crazy. And the stupid thing is; part of me regretted it almost immediately. My music was something I had, at least. But now my life felt even more completely empty and worthless. I stood there for ages, in a sort of trance, gazing out across the river, like I was separated from all reality. People walking past, going about their business, getting on with their lives, being happy, must have thought I was a loony or something. I felt so wretched, I couldn't even cry. I felt completely drained. Utterly. And then I thought, "well, I've lost everything now, my livelihood, and my hopes; there's just no point in carrying on".

'But I wanted to leave the world in a nice safe place: a sanctuary, a place that's been home these last few weeks. So I walked slowly back home, calling in a drugstore to buy paracetamol on the way. They would only sell me one pack though; that's the law. So I had to visit another one to get another pack. I didn't know how many it would take. And I bought the vodka and Coke, so I'd get drunk as well, and to help swallow the pills. I thought that would be a fairly painless way of doing it.'

I interrupted, feeling a sudden spike of anger. 'Well it wouldn't have been if you hadn't had prompt medical intervention to save you, you stupid woman! It would have been a slow horrible death from liver failure and God knows what else besides. I looked it up on the internet this morning, before I came to fetch you.'

She sighed again. 'Yeah, I've been a complete idiot. I'm sorry.'

I softened. 'No, not really. Just very troubled and unhappy. So what was the loud music and being naked in my bed all about?'

'Oh, I don't know. Sort of emotional anaesthetic, I suppose. Or sensory numbing, or something. I got back at about half-past-four and started drinking, and put some of the music we both like on the stereo, and sat and listened and brooded and got more and more depressed. It just reminded me of what I was losing, I suppose. And will still lose anyway, when I go back. And then, some time before six, I put on the Tchaikovsky, because it held a special memory, and decided the time had come to do the deed. So I took my clothes off and got into your bed. I tried to imagine you there with me, and I wanted to be naked for you. Give myself to you. Having failed in that little plan once, hoping if I did, you wouldn't want me to go back to the States, I thought at least I could imagine it as I drifted into unconsciousness.

'Then I started swallowing the tablets, one after the other, but nothing seemed to be happening, and after the first packet had gone it got more and more difficult; I was getting ever-more drunk and had more and more difficulty getting the pills out of their foil and swallowing them. And that was how you found me. Pathetic, isn't it. And now I feel like I'm falling into an abyss; a black, black abyss, because nothing's been solved.'

Dusk was falling, cocooning us in intimacy, but it was better without the light. I didn't switch the bedside lamp on. Her tears were falling freely now, wetting my hand. I turned towards the fragile weeping woman by my side, feeling a gush of protectiveness; drew her tighter to me. 'No, you're not falling, sweet girl.' I croaked, emotional. 'I've got you. I won't let you fall.'

Chapter 23

Eventually her tears subsided, but still she clung to me, as if I were an anchor against the cruel currents of a sea of misfortune, trying to sweep her away to a cold watery demise. I continued to stroke her wet cheek. 'It's all right,' I soothed, 'It's all right. Like in the words of that Bob Marley song. Do you like popular music?'

She snuffled. 'Yeah. Some. Which one?'

'"No, woman, no cry." That one. "Everything is gonna be all right" in the second part. Do you know it?'

'Oh Paddy, will you stop it? You'll get me going with the tears again. It's a bit before my time but yes, I know it.'

'I've got it on CD. On a Joan Baez album. Perhaps you noticed it when you were going through my record collection yesterday.'

'No,' Leah said, unhappily. 'I was just looking for things to play; things we'd listened to together and both liked. I told you that.'

'Oh. Sorry.'

I tried to lighten the mood. 'It's just occurred to me. That's who you remind me of, without your specs. When she was young, of course, and her hair was black. Before it became dignified grey.'

She took her hand from my chest and fished out the other, which was trapped somewhere down between us; rolled onto her back and gathered fistfuls of duvet to dry her eyes. Rolled back towards me, back into my re-encircling arm. Returned her hand to my chest. The other one burrowed down again, finishing up uncomfortably brushing my thigh. I tried to ignore it. She managed a chuckle. 'Oh no! You're comparing me with Joan Baez? I'm nothing like as beautiful as her, you Irish charmer, you!'

'Yes you are, a bit! In a slightly more delicate sort of way. Your nose is just like hers, in profile.'

'What; this beak? Yes, well I've got the classic stereotypical Jew's nose all right. Got it from my mom.'

But she quickly fell back into melancholia. 'Yeah. Speaking of whom, I suppose I'll end up crawling back to her and dad eventually, when I do get back home, unless I start to make a better fist of running my life.' She sighed heavily; lapsed into silence.

It was difficult finding an encouraging response to that. 'I'm sure you will. I didn't realize you were quite so unhappy about going back home though.'

'Didn't you? I thought I was making it pretty obvious. Not the least in trying to get into your bed the other night.'

I smiled. Of course I'd noticed her unsubtle attempt at seduction. But I hadn't understood the reason for it. 'So why did you?'

'You really don't know, Paddy?'

'Not really. I'm just a stupid, obtuse man; not well-versed in the wiles of women, remember.'

She looked up at me in the gloom. 'No, you're none of those things. Don't say that! Do I really have to spell it out?'

'Yes, perhaps you do.'

Leah Weisman took a deep breath. 'Okay then . . .'

Another protracted pause.

'Go on?'

And then the words came, in a flood. 'Well alright, Patrick Brennan, I'll tell you. I thought that if I came into your bed, and gave myself to you, completely, showed you just how much I could love you, how much I do love you, you'd want to love me just a little bit back. Enough to not want me to go back to the States. That's what I thought. But I was just being stupid, I suppose. I was the stupid one, not you; a stupid clinging naïve woman getting carried away and reading too much into things because you've been very kind to me. But why the hell should you see anything in me? You're a mature, educated, intelligent man of words. A really kind man. But nearly old enough to be my father. I'm just a silly little girl from Long Island who can't even get it together enough to make a living. And I'm not even supposed to be in your country now I'm not married to a man who was here doing a high-powered job. So I've got to go back, before I get thrown out because I haven't got a job here. Haven't been able to get one, not a proper one, in four years. And I've got to leave the one man in my life who's been really kind to me, unconditionally, without wanting anything from me in return. Who hasn't made demands on me that I didn't really want to meet. Who doesn't use me. I should have known it was too good to be true though. It's just been a fleeting dream. Good things, really good things, lasting things, just don't happen to little ol' me . . .'

Her voice faltered, threatening to dissolve into despair again.

I put two fingers to her quivering lips. 'Shush! Don't cry again. No, woman, no cry.'

She sniffed. 'Sorry.'

'So shall I tell you my feelings about all this, now?'

I felt her staring at me again. She nodded. 'Yeah?'

'Okay. Well, remember how upset I got the other night, after we heard about Benny's cancer?'

'Yes, you *were* upset.'

'But it wasn't only because of that bad news. It was hearing that that started me off, certainly, but I was already feeling pretty despondent, although I couldn't quite pinpoint what was causing it at the time. But it was the two things conspiring together that really got to me. Thinking about it later, in bed, I realized what it was that was making me depressed.'

Now *I* ground to halt, embarrassed about baring my soul in spite of just volunteering to do so. I felt Leah tense beside me. 'Go on?'

'Well, I feel the same as you. About you going back, I mean.'

'You do?'

'Yes, I do. Hadn't you noticed *my* mood? Oh, Leah! It isn't all one-way, believe me. It's not just what I do for *you,* giving you a roof over your head and all the rest of it. Not by any means. These last few weeks have been wonderful, having you here. You've brought light into my dull grey bachelor life, you really have.'

'I have?'

'Sure you have!'

'But what do you see in me?'

'Well, like you say about me: your intelligence. You're far brighter than other women I've had in my life. Emotionally intelligent, I mean Intelligent at a more profound level than just being super-educated. And clever. I really admire that you're a musician. It seems such an incredible skill. And lovely company, in a quiet, undemanding sort of way. And there's the way we seem to have a natural rapport; the way I just feel completely at ease in your company. And your kindness too. Not everyone would sing to a complete stranger; a little girl having a panic attack on a canal boat going over an alarming aqueduct, to calm her down. Most of the British would just curl up with embarrassment and keep well out of it. It really touched me when you did that. Oh yes you've given me a lot, believe me.'

Leah still stared, 'Oh, Paddy! Yes, that's what I think, about the rapport thing. Other men I've known – not that there've been many – don't come close to you. But you were going to let me go back to the States, weren't you.' She spoke quietly with the hint of an accusation in her voice.

I sighed. 'No, it wasn't a case of "letting" you go. I just assumed you'd made up your mind about it, because of the visa thing, and because you were having no luck finding proper work over here. And you didn't say anything to the contrary.' I added, slightly petulantly lobbing the accusation back.

'Well okay. Touché. So neither of us really knew what the other was thinking. Rather a *lack* of rapport there, then.'

'Yes, I suppose so. And I didn't want to throw a spanner in the works and complicating things for you, asking you to stay. Because, after all, you did you *would* be intentionally staying in Britain without a visa. You'd be an illegal immigrant, for God's sake!'

She laughed bitterly. 'Yeah; well so much for the "speci

relationship" between the US and Britain then. It doesn't mean very much when it comes down to real people, does it?'

'No, but I suppose the government has a point. There's a lot of political capital in appearing tough on immigration, even when it's from nice white Western countries where there's no racial element involved. Except for the European Union, immigrants, even from the British Commonwealth, never mind the US, have to prove they can be self-supporting and not be a burden on the state. So the Commonwealth is a bit of a mockery too. In other words, people have to have a decent-paying job to come to.'

She sighed unhappily. 'Yeah.'

'And apart from the practical problems of you staying over here, there's the emotional aspect. This all started out with me feeling sorry for you because you were down on your luck and on the streets. I rather blundered in, without thinking of possible consequences, offering you a roof over your head, as a sort of lodger, most weeks on a minimal-rent-paying basis – which I've been perfectly happy about – but now things have sort of . . . developed.'

'Developed?'

'Yes. Well. What began a few weeks ago as helping out a damsel in distress has become feeling very fond of said damsel. Extremely fond. And yes, dammit, I really didn't want you to go back to the States today anymore than you did.'

She raised her head again. 'Really, Paddy?'

'Yes, really.' I teetered on the edge of blurting out what I really felt, the two immortal words, as she had done, but I held back, inhibited. Instead I said, 'And please don't think that just because I wouldn't let you into my bed before, it was because I didn't want to, or didn't fancy you, or whatever. Far from it! I was just trying to act responsibly, for both of us. Trying to head off an impossible situation.'

'And what would that have been?'

'You know perfectly well! I could have really fallen for you, but then we couldn't have, well, been together, long-term, could we? There would have been no future in it. Sort of like having an affair, but without the infidelity. It could have resulted in terrible hurt. I don't mind so much being hurt myself. It's happened before, more than once, and I've got over it, but I really don't want to hurt you. It would have been very easy for me to exploit your vulnerability, if I was a selfish bastard. Good God; I didn't, I hope, but if I had, and had really got you to rely on me emotionally, even more than you've already come to, I dread to think what might have happened when this interlude ended and you had to leave me. You tried suicide as it is, and if you'd been even more distressed you might have tried something even more extreme and actually succeeded.'

Her hand came up to cup my cheek. She said, her voice unsteady again, 'Oh, Paddy! My sweet, sweet Paddy! No, you haven't exploited me. You're the most honourable man I've ever met. I admit I was a little wary that first night when you rescued me from the rain, but ever since then I've trusted you completely. I've never felt so secure, so cared-for, living here with you.'

'Yes, well, I'm just not the sort of guy to mess around, breaking hearts all over the place, love 'em and leave 'em style. I'm just old-fashioned, I guess.'

I felt her moving, and then a kiss fall on my cheek. 'Yes, you are old-fashioned. And I love it. You're a proper old-fashioned Irish gentleman so you are!'

I smiled, noticing her falling into my north-of-Ireland dialect.

'Mm. Or just a stupid, soft old eejit, more like.'

'Well, that's okay too.'

'Er, Leah . . .'

'Mm?' She was stroking my beard now.

'Sorry to go all morbid. But last evening. They were telling me at the hospital that suicide attempts are often cries for help. That doctor was saying he thought it interesting that you began taking the pills not too long before I was due home; that it was almost as if you actually wanted to be discovered. Is that true, do you think?'

She sighed. 'Well, I didn't consciously figure that. I don't think so. But perhaps there was a bit of it, subconsciously. Perhaps I wanted to show you just how desperate I felt; demonstrate it in the most dramatic way I could. And perhaps that was what the being-naked-in-your-bed thing was all about. I petulantly wanted you to see what you'd lose if you found me in time but then still sent me away, or I just wanted to have you find me like that and realize what you'd lost if you were too late. Oh, *I* don't know! It was pretty childish, really.'

I gave her a squeeze. 'No, no. Not at all. We often act irrationally in extremis. I think it's called being normally human. And as for the nakedness: well, under any other circumstances, I would have thought, what's this gorgeous, desirable woman doing in my bed? But I was in too much of a panic, believe me. Feeling desire never entered my head; it was the *furthest* from my mind.'

She said, wryly, 'Oh. I don't know whether to be pleased that you acted with such propriety or disappointed.'

There was nothing I dared say to expand upon that; better not to get into the tricky territory of physical desire; better to steer the conversation into safer waters. So I said, lamely, 'Well, anyway, would you like another drink? Something else to eat? How's your stomach feeling now?'

'Oh, yes, please. Another drink would be nice. Coffee again. Nothing else to eat though, thanks. Stomach's still a bit sore. Not very hungry and don't want to push my luck.'

I switched the bedside lamp on and got up. Went into the kitchen to put the kettle on. As there seemed to be the assumption hanging unspoken that Leah would be spending the rest of the night in my bed (and I certainly wanted her to), returned to the bedroom and rummaged for a clean tee-shirt from the chest of drawers as she lay watching me, wearing her sad smile. Coyly took it to the kitchen to change into, and made instant coffee and a cheese sandwich for myself. I took the food and drink back to the bedroom. 'Will I put some music on for us?'

'Ooh, yes. That would be nice. Play something for me, for a change.

Some of your pop music, as long as it's gentle stuff. Like that Joan Baez you were talking about.'

So, after I'd fetched the pillows from her bed and we'd sat side–by–side propped up in bed drinking and in my case eating, we lay down again in chaste embrace and I turned out the light and we listened to my music, my Baez and Carpenters and John Denver and Irish Furey Brothers, all my gentle, soft, sentimental stuff, because heavy rock isn't my thing at all; never has been. Halfway through the fourth CD I became aware that I'd been muttering without response for some time. She'd fallen asleep. After a while she turned over, facing away but staying close, drawing knees foetally, vulnerably up. I've always thought that women lying like that, exposing their intimate place, look touchingly vulnerable. I duplicated her shape, fitting to her but with a whisker of space between us; her full buttocks brushing a groin I hoped would, but feared might not, stay quiescent, burying my face in the soft cascade of her hair, my hand groping for hers. She wasn't fully asleep couldn't have been, because she found mine and took it to her lips, and murmured goodnight, leaving me wishing, my heart aching, that this woman could stay with me forever.

And of course, once the precedent had been set, it was a given that after a long day and evening trying to catch up with work to meet our publication deadline, because of course I hadn't written a single word the previous day, she would want to share my bed on the second night too. I feared she might want to listen to love songs again, but thankfully the request didn't come. I really didn't think I could have coped with the emotional overload, the aching need for her, if she curled up in my arms serenaded by Karen Carpenter's dulcet tones again. She declared herself tired (it was probably the after-effects of the trauma catching up) and, after making me coffee, went to the bedroom before I finished my piece and emailed it to the paper. When I finally went to bed myself she was sound asleep. I climbed in carefully, trying not to disturb her, and lay without touching, nerves a-jangle, wondering how long I'd be able to keep up this unbearable chasteness.

On the third evening, while she was in the bath, I telephoned Esther to enquire about Benny. Esther sounded weary too, although she was clearly trying to put a brave face on things. 'Oh, he's about the same. Perhaps a little tireder. He starts his chemotherapy the week after next, so that'll be a relief. There'll be some positive action then, anyway. It's the being in this limbo state that's so difficult to cope with.'

'Yes, Esther, that'll be good,' I said, searching for words of sympathy and support but, as usual, feeling hopelessly inadequate.

'Yes.' A pause. 'And how's Leah. Has she gone back to America yet?'

'Erm, no, not yet.'

'So you're still getting private flute performances then? She really is a very talented young lady.'

'Er, well actually she was meant to go back the day before yesterday but there was a . . . change of plan.'

'Oh, I see.' Esther clearly didn't though.

I really hadn't meant to spill the beans to her. She had enough worries of her own without being burdened with mine. But, as always, I found myself opening up, telling all. 'Well, as a matter of fact, she took an overdose of painkillers on Wednesday, the day before she was due to fly back, so obviously, that put paid to that.'

'Oh, no! The poor girl! Why ever did she do that?'

'Well, she just got very depressed about going. She's enjoyed living with me. And I enjoyed having her. She's a very nice person to have as a lodger, even if she can't afford to pay me very much in the way of rent.'

Esther scoffed. 'Oh, come now, Paddy; you can do better than that! It's we British who are supposed to be masters of understatement, not you Irish! You're telling me she tried to kill herself just because a mutually enjoyable time spent living under your roof was coming to an end? I suspect there's rather more going on between you two than you would have me believe.'

'No, really; we haven't been living together in the usual sense. It's like I told you. I took her in because I felt sorry for her being on the street. And she wasn't just being depressed about going, anyway. She lost her flute, the day before she was due to fly back, and the two things just added up to a major crisis, I suppose.'

'I take it she's not with you there at the moment? Or is she in hospital?'

'Yes, she's here. At home, I mean. Fortunately I discovered her before she'd taken too many paracetamol and phoned for an ambulance, and they took her to Saint George's where they got some sort of antidote into her pretty quickly, and they say she shouldn't have any long-term damage to her liver or anything. Thank God I did intervene so soon. So she was only in hospital for Wednesday night and I brought her home on Thursday. But no; she's not right here at the moment. She's in the bath.'

'Oh, of course!'

'What? Oh, yes. No, but seriously, it was losing her flute as well that really tipped her over the edge, it seems. Her flute was her life.'

'Yes, I can believe that. Like Benny's is to him. And so how did she come to lose it, on the very day before she was due to go back?'

'She, er . . . had it stolen.' The white lie slipped out. I didn't want to betray Leah's trust on that point, even to Esther.

'Mm,' Esther said, doubtfully. 'Well, I still think there's more going on between you two than you're letting on. Or admitting to yourself, at any rate. Perhaps Leah's more honest with her emotions, as she's young and not a hard-bitten cynical old journalist like you, Mister Brennan.'

I laughed mirthlessly. 'Yes, maybe so. Well, anyway, whatever there is or isn't between us two – and we aren't sleeping together, in a sexual sense – the problem is, she can't stay in Britain without a job, and now she's divorced, so she has to go back. That's the difficulty. And that's why any relationship we might have is rather doomed, really.'

'And how do you feel about that?'

'Well, not happy, if you really must know, love. To be honest, I'm desperately trying not to fall for the woman, knowing there'd be no future in it.'

'Mm. Well, you know what they say: "love will find a way".'

'Yes, well, that's an easy cliché, isn't it, Esther? But anyway, I was ringing to talk about Benny, not rabbit on about *my* emotional troubles. Let's hope he goes on all right with the treatment, when he starts it. I'm sure he will though.'

Esther sighed audibly on the other end of the line. 'Yes, that's all we can do: hope. And thanks for enquiring, Paddy. I do appreciate it.'

'Yes, well give him our love, won't you?'

'Yes, of course I will. Thanks for ringing. And I'm sure your problem will sort itself out.'

'Well, maybe. And take care yourself. I'll ring again soon.'

'Thank you Paddy. Bye.'

'Goodnight Esther.'

Leah emerged from the bathroom wearing a towel-turban, her pink jumper, best jeans and usual aura of post-bath fragrance. But still a sad expression although she declared herself pretty much over the effects of the overdose now. She plonked down beside me on the sofa, reaching for my hand, taking it into her lap to hold in both of hers.

I said, 'I've just been on the phone to Esther, to see how Benny is.'

'Oh yes? And how is he?'

'Tired, she says. He's starting chemotherapy the week after next.'

'Poor Benny! Why does he have to wait that long to start it? You would think they'd be getting on with it straight away, as it's such a serious illness.'

'Yes, well this is the good old NHS, remember. It's not like your insurance-based system in the States, with oodles of money sloshing around in it. Our – the British – system is funded from government. It has a huge budget but it's still a finite one. So it's a matter of resources. There's a high degree of egalitarianism but on the other hand you have to wait your turn, unless you're an absolute emergency, of course. Then you get seen to straight away. As you've just found.'

She sighed heavily. 'Yeah. And I'm very grateful for that. But that's a point: should I have even *got* treatment, as I'm a foreigner?'

'Well, strictly speaking no; not if you're not from the EU. I'm not quite sure what'll happen in your case. Of course I had to give your name at the hospital, but I said you were a visitor so not too many searching questions would be asked. And gave this address. So I suppose there'll be an invoice coming through the letter box in due course.'

'Oh, Paddy! That'll be more expense I've caused you then, just through being stupid! I'm costing you a fortune!'

I grinned. 'It's okay; don't worry about it. You're worth it!'

She scowled, rubbing her hair (which smelled wonderful). 'Don't joke about it! I don't want to be a financial burden! I'm between the Devil and the deep blue sea, aren't I? I could stop being heavily dependent on you and go back to the States, except that I haven't got an airplane ticket now and can't afford to buy another one. But I don't want to, and you don't want me to, either. Do you?' She looked at me anxiously.

'No, I don't.'

'Right. Or I stay, but then I risk being discovered and thrown out of the country. And if I do stay, having stupidly thrown my flute away I've now lost my means of at least making a little bread, so now I'm a complete millstone around your neck. I really don't want to be that. I've got some pride left, even if you *were* prepared to have me living here free.'

Leah had me there. 'Yes, it is a problem,' I agreed, unhappily.

We sat in melancholy silence for a while. Then she said, cautiously, 'I was thinking, while I was in the tub –.'

'Don't!'

'Don't what? Think?'

'No; don't present me with images of yourself in the bath. It's bad enough, imagining you in there every evening, as it is!'

She actually managed a chuckle. 'Sorry! Well, what I was thinking was; what if I did some piano teaching? After all, I've got a diploma from Juilliard, even if it's only a C. But it's a qualification, all the same. And besides I could teach at a fairly basic level: just small kids starting out, say. What do you think?'

'Well, aren't you forgetting one small detail?'

'What?'

'The fact that there isn't actually a piano here!'

'Ah, but what if I were a sort of travelling tutor? Going into the homes of the wealthy people to teach there, to save their little brats the bother of visiting a teacher?'

I pondered the idea. 'Well, it's a possibility, I suppose. It certainly beats busking on the street, so it does. I bet there are loads of rich doting parents in London who'd like such a service. Yes, it might work.'

Now she laughed. 'Right! Shall I give it a try then?'

'Yes, why not? We'd have to think how best to publicise you. Maybe with an ad in the local free paper. Or I think you can advertise online nowadays. Something like that. And you could keep your fees fairly modest, although not so cheap as to lack credibility. Yes . . .'

She turned her face to me, flushed with excitement; planted a smacking kiss on my cheek. 'Wonderful! I thought you might think it was a stupid idea, or something!'

'Yes, well don't get too carried away. You'd be doing it illegally, remember. And I'm sure you'd never get a work visa for doing it. But yes, as long as you were fairly discreet.'

'Great! So will you do an advert for me? You're the one who's good with words.'

'Yes, all right then.'

Her face was transformed. For the first time in many days her dark eyes shone; she looked positively happy. 'Well I think your acceptance of my brilliant moneymaking idea calls for a celebration, don't you?'

I grinned. 'What did you have in mind?'

Then I remembered. There was a bottle of red in the fridge, bought for the sad final dinner three evenings ago that never happened. 'Ah! There's a nice Burgundy in the kitchen that's seeking a special occasion. We could crack that open.'

She chortled. 'Well, that would do for starters. Just to get us in the mood, as it were.'

I opened my mouth to ask her what she meant but stopped mid-gape. Her meaning was only too clear. 'Oh. Yes, right then.'

'Good. So here's what we do. You go and get the wine and glasses. I put some nice smoochy music on the stereo. Then we go and get into bed and polish off the wine as quickly as possible. Or we drink it slowly. Deferred gratification, and all that. Whichever you prefer.'

I chuckled. 'Oh, I think plan A. Yes, has to be.'

'Yes,' she said. 'I agree.'

And so, nerves tingling, I went to uncork the wine and find glasses, and carried them through to the bedroom. Then I went to shower. Well, I had to be super-clean and sweet-smelling too. And brushed my teeth. It didn't take long to dry the little hair I've got left. But then ran up against a small dilemma. I was dried off but still naked. What to do? Parade through to the bedroom like that? I became acutely conscious of my still-too-ovoid, ginger-hairy belly, which hadn't shrunk significantly during the past weeks of eating healthily and exercise. Only a crash diet would do the trick as far as that was concerned, I'd gloomily concluded. It was still impossible to see my little dangly friends without leaning well forward. I hurriedly put my boxers and shirt back on and left the bathroom as Leah hovered outside, grinning awaiting her turn.

Then, as I climbed beneath the duvet, I worried vaguely about the bedding. It had been over a week since I'd last changed it. But no; there wasn't time for that now. And after all, she'd spent the last two nights between my sheets. She probably wouldn't give it a moment's thought. propped up the pillows against the headboard, poured the wine and waited, my heart hammering ridiculously, like a teenager about to lose his virginity. The stereo started up from the sitting room: my sentimental Fureys' CD of love songs. That pizzicato banjo intro preceding *When You Were Sweet Sixteen*. Jesus! You could cut the schmaltz with a knife! But she'd clearly chosen Irish easy-listening music deliberately.

Leah entered the bedroom, her hair falling free, still damp and uncombed, and still wearing her clothes too, apart from her jeans. She climbed in beside me, settling close, minty of breath, and I handed her her wine. My groin was beginning to ache like mad. 'Well, here we are then,' I said, inanely.

'Yes, here we are.' She took a deep draught of her wine, half-emptying the glass. I followed suit. 'You chose the music well,' I said, trying to sound casual, although my teeth were chattering.

She laughed an odd tinkly laugh, sounding nervous too. 'Yeah, well it seemed kinda appropriate, one way and another.'

'It is.' I drained my glass with a second swig. She did too.

I love you as I loved you . . . wafted through from the sitting room.

I refilled our glasses, emptying the bottle. Took another long drink. As did she.

When you were sweet, when you were sweet, sixteen.

We both drained our glasses.

'Sure well that bottle didn't last long, did it?' I chuckled.

'Sure didn't.'

I put my glass on the table. She handed me hers, with which to do the same. She shuffled down the bed a little to make herself relatively shorter, as I wrapped my arm around her delicate shoulder. As she nestled, sighing, into mine, I wondered where I dare place my other hand. I settled on her abdomen.

'No, not there,' she said, taking the hand and moving it under her jumper to cup a soft, bra-less breast. 'There.'

It felt wonderful. My small friend leapt enthusiastically, agreeing. 'Er, do I have your permission to look?' I quipped, ridiculously.

She giggled. 'Always the perfect gentleman, aren't you! Of course!'

Not until that moment did I see. I never realized what you meant to me. Finbar Furey sang a new song in his rich Dublin brogue.

She lifted her sweater to expose it, as I lowered my head to take the erect soap-scented nipple into my mouth. A hand came up to the back of my head, clasping me to her, as the other fumbled awkwardly down the waistband of my pants for my erection. 'Ooh, Paddy, you're so big!'

I certainly felt big; big enough to burst. I removed my hand and tugged her jumper. 'Please! Take it off!'

She unhanded me to cross her arms and pull the garment over her head as her small perfect breasts, suddenly freed, jiggled into view. 'There. Now you can look, even if you didn't before!' The jumper was tossed onto the floor and she wriggled out of her pants; threw the duvet back. 'There, darling Paddy! Look!'

She was utterly beautiful, I could have cried. 'Now,' she implored, 'you!'

You fill up my senses . . .

I unbuttoned my shirt, frantic, all fingers and thumbs, threw it aside as she scrabbled at my boxers, getting them comically entangled with my rampant penis. But then they were off.

She shifted to lie prone, her face flushed in anticipation, ebony eyes wide, wild with desire, opened her lovely, surprisingly fleshy thighs to me as I moved between them; pushed my head urgently down to the lurking female cleft below the raven-black bushy triangle below that eternally-teasing navel. 'Please . . .'

Come let me love you . . .

I kissed her down there but I was in a desperate hurry, and clearly she was too. There was no time for preliminaries. 'Quickly!' I gasped 'now!'

She urged me back up, pulling my face to hers, and our lips met hungrily. Slippery with readiness, she quickly guided me in, enveloping in her exquisite softness, subsuming me into herself in tender union.

'Oh, Leah! My love!'

My brain fit to explode and all restraint abandoned, I quickly came as she, too, spasmed and cried out in her need, clasping me so tight, so, so tight to her, into her, and in her release wept joyful tears.

Chapter 24

I could have lain there for hours, lost in her until sleep came, captured; a willing victim in her arms; arms which were wrapped fiercely, fingers clawing, around my back.

Hold me close, never let me go, My fellow-countryman now sang from the other room.

But, conscious of my weight on her delicate white body, I rolled to one side. She followed, determined not to loosen her hold, and we finished, a glorious tangle of limbs, facing each other, cheek to cheek. Her body felt like a fragile bird and her face was wet, osmotically wetting mine, aping the other shared intimate wetness in our groins. My heart rate began to return to something resembling normal.

'Oh, I do so love you, Patrick Brennan! I really do!'

'And I you, my sweet.'

'Do you? Do you really?'

'Yes, really. Scout's honour.'

That seemed to set her off again. She gifted me new tears. I pulled back a little to look into her red-rimmed, liquid-black eyes. 'Hey, don' cry!'

She managed a rictus smile. 'I'm okay. It's happy-tears, not sad ones.'

'Good. Well that's all right then.' I moved close again to kiss her fluttering eyes. 'Let's get comfy.' I lifted her head to pull the pillow down; did the same with mine. Reached to turn out the light. W settled, still locked together. I caressed her back, the swell of her buttock.

'Of course,' I murmured, 'You do realize, don't you? We've crossed the Rubicon now.'

'How do you mean?'

'You know. The point of no return.'

'Oh, Paddy! I passed that ages ago.'

I smiled in the dark. 'Yes, I suppose I did too, if I'm honest. I just didn't want to admit it to myself. As I say, I was trying to act all responsible. But I knew that once you came into my bed that would be it. It would put the kibosh on things. Good intentions would crumble. I'm only a weak old eejit, a man, after all.'

'Well I'm glad you are. That's fine by me. And I'm just a silly weak woman who keeps messing up. I don't deserve a wonderful guy like you.'

'Nonsense!'

I chuckled.

'What?'

'Well, I must confess, apart from all your other charms, and apart from feeling desperately sorry for you when I first invited you into my life, there was a quite a lot of simple straightforward fancying going on too, believe me.'

She laughed. 'Well good! I did rather wonder about it, sometimes. I know I'm no raving beauty. All those evenings watching you sat in your armchair, a few feet away that might as well have been a million, when I wanted you on the couch beside me. And when I made that first clumsy attempt to seduce you and you acted like a scared rabbit!'

'Yes, well I've explained why that was. You've no idea how difficult it was though, rejecting you like that, my sweet!'

Leah squeezed me. 'Oh, I'm sorry, baby! I'm not as good at discipline as you, am I? I shouldn't have come on to you like that. It was shameless. But I was feeling so desperate with the departure date looming. I was trying anything to make you ask me to stay. I'm sorry.'

'You're forgiven. Yes, well as I was saying; as soon as you scrubbed up clean and put decent clean clothes on . . . yeah . . .' My words fizzled out.

'Go on; finish it.'

'Well, I was just thinking of your second night here, after you formally became my lodger, and you bought that outfit for the dinner party with Benny and Esther. Your pink top.'

'Oh yeah.' She sniggered. That item from my extensive wardrobe that I seldom wear. What about it?'

'Well, you had a bath and then put it on to show me. Like you took it off a little while ago to show me something very sweet . . .'

I paused, nursing a recent fond memory. Resumed. 'Er, sorry, I'm digressing. What was I saying?'

'Dunno. Something about my sweater?'

'Oh yes. You had a bath and wrapped a towel round your head, and you'd turned the top of your jumper down to keep it dry, showing the back of your neck.'

'So?'

'Well, it may surprise you to know that the nape of the neck is one of my favourite women's places.'

She laughed. 'Seriously?'

'Yes, really! It's so . . . elegant. The way it merges smoothly into the shoulders. I love it. Especially on someone I'm very fond of. I suppose that's why a woman's hair worn up is so attractive. To me, anyway.'

'But you weren't back then, were you? Very fond of me?'

'Well, no, obviously not. But perhaps I was having prescient feelings or something.'

'Mm. And do you have any other favourite women's places, lovely man?'

'I certainly do!' I enthused. 'Many. Like the crease of the elbow when it's bent just a little. I love that. And ear lobes. And knees. And so insides of thighs. And navels. But that's possibly because female bellies are nicer than men's, because they're hairless, until you get to the nice furry bit lower down. I've been driven crazy by occasional glimpses of yours, you know.'

Another laugh. 'Really? Oh, you charmer! Er, which: navel or pubes?

'Your navel of course! I haven't seen your bush until just now.'

'You did the other night, when I tried to . . . you know,' she reminded me, suddenly sombre.

'No I didn't, not really. You were under the duvet and it was pulled up to your . . . and then I pulled it right up, when I realized what was going on. There might have been a quick glimpse when the ambulance men got you out of bed and onto their chair thing to carry you out, before they put a blanket over you, but as I said before, ogling you was the very last thing on my mind.'

'Oh, baby, I'm sorry! Well anyway, how have you been glimpsing my navel then? I don't remember allowing that.'

I laughed. 'I'll tell you. All those times you stuffed your flute down your jeans, after you lost the case. You'd lift your top, showing a bit of delicious midriff, before stuffing the flute down your waistband. Which was also pretty erotic, if you must know!'

She hooted with merriment. 'Oh; I'd no idea I was behaving so wantonly! Right. And is that all of your favourite places, then?'

'No, not yet. I haven't got onto the obvious places. But it's not cleavage, particularly, because it isn't natural. It's a more subtle thing: when you're au naturel, as it were, and wearing a very low top, and there's the beginning the edge of breast showing, that's definitely nice. You probably knew that when you tried to lay me before though. And proper, generous, bobbly nipples; not the inverted sort.'

'Ah; well you're all right there, then.'

'Yes, so I've just found. Yours are lovely. And your breasts generally.'

'Uh; they're not very big though. They've always been a bit of a disappointment to me. That and my skinniness.'

'No!' I protested. 'Big ones aren't everything; contrary to what you might assume, men don't necessarily go for large ones. And besides, it's the person behind them who matters, anyway. Literally.' I chuckled at my inadvertent pun.

'Well thanks for that!'

'You're welcome. And then there's the really obvious place, of course.'

She snorted. 'Mm; I don't think it's terribly pretty either. It's not very, er, neat, is it?'

I laughed. 'I don't know. I haven't had the chance of a very long look.'

'Well have a look now. You'll probably go right off me!' she teased.

'All right.' I turned the lamp back on, blinking for a moment or two as my eyes adjusted to the light. She disengaged herself, threw back the duvet and rolled onto her back, lasciviously opening and drawing up her thighs. I shifted to get a closer look. Her inner lips were certainly quite fleshy and generous, it was true, although poignant, in a curious sort of way. I placed fingers there, caressing, and grinned up at her. 'No, it's fine, really. It's lovely. It's like a, er, florid fleshy oyster, or something.'

'"Florid fleshy oyster"?!' She hooted again. 'I've never had my vaggie called that before! You have a very colourful turn of phrase sometimes, you wicked Irishman!'

'Yes, well, I'm a man of letters, you know. Master of the expressive simile!'

'Yeah, yeah!'

'Or an iris, perhaps. But no; oyster is better. Irises aren't fleshy are they? Well anyway, it's very sweet, in my opinion, now I'm able to look it. And so is the rest of you. And you're slender, not skinny. You're beautiful. Honestly. Like an elegant antelope.'

Her eyes softened, threatening tears again. 'Really? I've never thought so. Poor self-image, I suppose. And certainly, no one's ever said that to me before. They just took what they wanted, as if I were some kind of sex aid or something.'

'Well the other men you've had have been selfish bastards then,' said crossly.

She nodded. 'Yes, you're right. Oh, honey! You make me feel so . . wanted. In every way. So; can you take me through it again, all those places you love on me? Please?'

So I did. I rolled her onto her front and pulled her hair aside and kissed the delicate nape of her neck on either side. I kissed the lobes of bot her ears from behind. I kissed the peach of her buttocks, a circle of five for each one, whilst I had her that way up, although they weren't on the list strictly speaking. I rolled her back right-side-up and kissed the delicious bends of both arms. Then that tantalising crater in her smooth creamy belly. Then both knees, which she again gaenocologically opened and raised. She closed her eyes, sighed and smiled serenely, lips apart. I traced the edge of each breast, all the way around, lifting each softness to kiss below the roll, and took each organ-stop nipple into my mouth again. I knelt to kiss a journey from the inside of a smooth thigh to caress and kiss the head, the oyster lips and probe her moist secret place. It still tasted salty-sweet from my semen.

I rose to kneel between her thighs. 'All right? Does that identify them comprehensively enough?'

She opened her eyes; smiled dreamily. 'Mm. I've got a terrible memory though. You might have to remind me again another time. Will you do that?'

'Well, all right then. Seeing as it's you.'

She noticed that I was engorged again. Reasonably so, at least. After all, I wasn't yet fully recharged, and I *was* forty-four, after all.

'Ooh, is he up for it again? As it were?'

'Well, he's willing to give it a try.'

She raised herself to grasp and mouth him in reciprocation for my attentions, then after a while lay back down, drew me to her, into her again, one hand clawing my back, the other clasping a buttock and this time we made slow, languorous love with all the time in the world, floating on lesser physical sensation but with no less emotional intensity, although it took me longer now, until I finally panted and groaned and shuddered and let go, and she moaned too, and cried out again that she loved me, and I, choked, returned the fervent declaration.

At last, sated, to my exhausted relief, she settled to sleep, turning away and curling up, staying close. I turned the light off again and fitted myself to her foetal shape, my aching groin and thighs now uninhibitedly tight to her buttocks and enticing, no-longer-secret place.

My face buried in the damp tangle of her ebony hair, I wrapped an arm around her body, hand cupping a sweet soft breast, with one of hers trapping mine, holding it there.

Soon her breathing slowed and she began to gently snore. It wasn't only my nether regions that ached with unaccustomed exertion. I ached with love too. And I worried, vaguely, still. Worried that this was really just a mirage. After all, it was ridiculous. Against my better judgment I had a young woman, a breathtakingly desirable lover, in my life. I'd realized every middle-aged man's dream. Although she was much more than a physical lover: she was a cozy quiet companion; a kindred spirit as far as tastes went; potentially a profound soulmate. And she said she loved me.

But there was the tyranny of years stretching between us. Nineteen of them. In six years' time I would be fifty, at the first staging post of the second half of my life. But she would be only thirty-one, with anything up to two-thirds of hers still to run. Ten years further on again, I would be sixty and she still only brushing middle age. The words of that song from long ago came, *but will you love me tomorrow?* She might have tired of me by then. Well, why would she be wanting a probably fat-by then, bald old Irishman, after all? Did she really know her own mind? Or was she simply, and understandably, confusing love with gratitude for her rescue?

And there was the nagging anxiety about her status. She shouldn't really be in this country. Yes, she might be able to earn a sufficient amount from piano teaching to pay her way, but there would be the constant sword of Damocles hanging on its thread: the ever-present danger of discovery followed by almost certain deportation. The Home Office demanded minimum salary-earning requirements from sponsoring, orthodox, regular employer (as opposed to uncertain self employment) for people wishing to work in the UK, I knew, from research I'd done for articles.

And apart from the work angle (although I was getting absurdly ahead of myself), simply wishing to live together in a relationship with a foreigner, even an American 'cousin', conferred no right whatsoever for that partner to live here in the cold bureaucratic eyes of the Home Office. I'd come across heartbreaking cases where even spouses of different nationalities had been refused permission to live together in Britain.

My brain tossed about in mental conflict. The emotional part of it argued: *thank your lucky stars for this serendipitous change of fortune; for the happiness and joy of Leah Weisman in your life.* The rational part cautioned: *nothing can ever be certain; just live for today; enjoy love while you have it, while you can.*

The following day was Sunday and there was no journalism to do, so we lay in late; drowsily talking; throwing back the duvet to enjoy each other's muted nakedness (by now I'd lost all inhibitions about mine) as a thin autumn sun rose and filtered through the curtains; drinking tea, eating cereal, making love, although not in that order. We finally got up and shared a bath, doing creative fun things with bath foam, which did nothing to assuage the ache in my groin and resulted in yet another awkward, giggling penetration before getting out, drying each other off and vowing to be sensible, for at least a few hours.

And we did have to be sensible; there were important matters to put in hand. Leah and I devised an advertisement for the Oh-yez! online advertising site. After playing around with many phrases we ended up with *PIANO TUITION. Juilliard-trained pianist offers piano tuition in the convenience and comfort of your own home. Complete beginners up to ABRSM grade 5. Competitive fees.* Ending with the mobile contact number for a phone she would buy the following day as well as my landline number.

And she would also have to buy another outfit of clothes more appropriate to her occupation than a shirt or jumper top, jeans and trainers. Something a little more sober and professional-looking, like a trouser or skirt-suit and blouse, possibly, and sensible shoes. Well, she needed to be credible; look the part. And tomorrow she would also have to buy contraceptives.

We wondered whether she ought to extend her services to include teaching organ or keyboard too, but thought better of it. After all, as she pointed out, she *was* a classically-trained musician after all. And there would perhaps be more money to be made educating the offspring of the comfortably-off, who would probably be more interested in formal piano tuition.

It occurred to me that she would possibly need some sort of keyboard instrument to have at home too, to keep her hand in, for practicing on. Wouldn't she be a little rusty, not having played piano for some time? She looked at me doubtfully. 'But honey, you're spending an awful lot of money on me again.'

I squeezed her hand; grinned. 'No, that's all right. I'm thinking of it as an investment, or you can think of it as a loan, which you can pay back in easy installments when you start earning. And you do need some smart clothes, and an instrument too, really, don't you?'

'Well, yes, ideally. A proper piano, just an upright, of course, would be best, with eight octaves; better than a silly little electric thing.' She glanced around the sitting room. Would there be space to get one in here?'

'Yes, I should think so, if we rearrange things a bit. And we're on a ground floor so it should be easy enough to get one in.'

'Mm. And it needn't be new, of course. I suppose a fairly decent second-hand one wouldn't be terribly expensive.'

'No, I don't suppose it would. We'll have a look on the internet, shall we, to get some idea.'

Leah smiled wryly. 'To think; when I was ten my doting parents bought me a brand-new baby grand. It must have cost a fortune, but expense was no object for their spoilt little brat. And here I am fifteen years later, getting excited at the prospect of an old second-hand upright.' Her eyes moistened as she looked at me. 'But having that something second-best, here with you, would mean so much more, really would. It's all a matter of context, I suppose.'

'Yes, maybe so.'

'Of course,' she mused, 'if there were a piano here, it would slightly defeat the object of me being a travelling tutor, wouldn't it?'

'Well, no, not really; not if you hope to teach the offspring of the wealthy, who'd probably be furnished with a super-duper instrument, like you had. The parents would probably prefer that you went to them than send their child here to learn on the sort of inferior thing we could afford.'

'*You* could afford. I can't afford anything!'

'Yes, well anyway, shall we see how you go with the teaching? If you find you're getting work, then we could get something and you'll be in a position to start paying me back. Okay?'

She leaned across and palmed my cheek; kissed me gently. 'Okay, my lovely Irishman. It's a deal.'

I smiled; clicked to submit the ad to Oh-yez!

Leah came out with me the following morning, after another glorious if exhausting night of love, accompanying me part of the way to work, and I stopped at a cash point, made a withdrawal and handed her two hundred pounds to hopefully not entirely spend on her new wardrobe.

When I returned in the evening, after a day spent finding it difficult to concentrate on matters journalistic, she was like a little girl again, like she'd been that other time when I'd outfitted her for the Benny and Esther evening out. She'd bought a nice, smartly-understated, just-above-knee-length mid-grey skirt and matching jacket, a dark blue ruffle-collared blouse and sensible, low-heeled black shoes and black tights. And as before, she couldn't wait to put them on; demonstrate them for me.

But of course there was no coyly going into her bedroom to change now; she promptly stripped down to her bra and pants as I gazed, mesmerized, and put the blouse, skirt, jacket and shoes on, leaving the tights in their box. It was the first time I'd seen her wearing a skirt. Her legs really were very nice. Especially her knees. She did a twirl, grinning. 'Well? What do you think?'

'I think you look absolutely gorgeous, my sweet,' I enthused, wondering whether I could now manage to wait until bedtime to demonstrate the fact.

Her eyes shone behind her specs. 'Do you really think so?'

I closed to embrace her, hugging her tight. 'Absolutely.'

She gave a tinkly laugh. 'Thank you kind sir! Yeah, and the whole lot only came to a hundred and thirty-nine pounds, so isn't that good! I've been really thrifty and careful!'

'Even better; clever old you!' I said, relieved.

She kissed my cheek. 'Oh. And I got you a little something too, as I felt a bit guilty about spending so much of your money all on myself. She pulled away and reached for a box lying on the sofa. 'Hope you like it.'

It was a shirt. Dark green. Exactly like the one she'd bought herself.

'Oh; lovely. Thank you!'

A grin. 'Don't thank me. It was your money!'

'Well, thank you for the thought then. It's really sweet of you.'

'No problem. Try it on then; we've got to check it's the right size.'

I fiddled about removing all the many pins and clips and cardboard shaping pieces and then undoing the buttons; gave it to her to hold. took off my jacket and unbuttoned the shirt I was wearing. She gazed a my bare, ginger-hairy chest as rapt as I'd looked at her. I slipped the new shirt on. Her judgment of my size had been correct; it was jus right. She moved back to me to proprietorially do up the button Slackened my belt and tantalizingly unzipped and unbuttoned m trousers so she could tuck it in. Redid my belt. Stood back again t admire. 'Oh yes! Very nice!'

'Thank you, too! Er, was there a special reason for it being the sam colour as yours?'

Leah Weisman sighed. 'Oh, you obtuse men! Can't you see th symbolism of it?'

'Er . . .'

'Well let me spell it out for you, slowly. Identicalness. It implics oneness. Two of a single kind. Peas in a single pod. Union. An item. We are, aren't we?' She looked suddenly anxious.

I laughed. 'Oh, you sweet woman! Yes, of course! If you'll have me!' Her expression changed to grave. 'Yes, Patrick Brennan. I'll have you.'

'Good! That's all right then! Oh, and did you get a mobile?'

'What? Oh, cell phone. Oh bugger; I completely forgot!'

Well, never mind. Get one tomorrow. Just something cheap and basic. Doesn't have to be a smart phone or anything; you just have to be contactable by all the many customers you're going to get.'

'Okay; right.'

'And did you get contraceptives?'

She smote her forehead theatrically. 'Shit! No, I forgot those too!'

I sighed; pretend-admonished, trying to keep my face straight, 'Oh, well now what are we going to do? I can't make love to you now!'

Her face fell. She looked stricken. 'Oh, Paddy! I'm sorry!'

I glared at her, until the corners of my mouth began to twitch.

The penny dropped. She grinned. 'You son of a bitch! Don't tease like that!'

I guffawed. 'Well okay then, just this once. But get some tomorrow, okay?'

She breathed a deep sigh of relief; looked contrite. 'Yes, of course.'

But when we went to bed later, after eating, my somewhat distracted Monday evening Skyping to Bella and listening to music curled up lying on the sofa, but still not very late, it of course turned out to be more than just the once.

Chapter 25

Leah bought a cheap mobile (and contraceptives) the next day and we settled down to wait for the flood of enquiries about her services to arrive. None came that day. 'Well, don't worry,' I reassured, 'it's early days yet. We only put the ad on yesterday.' On the Wednesday, at lunchtime, I rang home to see if there'd been any calls. 'No,' she said, her voice a little flat, 'only a nuisance-call about reclaiming PPI, whatever that is.' There'd been nothing during the afternoon either, she told me glumly, when I returned in the evening.

'But there's still plenty of time,' I insisted. 'People looking for piano tuition won't be browsing the net every moment of their lives.'

We ate the meal she'd ingredients-shopped for earlier, prepared and now cooked on my arrival home. (She'd also done clothes washing and changed the bedclothes; they were in slightly odiferous need of it after three nights of concentrated passion). Already, as she wasn't earning any sort of income, our roles were defined: I was breadwinner; she housekeeper and warmer of my bed. And my soul. She'd quickly become a surrogate wife, almost. Although a very willing one, she earnestly assured me, until such time as she became an equal financial contributor, anyway.

Then, as there was nothing either of us wanted to view on television, we settled on the sofa, prone, like two sardines willingly crammed into a rather-too-narrow can, to listen to music. It was strange, although perhaps it wasn't, how our tastes had suddenly and markedly changed. When I offered Leah the choosing she plumped for pop music again and as I only had the gentle romantic sort, it had to be that. But I could no more imagine her being interested in heavy rock than I could myself, anyway.

She had no sooner got up, the buttons of her shirt undone and her br in some disarray, to change the CD to the Carpenters and rejoined me in my arms, when the phone rang.

'I'll get it'. She rose again, straightening herself, grinning at me, and turned the volume down low before picking up the receiver.

'Hello?'

. . .

'Yes, it is?' She moved to the armchair.

. . .

There was a longer pause. 'Yes, certainly.' The colour was rising in her cheeks. Her voice rose an octave and began to tremble slightly but she maintained relative composure. 'I graduated from Juilliard in twenty-eleven. I've lived over here since then. Oh, sorry, I'm American. Er, I've always liked working with children. I find it very rewarding –'

. . .

'Yes. I charge twenty-five pounds per session. For forty-five minutes – erm, or it can go to an hour, if I feel the child can sustain a longer session. It's the same price for the longer period –'

. . .

'Yes, well, I like to keep my charges reasonable. Keep them within the reach of most people, you know? –'

. . .

'Oh yes, sorry, Mrs Jameson. My name's Leah. Leah Weisman. I live in Canning Town. And you? . . . Er, just a moment please.'

Leah made frantic writing-down signals at me. I got up and moved to the telephone dock beside which there was a pen and pad ready for just such an event as this; picked them up and put them on the arm of the chair; grinned, mouthed, *'Calm down!'*

'Ah, sorry about that. You can never find a pen when you want one, can you? Right; fire away.'

. . .

'Lucinda. Right. And she's how old?' Leah scribbled frantically as I held the pad steady to stop it sliding around.

. . .

'Right. How long has she been playing, or is she right at the beginning?'

. . .

'Okay, well I look forward to meeting you –'

. . .

'Oh, yes. Now let's see; when can I fit you in? What sort of time suits you best? Afternoon, after school? Early evening, possibly?'

. . .

'Yes, the evening's fine. Let's see what I've got now.' I watched amused, as she silently counted up to ten, determinedly refusing to meet my eye. She resumed. 'I could do you this Friday, the day after tomorrow, seven o'clock, say; how would that be?'

. . .

'Lovely! Right, I'll see you then, then.'

. . .

'Yes, thank you so much, Mrs Jameson. Thanks for your enquiry.'

. . .

'Goodnight.'

Leah sagged back in the chair, closing her eyes, puffing her cheeks and blowing like a Titian cherub. I took the phone from her; replaced it in the dock. 'There you go! Your first customer!'

Her eyes stayed closed. 'Oh my God, now I'm panicking! I haven't got any teaching material or anything! No tutors or exercises to give the child. Or even a case to carry them in. Oh hell!'

I knelt down in front of the chair, opening her legs so I could close in and put my hands on her hips. 'Calm down; you'll be fine. Now then, tomorrow you visit a music shop and get all the material you think the child needs. And go to a stationers and buy an invoice book, so you look professional. Best to make it a case of pay-at-the-end-of-the-session. So whether they give you cash or a cheque, which you ask to be made out leaving the payee's name blank, so we can add my name and pay it into my account, you write an invoice for services rendered, on which you then write "Received" and the amount and date on, when they've paid so you look nice and authentic. And I've got a document case you can use. You don't want to turn up with everything brand new, looking like you've only just started. You can always say you've just started a new invoice book to explain that. Okay?'

She opened her eyes and looked at me. 'Mm; it suddenly sounds really daunting now it's coming to it!'

'Ah, sure you'll be fine! You've obviously got enough technical expertise to be a tutor. Think back to how it was when *you* were first taught as a child. How your tutor taught you. I don't suppose the method has changed that much over the years.'

'No, I don't suppose so.'

And how old is the child? Is she just starting?'

'She's six, apparently. And yes; pretty well a beginner, according to her mom.'

'Well there you are then. It'll be absolutely basic stuff: learning scales, or whatever you do to begin with. Get your first tutorial out of the way and it'll be easy after that.'

She put a hand on one of mine. 'Mm, maybe so.'

'I know so. And when you go out tomorrow, make a list of what you want; you know what your memory's like!'

'Yeah, that's a good idea.'

'Come on, love. You can do this. And it sure beats busking on the street, doesn't it?'

Leah smiled. 'Yeah, it does. I guess you're right. It's just that I so want this to succeed. I want to get things right in my life, for once.'

'You will. Just you see. Now then.'

'Now then what?'

'Well, what were we doing before we were so rudely interrupted, do you remember?'

She looked down at her opened shirt. Giggled. 'Er, I think I do , , ,'

The phone rang again.

I cursed, left Leah and picked up the receiver. It was a familiar number on the display.

'Hello Esther.'

'Hello Paddy. How are things with you?'

'Oh, fine thanks. How's Benny?'

'About the same. Still feeling very tired. He's due to start his chemo very soon now.'

'Oh good. The sooner I starts it the better, I should think.'

'Yes. And how's your Leah?'

I didn't contradict Esther as to Leah's status now. I didn't want to. 'She's fine too, thanks. She's feeling much brighter now.' I glanced at Leah as if asking for permission to discuss her. She smiled permission back. 'As a matter of fact she's going into the piano tutoring business. Got her first job to do on Friday.'

'Oh, right.' Esther sounded faintly discombobulated.

'Well, she thought she'd make use of her piano training now she hasn't got a flute.'

'Yes. Er, actually I was ringing to invite you two to pop over sometime. Benny has a little proposition for Leah.'

'Oh, what's that?'

'Well, we'd rather you came over really, rather than discuss it over the phone. When would suit?'

It sounded intriguing. 'Er, tomorrow evening then, perhaps? After dinner, obviously. We don't want to put you to any trouble. Just a quick visit; we won't stay too late. How would that be?'

'Yes, that's fine, Paddy,' Esther said, sounding tired. She was probably feeling the strain of the situation.

'Right. About eight then? We'll see you tomorrow, love. 'Night.

'Goodnight, Paddy.'

Poor old Benny certainly didn't look well when we walked into their sitting room the following evening. He looked utterly listless, as if all enthusiasm for life had fled. He made to politely rise to greet us, as he always did, but I said, 'No, Benny, stay where you are.' Leah crossed the room to him and bent to kiss his pale cheek, putting a hand on his shoulder taking his hand with the other, as he raised his free one listlessly to her arm. 'Hi Benny. How are you?'

He managed a weak smile. 'Oh, mustn't grumble, you know.'

Leah sat down in the armchair next to his, her eyes on him. They were glistening.

Esther hovered. 'Right. I'll make us some tea. Come and help me Paddy.' She looked at me meaningfully.

I followed her into the kitchen. She filled the kettle, determinedly busying herself finding her best teapot, cups and saucers and mugs for Leah and I, a dainty milk jug, a plate onto which she decanted a ring of rich tea biscuits.

'So how are things going?' I asked, wishing I could think of intelligent, empathetic words. My usual facility with the English language seemed to have deserted me again.

Esther sighed tiredly. 'Well, we'll see if the chemo helps at all. Just have to hope that it does. He'll be getting a blood transfusion too. That'll buck him up a bit, hopefully. Thank goodness for blood donors.'

'Yes indeed,' I said, feeling a twinge of guilt. It was something I'd occasionally thought I ought to do, with my outlook, but had never got around to.

We were skirting around the unspeakable subject; Esther for her own good reasons, I because I simply didn't know what to say and didn't want to cruelly take her into bleak, hopeless territory. She must have been there many times already and didn't need me sticking my clumsy insensitive nose in.

She forced a smile. 'Anyway, so how is it with you and your young lady now?'

There it was again: the possessive adjective. I lolled against the worktop, relieved at the change of subject but still feeling guilty, to be talking about my happier affairs.

'Good, actually, Esther. Yes; very good.'

'Well that's nice to hear. So you're an item now, as they say nowadays, are you?'

'Yes, we are.'

'Oh, that's wonderful! I'm so happy for you! She's such a lovely girl. And you're really smitten, are you, Paddy-boy?'

I grinned sheepishly. 'Yes, I am, I must admit. I never thought it would happen again. I thought I was too cynical about women now, after two failed marriages. But now; here I go again. She brings light into my life, she really does. I can't believe my luck. I don't deserve her really.'

Esther looked at me sharply, kettle poised over teapot. 'Nonsense! Of course you do! After what you've been through this last couple of years with that other dreadful woman, you deserve some happiness, my dear.'

'Yes, but I do worry a little.'

'What about, for Heaven's sake?'

'Well, the age difference, for a start. There's nineteen years between us, you know. And I've been desperately trying not to fall for her because she's so young and . . . well, you know. I'm nearly old enough to be her father, after all. I don't want to be some sort of sugar daddy. Not that I'm particularly rich, of course.'

Esther laughed. 'Oh, Paddy, listen to you! You'd never exploit someone like that, for sexual favours. So you started out just being very kind to her, because she was really down on her luck, poor girl, and now things have . . . developed between you. And no doubt, she began simply being grateful for what you were doing and ended up loving you. I don't blame her; I would have done exactly the same. You're lovely man, after all, Paddy.'

'Well that's sweet of you to say so, Esther,' I said, smiling wryly. 'But there *is* still the age thing.'

'But it clearly doesn't bother *her*. I get the impression she's a very sensible young woman; not an impressionable, flighty young thing.'

I sighed. 'Yes, she is, that's true. And she's not without experience men, after all. Her ex-husband sounds as though he was a selfish swine and that pop star she was with doesn't sound much better. Pretty irresponsible. So yes, I suppose she has not particularly prepossessing yardsticks to measure me by.'

'Well there you are then! Age difference isn't important, comparatively speaking. Anyway, it's not as if she's eighteen and you're eighty, for goodness sake! You're not so many years different. And it's the relationship that counts, isn't it?'

'Mm. But the other thing is: would there be a future in it, anyway? From a practical point of view, I mean. She's technically an illegal immigrant at the moment, as she's no longer married to someone working over here on a visa. She should be applying for a work permit really, but the trouble is, she hasn't got a full-time job to point to. And I've heard whispers in high places that our wonderful government is thinking of tightening the eligibility rules for people coming to work here: raise the minimum salary requirement to thirty-five thousand a year. So that would debar many younger people who'd often earn less than that. And my saying I'd be prepared to support her, like I'm doing now, wouldn't cut any ice with the Foreign Office. So I don't know what she'd do about that, other than become a bloody banker on an obscene salary, like her ex. Then she'd be welcomed with open arms, of course, as I imagine he was.'

'But didn't you just say she was going to do piano teaching?' Poor Esther didn't seem to have all of her mind on the conversation.

'Well, yes, but a bit of freelancing here and there isn't going to add up to thirty-five thousand, is it? Besides which, as I say, it has to be regular work from a sponsoring employer, who can prove she's earning an income.'

Esther looked up from pouring the tea; cast me a sympathetic look. 'Oh yes, of course. Sorry. Yes, this country isn't as welcoming to immigrants as it used to be, certainly; a fact that UKIP is only too willing to exploit. I feel so sorry for them. Immigrants I mean. Speaking as one myself. But anyway, let's join the others. You haven't heard what Benny has in mind yet.'

Leah and Benny were talking about music of course when we rejoined them, me bearing the tray of drinks and nibbles. I set it down on the coffee table and sank onto one end of the sofa. Esther took the other. She looked at Benny. 'Have you made your suggestion to Leah yet, darling?'

Benny smiled tiredly. 'I was just getting round to it.' He turned his head to Leah. 'This is only a thought, but now I've retired from the orchestra, there's a vacancy. I've heard that Marion Barker is moving up to First Flute so there'd be an empty seat left, so to speak. As far as I know, it hasn't been filled yet. Why not audition for the job? You're certainly very capable of doing it, from what I've heard of your playing.'

Leah stared, open mouthed. 'But . . . is the job being advertised?'

'Well I don't know, for certain,' Benny conceded. 'But I'll give Henry our orchestra manager – I mean *the* manager – a ring and tell him I know of just the candidate. Henry and I go back a long way. He's another of "immigrant stock", as they say. His parents came from Latvia though, in nineteen fifty-three, fleeing the Soviets. So he'd probably be quite sympathetic, if I explained the situation.'

Leah's eyes were beginning to glaze. 'Well, that's very nice of you . . .'

'No problem. I'll do it tomorrow. I like to help my friends, if I can.'

I interjected. 'As a matter of interest, Benny, what sort of salary do the foot soldiers in your orchestra – the orchestra – command?'

He looked at me quizzically. 'I've no idea. Is it important?'

'Well, it's really very nice of you to want to help like this, but yes, it might be. I was just saying to Esther; our lovely government is pandering to the anti-immigrant lobby and making noises about lifting the salary-earning requirement for non-EU people working over here just to cut the numbers. The salary might not be enough.'

Leah looked at me, aghast. 'Oh, don't say that, please!'

Her eyes pleaded with me. I cursed myself for my negativity; tried to rescue the situation. 'But on the other hand, if you fitted some piano tuition too, it might bring your earnings up to the bar. You could perhaps, er, exaggerate earnings from that a little . . .'

Her shoulders sagged. 'But there is one other small problem of course. I don't actually have a flute any more, remember? How can I be a flutist

– flautist – without a flute?'

'So we'll buy you one!

'Yeah; like you're going to buy me a piano, too. And clothes, and everything else. I'm an ever-growing money drain on you, Paddy!' Her lower lip began to tremble.

'Yes, well I've been thinking about that,' Benny interjected quietly. 'Since you lost your other one, and since I've no real use for it now, you could have mine.'

'What?' Leah stared again, incredulous. Tears were squeezing out behind her specs now. 'Really?'

'Yes; why not?'

'But . . . I couldn't accept it. Oh, Benny!'

'Yes, you could.' Benny shifted awkwardly, a picture of typical British discomfiture in the face of threatening emotionalism. 'After all, I've no one else to give it to as neither of ours are musical, are they, Essie?'

'No,' Esther murmured, her eyes bright too. 'You take it, Leah. It would make Benny happy.'

Leah's tears were in full flow now. 'But I don't deserve it! Not after throwing my own away!'

I felt a gush of protectiveness and love, but Esther beat me to it and crossed to her chair; perched on the arm; put one of hers around Leah's shaking shoulders. 'Another one saying they're undeserving! It's all right, lovie, don't get upset. I thought you had it stolen?'

'Er, no, Esther,' I said. 'That was a small porkie, I'm afraid.'

Esther ignored me. 'But why? Why did you do that?'

Leah had put her palms to her face, dislodging her glasses. Her words were barely audible. 'Because I was so desperately unhappy about going back to the States. I was in such a state; I didn't know what I was doing. I didn't see any point in carrying on . . .'

She petered out.

'You mean carrying on without Paddy?' Esther prompted gently.

Leah snuffled. 'Well, it was everything, really. The whole situation. But yes: especially that.'

'Oh, you poor thing!' Esther stroked Leah's hair.

Leah pulled herself together, wiping her eyes on her sleeve and replacing her specs. She looked at the embarrassed Benny. 'Well thank you so, so much, Benny. But I think you should keep it for now. If I do get an audition with the orchestra, I'd love to borrow it. And if I get the job, then yes, I'd love to have it. I'd cherish it. I really would.'

Leah came back from her first piano lesson her face flushed with excitement. I'd taken on cooking duties, getting everything prepared ready to cook when she returned. She strode, grinning from ear to ear into the flat and threw my document case onto the dining table. I got up to commence cooking. 'So how did it go then, love?'

She threw her arms around me, her eyes shining. 'Brilliantly! It was easy, really. Like you said it would be.'

I kissed her. 'Well there you go then. Told you so!'

Leah let go of me to open the case; drew from it two crisp new ten pound notes and a five and waved them at me. 'Look! My very first fee' She thrust the money into my hand. I took the tens and returned th five. 'This is yours.'

'No; I don't need it! I want to start repaying!'

'And you need to have a little pocket money of your own. Don argue!'

She grinned. 'Okay; thanks.'

'So have you got another lesson lined up?'

'Yes! Amanda seemed very pleased with what I'd done, and litt! Lucinda – Lucy – seemed to enjoy it. She's a sweet little kid. Amanc asked whether I could do two lessons per week, so I pretended mentally check my appointments book and said I could do Monda evenings too. So that'll be fifty pounds a week from just one client. Fc less than two hours' work!'

'Mm, plus your travelling time, of course.'

'Yeah, well, that doesn't really count. Everybody has to travel work.'

'Yes, all right then. So; it's a good start. Get a few more clients like this and you'll be making fairly good money. And if, just supposing, you got that orchestra job too, you'd be well away then. You'd be working all hours and I'd have to pack in my job to be a house-husband!'

She giggled. 'Whoa there; just a cotton-pickin' minute. Don't get too carried away!'

I laughed too. It was good to see her so radiantly happy. I suppressed my pragmatic anxieties. 'Well, it seems to me, this calls for an appropriate celebration, don't you think?'

'What; now, this minute, do you mean, honey?' she purred.

'No! I've got cooking to do! Restrain yourself, woman!'

'Oh, all right then. Killjoy.'

A pause.

She continued. 'Anyway, there's a snag.'

'What's that?'

'We haven't got any wine. For the mood-creating part.'

I grinned; she was learning the banter.

'Well, we could dispense with that bit. We're not very good at it anyway. We tend to rush through it.'

'Mm, yes, I suppose so,' Leah Weisman said, smiling at me wickedly.

There was another enquiry the next day, from someone in Hampstead, no less. I began to wish I'd suggested a higher fee; someone living there would probably be loaded and wouldn't blink an eye at thirty, forty, perhaps even fifty pounds a go. Leah handled that one more confidently and an appointment was made for the following Tuesday afternoon. That was three bookings for the week now. Things were cautiously beginning to look rosy.

But when I got home the following Monday evening her mood had changed. She was dressed up ready for her lesson with Lucinda, green shirt replacing blouse to ring the changes, but her face looked tight with anxiety.

'I've had another enquiry.'

'Good! They're coming thick and fast now!'

'Yeah, but I'm a bit worried about this one.'

'Why?'

'Well, the woman who enquired started asking whether I minded having a DBS check done. She said her husband worked in the Home Office and he was a stickler for doing things by the book as it was a child-protection issue, not that she doubted my credentials for a moment, she said. I hadn't the faintest idea what she was talking about. I wished you'd been here; you would have known. What is "DBS", anyway?'

'Disclosure and Barring Service. It's a system for checking the credentials of people seeking to work with children. To guard against paedophilia and so on. A child-protection thing, basically.'

'What? The woman – or her stupid husband – was checking me out in case I'm a pervert?'

'Yes, well, it's the law. Teachers, people who work in nurseries, anyone like that, have to be vetted. It's fair enough of course. There have been shocking cases of child abuse, even murder, by people like that.'

'Well okay; fair enough. But I'm going to other people's homes, for God's sake, to teach kids with their parents present. It's not as if they're coming into my home and I'm alone with them, is it!'

'No, but that's just the way it is. Some parents are hyper-careful with their kids nowadays. I suppose I should have thought of someone possibly bringing that up, but we don't want you getting too much involved in officialdom, or they'll soon twig that you shouldn't really be in this country.'

'Mm,' Leah murmured dejectedly.

'So tell me what happened.'

'Well, as I say, I was stuck for words, and then the woman asked me if I knew what DBS stood for, and I said I thought so, but fortunately she didn't ask me what it was so I could prove I did. And then she realized I sounded American, and asked me if I was, and I had to admit it, and then she said she'd enquire elsewhere and ended the conversation.'

'Oh, I see . . .'

'Oh, Paddy, I've got a horrible feeling I've fucked up, somehow! I don't know whether she meant she'd be checking up on me, or just meant she'd look for another tutor. Oh, shit!'

'Did you give her your name?'

'No, it never reached that point. But she did say her husband worked in the Home Office. And she has our landline number. I could be traced back here from that, couldn't I? But then they'd find I don't seem to exist. And then things would start to look very suspicious, wouldn't they? Oh, Paddy, I'm scared!'

'No, it's all right; don't worry.' I tried to calm her. 'It would take quite a lot of digging and making connections to establish that there's a non-person living here – even supposing that person who rang could be bothered to report suspicions – without pretty strong grounds for them. They have only so much time and so many resources available. There are many departments of the Home Office and I doubt that, unless it was the Border Agency, they'd be all that bothered. They tend to work within their own little pigeonholes. I'm sure you'll be all right. Now you go off to your lesson; it'll be fine.'

But I worried myself, all the same. But then I'm often a glass-half-empty sort of guy; a natural pessimist. I was distracted and monosyllabic during the Skype to Bella and was quite relieved when seven-thirty came. When Leah returned at twenty past eight she was subdued too. But we spoke no more of fears which, I tried to convince myself, were probably quite irrational anyway. We didn't want to contemplate the unthinkable. Later, in bed, I held my sweet girl tight to me, fiercely, protectively tight, with a leaden lump of dread in my heart. The thought of losing her was beyond bearing.

November

We sat in the departure lounge of Heathrow Airport holding hands. It was alive with the chatter of humanity, of the world still turning: people going about their daily untroubled lives. Happy people, perhaps jetting off to visit loved ones on the other side of the Atlantic, or looking forward to the holiday of a lifetime, or returning souvenir-laden from visits to Britain or Europe. Sober-faced businessmen reading documents of doubtless great import. Young people, expressions happy and carefree, sitting beside enormous rucksacks, joshing with companions or, heads down, absorbed in their smartphones. Children running around, impatient, excited by the adventure of it all.

But Leah sat empty-eyed, as if she had no more emotion left. She'd cried several times in the car travelling there, in such misery, breaking my heart listening to her sobs every time. And now we sat, close craving every last minute of physical contact as we waited for the inevitable. Words of tear-jerking pop songs kept flitting insistently masochistically through my brain although I tried to chase them away.

I'm leaving on a jet plane; don't know when I'll be back again.

Your eyes are soft with sorrow; hey, that's no way, to say, goodbye.

And let me hold you one last time, before the whistle blows.

We said little. Her knuckles were white, such was her desperate grip on my hand. I looked at her desolate face as she looked back at me, red-eyed, lips clamped in desperate control, trying to drink her in, to lay down a reservoir of memory on which to draw through lonely nights come. All my clever, apposite words had deserted me again. Whatever said, no matter how much forced, trite, determined casualness I tried bring, it wouldn't change a damn thing.

The tannoy suddenly burst forth, with brutal finality, sinking n heart like a stone.

Passengers now boarding flight Pan-Am 762 for J F Kennedy, New York.

Fourth Movement

Adagio – diminuendo, lamentoso

Chapter 26

The phone call finally came, puncturing the silence of my arid, now-empty flat, at gone eleven forty-five. Although she had some money (I'd given her a thousand pounds for expenses, incidental and otherwise), I called back.

Her voice sounded a little less sorrowful although still far from upbeat. 'Hi, baby. It must be quite late there. Nearly twelve?'

'Yes, that's right, sweetheart. No problem though; you know that. You could have phoned at four in the morning if you'd wanted.'

'Yeah. I'm all confused about time now. I'm still thinking of the hours it's been since I had to get on that goddamn plane and leave you: I can't make the adjustment for the time difference.'

'Mm. It's strange isn't it? Like another degree of separation. Different continent and different point in time too. So you're with Judy now then?'

'Yeah. I got here three hours ago and then had a little nap to get over the lag, and we've just eaten. I couldn't wait any longer to hear your voice.'

'Yes, likewise, love. I think I've got lovesick-teenager syndrome, or something.'

'It's awful, isn't it? I'm missing you like mad already.'

'And I you. Well, it shouldn't be for too long; just a few days. We'll just have to grin and bear it.'

Leah's voice was dull; resigned. 'Oh, honey, I hope that's all it is. I do hope nothing's going to go wrong.'

I tried to strike an upbeat note. 'Don't worry. I'm sure it'll be all right. We've got Henry at the orchestra on our side, telling that little untruth.'

She managed a tired little laugh. 'Yeah. I'm ostensibly being hired as first Flute, on the higher salary of thirty-six thousand, although the true one as an ordinary orchestra member is twenty-nine and that's what I'll actually get. But I hope the Border Agency isn't going to check up with Henry; ask for evidence of the job offer, or something.'

'Yes, well Henry's quite prepared to pull the wool over the eyes of any jobsworth who comes snooping. He's done that fake letter with the wrong salary for you to show the embassy with your visa application, after all. And he'll confirm it if any one comes asking. Say that's the sort of realistic figure a senior musician would get in a prestigious orchestra like the Philharmonic. And then as confirmation he'll start paying you the pretend-salary, so it shows on your bank statement, and I'll pass him the difference back again, as a "supporter" of the Philharmonic.'

I laughed too.

'What?'

'Well; I get the impression that Henry doesn't suffer bureaucracy too gladly. I suppose it's his job to negotiate funding from the public purse and strike hard bargains and he's pretty hard-bitten about it. When spoke to him the other day, he said his first instinct if anyone came nosing around would be to roundly tell them to fuck off, but he won't do so of course. He'll bow and scrape and be generally obsequious whilst raising two fingers behind his back, and meanwhile quietly work this little fraud.'

Leah sounded both resigned and anxious. 'Yeah, well I hope to God it's all going to be all right and I don't get found out. I couldn't bear the thought of not being able to come back just because, having been offered a job, it isn't for as much money as your government thinks ought to be. I just don't understand how governments can be so heartless, not allowing people who love each other to live together they want to.'

'Well, as they see it, it's just a numbers game. Set the entry requirements higher and, *voila,* you reduce the number of damn foreigners coming over here placing a burden on the public purse. And upsetting the voters. They can't limit migration from Europe so they hit everyone else instead.'

'Yeah; well it's just not fair, playing softball with people's happiness like that, as if it's just some bloody political game.'

'No, it isn't,' I agreed.

I tried reassurance again, although I felt far from confident myself. 'But I'm sure it'll be okay. After all, we worried when we thought you might have been rumbled after that teaching enquiry, didn't we? Although no repercussions came from that. You're playing by the rules now and applying for a visa from overseas; you aren't giving them any excuses to refuse you. And you want to come to take up work that's been firmly offered. It's better doing it this way, perfectly above board, than carrying on as you've been doing, as an illegal immigrant. It'll be fine, you'll see.'

'Mm. Oh, baby! I do miss you; so much, it hurts. It's going to be horrible sleeping alone tonight, not being in your arms, not having the feel of your gentle hands on me. Not hearing your sweet voice murmuring sweet nothings.'

'And I'll miss you too, sweet girl. For all the same reasons. Yes, I'll ache for you.'

She suddenly sounded coquettish as if determined to be cheerful. 'Really? Will a particular part of you ache for me?'

'Physically, yes. And you know which ones. That little trio.'

'Oh, I know the ones. One's not so little though, when he gets over-excited. And which particular parts of me will they ache for, do you think? Tell me!'

So I did. I took her through the usual litany, the one I'd regularly described over the last three weeks with accompanying demonstration, making her giggle. It helped a little; helped assuage the aching need. But only a bit. In another sense it amplified it. It was somewhat masochistic really. She sighed, but the lurking sadness was unmistakable. 'Thank you baby. Thank you for that. Those are some nice thoughts to take to bed with me, anyway.'

'Yes, well try using your own hand but pretend it's mine. It might help a little bit, perhaps.'

'Yeah, I will. And you could do the same, couldn't you?'

'Yes, that's true; I could. I will'

She sighed again. 'It's not the same though, telephone sex, is it? Not the same at all.'

'No, it isn't, my sweet, but it's all we have.'

We chatted on, as I tried to keep the conversation light and hopeful, trying to keep our spirits up. But in truth, I still didn't feel positive. Finally I reluctantly brought the conversation to a close, told her how much I loved her, as she fervently boomeranged the words back, and returned the handset to its dock. Then went to my cheerless bed and lay and worried. Well, it was a worrisome situation. More than once, writing pieces for the paper, I'd unearthed desperate tragic stories of couples, spouses and families even, being torn apart by the cold uncaring hand of authority.

The outcome was by no means cut and dried. There was the risk Henry was running with his obliging little fraud to help out a friend of his old friend Benny. You couldn't really play ducks and drakes with government; if he were found out, officialdom wouldn't take kindly to being made a fool of and he'd be for the high jump.

And me too, probably.

Two evenings later I visited Benny again. I didn't really expect him to look any better, and he didn't. He was even paler, even more shrunken. Even more a desiccated husk of a once-dignified man. Esther had told me on the phone the previous evening when I'd rung that the inductive chemotherapy hadn't been a success. His blood tests weren't significantly better and it had simply made him feel even more wretched. The heamatologist had suggested that it really wasn't worth asking him to suffer unnecessarily for no good reason, and suggested switching to simply palliative management. Benny had agreed although, Esther had told me, it had been a listless agreement, as if he knew perfectly well that the fund of his days was almost exhausted; as he was resigned to the fact that life was ebbing away and he couldn't really be bothered to make any more decisions; all he really wanted was to be left in peace to pass away as free from discomfort as possible.

Esther had said, tiredly, that a Macmillan cancer nurse was coming in now, several times a day, to administer pain relief and general care, and that Sam and Ruth were visiting daily too, as if trying to glean as much final contact from their father in his limited remaining days as they could. And the grandchildren were coming in too, particularly the girls, who were more sensitive to the gravity, the finiteness of the situation, especially Daisy.

In fact Sam was there that evening, sitting on the sofa, casting frequent concerned glances at his father, when I walked into their sitting room. It was the first time I'd met him: a tall, graying, slightly portly middle-aged man with something of the look of Benny about him. And the look of affluence too. Esther introduced me as Patrick Brennan, their good friend. We shook hands, exchanging the conventional salutations. Esther told Sam what I did for a living and for which paper. Sam raised his eyebrows slightly, looking politely interested, possibly relieved at the opportunity for non-illness-related conversation. To tell the truth, I, guiltily, felt a ripple of relief too. 'Oh really? he said. 'What; as a news reporter or do you do features?'

'Features.'

He nodded vaguely. It seemed my name meant nothing; presumably the Clarion wasn't his paper of choice.

'Sam works in property,' Esther said, sounding slightly embarrassed.

'Oh yes? What do you do? Development? Estate agency?'

He smiled. 'Agency. Durrells. You may have heard of them. On the letting side.'

'Oh; right.' I left the words hanging; not wanting to imply interest. Letting agents were not my favourite type of people. But then I perhaps had a jaundiced view of rentiers after the piece I'd written about Leah and homelessness. And I wasn't here to be bored or irritated by a dull estate agent but to give whatever comfort, support and love I could to Benny.

I sat down next to him, in the chair Leah had sat in when we visited last, and wondered what on earth I could say to my dear old friend, my virtual-father, but no sensible words would come, none that wouldn't sound ridiculously trivial or preposterously faux-encouraging or downright banal.

Esther went to make me a cup of tea but I didn't follow her into the kitchen this time. It would somehow have felt like cowardice; fleeing from a situation I didn't have the wit to deal with. Besides, there was nothing to cozily chat to her about regarding Leah. My girl had put in her application and was at the beginning of her waiting game; there was nothing more to say about it. And Esther had got far more pressing concerns on her mind than my love life, anyway.

No; I felt that my place was beside Benny, even if I spoke not a word. All I could do was simply, in the tired old cliché, be there for him. I looked at him now, sunk listlessly in his armchair, wondering what could be going through his mind, waiting for him to talk; talk about anything at all, whatever he wanted. But he simply gazed into his lap, miles away. I tried to break the silence. 'So, you're getting lots of visitors, are you, Benny?'

He looked at me tiredly. 'Yes, I am, Paddy. I'm being spoilt really. Daisy came yesterday, with her young man. I do like him. And the baby. She's a beautiful little thing. Going to be very like her dad, I suspect. Won't take after our side.'

'Yes, I bet she is.'

A faint smile fluttered across Benny's lips. 'Indeed. And Leah hasn't heard anything about her visa yet then?'

'No, not yet. I suppose it'll take a few days for the bureaucratic wheels to slowly grind.'

We were interrupted by the return of Esther bearing a mug of tea for me, giving it into my hand.

Benny continued. 'Yes, I suppose so. Well, let's just hope Leah comes back soon. Perhaps she'll accept my flute now.'

Sam spoke. 'What's this, Dad? You aren't giving your flute away, are you?' He transferred his stare to me. 'And who's Leah?'

Esther interjected, 'Leah is Paddy's yo . . . partner. Dad is giving his flute to her. She's a flautist. And a very good one.'

'But . . . hasn't she got a flute of her own? And your flute is very expensive, isn't it, Dad?'

Benny smiled weakly again. 'Yes, but that's neither here nor there now, is it? I want someone to have it who'll really appreciate it.'

Esther interrupted again, 'And Leah hasn't got a flute at the moment. And Dad wants her to have it.' She shot Sam a warning, don't-argue look.

Sam shook his head, taking the hint but clearly puzzled. I could see how his mind was working; in cash-register terms. The concepts of gift-giving and intrinsic emotional worth were perhaps alien concepts. 'Oh, well it's up to you of course, Dad.'

'Yes it is,' Esther affirmed.

Sam got up to leave soon after that, shaking my hand again and saying, 'See you then, Patrick.'

I didn't stay too much longer either, as Benny was clearly tiring. I put a hand gently on Benny's frail shoulder and told him inadequately to take care. He smiled up at me, eyes heavy, and nodded, mute. Esther saw me to the door. She looked drained. 'I don't know how much longer he's got, Paddy.'

'No,' I murmured, unable to think of anything else to say. 'Poor Benny.'

'I'm really sorry about Sam,' she said, 'letting himself down like that. Being rude about Leah. I expect he was assuming that the flute would be sold and we'd share the proceeds, or something. He sometimes only thinks in monetary terms, I'm afraid. Because of his job, I suppose.'

I placed my hand on her shoulder now. 'Ah; don't worry about it, love. No offence taken. Anyway,' I continued morosely, 'it's all rather hypothetical still. If Leah doesn't get her work permit she won't be able to accept the flute. Or wouldn't want to, I suspect.'

'Oh, don't say that, Paddy. Try and be positive.'

I smiled wryly, feeling the old familiar lump rising. *'You're* telling *me* to be positive, Esther, with what's going on with Benny?'

She smiled too, infinitely sad. 'Yes, well; you know what I mean.'

I continued to get nightly phone calls from Leah; increasingly despondent as none of them bore good news. Although I tried to sound upbeat, it was a struggle. My mood was as low as hers really. Even the mild telephone sex petered out after she stopped asking for it.

It had been eleven days since she'd left. Monday came around, and the regular Skype to Bella. It was a pleasant enough chat. Bella happily told me that she was getting back into her piano playing and really quite enjoying it. I was pleased for her, of course I was, but saddened too, fantasizing, imagining her and Leah together; Leah being the one teaching her. Now that would really be something, I thought. But it was a ridiculous notion, a hopeless dream; there was no point in masochistically wishing for the unattainable.

But there was something I had to sort out during this Skype. Christmas wasn't so many weeks away now and there was a visit to Bella to arrange. This might be the time to open negotiations about it with Catarina. So at seven-thirty I wound down the conversation, said goodnight to my daughter, with two fingers transferred a kiss from my lips to the computer screen, and asked if she could bring her mother to the screen. She receded from view and two minutes later Catarina appeared. I had tensed while waiting, remembering the hostility between us five months earlier when she'd gone out of my life for good, taking Bella with her. Five months; was that all it was? It felt like years already. Although it *was* getting on for three now, in living together, caring-about-each-other terms.

But I needn't have worried. For her part she seemed relaxed and even friendly.

'Hello Patrick. How are things with you?'

'I'm fine thanks. And you?'

It was like making polite small talk with a total stranger; impossible to imagine that I'd once worshipped her, mind and body, as I now worshipped Leah. But no; it hadn't been a case of worshipping her mind, as I'd fairly soon come to realize. With Catarina it had largely been the attraction of her olive-skinned beauty and voluptuousness. The only physical feature the two most recent women in my life had in common was black hair; as people they were as molasses and delicate, amber honey.

'Yes, I'm fine too. What can I do for you?'

'Well, I was thinking about a visit to see Bella at some point before Christmas. We need to arrange something.'

'Yes, fine. So will you come over here or shall I send her to England for a few days?'

I was taken aback. 'Oh; I thought the agreement was that I couldn't have her?'

Catarina smiled; that smile that had once so bewitched. 'Yes, well hopefully we can be a little more civilized about access now, can't we? I was trying to defend my interests so forcefully after the divorce because we were so at each other's throats.'

'Oh, right. Yes, things were a bit of a nightmare, weren't they? Fine. Er, well I suppose it's up to Bella really; whether she'd like a little holiday in England. I could give her a nice time and there's a spare bedroom in the flat.'

'Okay, I'll ask her. I think she might like that, although she's settled in well here, liking it at school, and her piano, and she likes Luigi, so that's good. There's nothing worse than a resentful stepchild, is there?'

'Stepchild? You mean you're? . . .'

She looked faintly embarrassed, casting her dark, mascara-thick eyes down for a moment. 'Yes,' she said gently, 'Luigi and I are engaged to be married. Sometime next spring. We haven't set a definite date yet though.'

'Oh, well congratulations. I hope you'll be very happy together. I mean that.'

Her eyes lifted again and there was softness in them now. 'Thank you

Patrick. That's kind of you. And I get the impression from what Bella says that there might be someone in your life too?'

'Mm, well there might be. It's a strange sort of situation; a state of limbo, really.'

'How so?'

'Well, Leah is American. She came over here in twenty-eleven with her then-husband when he got a job in the City. Then after they divorced she stayed over here and, well, to cut a long story short we sort of got together. But now she's applied for a job as a flautist with the Philharmonic orchestra and has gone back to the states to apply for a work visa from over there. But there's the question of whether her salary will be enough to satisfy the government – they're going to raise the minimum requirement next year. Even if she qualified under present rules, when they increase the threshold they could simply boot her out of the country if she didn't qualify then. So, we're trying to pull strings to get around it. But at the moment we're waiting to see what's going to happen. Or she is.'

'Oh, that's very cruel, isn't it? Governments can be so callous. I do hope it works out all right for you both, Patrick.'

I heaved a huge sigh. 'Yes, thanks, Catarina. So do I.'

But I didn't want to dwell on the subject and depress myself again. 'Well, anyway, so you'll talk to Bella and see what she thinks about visiting, will you?'

Catarina smiled. 'Yes, I will, Patrick. Leave it with me. I must go now. Goodnight.'

'Goodnight Catrina.'

Ten minutes later, in the middle of cooking dinner, the phone rang. I cursed as I walked out of the kitchen to the dock. It was probably yet another nuisance call. But the displayed number was a now-familiar one. I snatched up the handset.

'Paddy! I've been trying to phone for the last half hour!'

'Hello sweetheart. Sorry; I've been talking to Bella. It's Skype-nig

Then I was talking to Catarina.'

Leah groaned. 'Oh, of course. I'd forgotten that. Still can't get the time difference right.'

'So anyway, why are you calling earlier than usual?'

'Because I couldn't wait . . .'

Her voice seemed to fade. I thought for a moment that we'd lost the transatlantic connection.

'. . . Because I've got it!'

'Got it?'

'Yes; GOT IT! Got the visa! Oh Paddy, Paddy! Honey! I've got it!'

I had to sit down quickly, as the import of the words registered and relief, like an inhalation of oxygen, flooded my brain. 'Really? Oh, that's wonderful!'

'Yeah, I still can't believe it! It came in the mail this morning. I waited and waited until I thought you'd be home but then I couldn't get through because you were always bloody engaged. I've been going crazy!'

'Sorry about that; I wouldn't have lingered talking to Catarina if I'd known you were trying to get through.'

'Why were you talking to her?'

'Oh, nothing really important. Just arrangements for visiting Bella. It could have waited.'

'Right. Well isn't this just brilliant? Of course it's only for up to five years, but you warned me that would be the case. After that I have to reapply for another period. But we can cross that bridge when we come to it. It's years away.'

She sounded deliriously happy. I felt pretty joyful too.

'Yes. Good. And as soon as you get back you can contact Henry at the Philharmonic to say you can definitely take up the job offer. And I'll let Benny and Esther know. They'll be so pleased.'

'Yeah. I'm kinda pleased too!'

'And me. You know I told you I went to see Benny the other night? Well I didn't want to tell you what he said in case it was tempting fate.

But I can now. He said he hoped you'd be coming back soon and that perhaps you'd accept his flute now. Well you'll be able to, now you're definitely joining the orchestra, won't you.'

There was silence on the other end.

'Lovie?'

Her voice was a croak. 'Oh, Benny! He's dying and he says something like that! How selfless is that, Paddy? Yes, of course I will! I wish I was there now, at their place. I'd give him a great big hug, if he could stand it. Oh, the sweet man!'

I was succumbing to emotion too. Finding word formation difficult too. 'Yes, well, you just get on the next flight back home, do you hear?'

Another silence. Then she spoke, quietly again. 'Do you know what you just said then, baby?'

'No; what?'

'You said, "The next flight back home". Home.'

'Yes, well I daren't use the term before. As I say: tempting fate, and all that.'

'Yeah, well you can bet your bottom dollar, darling man; I certainly will be on the next flight back home!' She sounded choked.

'Okay; be sure you are. It's that Bob Marley song again, isn't it?'

'What?'

'You know; the one we've listened to. No Woman No Cry. Remember the last chorus of it?'

'Remind me, sweet Irishman.'

I crooned, *Everything's gonna be all right* to Leah Weisman on the other side of the world, several times, like in the song, and finally dare to believe it might be so.

Chapter 27: December

We were back at Heathrow, Leah and I, on the Saturday evening of the second week in December. But this time the occasion was excitingly anticipatory, not about parting in sweet sorrow. I'd allowed plenty of time in case of heavy traffic – well, I didn't want her getting off the plane with no one there to meet her – and we'd arrived over forty minutes before its arrival time.

We sat holding hands again, although this time our hands were relaxed, not clinging onto the other for grim death. 'I'm dying to meet her again,' Leah murmured. It seems a long time ago now since I saw her last, in twenty-eleven, doesn't it, honey?'

I smiled. 'Yes; like a lifetime. There's certainly been a lot of water under both our bridges since then – and mostly pretty turbulent stuff too.'

'Yeah; true. Don't remind me. Well, until four months ago, anyway.' Leah squeezed my bicep with her free hand.

'Mm; I'll certainly go along with that.'

I reflected on that for a moment before continuing. 'Yes, you'll find Bella's grown a bit since then. I know you've seen her face on Skype so you know what she looks like now, but she was getting quite a tall girl for a twelve-year-old when I saw her last back in July and I expect she's put on more inches since then.'

'Yeah; she sounds like me at that age. I was a beanpole though; gawky and bespectacled. I didn't like my appearance at all. Whereas Bella's much prettier and looks as though she's not as skinny.

'Well, it's all in the genes, isn't it? She's probably going to take after her curvaceous mother, whereas you say your mum's skinny. Not that you are, lovie. You're slender and elegant. And no; she's not prettier. Just different.'

Leah laughed. 'Yeah, I know, like an antelope. That's what you always say. Wicked flatterer! And as for the other thing: well, you're biased now, of course.'

'No, not at all! Well, okay, you and Bella are certainly my two favourite females, sure.'

'Charmer!'

'Yes, well . . . But seriously; you two are similar in some ways, aren't you? Physically both dark and slim, and both musical. Even the same instrument if you discount your flute. Although I don't know whether Bella would ever progress as far as you did, and go to a world-renowned music school.'

'Oh, you never know. She might. I didn't go all that far, after all. Just got a very expensive training. And became an occasional piano teacher. I'm looking forward to hearing her play on that old Joanna we've got now.'

'Yes, you'll be able to give her some pointers, so you will.'

'Mm. She'll be almost like the little sister I never had, really. It'll be great getting to know her.'

We chatted contentedly as we waited for the plane to arrive, looking forward to the future. After an emotional and tearful visit to Benny on her return from America to receive his flute, and with several rehearsal sessions now under her belt, Leah had her first concert to look forward to in a week's time; a special Christmas one. Again I was helping her on expanding her wardrobe while she waited for her salary to kick in including an early Christmas present of a black evening gown to wear for performances. The look on her face when she'd tried it on in the shop and emerged from the fitting booth for my approval (which had been enthusiastic) had been priceless.

One day she'd brought home her copy of the twenty-sixteen performance schedule to show me. Inevitably it had included tours three of them overseas: two weeks in Germany, four in Australia and a lengthy six-weeker in the States; which would mean separation course, but we could handle that now. We were happy in the secu knowledge of knowing we could stay together. It wouldn't be like the worry of the last time we parted, for her to apply for her visa from New York. And besides, after learning of the schedule I'd been seriously considering taking all my leave at one go (Ken would just have to manage without me) and spending it in Australia when she toured there. So there would only be two foreign tours actually spent apart. It wouldn't be the end of the world.

The announcement came booming that the Alitalia flight from Palermo had arrived. We waited, watching the airside exits until passengers began to filter through, some of them rushing into the arms of waiting relatives. We got up and took up station, and suddenly there she was, my little girl, slender in a vivid magenta parka and skinny jeans, carrying an enormous rucksack nearly as big as herself, entering the lounge, looking anxiously around before quickly spotting us and pointing and grinning, and apparently thanking a middle-aged couple who presumably were guiding her through the disembarking and customs process, before making a rapid beeline in our direction.

Yes, she certainly had grown in five months, and was filling out too. I stood with my arms open, she came into them and I hugged her tightly. It felt so, so good. The top of her dark-haired head was only a hundred millimeters or so shy of the tip of my beard. Yes, she would be tall, like her mother. I kissed her hair. 'Hello sweetheart!'

'Hi, Daddy!' she said, excited, into my chest. I held her like that as long as I dared, before it ran the risk of becoming embarrassing for her, then held her away from me. 'My, it's so nice to see you!'

'And you, Daddy.' She beamed at me.

I was forgetting Leah, who was standing deferentially back, waiting patiently. 'Look, Leah's come to meet you too! Say hello!'

If she was embarrassed about meeting my girlfriend she certainly didn't show it. I'd been slightly anxious about her reaction on meeting Leah in real life as opposed to the safe distance of Skype. But she was fine. Well after all, there was a day-to-day replacement for me in her life too. 'Hi, Leah,' she trilled.

'Hi Bella,' Leah said, pecking her cheek, perfectly at ease too. 'My, you *have* changed since I saw you last!'

Bella looked puzzled. 'Sorry?'

Leah laughed. 'Oh, didn't your dad tell you about that? About us meeting before in North Wales?'

'Er, no?'

'Oh, sorry. I thought he had.' Leah looked at me mock-sternly. 'I thought you'd told Bella, Paddy!'

'Didn't I, Bella? I thought I had done. My memory's like a sieve sometimes.'

'No,' Bella chided her absent-minded old dad, 'you didn't.'

'Oh, well Leah will tell you all about it on the way home, won't you love?'

Lea smiled. 'Gladly!'

It was a wonderful eight days (well, ten counting arrival and departure Bella spent with us. As it was so close to the twenty-fifth now, we made it an early Christmas celebration. It was certainly infinitely better than my previous one had been, spent alone and estranged from wife and daughter with the gloomy prospect of acrimonious and expensive divorce looming, in the dismal bedsit I'd moved into after living with Catarina had become completely intolerable, before the property division had been sorted out and I'd bought all I could afford supplemented by a small mortgage: the flat. But that was last year; this Christmas – well, pre-Christmas – was joyous, filled with love and laughter.

It gladdened my heart; it really did, to see Leah and Bella so obviously getting on well together. It might so easily have been otherwise. You heard such horrible stories of children not getting on with their parent's new partner sometimes. Bella seemed quite unfazed by my having a so much younger girlfriend, and Leah really took her sort-of-stepdaughter-cum-little sister to her heart. The girls spent many hours sitting side by side at the piano as Leah passed on her knowledge and showed Bella new pieces to explore, as I watched them happily. And when they weren't doing that, they were forever giggling together, wrapped up in girl-talk.

One evening, after dinner, after a piano session had drawn to a close because they'd decided they wanted to do some internet browsing and retired to the sofa, shoulder-to-shoulder with the laptop, I asked Bella the question that had been burning my lips. 'Would you like to take up piano playing seriously, lovie?'

She looked uncertainly across to me in my temporarily-relegated-to place in the armchair. 'What; you mean, like, do it for a living?'

'Well, it's a thought, unless you'd rather be a brain surgeon or astronaut or something.' I shifted my gaze to Leah. 'What do you think, love? Does she have the potential?'

Leah deliberated for a moment or two. 'Well, she's pretty accomplished, technically, for her age. As good as I was then, as far as I can remember.' She looked sideways at my daughter. 'But it depends on several things of course, Bella. Most important: you've got to really want to do it, honey, and if you feel you do, there has to be a hell of a lot of dedication and commitment on your part, almost to the point of being obsessive. There can't be any half-measures. And then; if you were talking about something really high-powered, like being a soloist, you do need to be pretty exceptional, have a real, innate gift. Be the best among the best. A few of us have it but most of us don't. The rest of us, like me, don't go very far beyond competent enough to earn a reasonable living, like I'm beginning to do. Not that I'm complaining; I'm really not. I'm glad I've got the opportunity to do what I really love . . thanks to meeting a certain someone I could mention.'

She looked across at me, smiling; her eyes bright.

Bella said, 'Well yes, I really do like music. More than any of the other subjects at school, to tell the truth. It would be great to actually do it for a living. I'd never really thought about it before though.'

'Well there you are then,' I put in. 'It's something to think about. A dream to have. Even if you didn't reach the top, it wouldn't matter.

Being happy and fulfilled, that's what counts. Look at me: I'm not a multimillionaire best-selling writer, just a humble newspaper hack, and I'm happy enough. I've got all I need.'

Leah said, glancing at me again, soft-eyed, 'Yes, your dad's right. It's all about doing your own thing and being happy doing it. Having loads of money is no big deal, as I've found out the hard way. But if that's what you want, as I say, you've got to work, work, work at it. And you do need lots of support. I know your dad gives you as much as he can but he's not living there in Italy with you. How does your mom feel about your music? Is she supportive?'

Bella studied the computer screen. 'Well, yes, quite a bit, I suppose. Perhaps not quite as much as Dad though.'

'Well then,' I said, 'Try and make it plain to her how much it really means to you, and work as hard as you can at your lessons, and do lots of practice. It's the only way, really.'

'Yes,' she said, 'I will.'

'And what about . . . Luigi? What does he think about it? Does he take an interest?'

'Erm, yes, quite a bit, I think. He often asks me how I'm getting on with it, anyway.'

'Oh good. I'm glad to hear that.' I felt guarded relief. *It would be much better if you could live here with Leah and me though,* I thought. *But that would be selfishly wishing for an ideal world.*

But I said no more about it, letting the subject drop. I didn't want be the typical pushy parent. And I wanted Bella's visit to be fun.

Although, obviously, Leah hadn't been brought up to celebrate Christmas, she wanted to have the proper festivities, with a proper, real tree and decorations and the whole shebang, so we'd spent a happy Saturday and a couple of evenings beforehand, the two of us, buying good-sized Norway spruce with all the usual accoutrements for it, and all the other necessary bright sparkly things to festively festoon our sitting room. Bella's eyes lit up the first time she saw it, and Leah was excited as a little girl by the whole thing too. It was wonderful to see her looking so bright-eyed, bushy-tailed and happy.

I worked at home again for the duration of Bella's visit as I couldn't really take time off completely (and besides, I wanted to build a fund of leave-days owed to me so that I could spend as much time away as possible with Leah when she was touring). And Leah was occupied several hours per day rehearsing, and the occasional one or two teaching too, so it would have been really unfair to expect Bella to spend hours alone in the flat.

But it wasn't all a case of me having to leave her to amuse herself and work. We spent a happy weekend together painting the town metaphorically red. And we went together, Leah in advance to prepare and Bella and I following, to her first concert. Bella seemed to genuinely enjoy it and I, sentimental old eejit that I am, came over all emotional and felt hugely proud, like a doting parent almost, of my bigger girl. We designated Bella's last Monday with us as official Christmas Day (well, it was close; it was the fifteenth) and did all the traditional things you do, like exchanging presents. Leah had helped me choose something nice for Bella, and Bella herself had come bearing gifts, small items that could be easily carried from Italy, not just for me but, touchingly, for a thrilled and slightly tearful Leah too.

There was the traditional Christmas dinner, but had in the evening before Bella was due to fly back, because Leah was rehearsing during the day, and we followed that with chocolates and drink and proper old-fashioned home entertainment: piano party pieces from Bella, giggly duets from the two of them and renditions on both piano and a certain precious flute by Leah.

And then, the following day and all too soon, it was time for me (Leah was working again) to drive Bella back to the airport and wave her goodbye, out of my life again for a few months. But there would be other times, I told myself. Oh yes, there would be many other times.

By the time I'd returned home from seeing Bella off it was gone half past eight. Leah was back of course and had dinner prepared ready to cook. She responded to my hug and kiss tenderly but seemed subdued.

'She got away okay then?'

'Yes, fine. God, I'm missing her already though!'

'Yeah. I will too. She's a lovely kid.'

'Mm, *I'm* quite pleased with her as well. I don't think I helped create a bad one there, really, did I?'

'No, you certainly didn't.'

Leah hesitated.

'Er, Paddy; Esther's phoned. It's Benny.'

'Oh no!'

She pulled me back to her, a hand going to cradle the back of my head. 'No; it's all right. It's not that. But she says he's fading. She wonders if we can go over there tomorrow. And she wants me to take his flute.'

Leah's rehearsal was a morning-only session the following day, and my work could wait, so when she returned and after a hasty lunch we headed straight over there. The door was opened to us by Sam, his face gaunt with stress. I unnecessarily introduced Leah. He nodded distracted 'Hi' and led the way into the sitting room, where a bed had now been fixed up. Clearly Benny's stairs-climbing days were over. He lay propped up, a pallid remnant of a man, his face almost as white as his pillows. Ruth, an astonishing similar middle-aged version of her mother, her dark eyes red-rimmed, was slumped in an armchair. Esther occupied the other, which had been pulled close to the head of the bed. She looked worn out, as if she hadn't slept for days, which was probably the case. But she managed a thin weary smile of welcome, looking relieved that we'd arrived. 'Hello Paddy. Leah. Thank you so much for coming.'

Her gratitude in itself was heart rending. I could think of no response that wouldn't sound trite, other than a murmured, 'That's all right love.'

We approached the bed and stood awkwardly looking down upon my old friend and Leah's new but transitory one. 'Hello Benny,' I said, throat tight. He seemed barely conscious judging by his almost-closed eyelids. It was as if the effort of even keeping *them* open was too much to struggle with. But there seemed to be a glimmer of recognition. He said something, or, rather, emitted a tiny, indecipherable, tired sound, shifting his languid gaze to Leah and then dropping it to her hands clutching his instrument case, repeating the sound, as if coherent speech was beyond him too, now. There seemed to be a faint parody of a smile on his face though. Sam brought up two dining chairs for us to sit, opposite Esther.

Esther said, 'The nurse was in half an hour ago. She's very kind. She's given him an injection for the pain. Morphine, I suppose. That's why he's so sleepy.'

'That's all right, love,' I said, the words coming out as a croak, 'he doesn't have to talk to us.'

Esther's sad eyes fell to the flute. 'I'm glad you've brought it, my dear. The reason I asked you to was; Benny was asking yesterday if you would play for him.'

I felt a rush of guilt. 'Oh, Esther! We should have come yesterday!'

Esther smiled wanly. 'No, that's all right, Paddy. I know you were otherwise engaged with your daughter going back home. Leah told me. Don't feel bad about it.'

Leah spoke for the first time. Her voice was strangulated too; barely more than a whisper. 'Well I'll play for him now.'

'Oh, will you, darling? He'd so like that.'

'Of course I will. What shall I play?'

Esther pondered. 'What about that Britten piece, from *Peter Grimes*. The Sea Interludes. He loves that. You played it when you and he first met, do you remember?'

'Yes,' Leah said, quietly, 'of course I do. I'll never forget. All right hen. It probably won't be very good though. I'm having a little trouble with my throat just now.'

Esther smiled again. 'Yes, I know. But that really doesn't matter.'

I got up and made Leah change seats with me so that she could be near to Benny. She took the flute from its case, which I relieved her of and assembled it. We waited. Benny's eyes were almost closed.

Leah placed her fingers, lifted the instrument to her lower lip and took a deep breath, as if to emotionally gather herself. She closed her eyes, whether to squeeze every last atom of expressiveness from the piece and give her all to Benny or suppress the tears that were squeezing from her tear ducts; I didn't know which. The sound began hesitantly, but then it must have been taking an enormous mental Herculean emotional, effort. But then it came; that atmospheric haunting melody, so evocative of a wild Suffolk beach. Like the first time she'd played it for our old friend, Leah made one or two mistakes either because she didn't have it committed fully to memory, or because of the overwhelming pathos of it all, but Esther was right; that didn't matter, didn't matter one jot.

I looked at Benny's pale, drawn face, his eyes now fully shuttered, trying to detect any reaction. It was difficult to tell if there was any. Could he hear Leah play his old friend Benjamin Britten's music? Or was he too far gone, senses too mercifully blunted by morphine? Or too far along his final journey to that good night of oblivion; beyond anything Leah could do for him now? I glanced at Esther. Her expression was oddly serene. 'Can he hear, do you think?' I wondered, speaking quietly, as if afraid to awaken a sleeper.

'No, I don't think so,' Ruth said from across the room, her voice unsteady.

'Yes, I'm sure he can,' Esther contradicted, with fierce certainty. 'Look, he's smiling. Just faintly. You can hear it, my darling, can't you?'

Perhaps she was right. Perhaps there was the ghostly flicker awareness, of a faint pleasurable response playing across those thin lips. Or perhaps not. But if Esther was simply finding something she wanted to see, that was absolutely fine. So I said, 'Yes, I think so too,' looking across the room to catch Ruth's eye, willing her to not to make argument of it.

Leah had come to the end of the piece; to the end of all she could remember, at least. She opened her eyes and lowered the flute; Benny's flute. Benny's wonderful gift. Rivers of wetness were streaking her cheeks. She looked at Esther. 'Do you want me to play anything else?'

Esther returned her look; smiled with infinite sadness. 'That was lovely. I'm sure Benny thought so too. Yes, if you want to, my dear.' She made no particular request though.

'Yes, please do,' Sam suddenly said, from his perch on the foot of the bed; his eyes moist too. 'That was beautiful, whether Dad could hear it or not.'

Leah looked at me, as if it were up to me to nominate something.

'Can you do the Ravel pavane? You know it, don't you?'

Her expression told me she understood what I meant. 'Yes, I do. Right.' She raised the flute again, paused and began playing the exquisitely sad, stately tune. Esther probably knew full well the title of it: *Pavane for a Dead Princess,* although it hadn't been written as a funereal piece. I glanced at her anxiously, fearing I might have made a terrible faux pas. But she didn't seem upset. She'd probably drawn her well of tears dry now, anyway. Although now, for the first time since we'd arrived, her eyes, which never left Benny's face, were slick with moisture.

We stayed for another hour or so. Leah played several more pieces that Esther said had special significance for Benny, getting up to go and find sheet music for those that she didn't know. But Benny was certainly asleep now; possibly on the edge of coma. Leah was really only playing for the rest of us now, as a balm for our sorrow. But it must have been a strain for her; it was unfair to ask her to carry on much longer. I caught her eye and sent a silent *That'll-be-enough-now* message, and when she'd finished the current rendition I gave the case back and she dismantled and put the flute away.

Ruth got up to make tea and coffee and we made desultory small talk, about Leah's budding career, Bella, and Sam and Ruth's jobs. And then we left, saying a final silent goodbye to Benny Walters, who was once the immigrant child Benny Wolfewitz, many years ago.

Sam saw us out. We hovered uncertainly on the doorstep. He spoke, looking down, somewhat embarrassed, but addressing Leah. 'Thank you very much for that, Leah.'

'Oh, that's fine. I wanted to do it,' Leah said, softly. 'If your dad heard any of it, that's good. It was a nice way for him to drift off to sleep, with music in his head. But if he didn't, I hope it helped your mom a little, at least.'

'Yes, I'm sure it did help. Thank you.'

He paused, looking as though he wanted to say something else.

He looked up, first at me and then at Leah. 'Yes. And Patrick; I'm sorry if I came across as a money-grubbing twat when we were talking about Dad's flute before. Yes, he was absolutely right in wanting you to have it, Leah. Ruth and I know you'll cherish it. It'll be like it staying in the family, in a way.'

That did it for Leah. She'd been keeping emotion firmly in check throughout our visit, but now the floodgates opened. Her tears came freely as she moved to hug Sam. 'Oh, yes; I'll certainly do that. You better believe it.'

The telephone rang at ten to eight the following morning, before I set off for work. As soon as I saw the number on the telephone display I knew who it was and what it would be about. His voice sounded flat, drained. 'Hello Patrick. It's Sam. Mum asked me to give you a ring. It's Dad. He passed away five hours ago.'

Encore

Adagio – ma non troppo

Chapter 28: January

The applause goes on and on. I steal another look at my companion. Esther is applauding enthusiastically, beaming. I hadn't been entirely sure about inviting her to Leah's fourth performance just three weeks after losing Benny, but it looks as though my worries were groundless. She'd said when I tentatively mooted the night out to take her out of herself, break her isolation, that she wanted to see Leah play, and she does seem to have enjoyed herself, in a sad sort of way.

The conductor, Miles, brings the orchestra to its feet, shakes hands with the leader, and goes through the time-honoured ritual of walking off and back on again several times. At his last re-entry he waits for the applause to finally subside. For some reason, he's now holding a radio mic and he's also brought a music stand onstage with him, which he places next to his podium. What's going on?

He smiles, raising the mic to his mouth. 'Thank you, thank you. Thank you. Now, by way of an encore, we would like to give you a little flute music. It's in tribute to the Philharmonic's late and sorely missed First Flute, Benjamin Walters, who sadly passed away recently.'

Esther emits an audible gasp. Neither of us had expected this at all.

Miles goes on, 'Benjamin – Benny – gave sterling service to the Philharmonic for over forty years and was one of our longest-serving members. He was a consummate musician and an inspiration to many players who came after him. But above all, he was a thoroughly decent and kind human being, a perfect exemplar of the civilizing influence good music well performed. I know that Benny particularly loved Mozart, so here, as our small tribute to a highly venerated gentleman, one of the old school, is part of the adagio of the Flute Concerto in D.'

Esther's hand has found my bicep and is gripping it hard. My hand finds her free one and squeezes it equally vigorously. She hisses at me, 'Did you know about this, Paddy?'

'No!' I hiss back. 'I didn't!'

Miles is still speaking. 'And here to perform it is the orchestra's new First Flute, Leah Weisman.'

Now it's my turn to gasp. *No! You madam! You kept this very quiet!* And then the significance of the 'First Flute' appellation sinks in and I smile. Good old Henry and Miles: they're keeping the little fraud going, presumably with the connivance of the actual First Flute, indeed all the flautists, probably, just in case some jobsworth from the Border Agency is watching and twigs that they've been hoodwinked.

The audience breaks into applause again, acknowledging Miles's tribute and anticipating the encore. Leah rises from her seat, picking up a score, and makes her way to the front; places the score on the stand and smiles nervously at Miles, who clips the mic onto the stand and raps the podium to get the orchestra's attention, before looking at Leah again to check she's ready. Her slight nod indicates that she is. Miles raises his baton and they begin, as Leah waits, eyes fixed firmly on her score, for the solo flute part to commence.

I'm finding the suspense unbearable and I sense Esther's tenseness too. It's one thing for Leah to be playing among her colleagues in the orchestra, an anonymous contributor to the general sound. Being a mere foot soldier she normally gets no solo parts, even brief ones, to play. Those are the privilege of the First Flute. But this is different; now she's completely exposed, has to perform flawlessly, her flute the dominant voice, for several minutes, depending on how much of the movement they'll be playing. Any errors will be as conspicuous as sore thumbs. And that's before you even begin to consider interpretation.

She raises Benny's flute to her lip, still waits.

And begins. The sound is muted at first, as if she's gathering confidence and courage. I don't blame her: I'd be terrified, standing in front of people, least of all a huge audience, doing any sort of performance, let alone something like that. But then she seems to become more confident as the music, pure, mistake-free, like an elegant, singing aria, like liquid birdsong, wings its way to us. I find I'm mentally counting seconds and minutes. Surely she isn't going to play the entire thing? Miles said it was only going to be partial. It's only an encore, after all. After three minutes or so I notice Miles glancing at her, catching her eye, and she seems to give a slight nod, and he turns his attention back to the orchestra.

The pure sweet sound is gossamer-light, a delicate celestial voice full of expression, floating above the orchestra which Miles is keeping *piano.* She's even getting the trills right, not stumbling over them, as far as I can tell. The performance goes on, flawless. Five minutes. Six minutes. And then there's an entirely solo part, a brief cadenza, which she seems to execute perfectly, before the orchestra comes back in for a final few closing bars.

It's over. She lowers the flute to hold against her chest, her head meekly bowed. There's a stunned silence. And then the audience breaks into rapturous applause, which goes on and on. A few people shout 'Bravo!' Esther's hand is still gripping my bicep. I look at her. Tears are streaming down her face. Fortunately I've got a clean unused hanky in my pocket, which I give to her.

Leah looks up, as if astonished by the warmth and magnitude of the applause. Her face is flushed, her eyes bright. Miles moves towards her, takes her hand and they bow together, before he gallantly kisses it. So does Kenneth, the Leader. The orchestra is applauding too. Finally the applause subsides. Leah is still standing there. She unclips the mic and holds it to her mouth. She speaks, her voice hoarse, nervous, looking out into the audience but in the direction of Esther and me.

'Thank you. Thank you so much. You're very kind.'

She hesitates.

'But this isn't about me. Benny, this is for you.'

Which only makes the audience erupt into applause again.

Rather than have Esther return home to an empty house, I invite her spend the night with us. So after an as-brief-as-we-can-get-away-with post-concert winding down in the green room (I reckoned Ester would prefer peace and quiet), we return to the flat. I'd disinterred the car again for the occasion, and the women sit together in the back as I play chauffeur. And they continue to sit chummily together on the sofa as I make coffee. The tribute seems to have been a release for Esther, giving her the excuse for a good old cry. Perhaps she needed to do that. Had the occasion been one of unalloyed celebration of Leah's triumph I would have been tempted to break out a bottle of wine, but it isn't. As she had so modestly and sweetly said, it wasn't about her, it was about Benny; it was a fitting elegy, a lovely final eulogy. Well, yes, mainly it was, I mentally agree. But not altogether.

Esther looks tired though, drained, as if the pent-up emotion and sorrow of the last three weeks have reached crescendo and suddenly been released, breached by a simple act of empathy. From the armchair, once again, I gently tease Leah. 'So the tribute was a little subterfuge between you and Miles then, was it?'

Leah smiles. 'Well, Miles, mainly. It was his idea. And then he recalled that I had a special connection to Benny, so he suggested I might like to play something, and asked if I knew whether Benny had any particular favourites, and I remembered he'd talked about Mozart, especially the second flute concerto. So it seemed exactly right. But I thought he meant I'd just play a bit sitting in the orchestra, not out front. So I was amazed when he said no, do it like a proper soloist. And pretty anxious, to be honest. So he said, well just do part of it to begin with, and when we were halfway through I could give him the nod if I wanted to carry on, or a head shake if not and we'd wind it up.'

'And so you played it all the way through, darling, even the cadenza. It was very brave of you!' Esther murmurs.

'Well, I don't know about that,' Leah says modestly, 'I was terrified to begin with; my heart was really thumping until I got started. But when I've got to the part where I could have aborted, I found I could carry on okay, so I gave Miles the signal and we did. And I wanted to finish it anyway, for Benny.'

Esther's eyes moisten again. She takes Leah's hand and squeezes it.

'Well that was extraordinarily kind of you, my dear. Thank you. It was a lovely tribute. As was your playing at the funeral.'

Esther looks at me. 'And so was that beautiful eulogy you wrote, too, Paddy.'

Leah smiles again. 'Well it isn't me who deserves thanks. After all, if dear Benny hadn't bequeathed me his flute, or given me the intro to the orchestra, I couldn't have done it.'

She pauses. Looks across at me, *her* eyes shining, too. 'And of course if a certain kind-hearted Irishman hadn't taken pity on me one evening in the street and persuaded me back to his lair, none of this would have happened, anyway, would it? I might still be on the streets busking, trying to get an airplane fare back home together. So the thanks should go to you, too, honey.' Her bottom lip quivers.

'Ah, think nothing of it,' I josh, 'I couldn't have left you out in the rain that night now, could I?'

'Well yes, you could have,' Leah says softly. 'Most people would have ignored a scruffy down-and-out. But you didn't.'

Both the women look tired, for their individual reasons, and we retire to bed soon after that. Leah and I don't make love, because I think we feel a little inhibited about doing so with Esther sleeping in the other room, in the bed that used to be Leah's and before that Bella's. And I feel such a cocktail of emotions anyway; there doesn't seem room for physical love, not this time. I'm so proud of my girl's achievement tonight; so happy for her; so profoundly touched by her tribute. And I ache with such tenderness, such love for her; it's almost painful. It almost makes me want to cry. We still climb into bed naked though, because I still want to hold her tight and feel her body and, all right, it causes a certain naughty stirring and she's aware of it and chuckles and briefly handles me, but that's fine. Tonight we can keep physical gratification low-key.

After a little more drowsy talk she kisses me and turns away without separating, as she always does, and soon falls asleep. But I'm too wound up. My brain is on a high. But I must drop off eventually, because the next thing I know, it's early morning and the bedroom is soft-lit by daylight infiltrating the curtains. We must have moved apart during the night because I find I'm on my back and so is she, her head turned back towards me but still asleep. I want to look at her, because I love doing that, and gently draw the duvet off, to halfway down her thighs.

The sight of her brings a lump to my throat. *Look at you,* I say in mental soliloquy. *Look at you. You look like a sleeping vulnerable child. So innocent. So porcelain-perfect. So precious. So fragile. I want to protect you from all the hurt of the world. Your body is blooming with health though. You're putting on obvious weight. Your face is less thin, radiant now, with the slightest suggestion of a double chin, even. That's another of my favorite female places: that little roll of flesh they often have there. Your sweet breasts are somewhat fuller and although it's not obvious lying down, you're getting a little bit of a pot belly. And your thighs are plumper too; they're even nicer to lie within, so they are.*

I do so want you to be with me forever, not ultimately leave, as the others did. I'd be utterly bereft if I lost you, darling colleen. I was thinking before I finally dropped off a few hours ago, about Miles's little subterfuge (he'll never go to Heaven) about your pretend-job title. It reminded me of the vulnerability of our position, really, should you ever be found out. Governments can be very heartless.

I'm going to gently awaken you in a minute. I'll kiss an eyelid, making the orb beneath flutter like a caged bird. You'll open those beautiful dark eyes. They'll register me watching you. You'll sleepily smile and say hi baby and stretch your arms out to me, and I'll take you into mine, and suggest something, and hope against hope you'll agree.

Reprise

2021

The narrowboat approaches the beginning of the Pontcysyllte aqueduct. I know what to expect now, so there's a slight frisson of apprehension, even though I know it's perfectly safe really. It's just the thought of that huge terrifying drop on the one side. No visual and psychological security of a guard rail, just the low rim of the iron water trough between us and a fatal plunge to the River Dee far below. I would have preferred it if we'd sat on the other side of the boat really, but presumably all the other tourists had the same idea and we were slow in getting onto the boat, so we have no option but to sit slightly nervously on the scary side.

We have our backs to the direction of travel. Roisin, my red-haired (just like her Aunty Julie and Cousin Amber) five year-old, is beside me, on this nostalgic holiday trip to North Wales, celebrating both my fiftieth birthday and something else of huge importance, revisiting the old haunts of fond memory. Unfortunately she's insistently taken the seat by the window in spite of my trying to dissuade her. I hope she's not going to be frightened when she suddenly realizes there's apparently only empty space outside it.

Across the table sits Leah, wearing her hair up in a bouffant today. I know what that usually signifies. She knows I love it like that and find her extra-irresistible, still, after nearly six years. There will be bedroom wickedness later. She has our little boy, three year-old Benji on her lap because there's another tourist occupying the other seat. Benji is named for sort-of granddad Benjamin, who, sadly, he never knew, although Roisin was in his presence, albeit as an embryo, in his final days on earth. He has his mother's dark hair and sloe-eyes, and is regarding the proceedings solemnly. He's beautiful, although I say it myself. He takes after his mammy.

But Benji knows and thinks the world of (as does Roisin) his Granny
Esther, who is now in her white-haired eighty-fifth year, and to a lesser
extent his other granny, Granny Carmel because, thankfully, Leah had a
reconciliation with her and Granddad Solomon before he died of excess
after she'd delivered them a fait accompli when we married: accept my
new Gentile husband and coming child or I'll certainly never speak to
you again.

I talk to Roisin, trying to divert her from coming possible anxiety. '
came here years ago, with your sister Bella. We came over the
aqueduct.'

I can see her little mind working, trying to work it out. 'Oh. Was
Mammy here then?'

I smile. I love the way she insists on calling Leah 'Mammy', just
because I do. I seem to be the dominant role model in some ways. I try
to explain. 'Well, yes, lovie, although she wasn't married to me then. '
was before you were born. I was married to Bella's mammy and
Mammy was married to someone else. If you see what I mean.'

Roisin frowns in concentration, causing the freckles on her forehead
to merge, considering that. 'Oh. So why was Mammy here with you and
Bella if she was married to somebody else?'

Leah is grinning at me. It's all going above Benji's head though.

'No; she wasn't actually here *with* me. She just happened to be here
at the same time, with her other, first husband. It was a coincidence. '
you know that word.'

'Right. And do you like being married to Mammy better than Bella'
mammy?'

Oh, the incisive power of a child's innocent question! My throat
constricts. 'Oh, yes, lovie. Much more. Honestly.'

Leah has stopped grinning. Her eyes have liquefied. Roisin seems
satisfied with the assurance.

I look at Leah, blinking a bit, my memory racing back through the
years. That heart-in-mouth marriage proposal, to really cement our
staying together, that morning I woke her up after the concert when

she played her tribute to Benny; her ready acceptance, her tears because she thought I'd never ask. The application for a fiancé visa the following Monday with the accompanying earnest assurance to the Border Agency bureaucrats that we were engaged to be married. The intense relief when it was approved in the April. The register office ceremony the following month (we hadn't wanted to tempt fate by marrying before visa approval, just in case) with Leah by now heavily pregnant and very few guests: just Esther, Bella over from Italy for the occasion, sister Julie and her husband Derek, niece Amber, sister Sorcha over from Ireland with her chap and divorced oldest sister Maeve. If all the Brennan clan had attended they would have overspilled outside and had to have loudspeakers. There had been a few raised eyebrows from other customers at the register office, I recall, smiling at the memory, concerning Leah's condition and age relative to mine, and we'd laughed about it at the do in the pub function room later.

And then, onwards another month, Roisin's birth and Leah's insistence that she have an Irish name. And, after her as-soon-as-possible return to work (but absolutely no overseas touring), because, still feeling insecure, she didn't want to push her luck and be seen to be economically inactive and a burden on the state, the touching palaver of her expressing her milk and me bottle-feeding it to Roisin when she was away briefly at performances, because she insisted on breastfeeding our baby. And the same thing happening for Benji twenty-two months later.

And then, in twenty-eighteen, the application for the second, extension spouse visa, and now, a month ago, at last, granting of permanent leave to stay in Britain, and the application in for naturalization, which should be a formality, so now, finally, there's no possibility that we can be torn apart . . .

I'm lost in my reverie with a stupid grin on my face. But then I'm jolted out of it. We're floating through space. Roisin tenses beside me; gasps. I look at her. She's staring, transfixed, down into the void. I pull her to me, turn her face away. 'It's all right, sweetheart. Just don't look.

You can't fall. I won't let you.'

Leah reaches a hand across the table to take one of Roisin's. 'Yes, you're quite safe, honey. Daddy won't let you fall.' Her eyes, soft, switch to me. 'He's good at that.'

I say (well, croak, really), 'Listen; Mammy will sing you a song to stop you being frightened.'

Leah smiles, a fond memory lighting her face. 'Yes, I will.'

And so she sings that song again, to drive fear away from another of my children.

Raindrops on roses and whiskers on kittens . . .

She sings it all the way through. My heart sings too. Roisin calm herself, entranced by the Pied Piper words. I let go of her for a moment to applaud my wife.

'Bravo Mammy' I murmur, bursting with love. 'Bravissimo!'

Thanks

My thanks go, as ever, to Gwendlyn Kallie for love, encouragement, support and proofreading; Michael Hawke for constructive comment; and Susan Allen, Chantelle Atkins, Steph Gravell, Shirley Hardy, Richard Hennerley, Susan Keefe and Marilyn Tomkins for their friendship and interest.

Printed in Great Britain
by Amazon

17607120R00208